STRENGTH FROM WITHIN

C.J. PETERSON

ISBN: 978-1-952041-29-7

Published by Texas Sisters Press, LLC. Lufkin, TX U.S.A.

The story, all names, characters and incidents portrayed and the names herein are fictitious. No identification with actual persons (living or deceased), places, buildings, and products is intended or should be inferred.

Texas Sisters Press, LLC

2020

Second Edition

DEDICATION

This book is dedicated to my loving husband and dear family who love and support me. You all mean more to me than you will ever know! Thank you!

*A portion of the proceeds from **Strength From Within** will go to "**Jenny's Hope**."*
"No one should ever have to grieve alone. There is healing found when we share our stories, our fears, and our memories. In 2017, we discovered Wise County Christian Counseling had 59 families with children needing grief counseling on the wait list. We could hardly bear it that 59 sets of parents were on the edge of their seats waiting for a call for help. We prayed, we dreamed, we sought advice. We decided to open Jenny's Hope, a free grief center for children and adults."
To find out more about Jenny's Hope, go to:
https://jennys-hope.org

To learn more about C.J. Peterson, you can find her online at:
http://cjpetersonwrites.com/
'While the stories are fiction, the journey is real!'

***Note: All quotes at the beginning of the chapters are found here (except for the Bible verse):*
https://wisdomquotes.com/strength-quotes/

SUMMARY

Pine Crest is a quiet little Ohio town just outside Cleveland. To the outside world, it seems to function as any other small town. However, upon closer inspection, Stacey and her father, Sam Spencer, discover the dangerous secret that is this town's reality. Corruption has such a massive stronghold; survival seems to be the way of life.

Asserting her normal independent attitude in this new environment as the new kid in town could find Stacey in trouble. However, the strength inside her forces her not back down. Once Sam figures out what is going on, he cannot turn a blind eye to it either. By fighting back, can the Spencer's help free this town from its bonds? Will it ignite a spark of hope or an all-out war? What would you do if your town was held captive? Would you comply or would you fight back?

Isaiah 40:31: But those who hope in the Lord will renew their strength. They will soar on wings like eagles; they will run and not grow weary, they will walk and not be faint.

CONTENTS

"I NEVER MET A STRONG PERSON WITH AN EASY PAST." ATTICUS

Sixteen-year-old Stacey looked up from her chemistry homework in surprise. The doorbell chime startled her. *Who would stop by in a snowstorm?* Before opening the door, she cracked the blinds to see a police car in the driveway.

"Jonah. Dan," Stacey acknowledged the police officers when she opened the door. She recognized the solemn expressions they wore. "Is everything okay?"

"Is Sam here?" Jonah asked.

"Yes. Come on in," Stacey said. "You guys can wait in the living room. Dad's in the study. I'll go get him."

They brushed off the snow before they stepped inside. "Thanks, Stacey. We'll stay right here," Jonah said. "If you could get your dad, it's really important."

Stacey ran to her dad's study and knocked.

"Come on in, Peanut," her father called.

When Stacey opened the door, she explained, "Dad, Jonah and Dan are here. They're asking for you."

Setting his pen and papers aside, he glanced out the window before he left the study. Stacey followed. Her dad was a lawyer and a good friend to the officers in the area, so their presence in the house was not unusual. However, something in their eyes made Stacey nervous.

"Jonah. Dan. What on earth are you guys doing out here on a night like tonight?" her father echoed her thoughts. Still, he greeted them with a smile and a handshake. "Do you guys want some coffee to warm up?"

"Thank you, but no. We need to talk to you," Jonah said, standing tall. "This is official business."

"Okay. We can talk in there." He gestured toward the living room. "Stacey!"

"What?" Stacey asked, coming out of the hiding spot where she was eavesdropping.

"Would you please bring us all some coffee? These gentlemen need to warm up."

"We appreciate it, but no thank you, sir," Dan said. "We need to speak with you and your daughter."

"Oh. Okay. Stacey?" Sam reached out to Stacey. When she got near him, he rested his hands on her shoulders as she stood in front of him. "What can we do for you?"

"Sir," Jonah said, "we wish we were here under better circumstances."

Sam furrowed his brow. "What's going on, gentlemen?"

"Lauren, was on the way home from work, when there was an accident," Jonah started. "She spun-out as she was driving on highway..." he continued.

The officers explained how Stacey's mom's car caught a patch of ice on the highway and hit the concrete median. They got to her within minutes of the accident. However, because of her injuries, the paramedics lost her on the way to the hospital.

Stacey gulped. Her heart felt as if it would beat out of her chest. She could not focus after the word *accident*.

For the next several weeks, everything sounded hollow as her world spun around her at a high rate of speed. She felt as if she were watching things from a distance. She felt disconnected from her world. She could not imagine how she would exist in a world without her mother.

The days slipped by as if she were on autopilot. Whether it was meeting with the doctor who explained the extent of her mother's injuries, family to explain what happened, or the funeral home representative working with them to set up the funeral arrangements, it was all more than she could handle and process. She went numb.

"...*THAN WHEN WE FIRST BEGUN*," sang those in attendance at the funeral, finishing *Amazing Grace*.

"Thank you for joining us in the celebration of the life of Lauren Spencer," the priest said. "Sam and Stacey will hold all the words spoken today close to their hearts. They are grateful for each and every one of you."

Stacey was torn inside. She bordered on angry and devastated. The same place she had been since the day Jonah and Dan delivered the news.

Her mother was cremated. That was her mother's wish. Her mother wanted her organs donated, and she got her wish there as well. Her mother did not want a casket or to be buried in the family plot. She wanted it plain and simple. After all, that was her mother to a tee. She was simple, but beautiful. She had a heart of gold, wore little makeup if any, and generally dressed casual in style, despite the money she and Sam made. Lauren was a cardiologist, so her time was valuable. She made time for the important things in life: her husband and daughter; working some evenings in the soup kitchen; and taking a trip every few years with *Doctors Without Borders*. Those were important to her. Having said all of that, she was a natural beauty. She would look stunning at events, yet turn around and look great in a pair of sweatpants and a T-shirt. Stacey admired her mom, and yearned to talk to her.

The coldness of the tan and white marble walls was not lost on Stacey. The March winter winds of Grand Rapids, Michigan whipped the snow around outside, adding to the bitter cold of the day. Even though Stacey was surrounded by friends and family, she felt cold and alone.

Catching movement out of the corner of her eye, she turned to see one of the graveyard workers leaving the mausoleum. When he did, it sent a deep chill into the room.

Although she knew she should be paying attention to the priest, instead she tucked her coat tighter around her body, sneaking looks at those in attendance. Her mother's entire side of the family was there, along with a good portion of her mother's co-workers. Some of Laruen's patients from over the years were there, along with many of the family friends. There were some representatives from her dad's side of the family up from Ohio as well.

Sitting next to her father, Stacey's mind wondered. With her mother being a successful cardiologist, and her father being a successful lawyer, Stacey's parents wanted to make sure she was a success as well. When asked what she wanted to do with her life, Stacey was only able to put off answering until she was fourteen. Going into high school, they wanted her to be focused and have goals. So, when they insisted on an answer, she told them she would be a doctor just so they would back off. She never said what type of doctor. She only said she wanted to be a doctor.

That was one of the few times she did not like being the sole focus of her parents. Normally, Stacey did not mind being an only child. It was a little lonely, but she did not have the normal sibling spats or competitions. She did not have to worry about working, and wanted for nothing. Her parents made sure her level of comfort was not lacking. Her only job was to get high grades in academics, and have a vast list of extracurricular and social activities for her college application.

"Everyone will be joining us at the house. Please be a good hostess," Sam said, bringing Stacey back to reality as they drove from the cemetery back to the house.

Stacey sighed while she looked out the window, tears crawling down her cheeks faster than she could wipe them away.

"You're sixteen," he continued. "You are strong enough to do this. You've done enough parties with your mom to know how to behave and where to help."

"Why did she have to be buried in that cold place?" Stacey asked. "Why couldn't she be buried in the plot with the rest of the family?"

"We've been through this," Sam said. "That's not what she wanted."

"She wouldn't want some party at the house afterward either."

"That's for us," Sam explained. "And it's not a party. It's more of a time to remember her."

"Can I just go to my room when we get home?"

"You need to be downstairs. You need to hear the stories. It will help you process."

"No. It won't. It hurts to hear the stories," Stacey said. "I won't have Mom to hold my hand through this life anymore. I won't be able to go to her for advice about life. Who am I going to talk to?"

"Me. I have quite a bit of life experience."

"You're always in Lansing. Are we going to move there so we can have more time together?"

"Your friends and family are here. Don't you want to stay with them?"

"I-I don't know what I want," she admitted. "I just want the pain to stop. That's the one thing I *am* sure of."

With a pained expression, he momentarily struggled to keep it together. "We have to be strong through this," he said, doing his best to convince himself as well as Stacey. "We can cry it all out after everyone goes home. Please work with me, Stacey. We'll get you counseling. We'll figure this out."

"I don't want to do this," she said as they pulled into their driveway. There were already several cars there. "Please don't make me go in there."

"Looks like your aunts, uncles, and cousins have beat us home. We may not have to do much for the rest of the day. They'll take care of it all," he said, turning off the car. "You *do* need to be downstairs for a bit. You have to go through this."

"I am telling you all I want is to go to my room."

"Unfortunately, I cannot let you do that. You have to hang out for at least a little while."

"For how long?"

"Stacey, these people are here for us."

"No. These people are here for themselves. They're here to do something to make themselves feel good," she said, her shoulders sagging. "They're here, because they want us to think they'll always be here for us. But here's the thing...in reality, they won't."

"What do you mean?"

"When the dishes are done, they'll go home to their families. They may check in on us over the week, or they may not know what to say and we won't hear from them at all," she said, tears streaming down her face as she raised her voice. Her emotions finally catching up with her. "When it's all said and done, they have their entire family at home. We don't. They have their moms to hug. They have their moms to ask for advice. They have their moms to tell them if they screwed up or if they're proud of them. They have their moms...period. I don't!"

Sam reached over and hugged Stacey as she cried. "I'm sorry, Stacey. I will do better. We'll figure this out together," he said and kissed her head. "I am *not* your mom, but I will do my best. We're in this together. After this all clears, we'll figure out what *we* want or need to do. We don't have to make any decisions right away. We do not have to listen to what others tell us. We will do what we want to do. Just give me a few hours downstairs, and then you can go lock yourself in your room. Can you do that for me?"

She sniffed, wiping her face. "I'll do my best."

Resting his hands on the sides of her head as he looked into her eyes, he encouraged, "You can do this. I know you are strong enough to do this."

"I'm fine. I'll be fine."

"You can do this," he said again. With that, they got out of the car.

As soon as they stepped across the threshold, Stacey saw all the people already bustling around the house. They were her family, but they seemed distant to her in that moment. Kids were running around, parents scolding them. Some people were laughing. Some were crying. Some were busy setting out food and plates. Everyone seemed to have something to do...except Stacey.

Her heart raced. Her chest hurt. She could not focus. "I-I can't breathe," Stacey said, grabbing her dad's arm. "Dad? Please?" She shook her head, tears streaming down her face. "Please don't make me do this."

"It's okay," Sam relented. "Go ahead to your room. I'll have someone bring you some food. You've been through enough."

Stacey could not get to her room fast enough. She closed the door behind her and leaned against the wall. Sliding down to the floor hugging herself, she lost herself in the tears and memories.

After a few minutes of crying, she wiped the tears from her eyes. Out of the corner of her eye, she saw a picture on her nightstand. She squinted to see better. Getting off the floor, she then went to her bed and picked up the picture. It was of her, her mom, and her dad on a skiing trip in Montage Mountain at Christmas. She ran her fingers over the picture of her mom, memories of the trip flooding her mind. Clutching it to her chest, she burst into uncontrollable sobs.

No one came to the door for over an hour. Stacey cried until she fell asleep on her bed still cradling the photo.

"COME ON, SAM," Mark Marshall, from the highly successful Cleveland Law Firm - Mannford, Marshall, and Adams Legal Services, said on his computer meeting with Sam. "We went to college together. I know your work ethic. I have followed your career. When I shared with my findings with my partners they agreed. They really want you, and are chomping at the bit to get you to come down here. They've been bugging me for weeks to talk to you. They told me that you can pretty much write your own paycheck. Give me a reasonable amount, and I promise I'll get it pushed through. They *really* want you here."

"I don't know," Sam said, stroking his chin. "Stacey's having a hard time. I don't know if I want to drag her to a big city. Cleveland may swallow her up. We finally got her into a counselor, but she doesn't like the her. I need to find her a new one quickly. I'm losing her, Mark."

"You've given it a few months up there. Every time we meet, I can see you falling apart. You cannot tell me that you're not drowning in memories of Lauren up there yourself."

"I am," he admitted. "Her family is doing their best to keep her memory alive by always sharing stories about her. What they don't understand is that it is tearing her –"

"You mean both of you," Mark challenged.

"Yes. It tears us *both* up inside. It's also tearing us apart. The fights about visiting family or going to the counselor are becoming more frequent. The more I push, the more she pushes back."

"Sounds like you need a fresh start," Mark suggested. "Look, you don't have to live in Cleveland. There are plenty of suburbs around here. There is Independence, Edgewater, Riverside, or hey, what about Pine Crest? You grew up there. You've said before that a lot of your old gang still lives there. Just do me a favor and do some research to see where you want to make your fresh start. Know there is a desk here waiting for you."

"I'll think about it," Sam relented.

"That's all I ask."

"PINE CREST IS a nice place to live, but it has its issues," Matt Slater said to Sam over the phone. "I also know you're having a hard time up there. My concern is there are some fractions around here that will be a challenge to work around."

"Matt, every town has its ups and downs," Sam said, "especially the small towns. I get it. It's a risk."

"Look, man, I don't want to discourage you. I really would love to have you live near us again. It would be bringing the gang back together. The only ones missing are Kara and Aaron once you're here. There's a lot here that you may not understand. If she lands in the wrong crowd, it won't end well."

"Stacey can handle herself. I can handle myself too. Stacey really needs guidance, and a small-town feel. When we get there, I'll find a new counselor for her. If you and Tina could help, that would be great. She really likes both of you and trusts you guys."

"We love her too. And if you want her to have a job, she can work at the restaurant. I will look out for her as if she were my own. Tina and I will do our best to help guide her through all of this with you to the best of our ability."

"Okay, then. Have your friend send me the listings for houses to rent. Once we're down there, we'll figure out where we want to buy."

"If you want my personal advice, Silverwood Townhouses is a safe place for you guys to start."

"Are there any townhouses available?"

"I'll send you the number. When are you planning to make the move?"

"Her seventeenth birthday is September nineteenth. I want her to be able to celebrate her birthday with her friends before we move."

"You do realize she'll be starting a new school after the school year starts, *and* in her junior year. That's going to make her transition rough," Matt pointed out.

"I have faith she can do it."

"When you guys get here, have her come by Slater's to officially fill out an application as a server. You know she has the job, but I have to have it all on file."

"Thank you, Matt. I look forward to being near the gang again."

"We've missed you. Just be careful down here. There are times where it's like the old west."

"What does that mean?"

"There are certain families who carry more weight than others in town."

"I'm not worried about that."

"Fair enough," Matt said.

"Thank you. See you soon. I have to have a conversation with Stacey."

Matt chuckled. "Good luck with that."

"Thanks. I'll need it."

∽

"STACEY?" Sam said, lightly knocking before walking into her room.

"What's up?" she asked, looking up from her phone.

"I need to talk to you." Going over to her desk, he grabbed the chair and brought it over next to her bed. Sitting down, he let out a slow breath of air. As he clasped his hands together in front of him, he rested his elbows on his knees and looked up at her.

"This looks big," she said, setting her phone down. Sitting on her bed cross-legged, she asked, "What's wrong?"

"Nothing is wrong. Well, that's not true. We're both struggling. I am painfully aware of just how much the passing of your mom affected both of us. We need a fresh start."

Stacey gulped. "What? What do you mean?"

"Things here are not working out. Everywhere we look, we see memories of your mom. We're fighting all the time. I am aware that the only thing holding us together is this house. I want us to make a fresh start in a new place. A place where we can make our own memories. A place where we won't see your mom around every corner. A place where we can go somewhere and not have more stories shared, gutting us each time without the chance to heal before the next one comes. I know they are trying to keep your mom's memory alive. I don't know about you, but I honestly feel suffocated."

"I feel the same," she admitted.

"Your panic attacks have finally slowed to a manageable level. Your hypoglycemia finally looks like it's back under control. I hate to say this, but the thought of the holidays coming terrifies me. The family Thanksgiving and Christmas will be brutal this year. Do you really want to be here to hear more stories? Do you want to see the looks on their faces?"

"Honestly? No."

"Do you really want to stay in this house?"

"I don't want to leave mom," she said.

"That's not what I asked."

"No. I don't want to be here. I don't want to face the holidays here. I'll miss my friends, though."

"I'm sure, but you'll make new friends."

"When do you want to move?"

"Well, in all fairness, I think your seventeenth birthday should be shared with your friends. So, what if we leave the Monday after your birthday? Then we'll take a few days to unpack and get settled before you start. That will give you three weeks before the move."

"Won't school already be started?"

"It will. But don't you want one more celebration with your friends?"

"Actually, yes. I appreciate that. Thank you."

"And you're okay with moving?"

"Knowing you, you didn't come to me without making a plan first."

"I have a plan."

"And, knowing you, you've got it all lined-up."

"Pretty much," he admitted.

"Okay," she said. "What's our new life going to look like?"

Sitting back in his seat, he explained, "Grand Rapids and Pine Crest are similar in size and pace. You've been to Pine Crest for visits before my mom and dad passed. You know what it looks like. You know Matt and Tina Slater and also know he owns Slater's diner."

"Yes. I love Matt and Tina!"

"He's willing to hire you as a server."

"A what? Wait. I have to work?"

"Stacey, I would not do you justice if I didn't let you work during high school. It's a rite of passage. It will give you extra money and help you understand the value of money."

"I've never worked before."

"I know. You're old enough to start working part time now."

"A server, huh?"

"Yes. There are a lot of kids from school and local colleges who work there. That should add an element of fun to it. You can get to know others in the area."

"Fine."

"That's your go-to phrase for *I don't care,*" he said with a smirk.

"That's my *I'll deal with it* phrase," she countered.

"All right, then. I'll make this move easy on you. I'll hire movers so we don't have to go through everything right now. They'll just come and box it up. We can go through it on the other end if you want to."

"However you want to do it is fine."

"There's something else we need to talk about."

She sighed, rolling her eyes. "What now?"

"When we move, we're moving into a townhouse."

She raised an eyebrow. "A what?"

"It's a two-bedroom townhouse."

"A two...what? What are we going to do with only two bedrooms? Where are we going to put everything? Why are we doing this?"

"What doesn't fit can be put into storage until we find a house. We need to get to know the area before we do that. I just got off the phone before I came up here. I rented a townhouse in a really nice place called Silverwood Townhouses. It has a pool, a clubhouse with games, and all sorts of fun things to do."

She huffed. "Fine."

"Okay. I'll let you process for a bit," he said, standing up. "Why don't you and your friends plan your birthday party. Get me the list for approval, and we'll go from there."

"How big?"

"However big you desire. This is a birthday slash going away party. Have as many or as little as you want. You are in control of this party. I'll just be there to chaperone so it doesn't get out of hand."

"Fair enough," she agreed.

After he left, she mulled around in her mind how many friends she wanted to have over for her party. Deciding to keep it small, she called her small circle of friends from school.

CHAPTER 1

"BEING MENTALLY STRONG DOESN'T MEAN
YOU WON'T FEEL AFRAID. INSTEAD,
MENTAL STRENGTH IS ABOUT FEELING
AFRAID AND DOING IT ANYWAY." AMY
MORIN

****Six months after the accident****

"Well, it's your first day. Are you ready for it?" Sam asked Stacey, as they pulled up to the school.

"Not really," she admitted. The school looked cold to her. The concrete was gray, while the steel framework of the structure was royal blue. This matched the school colors of silver and royal blue. "Glad we spent most of the week unpacking. I'm still really nervous about this whole starting over thing."

"You'll do great." He smiled, trying to ease her anxiety. "Just show them that Spencer charm."

"Yeah, sure, ya betcha," she said on a sigh. As she went to open the door, he put his hand on her arm. "What?" she asked.

"I know you've had a rough time since your mom died. We need to make new memories here. A fresh start. We've settled into the townhouse. You start a new school today. Tomorrow you start your new job at the restaurant. Things will work out if you stay focused until all of the Newbie 101 situations pass."

"I know." Stacey hung her head, taking a couple deep breaths. Glancing toward the school, she saw the students scat-

15

tered throughout the front lawn in little groups, laughing and having fun. Anxiety and panic threatened to overtake her, but she knew she could not stay in the vehicle forever. "I don't know if I really want to do this. I miss my friends," she admitted.

"You don't have a choice. Come on, Stacey, you'll make new friends. I promise. It won't be as bad as you are imagining."

"I'll be fine," she said, trying to psych herself up for the challenge.

"Just do your best. And don't forget to smile." He reached over and hugged her. "Love ya, Peanut. Just think, stay focused on these first few days, and you'll be settled in no time."

"Yep. Thanks," she said, opening the door, voluntarily leaving the safety of their black Jeep Cherokee.

As he pulled away, Stacey awkwardly stood there for a few moments in the chilly mid-September breeze. Tucking her dark blond hair behind her ear, she sighed. In her old school she was one of the confident popular kids who usually had at least five to ten people hanging around her as soon as she set foot on school grounds. Now she would be one of the self-conscious, uncomfortable, and lonely new ones. It also did not help that she stood a head taller than most girls. She was five-foot-nine, and thin. Growing up in her old school, it was not such a big deal. She understood it would be a different story here. In her other school, she saw how merciless kids could be to others. One girl in particular stood out. She was almost six-foot and thin. The guys teased her relentlessly. Stacey stood up for her. She and Andi turned out to be really good friends.

"It's now or never," she said to herself. Letting out a slow breath of air, she then negotiated her way through the minefield of students to the office to get her schedule and locker assignment.

"Welcome to Pine Crest, Ms. Spencer," said the office secretary. "Here is your schedule, homeroom, and your locker with the combination. There's a map on the back of this folder to help you navigate the school."

"Thank you." Stacey held up a lock. "I already have a lock for my locker."

"You won't need that," the secretary said. "The lockers here have the locks permanently installed."

"Is that secure? Wouldn't the person before me have the combination?"

"No. Between each school year, or if the locker changes hands, the maintenance staff changes the combination. Please verify it works before you head to your first-period class. If it doesn't, then come back to the office and we'll get it fixed."

Stacey heard the first-period bell ring. "I'll be late to class."

"Don't worry about it. Just hand Mr. Wexford this admission slip. There are admission slips in your folder for each class you will be entering today. You only need to hand these to the teachers for today. After you finish today, you should be good to go." She smiled pleasantly. "Here's your hall pass if a teacher stops you."

"Thank you," Stacey said.

Leaving the office, she looked around what would be her new school for the next two years. It was a fairly new school, so it had a modern industrial style to it on the interior. In keeping with the exterior pain, the brick walls and steel framework were painted royal blue, while the ducts were also exposed and painted gray. The outer walls of the cafeteria consisted of clear plexiglass strong enough to withstand the spring storms and tornadoes that hit the area. The classrooms each had a few windows, while the rest of the walls were concrete. The hallways were lined with tall, thin lockers, all painted gray.

Walking through the cafeteria, a study hall was currently in session. Many of the students looked up and watched her walk through the cafeteria to the other side, toward her homeroom.

Awkward was a mild term for it, but she understood that would be the theme of the day.

After the cafeteria, she passed an award case. This had athletic, band, academic, drama, and choir awards through the years on display. There were photos next to many of the trophies of the individuals or teams who won the award. There were also various articles from newspapers in frames regarding different events and special mentions of the school in the case. She noticed certain names were repeated through the years, so she filed them in the back of her head, thinking maybe they were founding families by how far they dated back.

Heading toward her homeroom, she had to go downstairs. She walked by the vast library, which was located below the cafeteria. The wall facing the hallway for the library was made of glass so she could see inside. There were shelves upon shelves of books, along with a computer lab. *Oh! She longed to get lost in a book at that moment!* She could get lost in a book for hours. Making another mental note to check out the library later, she continued toward her homeroom.

When she arrived at her homeroom, she located her locker. Quickly dialing the combination, she was relieved to find it open immediately. "This is a good start," she said aloud to herself. "Okay," she glanced at her schedule for the first-period classroom number, and then scanned the map, "I just need to get there."

Realizing it was on the other side of the school, she made sure to circumvent the cafeteria by staying downstairs this time to go to class. Relishing in the quiet of the school on her way to class, it was almost peaceful. She really did not want to go into the classroom, knowing she would be walking into another awkward situation.

Resting her hand on the door handle as she stood in front of the door to her math class, she took a deep breath, and then slowly let it out. Regrettably, she was going to make a poor first impression by being late.

"May I help you?" asked the math teacher, Mr. Wexford.

Holding the notebook and folders she carried as close to her as possible, Stacey walked over and handed him the admittance slip to the class.

"Oh! A new student. So, Ms. Spencer, where are you from?"

"Michigan," she said quietly. Looking solely at the teacher, she did not want to look up and see the entire class staring at her. Shoulders hunched, she nervously cleared her throat as she tucked a portion of her hair behind her ear.

"Where in Michigan?"

"Grand Rapids." She hoped that would satisfy him enough to let her sit down.

"Well, welcome to Pine Crest. I hope you enjoy your time here. I'll get you a book, while you get settled over...um...actually, over there behind Mr. Chandler."

Stacey could not believe it when he pointed to probably the hottest guy in the classroom. He was stocky and gorgeous. Brushing his dark-brown wavy hair out of his face, he then leaned forward to talk to the guy sitting in front of him. He almost seemed too big for the desk where he sat. He glanced up at her, his green eyes twinkling as he smiled.

Stacey quickly looked away. While she passed his desk to get to hers, she avoided eye contact with as many people as possible – especially with *Mr. Chandler*. She knew her face was bright red from embarrassment.

"Here ya go, Ms. Spencer. Please turn to page fifty-seven. That's where we're starting today," Mr. Wexford said. Then he added, glancing around the room, "That was *supposed* to be your homework from last night for those who did it." He raised an eyebrow when a couple of people turned away.

Stacey sighed as she opened the book. She hoped to blend

into the crowd for the rest of the day, but that would obviously not be happening.

As Mr. Wexford went through the calculations, Stacey scribbled the remaining equations on the page, completing them as she went. Stacey did well in math, and calculus was no exception. She swiftly breezed through the remaining equations to turn it in after class. She decided it was the least she could do since she was late that morning.

Going around the class, each student answered an equation. When it got to Stacey's turn, Mr. Wexford asked Stacey if she wanted to answer one. She promptly answered, so he went on to the next person. She did not mind, since everyone had to do one.

About forty-five minutes later, Mr. Wexford gave the homework assignment for the night, followed by a few minutes of free time before the bell rang to change classes.

By that time, Stacey was finally feeling a little more relaxed. The math problems they worked on in class took her mind off the anxiety of starting her first day. Stacey's intentions were to keep to herself for the rest of the day, doing her best to break as little first-day newbie laws as possible. Deciding her math homework should be safe, she pulled out her paper and pencil, and then flipped to the homework page.

However, no sooner had Mr. Wexford gone to his desk, then *Mr. Chandler* turned around to talk to her. "So, you're new, huh?" He put his hand out as he introduced himself. "Kyle Chandler, at your service."

Stacey shook his hand. "Stacey Spencer."

"Well, Stacey Spencer, it seems you're a math whiz."

She shrugged off his comment. "Not sure I'd classify myself there."

"So, what other classes do you have?"

She handed him the paper with her schedule on it. "Here. Take a look for yourself."

"Well, looks like we have lunch and P.E. together, too. You're also in the same homeroom with a couple of my very good friends, Amber Ross and Brad Strong."

"That sounds about right." She nodded, thinking through the alphabet as to who would be in her homeroom.

"So, what do your parents do?" he asked.

"My mom passed away last March, and my dad's a lawyer."

"Oh, wow! I'm sorry," he cringed, "on both counts." When she raised an eyebrow, he explained, "My dad's a lawyer, too. I'm really sorry about your mom."

"Thank you. What firm does your dad work for?" she asked. He looked like his family had money by the designer clothes he wore.

"Chandler, Marks, and Simmons."

"Oh."

"Yours?"

"Mannford, Marshall, and Adams."

"Oh! They're good," he exclaimed, impressed.

"Mark Marshall is one of my dad's friends from college."

"What college did he go to?"

"Harvard Law."

"Oh!" he said, pleasantly surprised. "Looks like brains run in the family."

"Guess so."

"What did your mom do before she passed away?"

"She was a cardiologist."

"Wow! You *do* have a lot of brains in your family." He smiled in delight as he asked, "Any brothers or sisters?"

"Nope. Just little old me."

"Gotcha. So, are you as good at your other subjects as you are at math?"

"I guess it depends on the class."

"So, what did you do at your old high school? Any sports?"

"Volleyball and ran track," she said, hoping with every bone in her body the interrogation would stop soon. However, since she was the new kid in school, she was certain she would face this line of questioning in every class.

"Well, you're too late to get into volleyball this year, but what did you do in track?"

"I did high jump, long jump, sprinting, and hurdles."

"Are you any good?"

"I lettered in both my freshman and sophomore years," she answered. "Guess that would be considered good."

"What about volleyball?"

"I was on the varsity teams my freshman and sophomore years, lettering both years. I might have been able to letter this year, maybe not. Guess I'll never know now."

"Well, there's always next year," he pointed out.

"Yep."

"Chandler, what are you doing tomorrow night, man?" the guy in front of Kyle asked as he turned around.

"Probably going out with Amber. Why?"

"Do you guys want to do Slater's for dinner, and then a movie afterward with Erin and me?"

"Sure," Kyle said. "It sounds like a plan."

Stacey groaned. *One of the hottest guys in school was bringing his girlfriend and two other friends on her first night at her first job? What could possibly go wrong?* She had a feeling this would not end well. She shook her head as horrid scenarios played in her mind.

Hearing her groan, Kyle turned back to Stacey and asked, "What's wrong? You don't look so good."

"Nothing. It's no big deal." Stacey started, as the bell rang to change classes. Closing her books, she then stacked her stuff and slid out of her seat, relief flooding her body. *Only seven more class periods until the end of the day.*

"Well, see ya in P.E.," Kyle said, and then left as the room emptied.

STACEY STUDIED her schedule while she walked out of the class-room, trusting she would get some sense of direction soon. There were three floors to the school, and the school was a quarter of a mile long. Time would be the biggest factor in getting to class before the next one started. Thankfully, her first and second-period classes were on the same floor.

While she walked through the school, she walked past the award case again. Browsing through the various awards, she found the most frequently used names were: Chandler, Ross, Phillips, Strong, Mason, Foster, Barnes, and the James families. They were repeatedly laced throughout the awards. Writing the names down in her notebook, she wanted to connect them with their current counterparts. Knowing Kyle Chandler was one, along with Amber Ross and Brad Strong, she was curious to see if the others were still at the school as well.

Making her way to her next class, she occasionally glanced up at the numbers to make sure she was headed in the right direction. The last thing she wanted to do was get to class late again.

"Watch it!" some girl snapped, as *she* ran into Stacey.

"S-sorry," Stacey stammered, scrambling to pick up her folder, notebook, and pen, face flushed bright red.

"Yes, you are," the girl said disgusted, as she picked up her books and purse. She then walked off with her friends, who were giggling and staring at Stacey as they walked away.

"Great!" Stacey sighed. So, newbie law number one she broke? *Always keep your eyes open and try not to purposely run into people...even if they run into you first.* Chances are, by the way she acted, she was probably popular too. Newbie law number two she broke? *Under no circumstances run into the popular ones.*

When she walked into her next class, Stacey handed Mrs. McCoy her admittance slip for English Lit. The teacher handed her the book they were currently using, before directing Stacey to an empty desk. This time Stacey was a few minutes early. Students were still arriving as she sat down, so that was a plus on her side.

"Well, if it isn't Princess Grace," the girl who ran into Stacey in the hall said snidely as she sat down in a desk two rows over. "Might want to keep your eyes open next time." She rolled her eyes before turning back to her friends.

"Don't mind her," a guy quietly said, turning around as he was sitting in the desk in front of her. She immediately noticed his friendliness and how his blue eyes stood out with his light-brown hair. "Erin Phillips doesn't care about anyone but herself," the boy continued.

"Well, we had a little run-in in the hall," Stacey admitted. "Actually, it was a literal one…and not all that little either."

He chuckled. "For a new kid, you sure know how to pick them. Of all the people to run into, Erin was not a wise choice. She and her boyfriend, Shane Mason, along with Kyle Chandler, Amber Ross, C.J. Foster, and Brad Strong rule the school."

"Did-did you say Kyle Chandler?" Stacey asked apprehensively.

"Yeah, you were talking to him in math. Shane was sitting in front of him."

"You were in my math class?"

"Yep. I was actually a row over and two seats back. You were hiding too much to see anyone else. Not that I blame you. Of all the people in that room to have to sit behind?" He shook his head and sighed. "That was an accident just waiting to happen."

"You said Erin is Shane's girlfriend, right?"

"Yep."

Stacey let out a frustrated groan. "Great."

"What?"

"They're supposed to be going to Slater's tomorrow night," Stacey explained. "They were talking about it in math class."

"That's pretty much where everyone goes. Well, there or Trina's. Why does that upset you?"

"I work there starting tomorrow night."

"Oh, man!" He laughed. "Boy, are you in for a fun night. Friday nights are a mad house."

"Yeah. And knowing my luck? I'll probably have them at one of my tables."

"Well, if you smile and do your best, you'll do just fine."

She rolled her eyes. "Easy for you to say."

"Actually, it is. I work there too. Adam Barnes," he said, putting his hand out for her to shake. "And you are?"

She shook his hand as she said, "Stacey Spencer."

"Oh! I didn't connect…I didn't hear your first name in math. You're Matt's friend's daughter," he said, as it hit him. "Well, this is funny." He smiled, putting her more at ease. "I'm your trainer for tomorrow night."

"Are you serious?" She grinned. "Well, at least *one* thing is going for me today."

"Have you ever worked as a server?" Adam asked.

"No."

"What *have* you done?" he asked, trying to assess how much training she would need.

"Nothing," she admitted. "This is my first job."

He smirked. "Oh, well this should be fun."

"Barnes!" Another guy came into the classroom, sitting in the desk behind Stacey. "Have you been holding out on me, brother? Who is this lovely lady?" He had brown eyes, along with light-brown, short, spiky hair. He seemed just as friendly and laidback as Adam.

"Brian Dalton, this is Stacey Spencer. She's new in school, *and* works with us at Slater's," Adam said, introducing her. "She's my trainee for tomorrow night."

"Did I miss it? When did you start there?" Brian asked.

"Tomorrow night." Stacey could not help the smile that lit

her face. She felt more relaxed with Adam and Brian than she did with Kyle and Shane. It was a nice feeling. The feeling of relaxation was almost foreign to her. Since her mom died, her life was turned upside down. She spent the last six months in survival mode or just plain shut down.

"Now *that* was what was missing in math," Adam hinted. "Smiling probably would have helped you this morning."

"Well, you know, new school and all," Stacey said.

"Hello, beautiful!" Stacey heard someone say. She looked up to see Shane from math class walk into the classroom and give Erin a kiss. Then he looked up at Stacey, and smiled as he asked, "Are you following me?"

"Nope." She shook her head. She was in such a good mood, she could not help the smile on her face...until she glanced at Erin, who was glaring at her. Stacey quickly turned back to Adam, wide-eyed.

"Yeah, watch that," he whispered. "She's a *very* jealous young lady."

"With a horrible temper," Brian added, stunned. "What did you do to her already? It's only second-period."

"Ran into her in the hall...literally," Stacey sheepishly admitted. "Guess that was a bad move, huh?"

"I'd say so." Brian chuckled. "Try avoiding her for a while."

"She can't." Adam shook his head. "They'll be at Slater's tomorrow night for dinner."

"Well, aren't you just in the pickle?" Brian smirked. "What a way to start."

"Thanks," Stacey mumbled.

Thankfully, at that moment, Mrs. McCoy got up to start class. Stacey was not sure exactly how to classify the day up to that point. While math and the time between classes did not go well, meeting Adam and Brian brought a bright spot into her day. It was her desire for the rest of the day to go well. She hoped to achieve that by avoiding Kyle and his friends and not breaking anymore newbie laws.

∼

HER NEXT CLASS WAS P.E., where she had swimming and lifesaving. This class would be for two class periods because the pool was at another school, and they had to travel.

Stacey looked forward to this class. Not only did she take swimming lessons while growing up, but she also had her own in-ground pool at their other house in Michigan. She was confident this was a class where she would do well. She also wanted to take it in order to be a lifeguard at the local pool, in case the server position did not work out. Her concern was once again her body. Along with her height, her thin frame was not well-developed. She cringed imagining the names they could come up with for her.

Walking out to the bleachers to sit until class, she crossed her arms in front of her chest. She cleared the distance in record time as she practically hugged herself.

Kyle walked out of the boy's locker room. Catching sight of Stacey, he strutted over to the bleachers next to her. A grin flashed across his face, as he said, "Looks like we meet again."

"Yep." Stacey said. "So, where's your girlfriend?"

"Oh, let's see, she'd be in social studies about now, listening to boring old Mr. Benton."

"Social Studies is a necessary evil," Stacey said, anxiously looking around for someone else to talk to...*anyone but him.*

"Yep. So, Shane tells me that one," he held up his pointer finger, "you really do smile, and two," he held up two fingers, "you've made a friend already in Amber and Erin. What happened?"

Stacey nibbled on her nails.

"Stacey?" he asked.

27

"She...well, it could have been my fault. I didn't think it was, but I'll take the blame."

"Anyway?" He gestured for her to go on, as he stretched out on the bench beside her, his elbows on the bench behind him.

Thinking through how to word it, Stacey struggled to concentrate on a single thought. Kyle sat there in just his swim trunks with his legs stretched out in front of him. He six-foot-two frame was well-sculpted for a guy in high school. She would not be surprised if he was a model. He was also tan, probably from hanging out at the lake or the pool all summer.

"*Anyway,*" she continued. "I literally ran into Erin, sending both of our stuff toppling to the ground. It wasn't good."

"Well, Amber said Erin wasn't very nice to you."

"She laughed too."

"She did it to stay on Erin's good side. She's a vindictive little –"

"Good morning, class," Mr. Baxter, one of the swimming teachers said, cutting him off. "Please start with your twenty laps while we take attendance. Make sure to grab a partner to count for you."

"Want to partner up?" Kyle asked Stacey.

"I...sure," Stacey said. "I need to take my slip to the teachers first."

"No problem." Kyle stood. "Come on." He grabbed her wrist to take her with him.

For some reason Kyle seemed to attach himself to her. While she did not mind, she was certain his girlfriend would have an issue with it.

"Hey, Chandler," Shane ran up to them, "ready for our laps?"

"Sorry, man," Kyle said, putting his arm around Stacey. Giving her a gentle squeeze, he winked at Shane as he said, "*Stacey's* going to help me today."

"Stacey?" Shane looked at her, and then smiled. "Ahh. Never mind, I get it."

Kyle grinned. "Just trying to make the new girl feel welcome."

Narrowing her eyes, Stacey crossed her arms as she took a step away. When he went to reach for her, she pushed his arm away.

"What was *that* for?" he asked.

She glared at him. "Why *exactly* are you being my partner?"

"To help you feel welcome," he said innocently.

"I'm not an idiot! I've seen how guys like you operate. If it's not going to benefit you regarding your social status, you don't do it."

"Hmm, stepped in it again, huh Chandler?" Shane chuckled.

Kyle shot Shane a look, before he turned back to Stacey and said, "If you don't want to, you don't have to. I was just offering."

"Stacey!" The trio turned to see a guy Stacey did not know come running up to them. "Glad I found you! Come on, let's get you set up and start our laps," he said, looping his arm through hers.

Stacey never saw him before in her life, so she attempted to jerk away but he held onto her arm.

"She's doing them with *me*," Kyle said, grabbing her other arm. "Sorry, Crestwood, no underlings allowed."

"I am most certainly *not* a person of inferior quality!" the guy holding Stacey's arm objected. "As a matter of fact, I am a person of *exceptionally outstanding* background *and* class. You, on the other hand, need your friend's help to count your brain cells, because they attain to a *slightly* higher level than the number of fingers and toes you possess."

"Why you –!" He went to jump at him, but Shane grabbed Kyle to stop him.

"Come on, man, he's not worth it," Shane said, struggling to keep a hold of Kyle.

"I'm worth more than your combined bank accounts will

ever reach!" the guy said, tugging on Stacey's arm again to go with him.

Stacey pulled back, and demanded, "Just *who are* you?"

"Alex Crestwood. I'm a friend of Adam's," he explained. "Trust me on this one."

"What is this?" Stacey demanded. "I'm not some new toy for you guys to fight over. This isn't elementary school!"

"You just want her because she's new," Alex said to Kyle.

"What about you? Why are you guys so interested in her?" Kyle asked.

Stacey's temper flared. "Excuse me?"

"We don't want her to have to put up with the likes of you," Alex said to Kyle.

"You would rather she hang with you guys? I mean, honest-ly!" Kyle rolled his eyes. "A prep cook, two waiters –"

"Doesn't matter what we do for work," Alex cut him off. "Who people are at their core is –"

"Enough!" Kyle snapped. "You seriously think you and your group of misfits could *ever* compare to us? Ha! I could beat you with my hands ties behind my back!"

Alex shook his head. "Brawn, but no brains, such a shame."

Kyle struggled in Shane's arms again, but Shane held tight.

"There's way too much testosterone here! I'm leaving," Stacey said, and left the three guys standing there. Walking up to the teachers, she handed one her admittance slip and said, "Hi. I'm Stacey Spencer. I'm new."

"Oh yes," one of the teachers for the class, Mrs. Nelson, said as she scanned the admittance slip. "I was just looking over your old school's transfer records the other day. I'm one of the track coaches, and I *fully* expect to see you on that track in the spring."

"Yes, ma'am. Um, is there someone I can partner with? Preferably *not* with Kyle Chandler?" Stacey asked.

"I'll tell you what. What if you partner with Marissa James

today?" Mrs. Nelson asked, pointing to a girl who walked out of the girl's locker room.

Marissa looked to be a little shorter than Stacey. She looked up at hearing Mrs. Nelson say her name. Walking over, she wore a one-piece suit with a pair of swim shorts to cover her fuller figure. "Did I hear my name?" Marissa asked with a smile.

"Hey, Marissa!" Mrs. Nelson greeted her. "Would you mind partnering up with Stacey? She's new, and it seems is already in the middle of things," she said, glancing at the guys, whose attention suddenly shifted to where the teachers and girls stood. "That way she doesn't have to worry about anything."

"Sure," Marissa agreed. "Let's go."

Stacey and Marissa went over to the pool and grabbed a lane to start their laps. Kyle and Shane ended up being in the lane next to theirs. Shane and Stacey did their laps first, while Kyle and Marissa counted for their counter-parts.

"Done," Marissa said, as she tapped Stacey's head when she finished her laps.

"Good! I haven't had a good swim like that in a while!" Stacey said. When Stacey climbed out, Marissa dove in and started her laps.

"Could have fooled me," Kyle said, looking Stacey over from head to toe as she got out of the pool.

Stacey just rolled her eyes as she sat down on the side of the pool to count for Marissa.

Kyle jumped in over top of Shane to do his. "You're done, Mason! My turn!" he shouted, just before he went under the water.

"Show off!" Shane yelled, getting out.

"That he is," Stacey said under her breath.

"Well, I'm assuming that was for *your* benefit," Shane said, as he laid down on his side next to Stacey, propped up by his arm.

"He has a girlfriend. Why is he acting this way?" Stacey asked.

"He's a flirt. He also knows what he likes."

"Well, that's too bad." Stacey shrugged. "He's not my type if he has a girl and flirts with another."

"Well, no disrespect, but you're more his type than Amber. I think he's just dating her until something better comes along."

"Oh, like *that's* going to make me want to date him." Stacey rolled her eyes. She turned her attention back to Marissa as she came back to turn around for another lap. Kyle came in right behind her faster than he should have, and took back off. "He's going to burn out before ten," Stacey said. "He's not pacing."

"It's a little hard to pace when you're trying to impress."

"Sorry, not in the mood for that type of guy. You might want to warn him to slow down. I'm not buying."

Shane smirked. "Nah, I'll just let him figure it out the hard way."

Stacey had to laugh at that one.

"He needs a couple hard lessons once and a while," Shane said. "It's good for him."

"Are you his conscience?"

"Well, someone has to keep the big oaf in line."

"So, that's your job?" she asked.

"Yep. You seem to be pretty good at it, too. Most girls fall all over him. You don't. Why not?"

"I've seen how guys like him operated in my old school. That's not really the type I want to connect with right now."

"Look, from what I've seen you have a great personality, and with what Chandler said about what you told him in math, you two are a much better match."

"Thanks, but I'm afraid your girlfriend doesn't share your sentiment."

"I'm afraid she does all too well. She, unfortunately, gets jealous easily."

"That's the way some girls are."

"Are you?"

"Not really."

"Insecure maybe?"

"Well, being that I'm in a totally new environment, yeah, a little," Stacey admitted. "And trying to figure out the social structures around here? Well, let's just say I'm pretty sure I've flunked Newbie 101."

Shane and Stacey talked while Kyle and Marissa did their laps. He seemed to be a genuinely nice guy. She had to give him credit for not hitting on her.

When everyone finished their laps, Mr. Baxter pointed to nine people, including Stacey and Shane, as he said, "You guys jump in and be our drowning victims with the dead man's float. The rest of you will rescue this time around."

The victims jumped into the water, while the others stood along the side. Mrs. Nelson gave those waiting to jump in some last-minute instructions, while those in the pool treaded water.

"So, what's a drowning victim like you doing in a place like this?" Shane asked Stacey as they treaded water.

"Just hanging around."

"How much you want to bet Chandler goes for you?" Shane asked.

"Over his friend?" She shook her head. "I doubt it. I think either Marissa or Alex will come for me. Or worse yet? No one, and I drown." Stacey pouted. "And on my first day no less."

Shane laughed. "You're funny!"

"Okay, victims…dive!" Mr. Baxter yelled.

Those in the water went under, and came back up floating face down in the water.

It only took a few seconds before Stacey felt an arm wrap around her waist, pulling her to the side of the pool. She looked up to see Alex pulling her over.

"Fancy meeting you here," Stacey said with a smile. "I was hoping you weren't Kyle."

"Well, I kind of got the best of him on this one. When I push it, I'm a slightly faster swimmer than he is," he said. "Now if the choice were either you or Marissa? I'm sorry to say that Chandler would have pulled you out."

"I see," Stacey said in understanding. "Are you two dating?"

"Not yet. Give me time though." He smiled. "I'm working on it."

"Is she aware?"

"I think so. Well, here we go." Alex climbed out of the side of the pool, and then reached down, pulling her out with him.

After all the victims were pulled out, Mr. Baxter said, "Good job. Victims, dive again. We'll do it one more time, and then switch people."

"I'll have Marissa and I both try to get to you, in hopes that one of us will beat Kyle," Alex whispered.

Stacey nodded, and then jumped into the pool.

Stacey did not have to go too far before Shane swam up to her. "This is getting to be a habit," Shane said.

"Oh, I'm sure there could be worse ones than drowning," Stacey joked.

He just chuckled, as Mr. Baxter shouted, "Victims...dive!"

The victims went under the water, and then came back up floating face down once again. This time when the rescuers jumped in, several people jumped in too close to Shane and Stacey. They got pummeled! Stacey got kicked in the head several times, along with the wind knocked out of her. She had no idea of how to even start to look to see if Shane was okay. She was trying to figure out how to move herself out from under the pile of legs above her without actually drowning.

Stacey's head spun. She shook her head in an attempt to clear it, but that only made it worse. When she tried to get to the surface, someone accidentally kicked her down as they tried to get their person to the side of the pool.

Stacey was going down fast. She ran out of breath as she

heard a bunch of yelling and shouting above the water. To her, it sounded distant, like a dream.

That's when she saw the blood. She was pretty sure it was not hers, so she guessed it was Shane's blood.

After a few more seconds, Stacey started to blackout. Forcing the black cloud back, she searched in vain for the surface, but she was disoriented. Heart pounding, she frantically tried to figure out how to get to the surface. She curled up into a ball and stopped moving, hoping her body would naturally float to the surface.

The yelling and screaming got louder. A couple more splashes landed in the water above her. Gratefully, Stacey felt an arm wrap around her waist, pulling her toward the surface. Unfortunately, she tried to get air too soon and sucked in too much water. By the time they breached the surface, as much as Stacey tried, she could not catch her breath. She continuously blacked out, until the black cloud took over.

"Come on, Stacey! Breathe!" Kyle yelled. "I'm trying to get you to the side. Stay with me!"

"She not breathing!" Alex exclaimed. "Her face is an ashen color."

"Get her over here now!" Mrs. Nelson ordered.

Kyle swam harder, pulling Stacey with him over to the side.

A feeling of sheer terror pulsated through Stacey's body. For some reason, she felt desperate and terrified. She thought when one died, they were supposed to have comfort and peace.

"Breathe, Stacey!" she heard Mrs. Nelson. Mrs. Nelson's voice sounded far away. "Come on! Work with me!"

Mrs. Nelson pumped on Stacey's chest, while Kyle did mouth-to-mouth. Finally, Stacey spit up the water. Gagging and coughing, Stacey fought for a few moments to get the precious air into her burning lungs.

"Good job!" Mrs. Nelson said, relieved when Stacey finally got her breathing under control. "Excellent work pulling her out, gentlemen."

Stacey turned her head to find Shane sitting next to her wrapped in a towel. Marissa was taking care of Shane by resting an ice pack on his head, while Shane wiped the blood from his mouth. Kyle and Alex were on one side of Stacey, with Mrs. Nelson the other. The other kids in class were gathered to the side, but trying to stay out of the way with Mr. Baxter.

Stacey closed her eyes, shaking her head to clear it before opening them again. Focusing was a struggle.

"Stacey? Are you in there?" Mrs. Nelson asked.

"I'm…yeah." She nodded, coughing. "That was –"

"Scary, I know," Mrs. Nelson said, cutting her off. "How are you feeling? Do you need us to call an ambulance?"

"My…um, my…No ambulance." Stacey pressed her hand to a spot on her temple where she got kicked the hardest. It throbbed, and she hoped pressing on it would dull the pain. She groaned when the pounding shifted to pulsating pain.

"Yeah, I know the feeling. My ribs, jaw, head, and arm got pretty beat up too," Shane said. "I *think* that *some* people need to watch for others before they jump in next time!" He snapped, glaring at Kyle and Alex.

"It was an accident, boys," Mrs. Nelson said calmly. "Just relax."

Stacey sat up, still holding her head. "Can I have some…I'll be okay…just need ice for my head."

"Of course. Alex, would you mind getting her some ice?" Mrs. Nelson asked. Alex nodded, then hustled off. "I think we're going to have you two sit out for the rest of class. Think you'll be okay? Do we need to call your parents?"

"I'll be fine." Shane shook his head. "Don't call."

"I'm fine too," Stacey said. As she slowly stood, Kyle wrapped a towel around her. Then he helped her to the bleachers, while Marissa gave Shane a hand over to the bleachers as well.

Stacey sat, then closed her eyes, resting her head on her hand. The pounding was almost unbearable.

"Hey, are you okay?" Shane asked.

"I'll be fine. I'm just tired and in pain," she mumbled.

"Here you go," Alex said, bringing Stacey the bag of ice. "You're going to…ouch!" He winced when he got a good look at her face. She felt the lump near her temple. "That's going to hurt."

Stacey mustered a smile and placed the ice on her temple. "Thanks for the vote of confidence."

"Well, I have to get back to class," Alex said. "Let me know if you need anything."

"Thanks," Stacey said, and he left them sitting on the bleachers.

"So," Shane said, "still having a good day?"

"It's been one of those roller coaster days," Stacey admitted. "I'll be happy when it's over."

"You know Kyle was the one who pulled you out, don't you?" He asked. Stacey lifted her head and he added, "I don't think he minded that he had to do the mouth-to-mouth either."

"He-he did *what?*" Stacey asked.

"You weren't breathing when you came up, so they had to do mouth-to-mouth resuscitation."

"You're kidding, right?"

"Nope."

"Great!" Stacey rolled her eyes. "That'll make Amber like me *so* much more." She dropped her head onto her arms again. "Why can't I just have a decent first day? I want to go back to Michigan."

"Oh, come on, we're not *that* bad. We may have our quirks, but every town does."

"Well," she looked back up at him, "I guess it would be safe to say that I *definitely* flunked Newbie 101 now."

"Don't worry about it. Everyone's had one of those days. Just relax and let things play themselves out. You never know what's going to happen next."

"I'm going to go ask Mrs. Nelson if I can get changed. I'm obviously not swimming for the rest of the day. I think I need some space anyway," Stacey said, stepping off the bleachers.

"Sounds like a good plan," Shane agreed. He stepped down with her.

They went into their separate locker rooms to get a shower and change, before heading back to the pool area to wait for the others. Of course, Shane was done first, so he was already on the bleachers by the time Stacey finished. He sat with his legs stretched out in front of him over a couple rows, resting back on his elbows.

"You're looking better," Shane said.

"I'm fine. A little nerve-wracked, but I'll be okay," Stacey said, sitting down beside him. She opened her math book to start on her homework, resting her still pounding head with her left hand, while she wrote with her right.

"Okay, so you're in my math class, lit class, *and* P.E. class. What other classes of mine are you in?" Shane asked.

"I don't know." She handed him her schedule. "Check it out for yourself."

"Hmmm, looks like outside of lunch, that's it."

"You mean I get a brain break from you guys? I was beginning to wonder," she said with a smirk.

Kyle walked up to the pair as the teachers dismissed the rest of the class to the locker rooms. "How are you feeling?"

"Fine." Stacey responded.

"Did you miss me?" Kyle sat down next to her.

"Not really."

"That wasn't very nice," he said, taken aback. "Is that the thanks I get for saving your life?"

"Well sure, after all, it *was* your fault we were in that position in the first place," Shane said. "If I wasn't hurt too, I'd half wonder if you did it on purpose just so you could give her mouth-to-mouth."

"You can be dealt with, big guy!" Kyle snapped.

"Oh, yeah?" Shane stood up. "What are *you* going to do about it?"

"Guys?" Stacey shook her head, disgusted with their display. "If this is for me, then you might as well cut it out now. I'm not biting."

"No. It's an alpha male thing," Kyle said, as he playfully shoved Shane.

Shane shoved him back. "Go get a shower. You stink!"

Kyle laughed as he jogged to the locker room.

Once he was in the locker room, Stacey asked, "So, who *is* the alpha male of your group?"

"He is," Shane said. "But we try not to tell him. It might go to his head."

Stacey chuckled, before turning her attention back to her math homework, while the rest of the class went to the locker rooms to finish getting ready.

WHEN THEY RETURNED TO SCHOOL, Alex and Marissa went with Stacey to the nurse to get her checked out. Stacey was cleared to go back to class, so the nurse gave her a slip to take home to her dad, notifying him of the accident report. Shane had to do the same.

Afterward, the group headed down to the cafeteria. The lunch line was a bit confusing, but Adam, Alex, and the girls of the group helped Stacey figure it out. It seems they did not have open lunches there like they did in her old school. They had to eat in the cafeteria, whether it was a lunch they brought from home or the hot lunch the school provided.

"So, a rough morning, huh?" Adam asked, as they sat down at a table.

"Have had better," Stacey admitted. "I've had worse too."

"Here," a girl who looked to be freshman age said, sliding Alex a piece of paper before she left.

"Well," Alex cleared his throat, scanning the paper. "It seems that…well, hmm." He studied it a bit more.

Adam smirked. "What has your intel provided now?"

Stacey sat between Adam and another girl. Her name was Harmony Kelley. Her twin sister, Melody, was on the other side of the table across from her. They had light brown hair with blond highlights and hazel eyes. Stacey noticed they were identical, with only a difference of a few inches in height between them. While they were identical in looks, that was varied in the area of make-up and hairstyle.

Next to Melody was Alex, and then Marissa. "Well, it seems that…well, read for yourself," Alex said, handing the paper to Adam.

"Do we *want* to know?" Marissa asked. "This looks serious."

"Could be a slight –"

"So, how are you doing?" Kyle walked up behind Stacey, cutting Adam off. He had Amber, Shane, and Erin with him.

"Oh-my-word!" Amber said, appalled. "I cannot believe you brought us over here for *her*! When you told me you saved someone's life, I didn't think it was her! We are out of here!" She went to leave, but Kyle grabbed her arm so she would not go anywhere.

"Judgy much?" Shane snapped. "We're just checking on her. Maybe if you took a second to get to know her, you might actually like her."

"I am not sharing the same personal space with these guys! They are just –"

Alex cleared his throat. Cutting Amber off, he pointed out, "Um, we may be out of your social league, but *she* is not."

"You have got to be kidding!" Amber said, disgusted.

"No. I'm not." Alex continued, "I have a source who works in the office. She has procured some rather interesting information you would appreciate." He gestured toward the paper in Adam's hand.

Stacey nervously glanced at the paper Adam was holding. She could only hazard a guess as to what information was on the precious piece of paper.

"It seems Ms. Spencer's attributes allow her to be more than suitable for your social status," Alex said.

Amber furrowed her brow. "Was that English?"

"She was one of you in her old school," Adam clarified. "Read for yourself. She had a 4.1 grade point average. She was in volleyball and track, lettering in both in her freshman and sophomore years. She was also one of the top girls in popularity in her old school. She was on the homecoming courts for both years, and even homecoming queen in her sophomore year. Unfortunately, her mother passed away last March, sending her and her father into a tailspin. Her dad is a lawyer. He graduated from Harvard Law, and is working up in a Cleveland law firm. Her mom was a rather successful cardiologist before she passed away."

"Knew that," Kyle said proudly. "That's why I was trying –"

"To hit on her," Shane cut him off, glaring at Kyle out of the corner of his eye.

Stacey sat there mortified. She dropped her head onto her hand, shaking it. She could not believe this was all going on... and on her first day no less.

Amber's jaw hit the floor. Stunned, she asked Kyle, "Are you serious?"

"I was trying to make her feel welcome," Kyle defended himself.

"Can we please stop?" Stacey begged. "My head still hurts from this morning."

"If you need some aspirin, you can go back to the nurse to get it," Shane suggested. "You did get hit pretty hard."

"Stop pandering to her!" Erin snapped. "Amber and I are done. We're going back to the table." She jerked her hand away from Shane, and pulled Amber with her as they left for the other side of the cafeteria.

Kyle and Shane both shook their heads as they watched the girls leave.

"Sorry for that," Kyle apologized. "They tend to get a little testy."

"There's the information." Alex nodded toward the paper in Adam's hand. As Adam handed the paper to Shane, Alex said, "You may verify its accuracy and authenticity for yourselves, but I assure you my sources are accurate."

"Go find your so-called ladies, gentlemen," Adam said, snidely. "They are in obvious need of your attention."

"Well, I guess we'll take that as a hint." Kyle shrugged. He leaned down near Stacey's ear, as he said, "See ya later, Stace."

Shane folded the paper Adam gave him, and then slid it into his back pocket. Then they left, going back to the table where Amber and Erin sat.

"Good riddance to that trash!" Harmony said, disgusted. "The whole lot of them are –"

"Harmony, be nice," Melody scolded.

She folded her arms in a huff. "I am!"

"Well, that was fun." Adam smirked. "Haven't seen Erin *or* Amber that riled up since...well, since Harmony and Randy started dating."

"Erin liked Randy too," Harmony explained, "but *I* won that one."

"Randy's in your homeroom," Alex said to Stacey. "You'll probably meet him in Psych," he said, as he finished eating. "We have that class together, along with Randy, Brian, and Melody."

WHEN STACEY WALKED INTO PSYCHOLOGY, it did not take long for her to figure out which one was Randy. He was just as Harmony described. His hair was blond and short, done in a military style haircut. He had blue eyes, and was slightly muscular, possibly a wrestler's build to him.

"Yeah, unfortunately Amber and Brad are in there with us, and it seems you've made just *such* a wonderful impression on that crew already," Randy said, while the group talked about Randy and Stacey's homeroom.

That was Stacey's eighth, and last class for the day. Their teacher's name was Mr. Freud. The irony of his name was not lost on Stacey.

The other classes Stacey had through the day were Art for her fifth-period class; Accounting for sixth; and Biology for seventh.

"So, newbie law number three I broke," Stacey said, as they evaluated her day, *"Don't tick off the popular crowd. Also, number four, don't drown, and have to have one of them save you either."*

"Actually, if you recall, he did mouth-to-mouth on you. I'm sure that is not helping Amber's disposition toward you," Alex added.

"Yeah, probably not," Stacey said. "So, newbie law number five? *Don't have it, so that one of the hottest guys in school has to give you mouth-to-mouth while you're at it."*

"Actually, I'd love for Kyle to give *me* mouth-to-mouth!" Melody piped up. She sighed. "Some girls just get all the luck."

"Hey, I had to be totally mortified and get kicked in the head to get mouth-to-mouth by Kyle. Nope, sorry, not seeing that it was worth it," Stacey said.

"I'm sure you'll break more of those laws before the day is done," Brian said. "You seem to be on a roll."

"Those newbie laws are funny!" Melody remarked. "I've never heard them before."

"They're just one's I made up. I was really trying to *not* break *too* many of them, but it seems I'm queen of them today," Stacey said. "And it looks like I didn't break any small-time ones either, just the biggies," she said. The others snickered, and Mr. Freud got up to start class, ending their discussion.

CHAPTER 2

"THERE ARE TWO WAYS OF EXERTING
ONE'S STRENGTH: ONE IS PUSHING DOWN,
THE OTHER IS PULLING UP." BOOKER T.
WASHINGTON

As soon as class let out, Stacey headed for her locker. While she shoved the books she would not need for homework into the locker, Adam walked up.

"So, break anymore newbie laws?" he asked, leaning on the locker next to hers. "From what I heard, you were pretty free and clear after the lunch escapade."

"I'm hoping I've graduated, and am finished with Newbie 101," she said. "I broke some pretty major newbie laws, and I *really* don't want to go through it again."

"Guess we'll find out tomorrow," he said. When Stacey shut her locker, Adam asked, "So, do you live near here? Want some company on the walk home?"

"Actually, I live about a mile from here," she said, as they started down the hall. "Company would be nice, if it's not out of your way. And hey, if the others want to come, there's a club-house in the complex where I live. We could go hang out there for a bit, that is, if you guys want to," she suggested as they walked outside. "It has a game room in it with pool tables, ping pong tables, air hockey, a retro pinball game, that sort of stuff."

"Pinball? Do people still play pinball?"

45

"Some do. Like I said, it's retro. It's actually fun. There are a couple old video games in there too. It's kind of cool," Stacey said.

"Sounds good. I'll ask the others, but it sounds like fun. Where do you live?"

"Silverwood Townhouses."

"Silv—wow! That's a nice area!" he said, stunned. "We usually meet over there after school." He pointed to a big tree where Randy, Harmony, and Alex were already standing. "Come on."

"So, any more screw-ups?" Harmony asked with a snicker when Stacey and Adam walked up to the trio.

Alex shook his head. "You have *such* a way with words, Harmony."

"I think I may be free and clear now," Stacey said. "We'll find out for sure tomorrow."

"She lives over in Silverwood Townhouses, and wants to know if we wanted to go over for a bit," Adam said.

"Silverwood?" Harmony's jaw dropped momentarily, but she quickly recovered. "Those are *way* expensive!"

"Is that a no?" Stacey cleared her throat as she tucked a portion of her hair behind her ear.

Randy reached over and wrapped one arm around Harmony, while covering her mouth with his other hand. Then he smiled, and said, "We'd love to." He then looked down at Harmony, and said, "And as much as I love you and your beautiful mouth, someday you'll learn to control it." He took his hand off her mouth, quickly kissing her before she could object.

"Okay." Adam chuckled. "All we need are Riss, Brian, and Mel."

"Hi guys!" Marissa walked up and stood on the other side of Adam. "What's going on? It looks like Harmony's stepped in it again," she said, as Harmony stood there red-faced.

"We're going over to Stacey's house. Want to come?" Adam asked.

"For what?"

"There's a clubhouse in the complex where she lives. We thought we'd just go to hang out," Adam said.

"Clubhouse? What? Does she live in Silverwood or something?" Marissa laughed. Then she looked at everyone, and her face red. "I'm...oh boy." She covered her face. "You do, don't you?"

Stacey nodded, her face flushed red. "Never mind," she said, nibbling on her nails. "Forget I asked."

"No, no, we want to come. It's just there's not, well, it's normally more of a place where people live who don't have kids," Adam explained. "They're more, well, professional, that's it," he said. "We've just never known anyone our age who lived there before."

"It is known as an exclusive place to live. It is rare to find kids or teens who live there," Alex clarified. "We would be honored to go. It merely comes as a bit of a surprise."

"That's okay," Stacey said. "I guess I...." her voice faded.

Adam rested his arm over Stacey's shoulders. "It's okay. You don't need to worry about Newbie 101 with us."

"Thanks. I just–I wanted...I don't know," Stacey stammered.

"Hey! Hey! The gangs all here!" Brian smiled, walking over with Melody. "What's the scoop for the afternoon?"

"I have to work later, but for now we have an invitation to the ever-elite Silverwood," Marissa explained.

"Are you –? Sweet!" Brian grinned. "How'd we score that one?"

"I live there," Stacey said, quietly.

Adam squeezed her shoulders again as a sign of encouragement, before he took his arm off, shoving his hand into his pocket. "So, who's riding with who?" he asked.

"You guys have cars?" Stacey asked.

"Yep!" Adam grinned. "Well, some of us do."

"I thought you were going to walk me home?" Stacey asked Adam.

"I didn't want to make you walk by yourself," he said. "Since it's about a mile away, I would have offered to drive you."

"I see," she said. "Thank you."

"Anytime." Turning to the others, he said, "Let's go." With that, everyone headed toward the vehicles.

Adam had an older car, which was not the best looking, but seemed to run pretty well. He bragged about his little maroon Ford Escort on the way to the parking lot. Mainly, that was because he saved his own money to buy it. He drove with Stacey in the passenger's seat, and Alex and Marissa in the back. Melody and Harmony shared a Ford F150 quad-cab truck their parents bought them, so they took Randy and Brian with them, following Adam's car to Stacey's townhouse.

The group entered Stacy and her dad's townhouse. During their unpacking, Stacey was the one who decorated. She kept it as close to how she felt her mother would have decorated the home as she could. Her mom had a rustic country style to her décor. Stacey's taste was a bit more modern, as was the townhouse style, so she blended the two. The townhomes were only a few years old, so all of them had modern appliances, as well as an industrial design to them. Most of the house was white with gray accents. The counters throughout the house were marble, while all cupboards and drawers were painted white.

"This is nice!" Melody said, looking around when the group entered Stacey and her dad's townhouse. "I've never been in one of these before."

"It's just until we find a real house," Stacey explained. "It's a lot smaller than our house in Michigan. It's taking some getting used to."

Brian smirked. "I could get used to it *real* fast!"

Stacey ran upstairs to put her books in her room, before she headed back down to get everyone a pop. Afterward, the group headed down to the clubhouse.

"Okay, I could *really* get use to *this*!" Brian grinned when they walked into the clubhouse. "Seriously! This is nice!"

"So, what do you guys feel like playing?" Stacey asked.

"Is that real pinball machine?" Melody asked.

"Yep!"

Melody grinned. "I want to play pinball!"

"Play ya?" Brian asked. She just nodded, so they took off with Harmony and Randy behind them.

"Pool?" Stacey suggested. "Or ping pong?"

"How about teams for ping pong?" Marissa asked. "I think pool is a two-person game."

"That sounds good," Adam agreed.

The four of them went over to the ping pong table. Stacey and Alex picked up the paddles.

The four of them stood there awkwardly a few moments before Stacey asked, "Um, girls versus boys?"

There was something in the group's dynamics that was off. Stacey could not quite put her finger on what it was at that moment. She decided to keep an eye on the group until she figured it out.

"That sounds good," Adam said. He and Alex went over to one side, while Marissa and Stacey went to the other. "How about the winners treat the losers to ice cream later at Trina's?"

"We want in on that one!" Harmony said over her shoulder. "Hold on!" Once she finished her game, their group came over to the ping pong table.

"Now, how are we going to do this?" Stacey asked. "There are four girls, and four boys, but only two paddles per side."

"Best two out of three?" Adam suggested. "Whichever team loses, they buy."

"We'll play in pairs, and then mix it up for the third," Alex offered.

The girls congregated to one side, while the boys went to the other. "Okay," Stacey said, "so, who's first for us?"

"Well, Harm and Mel are our best players," Marissa said thinking. "So, how about –?"

"We don't know how she plays," Harmony interrupted Marissa. "She could beat us all hands down."

"Fine," she said sharply. "Then, *you* divide up the teams."

"What is wrong with you?" Harmony asked, surprised by her reaction.

Marissa huffed as she crossed her arms. "Nothing."

"Okay," Harmony said on a sigh, shaking her head. "How about me and Stacey take the first game, and then Riss and Mel grab the second? We'll sort out who gets the third once we see how we all play."

"Sounds good," Stacey agreed. Stacey did not care for Marissa's attitude. While she did not think she did anything to deserve it, she would have to figure out where it was coming from before it became an issue.

Stacey and Harmony went to the table first. When the guys saw who was there, Randy and Adam walked to the table.

"But–" Marissa started, but quickly changed her mind. "Never mind. Have at it."

"Glad we have your permission. *Anyway*," Harmony rolled her eyes, "who serves first?"

Randy tossed her the ball. "Ladies first."

She caught it. With that, the game started. Stacey thought it would go on forever. Both sides had really good players.

"Finally!" Harmony smiled. "Yes!" She said, as she and Stacey did a high-five. Stacey and Harmony beat Adam and Randy by two points.

"About time," Marissa grumbled, as she and Melody stepped-up for their turn against Alex and Brian.

Stacey chose to ignore Marissa's actions, and enjoyed the fact that they won the first game.

"You play great!" Harmony said to Stacey, while she, Randy, Adam, and Stacey went off to the side.

"Not as well as you," Stacey complimented Harmony. "Ping pong is not my best game."

"You did really good! After those two beat Alex and Brian, we'll be good to go for free ice cream," Harmony said, excited.

"I don't know about that one." Randy shook his head. "Marissa's playing is way off. Her mind elsewhere," he said, glancing at her over his shoulder.

Instead of paying attention to the game, Marissa was looking at the group on the side. Then she quickly looked back to the table in time to hit the ball. She hit it too hard. It went off the table on her side of the net, giving the guys the point.

"See?" Randy said. "Way off."

Adam shrugged. "She'll get over it."

"Was there, or *is* there something between you two?" Stacey asked when Marissa glanced their way again.

"No. She wants it, but it's not happening." Adam shook his head. "She's nice, but not my type."

Stacey nodded in response. She understood his perspective, but felt for Marissa.

The four watched the remainder of the game. When Marissa and Melody lost to Brian and Alex, the guys cheered.

"Winner takes all!" Adam grinned. "Pick your team wisely," he warned.

The two teams divided to decide who would be the final two teams.

"We have to mix this last one up," Harmony said, thinking through the games and how everyone played. "So, how about Stace and Mel?"

"Sounds good," Melody agreed.

Stacey nodded. "That'll work."

"Ready?" Randy asked. The girls nodded, and he and Brian

got up to play. When Stacey and Melody walked up to the table, Randy said, "Well, *this* is a mix-up."

"I think the ice cream will be delivered by the ladies today," Brian teased.

"*I* think you'd better check your wallet to make sure you have enough money for us girls," Stacey shot.

Cocking his head to the side with a smile, Brian said, "That sounds like a challenge."

"I'm very competitive. I don't like to lose," Stacey said, "*especially* when it involves ice cream."

"Good!" Melody grinned. "I don't like to lose either."

As soon as they started playing, they heard Adam and Marissa yelling at each other.

"I don't care!" Adam said angrily. "It's not your place!"

"Guys!" Harmony snapped. "That's enough!"

"Um…"

"Don't worry about it," Melody said. "Harmony and Alex will calm them down. We have a game to win."

"True," Stacey said. She turned back to the game just in time to hit the ball back to Brian.

"Nice." Brian shook his head. "I can't even throw her when she's only half in the game."

They played for twenty brutal minutes. Periodically, they heard Adam and Marissa yelling at each other.

"Excellent!" Stacey smiled when Brian missed the last ball, allowing the girls to win the game.

"Good game," Randy said. He and Brian gave Stacey and Melody each a high five. "You guys did great!"

"So, do we conclude the guys are paying?" Alex asked.

"That would be an accurate assumption, my good man," Brian said, as he half-bowed, using a fake English accent.

Stacey's dad walked into the clubhouse. "There you are," he said. Holding up a piece of paper, he added, "I got your note."

Stacey smiled as she ran over, giving him a hug. "Hi, Dad!"

"There was also an accident report on the counter. What happened?" he asked.

"I had an accident in swimming/lifesaving class. Not a big deal," she said, not wanting to worry him. "It was more the rest of the day that was the issue. I broke some *major* newbie laws."

"Is that where that bruise came from?" he asked, pointing toward her head.

"That came from swimming/lifesaving. I'm fine, though. I just have a bit of headache. Some kids jumped in too close to me and another guy from class." She purposely omitted the fact that she had to be given mouth-to-mouth. "It wasn't pretty, but I'm okay."

"Gotcha. All I care about is that you're okay. So, you broke some major newbie laws, huh? *How* major?"

"Major enough to tick off the most popular girls in school."

"Oh, that's bad!" He shook his head, chuckling. "You always seem to go for the big stuff. So, rough day?"

"It was more of a roller coaster one," Stacey admitted. "I might have ticked off some people, but I made some new friends while I was at it." She gestured toward the group.

"Sam Spencer," he introduced himself. He shook their hands as they introduced themselves.

"Adam Barnes."

"Randy Taylor."

"Melody Kelley."

"Alex Crestwood, sir."

"Harmony Kelley."

"Brian Dalton."

"Marissa James."

"Well, nice to meet all of you," Sam said. Then he turned to Stacey and hinted, "It seems you didn't have *that* bad of a first day."

"No. It turned out really good. Oh!" Stacey remembered.

"Adam is my trainer at Slater's tomorrow night." She pointed to Adam, who nodded in acknowledgement.

"I've heard your name before," Sam said. "You're one of Matt's kids."

"He tends to call us that, yes," Adam said. "I've worked at Slater's for a year now. I started as soon as I turned sixteen."

"Aren't you his neighbor, too?" Sam asked.

"Yes. They're also youth leaders at my church."

"He and Tina are youth leaders for all of us," Melody added.

"Nice!" Sam said, pleasantly surprised Stacey found some good kids to be friends with on the first day.

"We were about to go out for ice cream," Stacey said. "Is that okay?"

"I'm not," Marissa said, flatly. "I have to go to work," she said and left, slamming the door behind her.

Stacey looked after her, stunned. "What happened?"

"Don't worry about her. She'll get over it." Adam shrugged. "She thinks she's the boss of everyone, and gets angry if we don't listen to her."

"Seems like a real peach," Sam remarked, watching her walk across the parking lot.

"She has her moments," Harmony said under her breath.

"How is she getting to work?" Stacey asked. "She rode with all of us."

"She only lives a couple blocks over," Randy said. "Her parents will get her to work."

Hoping to change the mood, Melody reminded them, "I think someone said something about ice cream. That sounds really good about now."

"Yeah. I think so too," Brian said, glancing over at Adam. "So, how about the guys drive together in Adam's car, and the girls ride with Melody and Harmony? We'll meet there?"

"But I want –" Harmony started, but Randy covered her mouth.

"Sounds good," Randy said, and then looked down at her. "We'll meet you there, *okay?*" She nodded in response to Randy's question. "I love you, but I have a feeling the guys need to chat." Harmony nodded again, so he took his hand off and quickly kissed her.

"Good. Since that's settled," Sam said, "what time are you going to be home? And are you eating while you're out?"

"I'll get something to eat while I'm out, and I'll also be home by curfew," Stacey said, hoping he would not give her a hard time in front of her new friends.

He pulled a twenty-dollar bill from his wallet and handed it to Stacey. "Have fun, Peanut," he said. He then gave her a hug, and left for the townhouse.

"Nice dad!" Brian remarked, while they headed toward the vehicles. "Can I have him?"

"Nope, sorry." Stacey shook her head. "He's taken."

"We'll meet you there," Randy said, giving Harmony a quick kiss before the guys got into Adam's car.

Adam did not say a word. He just got into the vehicle and closed the door.

"So, what did we miss in regards to Marissa and Adam, if you don't mind my asking," Stacey asked, as they got in the truck. "He seems pretty upset by it."

Harmony shook her head. "Nothing."

"You're not talking?" Melody's jaw dropped, as she sat between Harmony and Stacey on the bench front seat. "It *must* be big!"

Harmony shook her head while she started the truck. "She was just being Marissa."

"Is Adam going to be okay? He didn't look too happy," Stacey pushed.

"He'll be fine." Harmony waved her off. "Don't worry about him. He knows what he has to do."

Stacey gave up. "All right." She watched the scenery pass out the window as they drove, with Adam heavily on her mind.

When they arrived, everyone got their ice cream from the counter before heading toward a circular booth. It sat Stacey, Harmony, Randy, Melody, Brian, Alex, with Adam on the other end across from Stacey.

"Thank you for making the rest of my first day fun," Stacey said, as they finished their ice cream. "It didn't start off that well, but ended good."

"We all have had to have our first day." Brian shrugged. "Let's just –"

"Well, well, well," Kyle said, as he walked up to the table with Shane, "long time no see."

"What do you want Kyle?" Adam snapped.

Whatever he and Marissa argued about really put him in a bad mood.

"Well, this *is* a club of sorts, so how about a dance?" Kyle asked Stacey. "There are a few people already dancing. Would you join me?"

Adam jumped up from the table. "Sorry, she's dancing with me."

He walked over and grabbed Stacey's hand. She quickly stood up beside him. She was not objecting. She really did not want to go with Kyle.

"Well, it didn't seem like it," Kyle said, blocking their way. "She was on one side, and you were on the other."

"Stace, will you dance with me?" Adam asked.

Stacey nodded in response.

"See?" Adam said. "Go find *your* girlfriend."

Kyle got in his face. "Do you need a lesson in respect?"

"Kyle, what's going on?" Amber nervously asked, as she and Erin walked up to the group.

"We were just talking," Kyle said.

"And *we* were just *leaving*," Adam said, taking Stacey by the hand out to the dance floor.

The club was called Trina's. It was generally for older high school students. It gave them another place in town to hang out besides Slater's. The inside was in a mid-century modern style. If Stacey had to describe the decade style, it would be the fifties.

"Not that I'm complaining, but where did this come from?" Stacey asked. Adam took one of her hands into his, and put his other arm around her waist in keeping with the slower song.

"Kyle's not the type you want to get mixed up with," Adam warned. "It could *literally* be dangerous to your health."

"Huh?"

"Please. Just trust me."

"All right." Stacey sighed. She looked around to see Harmony and Randy, and Melody and Brian get up and come out to dance with them.

"So, is Alex our chaperone for the night?" Stacey asked. "He looks lonely sitting there by himself."

"It's usually him or me sitting there while the other one dances with Marissa. But I get the company tonight, if you don't mind."

"I don't mind," she said.

He nervously cleared his throat before he asked, "So, you're from Michigan?"

"Yep."

"You're a good ping pong player."

"Thanks. So, if you don't mind my asking, what happened with Marissa today at the clubhouse?"

"She, well, she's not always the most, um, she was trying to, uh…" he stumbled through his thoughts.

Stacey furrowed her brow.

"She was trying to tell me who to be friends with," he said in one breath. Then he quickly added, "and I didn't agree with her assessment."

"That sounds like an Alex statement."

"That was his summation."

"Is that why the guys *had* to ride together?"

"Well," he smiled, "it's not just the girls who need to talk."

"Hmm."

"What?"

Stacey shrugged. "Just thinking."

"Is that good or bad?"

"Good." She nodded. "I think." Stacey thought about her new friends before she asked, "So, I'm pretty sure I've got a pretty good idea, but can you give me the low-down on this crew?"

"Well, Kyle and company rule the school, and not in a nice way either," he said. Then he glanced around the dance floor as he continued, "As for the rest of us? Well, hmm, Alex is our brains and information guy. If you need to know something, he usually already knows it, or has a person who has access to it."

"Figured that one already."

"The Kelley twins are a treat!" He smiled. "Mel is the sweet, kind, quiet, gentle, peacemaker of the pair, while Harm is funny." He chuckled. "She's honest, blunt, outgoing, and, well, she's honest."

"That's a nice way of putting it."

He smiled as he thought of each of his friends. "Then Brian is our group comedian. If he can't get you laughing, no one will."

"Are he and Melody dating?"

"Not yet, but that's not entirely by his choice. He doesn't want to assume she feels the same way. He doesn't want to push her away either by being forward. He's taking it slow."

Stacey filed the information in her mind. She liked this new group of people she now called friends.

"Then there's Riss," he said, interrupting her thoughts. "Someday I hope she gets her head screwed on straight. She really is a nice girl. She just has some misguided thoughts and feelings."

"On?"

"Me, mainly," he admitted, as his face flushed.

"I see," Stacey said. "So, from what I've seen, you're the leader of this bunch?"

"I don't know if I'd call myself that."

"I would. I've watched."

"Well," he cleared his throat, as he looked away for a second. Then he said, "Um, Randy? I haven't told you about him yet."

"What about –?"

"He's more our muscle, and the level-headed thinker of the group," Adam explained, cutting off her objection. "He also keeps Harmony in line when Mel isn't available."

Alex walked up to Adam and Stacey. "May I cut in?" he asked.

"Sorry." Adam shook his head. "We're talking."

"Just for one song?" Alex shoved his hands into his pockets. "It's a little lonely over there."

"How about –?" Stacey started, but the song shifted to a fast, fun one, so as a group they danced together.

"WHEW!" Harmony said when they finally sat back down at the table exhausted after a couple hours of dancing. "That was fun!"

Melody smiled. "It was! I think we all needed that!"

"I'm going to go get something to eat dinner wise. Anyone want anything while I'm up there?" Stacey asked. She was starting to feel drained, and knew she had to eat. If she did not eat by a certain time, she got shaky and dizzy. The doctor called it hypoglycemia. While she had ice cream earlier, with dancing for a few hours and not eating anything else, she went from a sugar high to a sugar low.

"No, but I'll come if you want company," Harmony offered, sliding out of the booth with Stacey.

"I'll go too," Melody said. Randy shifted, so Melody could get out with them. Together, the three ladies headed up to the counter, leaving the guys.

"Want to go to the bathroom first?" Melody asked. "I really need to go."

"How about if you two go?" Stacey suggested. "I really need to eat something."

"You look a little pale. Are you okay?" Harmony asked.

"I'll be fine," Stacey said. "I just need to eat."

"Didn't you eat lunch? And some ice cream just a bit ago?" Harmony asked.

"My sugars don't regulate very well. I need to get dinner," Stacey said, as she began to feel on edge from low sugar. "The ice cream spiked my sugar, and then we did a lot of dancing. Now it's low, and past time for my dinner. I should have kept better track of time."

Seeing Stacey's hands shaking, Harmony grabbed Stacey's wrist to take her back to the table. "Yeah, okay," Harmony said. "Come on back to the table and we'll get it for you."

Stacey pulled her hand back. She knew she needed to eat or it would not end well. "I need food."

"All right." Harmony put her hands up in surrender. "We'll be right back. Don't go anywhere."

Taking deep breaths, Stacey glanced around the club doing her best to stay focused until it was her turn to order. She felt light-headed, and hoped the line would be quick.

After a minute of standing in line, Kyle walked up behind Stacey. "Boo!" He said, grabbing her sides.

She gasped, as she jumped. She placed her hand on her chest in hopes of keeping her heart inside her body. "Don't do that!"

He laughed. "Sorry."

"It's okay. I–I just…you scared me."

"Amber decided she wanted a Coke, so I came to get it for her."

"Nice of you," Stacey said, her heart still racing.

"So," he put his arm over her shoulder, "how do you like Pine Crest so far?"

Stacey reached back, shoving his arm off her. "Not too sure."

"Stacey, can't leave you alone for a minute, can we?" Brian suddenly popped up beside her. He put his arm over her shoulder, and turned to go back to the table. "The table's this way," he said aloud. Then he quietly added, "We'll get you something to eat in a minute, but you need to get to the table now. Amber's shooting daggers at you!"

"Oh," Stacey nodded, struggling to concentrate. "Okay. Thank you."

Brian guided her to the table and sat her down next to Adam. The guys shifted so Stacey was sandwiched between Adam and Brian.

"Um, guys, I, um…." Stacey put her head down. "I needed to eat twenty minutes ago, but I *really* need to eat now."

"Are you a diabetic?" Adam asked, concerned.

"Hypoglycemic," she mumbled. She closed her eyes as the world spun around her.

Randy jumped up from the table to go get food. "Got it."

"Word of warning?" Adam leaned down near her ear when Randy left. "You need to stay away from Kyle. It's *really* not a good thing."

She tilted her head to look at him as she said, "*He* keeps coming to *me*. Look, I need…" she started, but dropped her head back down.

"I think Randy had better pick up his pace," Alex said looking at Stacey.

A few minutes later, as Harmony stayed with Randy, Melody returned to the table.

"What's wrong?" Melody asked, sliding into the booth. "Did something happen while we were in the bathroom?"

"Well, it seems that our new friend is not only an attractant of Kyle's, but is also hypoglycemic," Alex explained.

"That's what she said. How bad is it?"

"She needs to eat," Adam said, gesturing toward her.

"Got it covered," Randy said. He and Harmony came back from the table with fries and a Coke for everyone.

Stacey mumbled a word of thanks, but kept her head down. The room continued to spin out of control.

Adam rested his hand on her back. "Stacey, I think you should eat something."

Stacey nodded as she slowly sat up. With the room spinning and her body shaking, she decided the pop would give her the quicker sugar dose. She also snacked on a few fries while resting her head back on the seat.

"I don't think Amber and Erin like you very much," Harmony said, glancing in the direction of their table.

Stacey picked up another fry. "Sorry. That's not my problem."

"It could be," Brian said.

"It's all her. Well, her and Kyle. Kyle keeps pulling me into their mess. I don't want anything to do with him. He seems cocky and arrogant," Stacey said. "He thinks every girl here wants him. He thinks all he has to do is smile and girls will fall at his feet doing whatever he wants."

"It's normally true," Alex said. "However, you don't seem to be bending toward him. I think he considers you a challenge at this point."

"Great," Stacey said on a sigh.

"Are you going to be okay? You still look really pale," Melody said, concerned.

"I'll be fine in a bit," Stacey said.

"That is, if you stay away from Kyle." Brian shook his head. "That guy is seriously bad news."

"Heard that," Stacey acknowledged.

Everyone was lost in their own thoughts while snacking on the fries and drinking pop for several minutes.

As he finished, Randy asked Harmony, "Want to go dance again?"

Harmony glanced at her watch. "I think we'd better start heading home. Our parents will worry if we aren't home soon."

"Can you guys give me a ride home?" Alex asked. "I have a report I need to work on. It's due on Monday."

"Me too." Brian slid out of the booth. "And I have to work the weekend, so I can't put it off."

"Let's go," Harmony said.

The group left after they said good-bye to Adam and Stacey.

Adam smirked. "Well, that was different."

"What?"

"They vacated quickly."

"Do you mind taking me home?" Stacey asked.

"Not at all. Whenever you want to go home, I'll take you. My mom's not going to be home for another couple hours, so no rush."

"I think I need more to eat, but I don't want to stay here and chance running into Kyle again."

"Want to go to Slater's?"

"Actually, that sounds good," Stacey said. They left, with Stacey bringing the fries and her pop with her to finish on the way to Slater's.

"So, you moved here why again?" he asked, as they headed toward Slater's.

"Well, my mom died in a car accident in March. After that, it was just not a good situation to stay in." Stacey shook her head. "Everywhere we turned, there were more memories. We also had family everywhere who were continuously reminding us of things she said or did. That wasn't helping us at all."

"I'm sorry."

"That's okay." Stacey sat up, finally starting to feel her sugars balance. "I'm just glad I've been able to meet some good people here already."

"Just do me one favor?" Adam asked.

"What's that?"

"Will you seriously stay away from Kyle if you can? He likes you, and that's a *really* bad thing."

"I'll take your word for it."

"Thanks," he said, as they pulled into Slater's. He parked the car, and then quickly went around to open her door for her.

"Thank you," Stacey said, pleasantly surprised.

"No big. It's ingrained in me," he said. "My mom makes me get her door all the time."

"That's not necessarily a bad thing."

"No. It's a habit now."

The hostess grinned when they walked into the restaurant. "Hey, Adam!"

"Hi, Ashley. We're here for dinner. Got any seats with a decent waiter?" he asked.

"Let me see…" she said, scanning the list.

"Who's on?"

"Um, there is Karalee, Jimmy, Carl, Vinnie, Shay-Lynn, Jett, and Mikey."

"Well, hmm," he said, thinking through the list. "How about Mikey? We could use a good laugh."

Ashley looked up and smiled as she nodded.

"Who's Mikey?" Stacey asked, while they followed her to a booth. The pair sat on opposite sides, facing each other.

Adam chuckled, taking his seat. "Oh, you'll see."

The waiter immediately came to the table. He half-bowed, as he said, "Hello, Sir Barnes, and his lovely lady who is…?"

"Hey, Mikey. This is Stacey Spencer. She's new," Adam explained.

"New at school?"

"New in town *and* at school."

"Spectacular!" He smiled a jovial smile. "That is simply delightful news!"

In an attempt not to laugh, Stacey covertly covered her mouth. She enjoyed this young man's attitude and did not want to offend him.

"So, Lady Spencer, what would you care to dine on this evening?"

"Any specials?" Stacey asked.

"Oh yes!" He smiled, and then did a dramatically funny presentation on the special. "We have a simply scrumptious meal of plump chicken breasts, smothered in a mouthwateringly delectable concoction of our very own homemade spaghetti sauce. It is topped with an enchanting medley of parmesan, provolone, and mozzarella cheeses, and served with a —"

"Okay, okay," Stacey said, laughing, unable to contain it any longer. "I'll take it." She was relieved when he smiled in pleasure of her enjoyment.

"Superb choice." Mikey winked. Glancing at Adam, he added, "Brilliant young lady who knows what she wants."

"You know what, I'll take that too," Adam said, as he closed his menu. He handed Mikey both menus.

Tucking them under his arm, Mikey said, "I will return momentarily with your crisp green salad, which includes crunchy croutons, along with several other freshly-cut vegetables. It is topped with our very own in-house made Italian dressing. I will also return with your, hot, fresh from the oven, homemade bread sticks. Would you care for some zesty marinara sauce, sprinkled with a little shredded parmesan cheese on top?"

"Um, I think so?" Stacey looked at Adam, who nodded.

Mikey bowed his head and curtsied before he left. When he was gone, Stacey and Adam burst out in laughter.

"I told you he would be a treat," Adam said. "And after today,

I'm pretty sure you could use a good laugh."

"He seems like a good guy."

"That he is," he agreed. "He's a walking Thesaurus. His tables usually tip him just for the extra adjectives they acquire while he serves them."

"Sounds like you've picked up a few of your own."

"You can't help it working around him."

True to his word, Mikey brought the salad and bread sticks. To Stacey's delight they were heavenly. Everything they had was delicious. With food this good, Stacey was certain she would make great tips as a server.

Mikey half-bowed, as he set their bills on the table. "I do hope you had a splendid evening at our dining establishment," he said, and left for another table.

Adam chuckled, after Mikey was out of earshot. "Well, ready to go home?"

"Not really, but I'd better go. I have Psych homework to finish."

"Yeah, and you wouldn't want to disappoint Mr. Freud. He might analyze that against you, and say you did it on purpose." He rolled his eyes. "All right." Adam stood. "Let's head out."

After they paid their bills, and left Mikey a healthy tip, Adam took Stacey home. When she walked in, she told her dad how the evening went, and then headed upstairs to do her homework.

All-in-all her first day was a good one. She chose to look at the good, and keep the bad in the back of her mind as to what to avoid when she headed to school the next morning.

CHAPTER 3

"THAT WHICH DOES NOT KILL US MAKES
US STRONGER." FRIEDRICH NIETZSCHE

"Well, ready to try this again?" Stacey's dad asked when they pulled up to the school the next morning.

Stacey yawned. "I think so."

"Are you going to be okay to go today? You were up pretty late last night between us talking and your homework."

"Should be." She stretched. Then she gave him a hug, and got out of the vehicle, slowly heading toward school to start her day.

"Stacey!" Adam called, running across the lawn. "I called for you five times," he said when he finally caught up to her.

"I'm sorry. I didn't hear you."

"That's okay. Mind if I walk you to class since we're in the same one?" he asked.

"Sure," Stacey said with a smile.

"So, how do you like our little corner of the world so far?"

"Pretty good. Of course, I haven't officially started day two yet. Considering the way Kyle was acting yesterday, I'm not sure if I want to. I can't imagine Amber appreciates me, and I *know* Erin hates me."

"Just ignore them and hang out with us. We don't have anything against you."

"Actually, I'm more relaxed when I'm with you guys," Stacey said. "With the others, I feel tense and on edge."

"With good reason," Adam said, pulling off a note taped to Stacey's locker. As he handed it to her, he explained, "That's Erin's hand writing. I'd recognize it anywhere. We've been going to the same school since elementary school. We were even friends up until Jr. High. That's when she got sucked into the rude crowd."

"So, what crowd are you in?"

"We're more of a laid-back group."

"Gotcha," Stacey said. Then she opened the note. It was from Erin, just as Adam thought. "Not good," Stacey said, passing the note to Adam. "She wants to meet with me."

"Want me to come with you? That way you have a witness."

"I wouldn't mind another person with me. It's probably not a good idea to be alone. However, I'm not going to purposely look for her. If she finds me, she finds me," Stacey said. Then she added with a smirk, "But I'm going to avoid it with everything I've got."

"Probably wise," Adam said as they headed to math.

"I see your choice in friends has sunk to a *really* low level," Kyle remarked when Stacey walked into math with Adam. "You need an upgrade."

"I like the ones I have just fine. Thank you," Stacey said, taking her seat.

Adam went to his seat a row over, keeping an eye on them. He dug his homework out as he eavesdropped on their conversation.

"Well," Kyle turned around, "I have to tell you, after checking out that paper Crestwood gave us yesterday, I'm surprised you would even talk to him. I'm shocked you hang around any of that crew for that matter."

"They're nice people. I also trust them a lot more than I do you guys."

"Well," he huffed, "that doesn't sound very friendly at all. Maybe you *do* belong with them."

"That's what I've been trying to tell you," Stacey said.

Mr. Wexford walked past them to the front of the class to start. "Please open your books to page fifty-seven."

"We'll finish this later," Kyle whispered. "In P.E. maybe, when *he's* not around," he nodded toward Adam, who rolled his eyes.

Stacey shook her head in response, while Mr. Wexford had the class open their books to the homework from the previous night.

After class, Kyle tried to talk to Stacey again, but she quickly got up and went over to Adam, hoping Kyle would get the hint.

"You are a wanted woman," Brian said, coming up behind Adam and Stacey as they walked to second-period. "You'd better keep your eyes open. Amber and Erin are on the warpath looking for you."

"Great," Stacey said on a sigh. "Just what I needed this morning."

"We could dawdle a bit, and sneak in at the last minute," Adam suggested.

"No, we'll –"

"Hey you!" Shane stepped in front of them, cutting Stacey off. He walked backwards a couple steps until they stopped. "Your presence is requested." They tried to side-step him, but he stepped in front of Stacey again. "Look, they're going to catch up with you sooner or later."

"We'll just make it later," Stacey said. "I'm trying to get through day two of school *without* being injured."

"Just lay off, Mason," Adam said, as he stepped slightly in

front of Stacey. Brian hung back a bit, so they would not get caught off-guard from behind. "She hasn't done anything. It's all Chandler."

"Well, that's the thing," Shane said in a low voice. "You see, it's *her* he wants. And what Kyle wants, Kyle gets."

Fire flashed in Stacey's eyes. "I don't *think* so!" she snapped. "I don't jump just because someone says so! And I'm *not* anyone's personal property either!"

"You might want to re-think that philosophy," Shane said. As he walked off, he said a little louder, "It could be dangerous to your health."

"Okay, that's the second time I've heard that." Stacey narrowed her eyes at Adam and Brian. With her hands on her hips, she demanded, "What *exactly* does that mean?"

"It means people tend to get beat up when they don't listen to them," Adam explained, as he grabbed her arm, hurrying them in a different direction. They went the long way around to class, and ducked in just as the bell rang.

"Well, a couple seconds later, and you three would have been counted as tardy," Mrs. McCoy mentioned while taking attendance for class. "Might want to watch that."

"Sorry, Mrs. McCoy," the three of them said in unison as they took their seats.

Stacey glanced back at Erin, Amber, and Shane. Amber and Erin glared at her, but Shane winked. Stacey quickly turned back to Adam, wide-eyed.

"Not good," Adam whispered. "Duck them for the rest of the day. I'll try to keep at least one of us near you at all times. You have to do your best to avoid them as well."

"I'll try, but I don't normally run," Stacey whispered back.

"Just for today. Give us the weekend to figure something out," he said, as Mrs. McCoy got up to start class.

After class, Adam and Brian walked Stacey to Alex and Marissa. They warned them not to leave Stacey alone in class that day. Alex and Marissa agreed, so the group set to meet up with Adam, Melody, and Harmony for lunch near the office after class. With that, they headed to P.E. for swimming/lifesaving.

~

WHILE THEY WERE in the locker room changing, Marissa was with Stacey. "Okay, what's going on?" Marissa demanded. "I haven't seen Adam this jumpy in a very long time."

"Erin and Amber have been looking for me today. It seems Kyle and Shane are in on it too," Stacey explained.

Marissa looked at Stacey wide-eyed. "Uh." She cleared her throat "Exactly *how* in on it are Shane and Kyle? And what do you mean by that?"

"Why?"

"Did something happen last night after I left?"

"Yeah, Kyle kept bugging us and hitting on me when we were at Trina's. So, after everyone else left, Adam and I went to Slater's to eat dinner. You know, to try and relax a little. Then he took me home. Why?"

"You...*what?*" She narrowed her eyes at Stacey. "What did... you ate...with who...*where?*"

"Adam and I went to Slater's." Stacey furrowed her brow. "What's wrong?"

Marissa acted as if she and Adam were dating, and Stacey was trying to take him from her. She was not sure whether to be angry by her rudeness, or be arrogant about the fact that they went out to dinner alone just to be a brat.

"Are you kidding me?"

"No. Why?"

"Who was your waiter?" Marissa demanded.

"Mikey. He was pretty funny too!" Stacey smiled, remembering the previous night.

"Why that little...Oh!" She growled. "I can't even!" she said, and stomped off.

"Okay." Stacey sighed, shaking her head. Then under her breath, she added, "Obviously I'm not making a friend out of her." She finished getting ready, and then headed out to the bleachers to wait for class to start.

"Here you are," Kyle said, as he sat on the bench beside Stacey. "And without your bodyguards."

"Where *are* Alex and Marissa?" she asked, looking for them.

"They're over there. She looks pretty mad," he said, pointing toward the other side of the pool.

Alex and Marissa were in a heated argument over in the corner. She was doing most of the yelling. He seemed to be half trying to calm her down, half standing up for the argument itself.

"Would you happen to know what that's about?" Kyle asked.

"Possibly me." Stacey looked down at her hands, upset. She strongly wished to be back in Michigan at that moment.

"What is she upset about?" Kyle asked.

"Adam and I went to Slater's last night after Trina's."

"And?" Kyle pressed.

"And well, she didn't like it."

"Why not?"

"Because she likes Adam, but Adam and I are connecting. She doesn't approve."

"We need to talk," Kyle said, as he reached over and took her hand.

"What? No, we don't. Let me go," Stacey said, trying to pull away, but he held tight.

"Listen," he said sternly.

"I don't have to listen to you," Stacey looked at him surprised. He squeezed her hand so hard, it hurt.

"They don't care about you," he persisted. "They just want to fight over you. If those are your friends, then you might want to rethink that choice."

Stacey glanced over at them. They were still arguing.

"I can protect you from all of that," Kyle said. "I can take care of you. All you have to do is ask me."

"I–I don't…" Stacey shook her head. She tried to pull her hand back, but he held tighter. She felt it pulsating under his grip. Stacey wanted to get away from him, but there was nowhere for her to go.

"*Yes*, you do," he said, locking onto her eyes. He would not look away. Then he shifted in front of her, blocking her view of Marissa and Alex. "Do you *really* want to spend your days looking over your shoulder to see what she's going to accuse you of next?" he asked. When Stacey shook her head, he continued, "Do you *really* want to have a so-called friend who hates you? Marissa *hates* you. You know that, don't you? She *despises* you. Do you want that? Do you *want* to have a friend who detests the sight of you?"

"No," Stacey said, his words swirling around in her mind.

"How can you handle going out with them *knowing* just how much she *loathes* you?"

"I…" Stacey looked up at him. He was staring directly into her eyes. She could not look away. His eyes were so green, yet as cold as ice. He looked deep into her eyes, as if he were looking into her very soul. Mesmerized by his eyes, she said, "I-I don't want to –"

"Stacey, I know you like me."

"I don't –"

"Yes, you do. You like me. I like you. Go out with me just once."

Unable to turn away from him, she continued to stare into his eyes.

"Just go out with me one time? If you don't enjoy yourself, I'll back off. I promise."

"I don't –"

"Stacey!" Alex ran up to them, with Marissa lagging behind. "I *really* need to talk to you," he said nervously.

"She's talking to *me*," Kyle snarled, as he grabbed Stacey's other hand. His hands were like a vise, progressively getting tighter. "Go out with me," he pressed. "Just once."

The distraction of Alex yelling, gave Stacey a brief second of release. When she looked away, she realized how much he was hurting her hands. "I–no! Let go!" she said, trying to pull her hands away. "You're hurting me!"

"Kyle, let go!" Alex demanded, tugging on Stacey's arm. "If you don't, I'm going to the instructors!"

"Ow!" Stacey winced and jumped. "Let go! That hurts!"

"You *want* to stay with me, don't you?" Kyle said, not looking away from her eyes. It was like he was telling her, not asking anymore. "You *don't* want to be with them, do you?" Kyle asked.

"Kyle! Let go now!" Alex ordered, while still trying to get her hands free. "You're going to break her hands! Marissa! Help me!"

Marissa just stood there watching the scene before her with her arms crossed.

"Kyle, please let go!" Stacey had tears in her eyes. "Please?"

His grip was strong and solid. Stacey felt the pressure on the bones of her hand start to buckle.

"What's going on over here?" Mrs. Nelson asked, coming over with Mr. Baxter.

Kyle immediately let go. "We'll continue this later," he said, and then he left, satisfied he made his point.

"Are you okay?" Mrs. Nelson asked, looking at Stacey's hands.

Stacey cradled the hand that hurt the worst. "They really hurt."

"But are you okay?"

Stacey nodded. "I will be. Just give me a few minutes,

please?"

"Try to keep those two separated today," she said over her shoulder to Mr. Baxter. Mrs. Nelson still had the first hand Kyle grabbed. "Can you squeeze my hand?" She asked, turning back to Stacey. Stacey did, but it was not to full strength. "Take it easy on that one today," she said concerned as she stood. "Do you want some ice for it?"

When Stacey shook her head, Mrs. Nelson said, "Okay. Just be gentle with it. I don't want to have to fill out another accident report for you." Then she and Mr. Baxter left to go talk to Kyle.

When she was gone, Alex sat beside Stacey to look at her hand. Seeing the bruises already forming, he said, "I'm sorry. I had to..." He shook his head, frustrated with himself. "Adam told me not to leave you alone today. I'm so sorry."

"It's okay," Stacey said. "I get it. I can't be babysat twenty-four hours a day. I have to stand on my own."

"Well, we'd better start laps," Alex said. "Do you want me to do them with you, or do you want to partner with Marissa?"

"Um." Stacey looked up at Marissa, who stood there with her arms crossed. Stacey decided if she did not make an effort to bridge whatever this gap was, it would only get worse. "Would you?" Stacey asked Marissa.

"No," she said snottily, and left them sitting there with their jaws dropped.

Alex shook his head. "I'm-I'm sorry. She's not normally like this. I *will* inform Adam as to what happened regarding her actions. Until then, come on. Let's begin our–no way!" He clicked his tongue. Marissa and Kyle were partnered together doing their laps. "Why that –!" He narrowed his eyes. "Come on!"

Alex was at Stacey's side through the remainder of class. Anything that had to do with partners, the instructors paired Stacey with him.

As Stacey got dressed after class, her stomach was in knots. At some point during class, Marissa moved her stuff across the locker room. That move got Stacey thinking on Kyle's words. *How could she go out with them as a group knowing Marissa hated her that much? Marissa loathes, detests, and despises her.*

Stacey shook her head as she wiped the tear that escaped. After she got dressed, she quickly did her hair and make-up, and then headed out of the locker room to go wait for the bus.

When she stepped out the doors of the school to wait for the others, she practically ran into Shane. "Well, haven't seen much of you today. Figured I'd run into you sooner or later," Stacey said, aggravated.

"We need to talk," Shane said. He wrapped his arm around her shoulder, pulling her to the side.

"If Kyle pops over here, I'm out of here. He bruised my hand earlier." She held it up for him to see. "I'm not thrilled about that one."

He shifted to block her from view of anyone who came out of the school. "I don't blame you. I just wanted to talk for a minute before we go back to school."

"Look, I don't want to date Kyle. He's dating Amber. I don't want to be in a group where someone hates me either. I just—I want to somehow be able to go to school with no one hating me," she said, and sunk to the ground, dropping her head onto her hands.

Shane crouched beside her. With his hand on her shoulder, he quietly said, "Look, I'm only going to say this once. If you tell anyone I said it, I'll deny it to my grave."

Stacey's eyebrows arched in surprise.

"In front of everyone, I will stand up for Kyle and the rest of them," Shane said. "But what I'm telling you right now to do is stay as far away as you can from Kyle. Stick with Adam."

She shook her head. "But I –"

"If Kyle were standing here, I'd tell you to go with him. Do you understand?" he said sternly.

"Why is everyone being so cryptic?"

Hearing Alex call for Stacey, Shane said, "Just take the warning. I'll deny I ever said it, so don't tell anyone. Got it?"

Stacey nodded.

"Good," Shane said, and left her to go find Kyle.

"Stacey!" Alex said, visibly relieved when he saw her. Seeing the look on her face, he asked, "What happened now?"

"Nothing." She shook her head. "I'm just frustrated."

Alex helped her off the ground. "Come on, let's get on the bus."

It did not take them long to find a seat. As they chatted, Marissa walked up to them. "Is there room for me?" she asked.

Stacey huffed. "Why don't you go sit with your buddy, Kyle?"

"Stace, look, I'm sorry for being mad at you. Would you please let me start over? What I did was wrong," Marissa said.

"You bet it was!" Alex said, sharpness in his tone. "And I *will* inform Adam of your actions. You made a promise to him. Not only did you break it, but you also had the *audacity* to partner with that cretin all through class. Go sit somewhere else."

"Alex, I…" She shook her head, tearing up. "I'm sorry. What I did was wrong. I'm so sorry."

"Do what you want." He crossed his arms. "I want no part of anything to do with you right now," he said, and then slumped back in his seat by the window, turning away from her.

Marissa turned to Stacey, who finally nodded. Stacey figured if she did not let Marissa sit down, she may end up with Kyle in the seat next to her.

Stacey pulled a book out of her backpack, and put earbuds in her ears. As she got the music going, she opened the book to read, making it obvious she did not want to talk to Marissa either. Needless to say, it was a very quiet ride back to school.

❧

WHEN THEY RETURNED TO SCHOOL, Melody, Harmony, and Adam were already waiting for them to go to lunch. So, on the way in to the nurse's office to check Stacey's bruised hand and get some aspirin, Alex gave Adam a full report. Marissa was embarrassed and humiliated as Alex explained everything that happened during class.

When the nurse handed Stacey another accident report for her dad, she mentioned, "This is getting to be a really bad habit."

Stacey accepted the paper. Tucking it into her folder, she grumbled, "Trust me. I know."

"You may want to consider changing classes."

"Hopefully this is the last issue," Stacey said, and the group left the office.

As soon as the door closed to the office, Adam spun toward Marissa and demanded, "*What is wrong with you? What were you thinking?*"

"I-I don't know. I was upset," she stammered.

"*So, you fed her to the wolves?*" Adam was livid. "You didn't help her! You left her to Kyle! You know better! You know what he does! *Then* you had the *nerve* to partner with him too? *Marissa*! What is wrong with you?"

"Um, can we just forget about it for right now?" Stacey asked. "I've had a rough day. I also have a really bad headache, *and* a sore hand."

"Sorry." Adam put his hands on his hips as he shook his head. "It's just...you don't understand."

"I *do* understand," Stacey said. "Please, let's just go to lunch? I'm reaching the point of too long here shortly. I need to eat."

"All right," Adam agreed, so they headed to the cafeteria. "By the way," he said a couple minutes later as they were in line getting their lunches, "Erin and Amber are still looking for you."

Stacey groaned. "Great. Can this day get any worse?"

"Time will tell."

"So, what do you have for fifth-period b & c?" Melody asked when they sat down at the table. "I missed that yesterday."

The school broke fifth-period into three sections, because the school had over two-thousand students. The sections were forty-five minutes long, and labeled as 'a', 'b', and 'c,' so the lunchroom would not get bombarded with all of the kids at the same time.

"Art," Stacey said, snacking on her fries.

"I've been looking for you," Erin said, as she walked behind the group.

Stacey's head pounded. She sighed, before she asked, "What is *your* issue?"

Everyone around their table stared at the group in shock.

"*You* are my issue." She leaned down next to Stacey's ear, while resting her hands on the back of her seat. "It *seems* you can't keep yourself away from my friend's boyfriend, *or* mine for that matter."

Stacey stood, and then turned to face her. They were both about the same height as they stared each other down.

Stacey's head throbbed from the headache, but she did her best to focus. She did not want to have to deal with this on Monday, or worse yet at work that night. "I don't want your boyfriend," Stacey said. Then to Amber she added, "Or yours. For the record, they're nice guys, but I'm not interested in either of them. Number one, Kyle's a flirt, so I wouldn't feel secure in a relationship with him. Number two, he almost broke my hand today, which I *really* don't take kindly to either. And number three, Shane's too smooth and confusing, so I wouldn't feel secure with him. Have at them ladies. I don't want them."

"I can't believe you just –"

"Believe it!" Stacey said, cutting Amber off. "I've grown up with guys like that, and I don't want them. Now, *these* two are gentlemen," she said, gesturing toward Adam and Alex. "Any girl should count herself lucky to have either of these guys. As for *your* two? If I were you, I wouldn't trust them as far as I could throw them. Now, if that offends you, have at me, because my head and hand already hurt, so a little more pain right now isn't going make that much difference. But just so you know? I work at Slater's, and I start tonight, so you'll see me there if you come. I'm not trying to discourage you, because it's a great place to eat. I'm just letting you know so there aren't any surprises."

They both stood there dumbfounded.

"Look, I'm not one who likes to start trouble. I'm really not a confrontational person. However, I try not to run either," Stacey said. "And to tell you the truth, I've just about had it with this school."

They continued staring at her, jaws dropped.

"Okay." Stacey took a deep breath, and then slowly let it out. "I'm going to eat now before I pass out. Please go find another table," she said, turning to sit down. Her body was not only shaking from the adrenaline, but also from lack of food and nerves.

Stacey picked up a fry and ate it, looking around her table. When she noticed the others looking behind her, Stacey asked, "Are they still there?" The group just nodded. Stacey turned back around and asked Amber and Erin, "Anything else?"

"No. We just..." Amber's voice faded.

Stacey picked up another fry and ate it. Then she turned back to them. While staying in her seat, Stacey calmly said, "Ladies, I don't want your boyfriends. If there is anything that seems fishy, it's from your guys. I'm just warning you, from a person who has been there and done that, that they should not be trusted. Now, I really do need to eat, so please move on," she said, and turned back around.

Stacey watched the faces of the group, as they watched Amber and Erin leave.

"I–wow!" Adam said, when they were out of earshot. "That was–wow!"

"I really don't want Kyle or Shane. They're cute, but they know it," Stacey explained. "Besides, Kyle almost broke my hand this morning, and I really can't figure Shane out. Any of those factors would terrify me in a relationship."

"Thank you for your kind words regarding us," Alex said. "That was perhaps the most pleasant thing anyone has ever said or done for me."

"It was the truth." Stacey shrugged, and then picked up her burger, taking a bite.

"Well, either way, I don't think Chandler or Mason are going to be a problem anymore," Harmony said, laughing. "Look at *their* faces. Pretty sure the girls are telling them what you said. Randy's going to love this one!"

"Now, if you don't mind my asking, are there any relationships in this group I should know about?" Stacey asked, looking at them. "You guys told me just Randy and Harmony, but I'm getting some feelings I wanted to check out. Were there any past relationships within this group?"

"Only Randy and Harmony," Adam said. "The rest of us are just friends, and have been that way forever."

They sat the same way they did the day before, with the exception that Melody was in between Alex and Marissa. Alex was still upset with Marissa.

"All of you have been friends since elementary?" Stacey asked.

"No, we came in eighth grade," Melody said.

"And I came in the sixth," Alex added.

"I've been here since the beginning though," Marissa piped up. She was quiet since her argument with Adam.

"Were you at your other school all your life before now?" Alex asked, ignoring Marissa.

"Actually, yeah," she said, and then finished her burger. Diving into the salad next, she continued to eat before anything else happened.

"So, is all your family still in Michigan?" Melody asked.

"Yep," Stacey said. "Almost all of them are there, except for my dad and me of course, and a few others who have managed to slip away. That's why it was so hard up there. Everywhere we turned, we were running into another memory of my mom. It was hard enough losing her to begin with, but to add that on top of it." She shook her head. "We honestly couldn't take it anymore."

"So, what did you do out there in your spare time?" Adam asked.

"Oh, things like skating, sled riding, going to the lake in the summer. The winters there were long, and we would make ice forts to…" She smiled in remembrance. Then she got a good look at everyone's face around her. She gulped. "They're behind me again, aren't they?" Stacey asked. The group just shook their heads, but continued to stare behind her. "The guy portion of it?" Stacey asked. The group nodded, not taking their eyes off Shane and Kyle.

Stacey turned to find Shane and Kyle standing behind her with their arms folded. They looked like a couple of bouncers from a club.

"Yes?" Stacey asked, innocently.

Kyle narrowed his eyes at her. "You just floored our girl-friends."

"Oh, you're claiming them now?" Stacey asked.

Out of the corner of her eye, Stacey saw Adam put his head down on his hand, shaking it. Then he looked up at Alex, and slightly covered his mouth, stifling his laughter.

Kyle growled. "We were claiming them before!"

"Then why were you hitting on me?"

"You're delusional!" Shane snapped.

"You asked me out," Stacey said to Kyle.

"You need a psychiatrist! I did not," Kyle said.

"I beg to differ," Alex spoke up. "I was a witness to a dalliance with her, and it did not appear to be from her end."

"A what?" Shane asked.

"Shut up, Crestwood!" Kyle said sternly.

Stacey stood. "Don't tell him to shut up when he's telling the truth!"

"Ya know, I don't know whether I want to beat you or –"

"Don't!" Stacey warned Kyle. "I don't want to hear the rest of that sentence."

"Probably not," Adam said under his breath.

"Did you say something, Barnes?" Shane asked, stunned Adam attempted to add to the conversation.

"I *said* she probably didn't want to hear the end of that sentence," Adam said. "Knowing your mouths, the way you think, *and* the mood she seems to be in, chances are she'd sucker punch you if she did."

"Is that a threat?" he asked, surprised by Adam's boldness.

"Nope. Just telling the truth."

"You can be dealt with!" Shane said, picking Adam up by his arm.

"Put him down!" Stacey said, trying to pull them apart. "I'm the one you have the problem with."

Kyle grabbed Stacey's arm. "Then *you* need to take a walk with us, *now!*"

"Let him go first," Stacey insisted.

"Fine. He's just a stick anyway. I'd probably snap him in half," Shane said, shoving Adam into the table.

Kyle pulled Stacey over to the side of the cafeteria, out of earshot of anyone. "What is your issue with me?" Kyle demanded.

Shane had his back to the pair, keeping an eye out for anyone who might try to interrupt them.

"You're a jerk and a bully!" Stacey said with her back to the wall, as Kyle stood in front of her.

Leaning one arm on the wall as he stood in front of her,

essentially boxing her in, Kyle leaned down so he was at eye level with Stacey. "I'm not a bully. I'm just a guy who knows what he wants. Besides, it seems you keep getting yourself in trouble. I could protect you."

"*You're* the one I need protection from," Stacey pointed out.

"Here's the thing, I know you like me. I like you too."

Stacey rolled her eyes. "You have a girlfriend."

"I would get rid of her for you."

"I don't want to date you."

Leaning closer to her, in a low voice, he said, "Yes. You do."

Crossing her arms, Stacey insisted, "No. I don't."

"Just one date. All I'm asking for is just one date."

Stacey stood her ground. "No."

"You know, I would hate to see you and your friends get into accidents," Kyle hinted.

Narrowing her eyes, she demanded, "Are you threatening me and my friends?"

"No. No. Not at all. I just know that you seem to continue to get beat up in class. I also know that truck the Kelley twins have is pretty new. Who knows if there are gremlins within the systems of the truck? I would hate to see their breaks fail, or have them breakdown in a bad part of town. Then there's Adam's car. It's old and beat up. I'm one-hundred percent sure there's an accident in there just waiting to happen."

"Stop it!"

"Oh, then there's Randy. He's powerful, but I remember him being a bit clumsy. You know what they say...the bigger they are, the harder they fall."

"Stop it right now!" Stacey said, balled fists to her sides.

"Then there's innocent Marissa. She's just a good girl, hoping to catch the attention of a guy...any guy at this point. She may just end up on the wrong end of a bad relationship," Kyle said.

"You are seriously messed up! You wouldn't do that, would

you? How could you get away with something like that?"

"Well, see that table over there?" he asked, pointing toward a table of guys. When she nodded, he said, "The one in the blue shirt, and the two in the black shirts all are taking auto mechanics. They owe me. See that guy in the green shirt at that table over there?" he asked her. She nodded, so he continued, "He's bad news. He has a bit of a temper. I'm certain I could convince him to take Marissa out on a date. I have quite a bit on him. Pretty sure he would be resentful, and may just take it out on her."

"You wouldn't dare!"

"I would. To stop it, all you have to do is go out with me."

"I don't want to."

"Meet me after school by the bench across the street in the park. If you don't, I cannot be held responsible for which accident gets unleashed first," Kyle threatened.

"That's blackmail! You cannot be serious!"

Hearing the bell ring for the next class, Kyle said, "Don't be late. I don't like to be kept waiting." With that, he left.

Stacey gulped as she watched Shane and Kyle walk away as if nothing happened. Adam walked up to Stacey with her books.

"Here." Adam handed her books to her. "What happened? What did he say?"

"I have to meet him in the park across the street after school," she said, pale and shaking. "He said if I don't, you guys would end up in accidents."

Adam gulped. "Oh boy."

Stacey looked up at Adam. "I don't want to go."

"I'll go with you. They may not do much with two of us there."

"They might hurt you," Stacey said.

"They *will* hurt you if there's no one else there. I'll let the others know, so they'll wait for us at the school."

"Are you sure?"

"Absolutely," Adam said. "Come on. I'll walk you to class. Don't leave your classroom without at least one of us with you for the rest of the day. Okay?"

"All right," Stacey agreed, much to Adam's relief.

"It's not that I don't think you can handle yourself. It's that I know exactly what they are capable of. We need backup."

"Agreed," she said, as they headed to class.

THROUGH THE REST of the day, Stacey was a nervous wreck. She was relieved when she walked into psychology, because a lot of the group was in that class.

When she sat down, Randy turned around from his desk in front of her, and said, "Harmony and Melody are fit to be tied. What the heck is going on?"

"Kyle is demanding to meet with me after school, or all of you guys will suddenly find yourselves in an accident of some sort."

"He can't touch me," Randy said confidently. "He knows better. I took him down a couple years ago."

"He didn't sound afraid of you earlier. He said the bigger they are, the harder they fall."

"Huh," Randy said with an amused smile. "That's rich coming from him. It seriously didn't take much to take him down. That's when Erin started liking me. Personally, I feel like a piece of meat anytime that girl is around. She creeps me out," he said, and shuddered. "Stalker material."

"I wouldn't doubt it," Stacey said. "She and Amber are a piece of work."

"You're not really going to meet him. Are you?" Randy asked.

"Adam said he was going to talk to all of you and let you know where we would be. He is going with me. Don't leave until we meet back up with you guys."

"Oh, that's not in question. If I had my choice, I'd go with you."

"I hope Adam will surprise him enough that he won't do anything," Stacey said.

"You cannot seriously go!" Melody said, walking into the class with Brian and Alex.

"Adam's going with me," Stacey said.

"We'll be on standby," Randy added. "We're not leaving until they're done."

"How are your head and hand?" Alex asked.

"What happened now?" Randy asked. "I missed that one."

"In class, Kyle just about broke my hand. The headache is from stress," Stacey said, showing him her hand.

"Seriously," Randy shook his head, "that guy needs to be put on a leash!"

As Mr. Freud got up to start class, Brian passed Stacey a note from Adam. It said for Stacey to stay in the classroom after class. He said he would meet her at the classroom, and they would leave from there. He also said not to worry, and that she was not alone.

"We're staying until Adam gets here," Brian added.

"Good," Stacey said, her nerves still on edge.

AFTER CLASS, Adam went to his locker, and then met the group at the classroom. "Ready?" Adam asked.

"Not really," Stacey admitted. "But the alternative is just not an option.

"Let's go," he said.

As the group dispersed to go to their lockers, Adam went with Stacey. Keeping an eye in every direction, they made their way to her locker without a word.

"I feel like I'm being hunted," Stacey finally said, putting the combination into the lock.

"In a way you are. Once Kyle sets his mind on someone, it doesn't take them long to succumb to his desires. He's really not a good guy."

"Quite honestly, he's downright scary."

A guy walked up to Stacey and Adam. "Stacey?"

"Let me guess?" Stacey said.

"I'm Brad Strong."

"Figured as much. What do you want?"

"I'm supposed to take you to Kyle."

"I'm going with her," Adam said.

Brad scoffed. "No, you're not. She's supposed to come alone."

"It's either he comes with me, or I don't come at all," Stacey insisted.

"Fine," Brad said on a sigh, rolling his eyes. "Just hurry up."

Stacey quickly changed out her books for the ones she would need for homework over the weekend, and shut her locker. "Okay. I'm ready."

As they walked down the hall, Adam and Brad flanked Stacey. She felt like a prisoner going to her execution. She did not want to do this, but the alternative was not a good one. She did not want anyone getting hurt because of her. She really did not want Adam to go, knowing he was a target as well. However, she was grateful for him being there, so she was not alone.

She reached over and grabbed his hand as they walked. He glanced at their hands, and then looked up at her. He smiled as he gave her hand a gentle squeeze, but did not let go. He kept ahold of her hand as they walked outside, passing their group next to the tree.

Stacey saw the looks from those in their group were of distain for Brad, mixed with anger that Stacey and Adam had to do this, along with pity and compassion knowing what others faced over the years. Stacey knew what they were all feeling. She had the exact same feelings churning within her so ferociously, she thought she would throw up.

Adam squeezed her hand again, as they walked across the street, away from the safety of the school yard. "You're not alone," was all he said, as they walked into the park.

While they continued to walk, Stacey finally asked, "Where are we going?"

"See that tree line over there?" Brad asked, pointing toward the other end of the park.

Where he pointed would be out of sight of anyone still at school or even in the parking lot. "Are you serious?" she asked.

"Yep. He wants privacy. That's why he said alone," Brad hinted, glaring at Adam.

"Where she goes, I go," Adam insisted.

"Fine," Brad huffed.

When they arrived just inside the tree line, Stacey was immediately grabbed by Shane, who wrapped one arm around her body, while he covered her mouth with the other.

Meanwhile, Brad grabbed Adam, looping his one arm through both of Adam's from behind him. "Don't say a word," Brad threatened as Adam's books fell to the ground.

"What are you doing?" Adam demanded, struggling in Brad's arms. "Let me go!"

Brad pulled up on Adam's arms, and Adam let out a groan. "Keep talking," Brad warned.

When he was satisfied that Adam would keep his mouth closed, Kyle walked over to Stacey. Putting one finger in front of her, he said, "One date."

"No!" Stacey shouted through Shane's hand.

Getting into her face, he said, "One date, or I'll let Adam *really* know what pain feels like."

Stacey looked at Adam in wide-eyed terror. Adam shook his head 'no,' as he mouthed, '*Don't do it.*'

Stacey's eyes pleaded with Adam, but Adam shook his head again. Stacey took a deep breath, and then shook her head. Her eyes widened in horror, as Kyle went over and pounded into Adam's mid-section in succession. Adam doubled over as much as possible, trying to protect himself, but Brad held strong.

"Now?" Kyle asked. "One date. That's all I want. You say yes, and I'll stop. You say no, and Adam gets a beating he won't soon forget."

Stacey looked at Adam, heartbroken. Adam stared at her with tears in his eyes, but still shook his head no.

When Stacey did not respond, Kyle insisted, "I need an answer."

"No!" Adam said. "She's not going anywhere with you!"

As soon as he said that, Brad kicked Adam's legs out from under him, and Adam hit the ground hard.

"Stacey?" Kyle asked.

"No!" Adam said again, as Brad put his knee in Adam's back to keep him down. "Tell him, Stacey!"

Kyle walked over to Stacey. When Shane took his hand off Stacey's mouth, Kyle demanded, "I need an answer. Yes, and you both walk away. No, and you both pay dearly."

Stacey looked to Adam, who shook his head again. Hearing her heartbeat pounding in her ears, she shouted, "No!"

"This is on you," Kyle said. As he went over to Adam, Shane re-covered Stacey's mouth with his hand, while he tightened his arm around her body to hold her in place.

Kyle and Brad took turns beating on Adam right in front of her. Stacey tried her best to try to get free, but she could not get loose. As she fought, she was also screaming and crying.

"Shut her up!" Kyle said to Shane, while they proceeded to kick and punch Adam.

Shane gripped tighter on her mouth, so Stacey screamed louder. "If you don't shut up, they'll literally beat him to death, and then you're next," Shane warned, down near her ear. Stacey gasped and froze. "Good girl. About time you learned to control yourself."

"He's done," Kyle said disgusted, as he gave Adam one more kick to the rib cage. Adam laid there in a bloody heap, moaning and groaning, but unable to move.

"Her turn," Kyle said, turning toward Stacey.

Wide-eyed, she stared at them in sheer terror. Glancing from them to Adam, she started crying and screaming again.

Kyle grabbed her shirt with his fists. The look on his face was frightening – it was so full of anger and hate. "You *will* shut-up right now, or you will end up like him!" He nodded toward Adam, who was still trying to do his best to get up to help in some way.

Stacey glanced from Kyle, to Adam, and then back to Kyle again. Panic took over as she vigorously wiggled to get free. After a minute, she stopped. Reality set in as to what was about to happen.

"That's better." Kyle smiled an evil smile. Stacey froze. "About time you cooperated. All I asked for was one date, and you refused. Refusing what we say will cost you around here. I'm getting tired of dealing with you and your stubbornness. So, allow me to explain how things work. When we tell you to do something, you *will* do it. You *will* respect our authority in this town, and you *will* do as we say. That includes the next time I ask you out on a date. Do you understand?" He asked.

Stacey did not move. She narrowed her eyes at him. She saw what they did to Adam. She knew what was coming. Her strong-willed attitude kicked in and she stood there in defiance.

"I said, *do you understand*?" He asked a little louder.

"Chandler, shh! Someone will hear you!" Brad hushed him, while Stacey stood her ground.

When she did not answer, he roared, "I SAID, DO YOU UNDERSTAND?"

"NO!" Stacey shouted with Shane's hand still over her mouth.

Kyle looked at her for a second. He glanced at Brad and Shane, before he turned back to Stacey and landed a punch square in her jaw. Shane let her go when Kyle punched her over and over again. With each punch Kyle landed, Stacey saw stars. Her body continued to take the beating, without any more objection from her. She could not catch her breath enough to even attempt to object.

Kyle was the only one hitting her. Shane and Brad stood back, keeping an eye out for anyone coming. Kyle kept it up for a few brutal minutes, before he finally stopped. "She's done too," he said disgusted, as Stacey dropped to the ground. "Pathetic!" He shook his head. And then the three of them walked away, leaving the pair writhing in pain and agony out of sight from help.

Stacey heard them talking while they walked away. "Man, I think I might have actually hurt my hand on that last one!" Kyle said, shaking his hand to try to get some feeling back into it.

"Think they'll talk?" Brad asked.

Shane shook his head. "Not if they know what's good for them."

From that point on they were out of earshot.

"Adam?" Stacey's voice was barely a whisper.

Adam raised his head. "Stacey, are you...ohhh," he moaned, holding his ribs.

Stacey slowly crawled to Adam. It took her a few minutes to make her way over to him. At that point, it was all she had, so she collapsed on the ground next to him, facing him.

He put his hand on hers. "Stacey? Are you okay?"

Stacey shook her head, and then closed her eyes.

"We need help," he said, looking up at the sky to the Lord for help. "Preferably sooner rather than...ohhh...sooner rather than later," he winced, holding his ribs.

Stacey gasped and jumped as a spike of pain shot through her entire body. Closing her eyes, she let the darkness take over. The peaceful, painless darkness

"Stacey?" Adam asked. When she did not respond, he asked again, "Stace? Oh, not good. Stacey? Please wake up?"

"Adam!" Adam heard his friends calling for him. "Adam! Stacey!"

"Over..." Adam started coughing up blood. "Over here!"

"*Adam!*" Marissa ran over, horrified at the bloody mess she found. "They're over here!" she shouted to the others. Leaning down, she said, "We saw Kyle, Brad, and Shane, and not you two. We waited a few minutes. And when you didn't show, we came looking for you."

"Where's...Oh! Oh wow!" Randy shook his head, running up with the rest of the group behind him. "Crestwood, call for help."

"Dialing as we speak," Alex said, going off to the side to call an ambulance. Melody and Brian took off back to the school to report what happened. They hoped the nurse was still in the office.

"Stacey?" Adam asked, trying to see her. "She's not good."

"We know," Marissa said, running her fingers through Adam's hair, while Randy and Harmony tried to wake Stacey. "We're working on it. You just relax."

"Come on, Stacey. Please wake up?" Harmony said to Stacey down near her face.

"Need to see...move," Adam said to Marissa. "I need to see her."

When Marissa moved, Adam reached over and grabbed Stacey's hand. "Please wake up?" he asked, and then laid his head down on the ground, closing his eyes.

Randy, Harmony, and Marissa looked at each other, wide-eyed. "They'd better hurry!" Randy shouted to Alex.

CHAPTER 4

"YOU GAIN STRENGTH, COURAGE, AND
CONFIDENCE BY EVERY EXPERIENCE IN
WHICH YOU REALLY STOP TO LOOK FEAR
IN THE FACE. YOU ARE ABLE TO SAY TO
YOURSELF, 'I LIVED THROUGH THIS
HORROR. I CAN TAKE THE NEXT THING
THAT COMES ALONG." ELEANOR
ROOSEVELT

"I don't care *what* you say. She was in *your* charge when this happened. She has only been in your school for *two* days, *both* of which she has been injured. This time she's even landed in the hospital," Sam Spencer shouted. "What type of a school are you running? How can I send her there, knowing this might happen again?"

"I assure you these are isolated incidents," Miss Schmidt said, trying to calm him down. Miss Schmidt was the principal for Pine Crest High School.

"Isolated or not, my daughter is a target in your school! You are *failing* to keep her safe."

"I'm sure the worst is over, and she'll be fine from now on."

"I want those boys prosecuted," he demanded. "If you do not file charges, I will. Not only against them, but also against the school district."

"You have to understand who their –"

"I DON'T CARE WHO THEIR PARENT'S ARE!" he roared.

"Mr. Spencer, there's no reason to overreact here."

"Overreact? Overreact? You think *this* is overreacting? You have not *seen* overreacting yet! I *will* file charges whether you do or not. I *will* follow this through. I have a lot of friends in *very* high places," he said, inches from her face. "And I have to tell you, the weight I throw around will not even *remotely* compare to the slim power they *may* hold!"

Miss Schmidt quickly looked around to make sure no one could hear. She got close to his face as she quietly said, "I pray you're right. And if you can get this taken care of, I will be more than grateful. However, I do not have the power to do it myself."

He looked at her, surprised for a moment. Glancing around, and then back to her, and quietly replied, "Are you trying to tell me something?"

"Yes."

"How bad is it?"

"Lawyers, judges, politicians, law officials galore. They rule this town. Chandler's dad is a partner in a rather large law firm. Mason's dad is a judge. Phillips's dad is the Mayor. Strong's dad is the Chief of Police. Foster's dad is the Fire Marshall. And Ross's dad is the Assistant Police Chief."

Sam's eyes widened. "Are you...wow!" He whistled. "That's going to pretty much take all the connections I have to pull this down."

"Can you do it?"

"I can if you don't tip my hand."

"Done," she agreed. "I want my school and town safe as much as everyone else. Right now, they have a huge hold. I can't fight this by myself."

"I can."

"Your daughter will have a battle on her hands as well."

"She can handle it," he said, confidently. "She can help me from inside the school."

"She's already off to a good start, believe it or not."

"Are you–? She got the tar beat out of her!"

"That's because they feel threatened. They haven't reacted

this strongly in a long time. They usually chase just about anyone who has come against them out of town before it reaches this level. So, how high can you go? How much power do you have behind you?"

"Are three FBI agents, one FBI supervisor, two CIA agents, one Supreme Court Justice, two District Attorneys, and the State Police Chief high enough for you? Is that enough power?"

Her jaw dropped. "Definitely!" She grinned, feeling a sense of hope for the first time in a long time. "Whatever you need, I'll do my best to get. If you can relieve the town of this, I'm behind it one hundred percent!"

"Mrs. Schmidt, I do believe we have an alliance." He put his hand out, and they shook hands in agreement.

"It's Miss…and yes, we do. Whatever you need that is at my disposal, is yours."

He smiled. "Excellent."

Stacey's blue eyes fluttered open as she moaned. "Dad?"

"Hey, Peanut," he said quietly. Sam walked over to her. Cradling one of her hands in his, he asked, "How are you feeling?"

"I, um, how's Adam?"

"He's an excellent resource as well," Miss Schmidt said in a low voice. "That whole crew is. As a matter of fact, as far as popularity goes, they are more popular and more liked than the others. It's just that the other group has more muscle and domi-nance. They rule with fear."

"Adam?" Stacey asked again.

"He's going to be okay, honey," her dad said. "He woke up a little bit before you did."

"Good." She nodded. "It was Kyle Chandler, Brad Strong, and Shane Mason."

"Figured as much. At this point, there's nothing I can do about it," Miss Schmidt admitted.

"Miss…what's your first name? If you don't mind, 'Miss' and

'Mister' sound so formal. And if we're going to be working on this together, I think a first name would be more appropriate. Don't you?" Sam asked her.

She smiled. "Becky."

"Well, Becky, I'm Sam, and you know Stacey."

"Yes."

"Well, Stacey, it seems we kicked a hornet's nest," her dad told her.

"Oh yeah?" she asked, shifting positions to get a little more comfortable.

"Yep. There's a power team at work in this town. Want to mess with them?"

"Would it happen to include Chandler, Mason, Strong, Phillips, Foster, and Ross?" Stacey asked.

"As a matter of fact, it would."

"Then I'm in," Stacey agreed. She closed her eyes, trying to control the pain emitting from all over her body.

"Do you want something for that?" he asked.

"Yeah." Stacey nodded. When her dad left the room to go get the nurse, Stacey said, "I'd like to see Adam as soon as possible."

"Well, he's down a floor, and a couple rooms over," Becky explained. "It's going to be a couple days before either one of you can go anywhere. Chandler packs a powerful punch."

"How are we going to do this?"

"Well, your dad somehow has these miraculous connections that are going to help out immensely," she said, sitting on the chair next to the bed.

"Can we trust you?" Stacey asked, studying Becky's body language to figure out if she would tell the truth.

"If it'll clean up not only my school, but also the corruption in this town then I'm all for it."

"Okay," Stacey said, satisfied. She closed her eyes, taking slow breaths in order to control the pulsating pain.

Becky looked at Stacey, concerned. "What did they do to you guys?"

"Beat and threatened. They got Adam first, and then me."

"Well, it's going to get really messy, but if you're willing to help out, then I am too. It's either that or I move. I'm getting sick and tired of what these people are getting away with around here. Did you know that what they're doing in the school, they're doing in the town as well?"

"Huh-uh." Stacey shook her head, and then winced. She closed her eyes again, doing her best to keep her pain levels under control until the nurse could get her medicine.

"Just rest, Stacey." Becky patted her hand. "I'm going to check on Adam."

"Tell him I'm sorry."

"He doesn't fault you."

"Please just tell him I'm sorry," Stacey said. She shifted to a more tolerable position, as Becky left the room.

"Okay, here ya go young lady," the nurse said, walking into the room. She injected something into the IV. "Your dad went to get something to eat down at the cafeteria since I am going to knock you out again. This shouldn't take too long to kick in. Sweet dreams," she said and left.

It only took a few seconds for Stacey to feel the warmth permeate her body. She hoped it would take over quickly, allowing her to get some rest. In the meantime, she drifted in and out of sleep.

MELODY WALKED into the room with Marissa and Harmony. "The nurse said she was awake a little bit ago," Melody said quietly.

Stacey barely got her eyes open enough to see the trio come quietly in the room about twenty minutes after the nurse left.

She closed her eyes again, hoping the medicine would knock her out soon. The pain was almost unbearable.

"She's not awake anymore," Harmony said as she cringed. "She looks awful."

"They said she asked for Adam first thing," Melody pointed out. "He's not too much better than she is at the moment."

"She did?" Marissa asked.

"Yeah, they said he asked for her first thing too." Melody grinned. "I think our friend has finally found a young lady he's interested in!"

Harmony sat down next to Stacey and picked up her hand. "Good choice too. She's strong and knows what she believes in. An awesome combination, I think."

"Now, if we can just get her to our side," Melody said.

"Do you know if she's a Christian?" Marissa asked.

Melody shook her head. "I can't judge her heart, but I don't think so."

"Would Adam date a non-Christian?" Marissa asked, rubbing the back of her neck as she paced.

Harmony studied her for a moment. "What is wrong with you?"

Marissa stopped pacing. "Well, I–I was…nothing."

"Adam found someone he likes. Why can't you be happy for him?" Harmony asked, irritation evident in her voice.

"I *am* happy for him."

"Riss, you've liked Adam since fifth grade, but he's made it perfectly clear he only likes you as a friend," Melody said calmly. She rested her hands on Marissa's shoulders. "However, there's actually someone here he *does* like. And I think she's a good choice."

Marissa sighed. "It's just that –"

"He likes her! Give it up already!" Harmony snapped, cutting Marissa off.

"Harm, chill!" Melody shot at her. "Look guys, we don't even know if she likes him. We don't know if he wants to ask her out. They've only known each other for two days."

"But he stood up for her, and more than one time. That's what got him beat up," Marissa said in an emotion-choked voice. "He's never stood up for me."

"You are *so* blind!" Harmony huffed, crossing her arms. "You might like Adam, but *Alex* likes you!"

"Are you...no way!" Marissa shook her head. "No, he doesn't!"

"*Yes*, he does! He's a great guy, but you don't see him, because you're pining over Adam!"

"Harmony, your name does *so* not match your temperament." Melody rolled her eyes. "You really need to try to be *more* harmonious."

"I'm perfectly fine!" She snapped. "I just have major issues with whiners!"

Stacey struggled to wake up. The intensity of the room was higher than she liked. It was halting her from letting sleep take over. "Um..."

"Was that her?" Harmony asked. Harmony lifted Stacey's hand. "Hey, if it was you, squeeze my hand."

Stacey barely got her fingers to move.

"Awesome!" Harmony smiled. "It *was* her."

"Great!" Melody grinned, coming over to the other side of the bed from Harmony. "Hi, Stace."

"Um, yeah." Stacey struggled to open her eyes. "Adam?"

"He's looking pretty bad," Harmony admitted, and then glanced at Marissa, who just looked away.

"Is he..." Stacey shifted her position. "Is he going to be okay?"

"He will be," Melody said. "It seems you picked a fight with the wrong people."

"No." Stacey shook her head. "Right people. They need to be

–" She gasped when pain spiked from her ribs. "Make it stop already."

"We understand," Melody said. "Just relax for now."

"Yeah." Stacey nodded. She rested her head back and closed her eyes. The medicine was difficult to fight, so she went ahead and gave in, succumbing to the blissful, painless sleep.

"Well, I'd say that was pretty obvious," Harmony said after a couple minutes. "I think we know where she stands."

"What are you thinking?" Melody looked at her suspiciously, as a grin spread across her face. "I know that look."

Marissa scoffed. "Well, count me out. I want absolutely *nothing* to do with *this* one!"

"You care more about your own feelings, which are *not* mutually felt by Adam, than you do about his feelings?" Harmony looked at her, taken aback. "That has got be one of the shallowest and most selfish things I've *ever* heard from you!"

"And that's the meanest that I've heard from you!" she snapped back.

"Do we even *want* to know?" Alex asked, seeing the girls having a stare-down as he walked in with Randy and Brian.

"No," Marissa said before Harmony could open her mouth.

"Well, I'm sure they know." Harmony shrugged. "It's not like we won't be telling them something they *don't* know, or haven't figured out by now."

"Whatever," Marissa said on a sigh.

"Well, you guys know Marissa likes Adam, right?" Harmony asked.

"*Everybody* knows Marissa likes Adam," Randy said, going over to Harmony. He kissed her cheek, before wrapping his arms around her waist from behind.

"Well, we think he might be interested in Stacey," she continued.

"Well, duh!" Randy smiled. Then he looked down at

Harmony, and added, "*But* we're *not* doing anything about it. *Right,* Harmony?"

"Well," she said, "sometimes people just need a gentle nudge in the right direction."

"No, let *Adam* decide what *Adam* wants. He's got a good brain in his head. Just let *Matchmakers Incorporated* have a rest on this one, okay?"

"Well, well, well, looks like the gang's all here," Matt Slater said, walking in. "No wonder Adam's feeling a bit neglected."

Marissa's face lit up. "He's awake?"

"Yep. Unfortunately, the one *he* wants to see, is not," Matt said, concerned, as he looked at Stacey.

"She's been in and out of it, but I'm pretty sure she's headed more toward out of it right now," Melody said. "She was awake a few minutes ago."

"Not since we've been here though," Brian said, leaning against the wall next Melody, shoving his hands in his pockets.

"Well, hmm." Matt walked over and gently shook Stacey's shoulders. "Stacey? Stacey?"

"I…what?" Stacey quickly opened her eyes, and then closed them again because the room spun. "Matt?"

"Yep. Can you open those for me? You have some very concerned friends here. You also have an extremely worried one down a floor who would like to hear a good report."

It took Stacey a minute, but she finally got her eyes opened and looked up at him. "Super tired," she mumbled.

"I know, but can I get you to at least sit up?" he asked.

Stacey shook her head.

"Even if I help?" he asked, hopeful

"Cracked ribs," she said, "and I'm medicated."

"I know, but I got Adam to sit up with broken ribs. How about you? The sooner we get one of you two going, the sooner we can let you guys see each other."

Stacey glanced around the room and groaned. She put her

head back on the pillow and closed her eyes. Taking a moment for the room to stop spinning, she then reopened her eyes, trying to focus. "Too many people."

"I know. Give it a try?" Matt coaxed.

"If I try, will you leave me alone?"

"That's all I ask," Matt agreed.

"Okay," she relented.

Harmony stood on the one side to help, while Matt helped with the other. Randy raised the bed so Stacey could stay sitting up.

"Pain!" Stacey shouted, partway up.

"Let it ease, and then we'll keep going," Matt said.

He and Harmony held Stacey in place, while she breathed through the pain. He waited until Stacey nodded before the pair slowly raised her the rest of the way.

"That's…Oh boy! That, um…ouch!" Stacey winced, after a few more minutes of waiting again. "Way too much stiffness and pain."

"What kind of pain?" Matt asked. "Sharp?"

"Not anymore. It just hurts."

"That's a good sign."

"I'm hungry too."

"We'll go tell the nurse, and vacate the room for a while," Randy said, grabbing Harmony's hand as they left.

"So, how about we get you some food, and then maybe see if we can take you on a field trip?" Matt asked.

Stacey furrowed her brow. "To where?"

"Adam *really* wants to see you," Matt said. "Every time he wakes up, he's asking if anyone's heard any news about you."

Stacey glanced at Marissa, who turned away at hearing Adam's name.

"I told him I'd try to see if I could get you out of bed to come down," Matt said. "So how about it? Want to go see Adam?"

"I do, but –"

"Okay!" Matt said, pleased.

Stacey glanced at Marissa again. "Marissa, is there something wrong?"

"No," she curtly replied.

"Then why do you look like *you* were the one who got beat up?" Stacey asked. "What's wrong?"

"Nothing," she said flatly.

"Uh, Riss, do you want get something to eat?" Alex asked. "You look like you need a break."

"No, I –"

"I think that's a wonderful idea!" Melody perked up, cutting Marissa off. "Brian, why don't we go too?"

"You really...sure!" Brian grinned.

The four of them left the room, with Melody and Brian seemingly the happiest.

"Ahh," Matt sighed. "I don't miss high school."

Stacey raised an eyebrow. "What does that mean?"

"You don't see it?"

"See what?"

"Well, Brian likes Melody, but I don't think Melody gets it. Marissa likes Adam, but he's bluntly told her he doesn't like her in that way. And Alex likes Marissa, but she's too enamored with Adam to see it." He shook his head, chuckling. "And from what I've heard, I think you and Adam might be headed down that path, too. Except you two aren't so blind to it."

"Really? You think so?"

"What do *you* think?"

"I'm interested, but it's too soon to tell just how much."

"He's a really good guy if you're interested in pursuing it. Also, Becky Schmidt and your father seem to be hitting it off."

"Well, aren't you just the matchmaker." Stacey smiled. "Your wife must have a field day with you."

"She's the one who pointed most of those out to me. The one with your dad and Becky though? I figured that one out on my own. They've been down at the cafeteria talking for quite a while." He shrugged. "Doesn't take an Einstein to figure it out."

"What's your take on her?" Stacey asked. "Do you trust her?"

"What do you mean?"

"Like, if you had a big secret, would you trust her to not tell it?"

He thought for a moment before he nodded. "Yeah, I would. I've known her for several years. She goes to our church."

"She goes to church? Does anyone *not* go to church in this town?"

"Yep, the likes of Erin, CJ, Kyle, Shane, etcetera," he said. "And you can see what good it does them."

"Yeah," Stacey said, her mind processing the information.

"What's going through that brain of yours?" he asked, sitting on the chair next to the bed.

"Well, I just–I don't know about this church thing."

"Have you ever tried it?"

"No."

"Want to?"

"I'm thinking about it," she admitted.

"Well, you get healthy, and we'll talk to your dad about it some more." He stood and patted her shoulder. "Until then, I guess I'll have to track down some food for you."

"Hey, Matt?"

"Yeah?" he asked, stopping at the door.

"Did Adam really ask for me?"

"Multiple times." He smiled. "I'm working on getting him out of bed as much as I am you. I think it'll be good for both of you to see each other."

"I would like that," Stacey said.

"Good. I'll go get you some food," Matt said and left.

So, there are more relationships within the group other than Randy and Harmony. Stacey was curious to see just how this would to play out.

CHAPTER 5

Stacey woke the next day. She and the nurse worked all morning to get Stacey out of bed. By the afternoon, Stacey was confident she could sit in a wheelchair to see Adam.

When her dad came in that afternoon, he helped her into the wheelchair. "You sure you want to do this?" Sam asked.

"Yes. I'm in pain, but I really want to see him," Stacey said.

"Fair enough. May I escort the princess?" her dad teased.

"Yes, you may, kind sir."

"Right this way," he said, as he pushed her wheelchair out of the room.

When they were at Adam's door, Sam poked his head in first to make sure he was ready. "Got some company for you." Sam said to Adam.

"Who is it?" he asked.

"Are you ready for company?" Sam asked.

Slumping back in his bed, Adam just nodded.

Sam pushed the door open all the way, before going back out to the hall for Stacey. When he pushed her into the room, both grinned at seeing each other.

"I'm going to leave you two alone for a bit. I'll be back in say ten minutes?" he asked Stacey.

"Yes, please." Stacey said. "I hurt, but I want to stay for a few minutes."

"Okay. Be back in ten, Peanut," he said, and kissed her head. "Please don't push it."

"I won't," she assured him. "Thank you," she said, and he left the room.

"Hi," Adam said, cradling his ribs.

"Hi. I don't have very long to visit, but I wanted to tell you how sorry I was that you got hurt."

"Sorry?" He furrowed is brow. "For what? You didn't do this."

"No, but I pushed them. You guys warned me, but I didn't listen. I'm sorry."

"I'm not. It's about time someone pushed back," Adam said. "Look," he put his hand out, so Stacey gave him her hand to hold, "that crew are a bunch of bullies. They have been getting away with this kind of stuff for way too long. Please, know it has nothing to do with you. They have done it to others. They take every chance they get to shove their power around."

"I understand. But if I went out with him, we wouldn't be in this mess," Stacey said. "Please, accept my apology?"

"I will, but there is no reason for it. It's not the first time they've beat me up, and it won't be the last. Having said that, I will *not* stand by anymore and let them push people around."

"Adam, can I tell you something?" Stacey asked.

"I would think I proved to you already that you're safe around us."

"I want to tell you something, but I need you to keep it from the rest of the group. Will you do that for me?"

Adam looked at her for a minute before he asked, "Is this something that could get them hurt?"

"I don't know," she admitted.

"Is it illegal?"

"It's something to stop the others. And no, it is not illegal."

Adam rubbed his chin for a moment before he finally agreed, "All right. What is it?"

"My dad has a lot of connections…like high up connections."

Adam studied her. "What *kind* of connections?"

"FBI, CIA, Supreme Court type connections," Stacey said.

"What are you trying to tell me?"

"There's going to be a battle. What side do you want to be on?" Stacey asked.

"Yours."

"We're going to take them down, Adam. There will be a fight. It *will* get worse."

Adam nodded in understanding. "I get it. Whatever you need. I'll help where I can."

"You cannot tell anyone."

"I won't. But if this is going to get as big as I think it is, we won't have to tell anyone. They'll figure it out."

STACEY'S DAD returned after the ten minutes. She was exhausted, so he helped her back into bed. Once tucked in, she took a nap until the group came in for their daily visit.

STACEY HATED THE HOSPITAL. The only portion she enjoyed were she and Adam's daily visits. She was relieved when the hospital released them both on Monday to go home. That way neither were left in that place by themselves. It also gave them a couple days to recover before returning to school.

Through those first few days at home, the girls brought Stacey her homework, and gave her a hand where needed. Meanwhile, the guys helped Adam. Harmony and Melody were great, and Stacey enjoyed her time with them. Marissa was another story. She continuously shut down whenever Stacey tried to talk to her.

Finally, on Wednesday afternoon, the day before Stacey returned to school, Harmony and Melody had to stay after school. This left Marissa to bring Stacey her homework by herself.

Marissa knocked on the door around three o'clock. "Hi!" Stacey smiled, as she opened the door. "Come on in."

"Thanks," Marissa said, not making eye contact with Stacey.

Stacey accepted her books, and went back over to the couch. That was where she parked herself during the day.

Stacey gestured toward the chair beside her. "Have a seat."

Marissa pointed over her shoulder toward the door. "I-I should probably –"

"Please?" Stacey asked.

"All right," she relented. She sat in the chair up near Stacey's end of the couch.

"I need to talk to you."

Marissa smirked. "Uh-oh, maybe I *should* go."

"Actually, I've *needed* to talk to you. Since we're alone, it's probably a good time."

"What is it?" Marissa asked.

"It's about Adam…I think."

"Say again?"

"I know you like Adam."

"That's okay. He doesn't like me. I'm pretty sure he likes you too."

"The problem I'm seeing is you get hurt and angry every time something comes up about me and Adam being together."

"I can't help how he feels."

"You can't help how *you* feel either," Stacey said.

"Every time we go over there, which usually right after we

leave here, he asks how you are," she admitted. "I feel like I'm –" She shook her head. "It just…" her voice faded.

"I'm sorry."

"You didn't do anything. He likes you. It's understandable. You're pretty, strong, confident…"

"But I'm not a Christian."

"He is," Marissa said.

"So are you."

"That's not why I am though."

"Then, why are you?" Stacey asked.

"Well, it's not about Adam. It's about Jesus, and what He did for us."

"Huh?"

"What do you know about Jesus Christ?" Marissa asked.

"That He was some guy who thinks He was a god or something."

"Not *a* god, but *The* God."

"I thought He was just some man?"

"Oh boy." She sighed. "This could take a while. Maybe, hmm…what are you doing on Saturday night?"

"Nothing."

"Do you work at all on Saturday?"

"I work until three. Why?"

"Because we're having a youth outing on Saturday night. Do you want to come?" Marissa asked.

"A what?"

"A youth group outing. You already know half the kids there. They are our friends from school. We're going roller skating with a couple other church youth groups."

"Are you sure you want me there? Wouldn't that be invading your territory?"

"There can't be territories when it comes to eternal security." She shook her head. "My feelings regarding Adam are just that. He has made it perfectly clear he likes me as a friend."

She thought through her words for a moment before she continued. "Stacey, if my feelings stop you from going and hearing about Christ, then I'm the one who has to answer to God. And that's not a good position to be in. If you don't go because of me, go because of Adam. He wants to ask you, but he is too nervous. If I tell him you're going because I asked you, then he'd feel less nervous about approaching you to skate."

"But that's…aren't you kind of setting us up?"

"Kind of." She smiled and added, "You can thank me later."

"Would I be able to do it a different way?"

"What do you mean?"

"Well, I happen to know there's a respectful, nice, kind, Christian young gentleman who likes you."

"Alex?" she asked.

"Yep. You might want to change those glasses, dear. He's sweet, *and* a nice-looking guy at that."

"He's not as nice looking as Adam…or as nice."

"I don't know about that one. I *do* know Alex has his good qualities. Adam has his too. They both also have their faults."

"I'm sure."

"On my first day of school during P.E., Alex said if you were one of the floaters, he would have let Kyle save me so he could save you. If he was willing to throw me to the wolves for you, there's something to be said for that."

Rubbing her chin in thought, Marissa acknowledged, "He's a possibility."

"Maybe a couple's skate on Saturday?" Stacey suggested.

She looked at her wide-eyed. "I couldn't!"

"What if it was lady's choice?"

"I always ask Adam for those."

"What does he say?"

"He makes it clear it's out of friendship, but he does it."

"So, would you rather skate with a guy you are *positive* likes you as a friend? Or would you rather skate with a guy you are *positive* likes you for *more* than a friend?"

"Good question."

"I have to tell you that if I go on Saturday, and there's a lady's choice, I'm asking Adam."

"I figured as much."

"You asked me to come."

"I know."

"Do you still want me to come?"

"Actually, yes. I think you need to."

"All right," Stacey agreed. "I'll talk to my dad."

"Thank you, Stacey."

"No problem. If we're heading where I think we are, I have a feeling we're all going to need to stick together."

"What does that mean?"

"I'm pretty sure there will be a power struggle when Adam and I go back to school."

"Over?"

There was a knock on the door before Stacey could answer Marissa. "Wonder who that is?" Stacey asked.

"Want me to get it?"

"If you would, that'd be great."

Stacey watched Marissa go toward the door, concerned. She was not expecting anyone.

Marissa opened door the to find Adam standing there. He looked rough, but better than when Stacey saw him last in the hospital.

Marissa said something about seeing Stacey on Saturday before she left.

"So, what's Saturday?" Adam asked, gingerly sitting on the chair near Stacey's end of the couch.

"Skating with your youth group."

"Really?" He sat up, excited. "You're going?"

"She asked me to. Do you want me to?"

"I…yeah!" he said. Then he realized he was a little too excited. He sat back in his seat as he nonchalantly added, "I mean, yeah, if you want to."

Stacey bit her lip to stop from laughing at him.

"It's actually pretty fun…that is, if you like that sort of thing."

"What do *you* think of me going?"

"I think it'd be good for you."

"All right," Stacey said. She wanted him to tell her how he felt. They got closer to each other through some great conversations in the hospital. She also had a good idea by what everyone told her, but she wanted to hear it directly from him.

"So, is she just…are you meeting us at the church?"

Stacey shrugged, working on her math. "Guess so."

"What's wrong?" Adam asked.

Stacey shook her head. "Nothing."

"Is it okay that I'm here?"

"Yep."

"Are you mad at me for something?"

"Nope."

He looked down, playing with his class ring on his finger. "What's…never mind."

Putting her pencil down, she ran her fingers lightly over her necklace in thought. She glanced at Adam. Before she knew it, she blurted out, "I don't like games, but I don't think you like pressure or forward women either."

He shook his head. "What?"

"Never mind," she said. She fumbled with her pencil for a moment before getting a grip on it. Working on her math homework again, she decided that would be the best way to distract herself from the embarrassment and anxiety that swirled around them.

"Maybe this was a mistake," he said, and went to get up.

Stacey sighed. She slammed her pencil down and asked, "Do you like me?"

He stopped mid-rise out of the chair. "Uh...what?"

"I'm...never mind," she said, flustered. Her hands were shaking, so she concentrated on the math equations in her head to keep herself under control.

"Did you just ask...?" He sat back down in the chair. "Stacey?"

Stacey glanced at him, and then looked away. He was staring right into her eyes. *He had the bluest eyes she ever saw.*

"What did you ask?" he asked.

"Never mind. It was too soon." She shook her head. "Let's just forget I –"

"No," he interrupted her. "What did you ask?"

"I..." she cleared her throat. "I just wanted to know...you see, the girls have some crazy idea that you *might* like me. Not that I'm insinuating anything. I'm just curious as to how you feel. Friends are fine."

"They are," he said cautiously, as he continued to stare at her.

"Okay. Um, drink? Do you want something to drink?" She slowly got off the couch and went to the kitchen, bringing back two pops. She handed him one as she slowly sat back down.

"Thanks," he said, opening his pop. As he settled back into his chair, he anxiously bounced his knee.

"This is awkward now. I'm sorry. Me and my stupid big mouth." She stood. "I need to walk, or run, or *something*."

"We could walk around your neighborhood," he suggested. "That should be safe."

"We could go to the clubhouse?" she offered.

"Sounds good," he agreed.

They walked to the clubhouse with an awkward silence hanging between them. It felt like a cloud of impending doom to Stacey. It was killing her on the inside. When they arrived, it took two rounds of pool before they both started to relax.

"So, did you get your homework done for Wexford?" Stacey asked, unable to handle the silence anymore.

"Yep, it was a piece of cake. You're turn," he said, as his ball missed the hole.

Stacey had stripes. "So, how come Melody and Brian haven't hooked up yet?" She asked, dropping the first ball in. "They both seem to like each other."

"Because Brian's a slow mover, and Melody's too sweet to say anything," Adam explained, as she dropped the second one.

Stacey lined up for her next shot. "Oh."

"Of course, sometimes…you know…a guy *might* need a hint…or two."

Stacey took her shot, dropping another ball into a pocket. As it dropped, she looked up at him.

"You know, just to make sure both people are on the same page sort of thing," Adam finished.

"Mm-hmm," Stacey said, taking another shot. "Missed. Your turn."

"Thanks."

"Would you hypothetically date a non-Christian?" Stacey asked, as he lined up to hit his ball.

He scratched. He started to open his mouth, but stopped. Looking at her, he grimaced.

"Sorry." Stacey cringed. "I mean, it *was* hypothetical."

"That's…it's okay."

"Take your shot again. I won't say anything until you're done," Stacey said.

He lined-up his shot again. When he went to take his shot, he glanced at Stacey and missed the hole anyway.

"My turn," Stacey said.

"You're good at this."

"It just takes concentration," she said. "Sorry I threw you."

He shrugged. "It's okay."

Stacey took her shot. The ball easily dropped into the hole. The next one was going to be tricky. She would have to bounce it off one side, and hope it ricocheted in the right direction.

"Hypothetically, possibly," Adam said, thinking aloud.

Unfortunately, he said it just as Stacey took her shot. The ball bounced off the side of the table onto the floor. Stacey dropped her head onto her arm.

"I'll, uh, get that," he mumbled, as he leaned down to pick it up.

"Yeah, thanks."

He handed Stacey the ball. "Here."

"Thanks. Um, so, what did you…never mind." Stacey shook her head, setting the ball back on the table.

"You asked, hypothetically, if I would date a non-Christian. I said possibly," he said, as he aimed for his shot. After he dropped the ball into the hole, he said, "If her heart was open to listening, then it would be a possibility. Since you are willing to go to a youth outing, it shows me that you are willing to listen. Knowing Marissa, she asked you to come because you brought up the subject."

"It was."

"Then, I would say you're willing to give Jesus a shot. Correct?" He asked, coming over, standing in front of Stacey. Looking down at her, he said, "That's all I ask."

"Hypothetically?" Stacey asked, looking up at him. He was slightly taller than her by about five inches.

"For real," he said, quietly. "I, uh…" He turned and went to shoot another ball into the hole.

"Nice shot. Do you want to play pinball next?" Stacey asked, leaning on her pool stick.

"Who goes first?"

"Whoever wins this round," she suggested.

"Sounds like a plan," he agreed. He and Stacey each only had one ball left. "By the way…" He leaned down and shot his last one in the hole. "That's the last one."

"Ah-ah-ahhhh." She shook her finger at him and smiled. "You still have the eight-ball left, and it can be a bugger…especially where it's at."

"I'm going to bounce it off of the right side, into the lower left one by you," he said.

"Yeah, uh-huh," Stacey said. "I doubt that."

"Yep." He winked, and shot, dropping the eight-ball into the pocket.

"Nice!"

"Thank you. Pinball?" he asked, taking her stick to put it away for her.

"Sounds good."

They went over, and he played his game. He got a high score. "How about whoever gets the lower score treats the winner to dinner at Slater's?" He asked, gesturing toward the pinball machine.

"Maybe," she said. "I hope you have enough on you."

"Oh, I'm sure I won't have to worry about it."

"We'll find out," she said. She played the first ball *way* wrong. It was horrible.

Adam smirked. "Need help?"

"No, I got it," she said. The next two balls were much better, but not good enough to beat his score. "Okay, let's go back to the house. I need to leave a note," she said. "Looks like I'm buying."

"You know I can't let you do that."

"Do what?"

"I can't let you treat me," Adam said.

"That was the deal."

"That was in fun. However, I cannot let a girl buy me dinner."

"Why not? We let you guys buy us ice cream the other day."

He shrugged. "That's not how I was raised."

"What if we each buy our own like last week at Slater's?"

He thought for a minute. "What if we play pinball for it again?"

"And you'll adhere to it if I lose?" she asked.

"Yes," he agreed. "You go first this time, since I went first last time."

"All right," she said. This time she did a lot better.

"My turn," he said, and bombed the first ball.

"Need help?" Stacey teased.

"No, I know what I'm doing," he said, and did a little better on the second two. "Gee, I guess it all depends on the mood of the ball." He shrugged. "Looks like I'm buying."

"Or the mood of the player maybe." Stacey raised an eyebrow. "I think you lost on purpose."

"To save face, yes. You see, it goes against my grain to take a lady out, and either have them pay their own way, or worse yet buy for me. I just cannot do it."

"What about when we went out as a group?"

"That's different."

"Why?"

"Because I didn't ask the group out," he said as he turned and looked right at Stacey. "On the other hand, I *did* ask *you* out. That is, if you're interested?"

"To Slater's? Or out on a date?"

He took both of her hands into his, looking into her eyes. "If you're open to at least listening with an open mind to what Christ has to offer, then I'm open to the possibility of dating. Nothing serious, mind you. Just testing the waters."

Stacey cocked her head to the side, and asked, "Are you asking me out or not?"

He chuckled. "Yes, I'm asking you out."

"Then, yes. Where are we going?"

"I think it was Slater's? Then skating on Saturday?"

"Anything after Slater's tonight?" Stacey asked.

"Why don't we just play it by ear?" He shrugged. Then he smiled, as he said, "The way our life has been going lately, that might be all we can handle."

"This is true."

"Dinner?"

"Dinner," she agreed. They left, walking hand-and-hand back to the house. She left a note for her dad, and then they left in Adam's car to Slater's. Holding hands, they walked into the restaurant.

Karalee was hostess that night. "Well, don't you two look like the belles of the ball," she said, concerned. "Now I see why you haven't been in."

"I'll be in tomorrow and Friday night," Adam said, "and on Saturday, day."

"Same here," Stacey added.

"Pretty sure that was on purpose," Karalee pointed out. "I think Matt has you two scheduled the same for the next three, well, now four weeks together. That way you can train her."

"Well," Adam smiled, "that'll work great!"

"Why?" Karalee asked.

"Just for scheduling purposes," he said, glancing down at their hands, and then back up to her.

When she followed Adam's gaze, Karalee's eyes got huge, as a grin spread across her face. "Wonderful!" She smiled, excited. "I'll, uh…I'll give you a nice table, and a good waiter. This is just so…" She grabbed two menus, and then headed out to the dining room. The pair followed her, snickering at her reaction. "Here ya go. Brian's going to be your waiter," she said, as she set the menus on the table. "Have a wonderful meal," she said, and then left.

"Brian? As in Dalton?" Stacey asked Adam.

"Yep. He and Marissa work here too."

"As servers?"

"No, Marissa works in the kitchen. Brian is a server."

"What about Melody, Harmony, Randy, and Alex?"

"They don't *need* to work."

"Why not?" Stacey asked.

"Because Alex's dad is a U.S. District Attorney. Melody and Harmony's mom is an Advertising Executive, and their dad is a news anchor for a TV station out of Cleveland. He does the morning and noon shows. Randy's dad works for the FBI in one of their crime labs up in Cleveland."

"Really? That's neat!"

"Yep! Needless to say, money is not an issue with any of them."

"What about you?"

"My parents are divorced. I live with my mom. She's a journalist for the town paper. My dad lives in South Carolina, down near Myrtle Beach. He owns a tourist souvenir shop."

"Interesting pair."

"Yeah, I know. I stay here for the most part, but I go in the summer to see him for a couple weeks. It's great! Alex and Randy go with me. We go and enjoy the beach all day, and then at night we go do things like miniature golfing, bowling, go-kart racing…that sort of stuff."

"You don't want the one-on-one time with your dad?"

"To tell you the truth, I don't think he wants the one-on-one time with me," he said, fiddling with his napkin. "He usually asks me to bring the guys. He *says* it's so I won't be bored all day. My thinking though? I'd be happy to help him in the shop all day, and then go out together at night. I only see him two weeks a year."

"Have you ever asked him about it?"

"Well, we're guys, so we kind of hint and hope the other person gets it." He looked up at her. "He doesn't."

"Well, well, well, if it isn't the bruiser twins," Brian said as he walked up to the table. "So, what can I get you two beat-up beauties?"

"Want a Coke?" He asked Stacey. Stacey nodded in response. "Two Cokes to start."

"Sounds good. I'll back in a sec," he said and left.

"So, what do you want to eat?" Adam asked Stacey.

"I had a really good dinner the other day," Stacey said, thinking, as she scanned the menu. "I'm sure just about everything is good."

"How about splitting a pizza, and we can each have a salad and some breadsticks with it?" he suggested.

"That sounds good," she said, closing her menu.

"Great! Then that's what we'll do."

They talked about what kind of pizza they wanted until Brian came back with their drinks. After they ordered, Brian disappeared into the kitchen.

It only took him a few minutes before he returned with their salads. "Freshly made by our very own, Marissa James," he said. "She, of course, left off the onions and cucumbers for you," he said, setting it in front of Adam.

"Thanks," Adam said appreciatively.

"And added a small note for you," Brian said, setting her salad in front of her. Then he handed Stacey a note. Sliding into the booth beside Adam, Brian said, "Just so you know? Your friends are on the other side of the restaurant. They are currently not aware you two are here. They got here a couple minutes before you guys did."

"Okay, try to keep it that way," Adam said. "I don't want them to ruin our date," he added, and then quickly glanced at Brian to see if he caught the hint.

"Well, that's understandable, no one would..." Brian's head spun toward Adam when it registered what Adam said. "Did you just say –?"

Adam grinned. "Yep."

"Nice!" Brian smiled, genuinely excited. "That's awesome!"

"Shh! That's going to attract attention that we *don't* want."

Brian covered his mouth, and then quietly said, "Yeah, sorry."

"Looks like I need to go to the kitchen for a second," Stacey said, reading the note. It was Marissa asking Stacey to come talk to her for a minute.

"Want me to come too?" Adam asked, concerned.

"No. I'll be back in a second."

"All right," he said. He and Brian continued talking at the table.

Stacey went to the kitchen. The only time she was in there was during her tour with Matt after her interview.

"Well, Miss Spencer, are you ever going to grace us with your...ouch!" the cook cringed when he got a good look at Stacey. "What happened to you?"

"The same thing that happened to Adam," Marissa said, filling an order. "Thanks for coming back."

"It's fine," Stacey said. "What's up?"

"Karalee said you were on a date with Adam. Is that true?" Marissa asked.

"Yes."

"Hmm." She placed some food on a plate. "Just thought I would ask."

"Hey Riss!" Brian came in, putting his arm around Stacey's shoulders, smiling. "Did she tell ya the good news?"

"Yes," she said flatly.

"Marissa, I'm –"

"No," Marissa said, cutting Stacey off.

Stacey felt bad for Marissa. Marissa was trying to hide it, but she had tears in her eyes.

"Marissa?" Brian looked at her concerned. "What's wrong?"

"It's–I…" She shook her head. "Here." She put a couple plates up on the counter from one of Brian's other tables.

"Maybe this is a mistake," Stacey said, tears brimming her eyes.

"What is? You and Adam? No way!" Brian objected. "Marissa, you have to understand he has the choice in who he dates."

"She's not even a Christian!" A flash of anger shot across

Marissa's eyes. "We're not supposed to date *those kind of people!*" She looked down her nose at Stacey.

Stacey's jaw dropped as she stared at Marissa, mortified. She wanted to bolt, but Brian put his other hand on her arm so she would not leave.

"Marissa!" Adam came into the kitchen, wide-eyed. "I heard you all the way out there! *What is wrong with you?*"

"You're – she's not – she's..." Marissa's voice faded. She sighed, looking away.

Adam walked over to the counter where she stood. "Riss, you cannot control who I date. I'm sorry for you that I don't feel the same way you do. However, to slam her like that, throwing it in her face was..." He shook his head with his hands on his hips. "It's just not something I *ever* expected to hear from you. A Christian doesn't behave that way! You know better than that." He went over to Stacey and grabbed her hand. Pulling her with him, they left the kitchen, leaving Brian and Marissa in the wake of Marissa's outburst.

When they sat down at the table, Adam sat on the same side as Stacey, his arm around her. "I'm really sorry, Stacey."

"I just..." Stacey shook her head, still in shock. "If that's what a Christian's attitude is toward the rest of the world, then why would you even look twice at me?" Stacey asked, tears in her eyes. She bit her lip, fighting them back.

"It's *not* how we look at the rest of the world. She said that out of hurt."

"What happens if I don't choose this Jesus guy?"

Pained, he calmly said, "That is your choice, but I don't want to look at that right now. Why don't we take it one step at a time?"

"What happens if I don't choose Him, though?"

"Are you willing to look at Christianity *with* an open mind?"

"Yes," Stacey agreed.

"That's all I ask. We'll go from there."

Stacey dropped her head down into her hands, shaking it.

"Stacey?" Brian came out of the kitchen. He sat down at the table across from them, and asked, "Are you okay?"

"No," Stacey said, not looking up.

"What she said was out of line," Brian said.

"She talked about me as if I were some disgusting, filthy piece of trash. You know, I'm going to just quit going out in public around here if this stuff happens every time I do."

"No, don't do that," Brian encouraged. "We would miss your smiling face."

"But –"

"No." Brian shook his head. "There are no 'buts' in this one. What she said was wrong. That's not a nice way to look at anyone. Look, you guys should eat your salads. The rest of your meal will be coming soon," he said, as he got up and left.

"I'm not hungry," Stacey said. "I lost my appetite."

"Well, I remember something about you being hypo-glycemic," Adam said, "which, I *do* believe means you need to eat."

"Yes."

"Just try to relax and eat," he encouraged.

"You don't think I'm a disgusting piece of humanity?" Stacey asked.

"I'm telling you I don't share her sentiments," he said, getting up and going back to the other side of the booth to eat. "Now, would you mind if we prayed first?"

"No, I–I guess not. I've never done it before. Is there some-thing I need to do?"

"Just bow your head and close your eyes," he said, taking her hands. "I'll do the rest."

"Okay," she said uneasily.

He said a short prayer, and then they started to eat. Stacey used her fork to push her salad around the plate. Her stomach was in knots.

"The idea is to actually eat," Adam said after a couple minutes.

"Well, I can handle the disdain from Chandler and crew, but from one of the people I just felt comfortable in calling a friend? It's just a little…well, yeah."

"She's just hurt."

"And hurt me back," Stacey said, setting her fork down. "What did I do to her?"

"You didn't do *anything* to her."

"Mind explaining that to her?"

"She knows it," Adam said. "Give her time."

"Whatever," Stacey said. Picking up her fork, she continued to toy with her salad.

"Stace, just try to relax. For me?"

Stacey rested her chin on her hand and sighed. "All right."

"I'll tell ya what. Why don't we get our meal to go? We can eat it at the park, or at my house or yours?" He offered. "Would getting out of here help clear your head?"

"Probably. Yeah."

"Okay, I'll be back in a minute. Will you be okay?"

"Yeah."

He left for the kitchen. He was gone for only a minute, when Kyle and Shane sat down across from her.

"My, my, my, it *is* true. She walks," Kyle said crossing his arms, as he slunk back into his seat.

Stacey rolled her eyes.

"Oh, I would *think* we'd get more of a reaction than that. Wouldn't you, Mason?"

"I would think so. After all, we *were* the ones who gave her almost an entire week off from school," Shane pointed out. "A thank you *would* be nice."

Stacey just shook her head in response. *Who did they think they were kidding? And what would it take for them to leave her alone?*

"Now, we're going to assume you haven't told anyone what happened the other day, because that would be *really* bad," Kyle said sternly.

Stacey stood. Bracing her hands on the table, she leaned toward them. "Right now, your little antics are the furthest thing from my mind. However, just so you know, I am on to your little game," she said, narrowing her eyes at them. "And I *do not* appreciate you coming back and threatening me after you already beat me up. *Everyone* knows it was you."

Kyle stood, leaning on the table matching her glare. Within an inch from her face, he sternly said, "Then you had better *shut up,* and keep any further conversations we have *to yourself.* By the way, just so *you* know, when we tell you to do something next time, you'd *better* do it *without* mouthing off."

"Like what?"

An evil smile spread across his face.

Wide-eyed, she asked, "And if I don't?"

"Next time, you and your boyfriend might not make it out quite so easily."

Matt walked up to the table. "Is there a problem over here?"

Shane stood. "We were just leaving."

"Then, just so *you* know? If you threaten another of, not only one of my customers, but also one of my employees again, you will no longer be welcome in this restaurant."

"We go where we please," Kyle said, daring him to say otherwise.

"Not as far as I'm concerned."

"Then maybe *you* need a lesson in respect."

Stacey gasped. "No, don't! He–it's okay. I'll cooperate."

Kyle smiled and nodded. "That's better," he said, and they left.

"What just happened?" Adam asked, coming out of the kitchen, noticing the look on Matt and Stacey's faces. "Stacey, you look scared to death."

"Just got a visit from the friendly neighborhood code enforcers," Matt said, crossing his arms.

Seeing how pale Stacey was, Adam commented, "Doesn't look like it went well."

Sickened, Matt shook his head as he crossed his arms. "They were throwing their weight around."

"Yeah, okay, we need to go anyway," Adam said, with the pizza box and a couple bags in his arms. "Can you check us out, so we can leave before anything else happens?"

"No, it's on the house." Matt waved him off. "I'll call Sam and let him know what's going on. Why don't you take her to your house? That way she's not at her home by herself."

"That sounds good," Adam agreed. "So, you'll just have her dad pick her up at my house?"

"Yeah. When's your mom getting home?"

"In a couple hours."

"Then don't answer the door unless it's me, one of your friends, or her dad. I don't care if it's the police. Do not open it. Understand?"

"Why wouldn't we open it for the police?" Stacey asked.

"Just trust me," Matt said. "Open it for *no one* but those I told you. Understand?"

"All right," Adam relented. Taking Stacey's hand, they left. "Okay, Matt's not normally the paranoid type," Adam said, when they were in the car and on the way to his house. "What exactly happened back there?"

"They threatened him if he tried to kick them out of the restaurant."

"As in...?"

"As in what they did to us. They threatened to quote, *give him a lesson in respect.*"

He glanced at Stacey in shock, before turning back toward the road. "*For real?*"

"Yes." Glancing out the window at the passing landscape, she admitted, "I just told them I would cooperate if they left him alone."

"You'll *what*? Why?"

"I created this mess. I'm the one who stirred things up. I don't want anyone else injured, or worse yet killed because of me."

"You didn't do this." He shook his head. "You're just one of the few who's trying to stop this."

"But people –"

"Are currently under their control, and they know it," Adam cut her off. "I'm willing to help in any way possible. But Stace, don't bend or give in to them. You're strong enough to fight this. I'm behind you. I'm sure the others are too."

"Including Marissa?"

"I'll talk to Marissa later. Don't worry about her."

"I'm afraid I have to. If she's that upset at me, she's going to be looking for a way to get rid of me."

"She's a Christian!"

"You've already said she's not thinking straight."

"She won't do anything," Adam said confidently. "She doesn't want to see me hurt."

"She may not want to see you hurt, but I promise you she doesn't want me around."

"Stacey, that group's families are holding this town hostage," Adam said, visibly agitated. "If anyone has even *remotely* challenged them in the past, they seem to suddenly run into a whole string of accidents. If you and your father, and yes, I've already talked to him, if you guys can free us, trust me there will be a lot of people behind you!"

"What exactly did my dad say?"

"He told me the power he has behind him. He also said it might take all the favors he is currently owed from them to do it, but he'll fight with everything he has. He's been recruiting. I gave him a couple names of people who might be willing to help, including Mr. and Mrs. Crestwood, Mr. and Mrs. Taylor, and Mr. and Mrs. Kelley."

"That'll work," Stacey said, thinking through what they were about to do.

"So," he reached over, taking her hand, "how are you feeling?"

"A little better, that is, until I go back to school in the morning."

"They think they have you. They might test the waters and try to provoke you, or they may just leave you alone."

"Hmm, great choices."

"I would personally prefer they left you alone."

"Me too," she said, looking out the window.

He squeezed her hand, and then held it for the rest of the ride to his house.

"THIS IS CUTE," Stacey said with a smile, looking around his house when they walked inside. It was cozy, and decorated in a country style. The outside of Adam and his mom's ranch style three-bedroom, two-bathroom house was made of brick.

Stacey walked over to a bookshelf with photos and books. Taking a good look at the pictures, she asked, "Is this your dad?"

"Yep. Do you want to eat out here or in the kitchen?"

"Whichever is easier," she said. "Is this you?" she asked, pointing to a picture of what looked like a younger Marissa and Adam of about five years old.

"Yeah. Marissa too."

"She *has* been around for a while," Stacey remarked.

"And thinks she can stake her claim on me because of that. She'll get over it sooner or later."

"I think I'd like sooner on that one," she said, as he came out of the kitchen with napkins in hand. He then set the coffee table for their dinner. Afterward, they enjoyed their food while talking about school and their friends. Adam shared stories from over the last few years. She shared some stories of her own from her life in Michigan.

"So," Stacey glanced at the photos again after they finished eating, "to look at these pictures, and to look at this town, it *looks* like happy-go-lucky everyday suburbia. Is there a page I'm missing?"

"In what?"

"Around here. There are a lot of things that don't add up."

"Well, you should stay away from Kyle and company *and* their families, *and* any public or government type officials of this town. Otherwise you should be fine."

"Great, that narrows it down." She rolled her eyes. Then she asked, "So, what happens if I don't stay away from them?"

Frowning, he asked, "You *want* to hang around them?"

"No. I'm having trouble knowing Marissa hates me so much."

"She doesn't *hate* you," Adam said. Then he got off the floor. Resting his arms around her waist as she faced him, he explained, "She doesn't like that we're connecting. She'll be fine regarding us in time."

"I don't know." Glancing at the pictures again, and then back to him, she pointed out, "There is a lot of history with you guys."

"It was only on her side. I assure you," he said, resting his hand on the sides of her face. "There's nothing there on my side except as friends."

Stacey nodded, and then looked up at his beautiful blue eyes that were staring into hers. She adored his smile. His cologne permeated her senses, as she stared into his eyes, soaking in the feeling of his body close to hers.

"You, on the other hand?" He smiled. "I love your gorgeous light brown hair. The highlights really make your eyes stand out. Your blue eyes sparkle when you look at me. Your face lights up when you smile, showing your adorable dimples," he said, as he brushed his thumbs over the dimples in her cheeks.

Stacey smiled. His words touched her soul.

He ran his fingers through her hair, watching it fall back onto her shoulders. When she looked back up at him, he hugged her tightly to his body.

"I'm looking forward to Saturday," he said. "The idea of skating all night with you sounds wonderful. I'm also curious to see what you think about what Matt's going to be talking about."

"I'm looking forward to it as well."

He savored the few minutes with Stacey in his arms, before he turned and let her go. "We should probably…homework? We have math we can work on. Since we're in the same class we can share the book and work on it together?"

"Sounds good," Stacey agreed. "Um," she looked around where she stood, "where's the bathroom?"

"Down the hall. It's the second door on the right," he said, cleaning up from dinner.

"Thanks," she said, and went down the hall to the bathroom. After she finished, she washed and dried her hands. When she opened the door to leave the bathroom, she heard him in his room, so she headed in that direction. "Like it." Stacey nodded in approval, as she leaned on the doorway, arms crossed. He was getting his math book and notebook out of his backpack.

He smiled as his cheeks turned red. "Thanks."

It was neat and clean. She was impressed that his bed was even made. There were numerous posters on the walls of various scenic shots of the ocean and waterfalls, Christian posters with versus on them, and a few posters with skateboarding scenes. There were also a couple skateboards over in the corner.

"Mind if I come in?" she asked. "I kind of want to see those." Stacey pointed toward the skateboards.

"Sure. Go ahead. Do you board?"

"Never have before. How good are you?"

"Well, we have a couple ramps and a half-pipe in the back-yard." He watched her as she picked up one of the skateboards and spun the back wheels. "Want to go try?"

"Well, I'm already bruised." She shrugged, smiling. "I guess it won't make that much difference if I add a couple more, huh? Let's just do our best not to break anymore ribs and I'll be fine."

He smirked as he got up off the bed. "Come on," he said, grabbing the other board with one hand, while his books rested in his other hand. He dropped off the books on the coffee table in the living room before they headed toward the backyard. It was dusk, so he turned on the porch light.

"Okay, so how does this work?" Stacey asked. She rested one foot on the board, with her other foot solidly on the ground.

Taking both of her hands into his, he said, "Up ya go."

When she got on the board, it moved under her feet. "Uh, this is –"

"Trust me?" he asked.

She glanced from her feet, to him, anxiously. "Okay. I'm nervous, but I trust you."

"Good. Now, keep your eyes on me," he said, and started walking backwards.

"It's…this is very –" Stacey faltered, "it's moving under me."

"It's okay. It's supposed to," he assured her. "Watch." He let her go, so she put a foot down to keep her steady.

Going to where the other board rested on the ground, Adam scooped it up. Taking it over to the ramps, he started at the top of the half-pipe, and took off. He was amazing! He did jumps Stacey had only seen on television. To his credit, he did not fall once. He did not have on a helmet or hand and kneepads either. Stacey was *majorly* impressed.

"Okay, I think you could cream Kyle at this any day," she said.

He looked up at her and grinned, as he landed smoothly at the bottom of the half-pipe. Then he picked up his board and walked back over to Stacey. "Wanna try?"

"I'm afraid if I do, I'll wipe out."

"Okay, let's start with the basics." Shifting on his board in front of her, he explained, "You put one foot here, and the other one there." He showed her on his board. After playing around on them for a little while, he confidently said, "Okay, you're ready."

"For what?"

"To try a one-eighty."

"A *what?*"

"This..." He tipped the board back with one foot, as he spun it halfway around before dropping it back onto the ground. "See, it's a controlled one-hundred-and-eighty-degree turn."

Stacey shook her head. "Oh, I don't know about this."

"Come on, try it? Please?"

Stacey looked down. Nervously, she positioned her feet how Adam instructed. Glancing up at him, she saw him staring at her feet, so she looked back down. "Like this?" she asked.

"Yes. Just give it a try," he encouraged.

In one quick movement, Stacey spun around as she shifted her back foot. Unfortunately, she spun the whole three-hundred-and-sixty-degrees...and way too fast! She felt the board slip out from under her, along with her feet. She hit the ground...hard. "Ow," she groaned, grabbing her elbow.

"Oh!" He ran over to help her. "Are you okay?"

"Not really." She winced. "I'm thinking math, for right now, is safer."

"I agree," he said, looking her over for injuries. "Do you...are you bleeding anywhere?"

"I think my arm is," she said, still holding her elbow. "My ego is pretty bruised too." She winced and jumped as Adam looked at her elbow. "Ouch!"

"Okay, let's go get you patched up." He helped Stacey off the ground. Heading toward the bathroom, he said, "Good news? You actually did a three-sixty before you lost it. That's pretty good."

"Just landed wrong."

"That's okay. At least you tried," he said, pulling the antibiotic ointment, band aids, and the hydrogen peroxide from the cupboard under the sink. "Hate to tell you, but this is going to hurt," he explained. "Going to apologize ahead of time."

"Go ahead," Stacey said.

He did his best to clean her arm gently. She jumped and winced. Biting her tongue, she tried not to yell as he cleaned the scrapes on her arm with the hydrogen peroxide.

"Okay." He stood up, satisfied, after applying a couple band aids and antibiotic ointment. "How's that?"

"Better."

"Good, let's, um…" He looked down at her, as she sat on the counter in front of him. "We should…homework?"

She nodded as she looked up at him. "Yeah. Maybe."

Stacey got off the counter. As they stood there, Stacey could not take her eyes off his.

After a few moments, the doorbell rang. "I should go get the door." He quickly kissed her cheek, and then took off for the door.

Stacey rested her hand on her cheek where he kissed it. She could not help the smile on her face. By the time she made her way out to the living room, her hand was holding the pulsating part of her arm from where she scraped it. Still a little lost in the moment, she barely acknowledged her dad when she walked in. "Hi, Dad."

"Heard you took a spill," he said.

"It was my fault," Stacey admitted. "Princess Grace strikes again."

"Well, are you ready to go home?"

"Sure." Turning toward Adam, she said, "Thank you for tonight. I enjoyed the time we had here."

"You're welcome. I'll see you in the morning," Adam said.

"At the tree?"

"Yes. Since we work at the same time tomorrow night, do you want me to pick you up?" He offered.

Stacey smiled. "Sure. Thank you. That would be great!"

"Sir," he looked at Stacey's dad, "if it's okay with you," he said, and then turned to Stacey, "and you. If you want, you can come home with me after school, and we could just take off from here."

"Thank you for asking," Sam said, impressed. "And it's up to her."

Stacey grinned. "That would be wonderful!"

"We can get a snack before work. That way there's no chance of your blood sugar dropping before our break," Adam suggested.

"I think that's a great idea! Thank you," Stacey agreed.

"Well, see you tomorrow," Adam said, and Sam and Stacey left.

"HE SEEMS NICE," Sam mentioned on the way home. "Do I miss my guess when I suggest that there might be some interest between you two?"

"He...well, we went on a date tonight," she admitted.

"Well," he said, taken aback. "That's nice. He seems like a good guy."

"Oh, he is, Daddy! He really is a nice guy!"

"He seems respectful as well."

"He is."

"You really like him?" he asked.

She blushed. "Yes."

He nodded. Rubbing his chin as he drove one-handed for a few moments, he finally said, "Since reading people is part of my job, from what I can tell, he seems polite, kind, honest, considerate, and a gentleman. I approve."

"Thanks!" Stacey wrapped her arms around his neck in a hug. He started laughing, as he swerved the vehicle before getting it back under control. Quickly kissing him on the cheek, she then returned to her seat. "There's also skating on Saturday night with the youth group. Can I go?"

"Is he going to be there?"

"Yes."

"Did he ask you?"

"Actually, Marissa did. Like I said, it's for their youth group. Matt Slater is speaking at the outing as well."

"Well, that sounds safe. Get me a time, how much, and you can go."

"Thank you!" She said, feeling butterflies in her stomach. Her mind filled with moments from her time at Adam's house while she watched out the window with a smile on her face.

"I love you, Peanut," he said, as they pulled into the parking lot of their townhouse. "I only want the best for you."

"I know. I love you too, Daddy," she said, still looking out the window. "I feel like there is some heavy stuff coming our way."

"I'm sure there is. This is just the beginning."

"If there is a God out there, I hope He's paying attention to us and this town, and keeps us all safe."

"Me too, Peanut. Me too."

When they got home, Stacey quickly filled him in on the events of the evening. Afterward, she headed upstairs to finish her homework before going to bed with thoughts of Adam on her mind.

∽

THE NEXT MORNING, Stacey got ready as quickly as possible. Since it was her first day back after the incident, she did not want to be late. Of course, Adam was waiting for her when they arrived.

"Hi," Stacey greeted him with a smile when she got out of the Cherokee.

"May I?" he asked with his elbow out.

They waved goodbye to Stacey's dad before they headed into the school. Once inside, they switched to holding hands. Making their way through the crowded halls, they went to Adam's locker, and then headed toward Stacey's.

"Hi…uh…" Marissa ran up to them, but stopped short when she saw them holding hands. "Uh…hi, I, um…how are…I'm sorry. I wasn't…okay, can I try this again?" she stammered. "How are you guys today? I mean, I'm sorry." She shook her head, unable to make eye contact. "I need to…I have to find… Alex. Yeah, I need to find Alex," she said, and left them standing there, baffled and confused.

"That was different." Adam said, as they walked up to Stacey's locker. "What *was* that?"

Stacey chuckled, inputting the combination into the lock. "I honestly have no idea. After last night, I'm not sure I *want* to know."

"Agreed."

After grabbing her books, they then headed toward math class. They made it just as the bell rang. He dropped her off at her seat, and then sat down at his seat a row over as class started.

Kyle passed a note behind him to Stacey after a couple minutes. Stacey really did not want to read it. She slightly held it up so Adam could see it, and then pointed to Kyle. Adam just shook his head, visibly annoyed.

As she scanned the note, she saw he wanted to meet with her

for a few minutes after school. She wrote that she could not, and passed it back.

She hoped saying she could not would be sufficient, but it was not. He wanted to know why. Wanting to pay attention to the class, she tucked the note into her math book. As far as she was concerned, she answered his question. She felt he did not need to know why.

Toward the end of class, Mr. Wexford gave the class about five minutes free time before the bell.

Kyle turned around. "So?"

"So…what?" Stacey asked innocently.

"Why can't you meet me?"

"Because she's meeting me," Adam said from his seat. "We're dating, just so you know."

"Oh!" He said surprised. Then cleared his throat, before he said, "You, uh, might want to change your mind on that one."

"No. I'm confident in my choice," Stacey said.

"We'll see," he said, and then turned back around.

Stacey just shook her head, and then turned back toward Adam to talk for the remainder of the class. She could feel Kyle fuming in front of her.

After class, Adam walked with Stacey to their next class, when Brian ran up behind them. He put his arms over their shoulders, pushing himself between them. "Okay, so there's this funky rumor going around that you two are dating. Now, I'd believe it if I had heard it directly *from* my friend, but since I didn't…" Brian's voice trailed off.

Tilting his head to the side, Adam said, "You knew we were on a date last night. Not sure where the miscommunication was?"

"Well, going on a date, and *dating* are two different things. Is there a commitment there I don't know about?"

"We're dating," Adam said bluntly. "If someone has a problem, or needs further clarification, then they can come to us directly. Since it's probably Marissa, she can just suck it up because I'm getting tired of it."

"It was partially her," he admitted, "but the other part is Kyle and company. He's not happy either. You should have heard him in the hall a few minutes ago."

"Oh well." Stacey shrugged. "Last time I checked this was a free country. I wasn't aware we had to get permission from anyone but our parents to date."

"Just warning you," Brian said, moving to the other side of Adam while continuing to class. "You guys need to stay on your toes until this situation cools down."

"I'm not *that* worried. He wasn't dating her." Adam waved him off. Then he reached down and grabbed Stacey's hand. She glanced up at him smiling, so he winked at her and returned the smile. "Don't think she'd date him anyway."

"Nope," Stacey said. "Pretty sure I made that clear the other week."

"I want to talk to you," Erin said sternly, jumping on the trio as soon as they set foot through the threshold of the class.

"Who? Me or him?" Stacey asked.

"You," Erin said, looking at Stacey.

Stacey sighed as she shook her head. They were at least five minutes early, so Stacey went with Erin. She did not want to have to deal with them later. "Erin, what is your problem with Adam and I dating? What will it take to make it perfectly clear that I *do not* want Shane *or* Kyle?"

"I want to know why."

"Why what?"

"Why don't you want them?"

"Why does that bother you? You were mad at me last week because you thought I *did* want them."

"Just tell me!" she demanded.

Stacey groaned in frustration. Crossing her arms, she explained, "Adam is sweet, kind, gentle, and very polite. Meanwhile, Kyle almost broke my hand last week, and *did* beat me up, breaking two of my ribs and three of Adam's! And to be honest, I just don't like his *king of the world* attitude."

"What about Shane?"

"What *about* Shane? I wasn't aware he was anywhere near this situation."

"You said last week you wouldn't date him either."

"And you have a problem with that *why* again?"

"Just tell me!" she said, impatient.

"He's a nice guy. I'm just not interested."

"But you said not to trust him. My best friend is dating him. I want to know why you wouldn't trust him?"

"Because he's...well, he's *so* comfortable to be around, someone *might* take that wrong and think he was interested in them."

"Do you?"

"Oh-my-word!" Stacey threw her hands in the air. Then she yelled, getting into Erin's face, "I like Adam! Not Shane *or* Kyle!"

Adam poked his head out the door. Grabbing Stacey by the wrist, he said, "Okay, this is done. Besides, class is starting."

"Thanks," Stacey said, relieved as they sat down in their seats. "I was beginning to get a little frustrated."

"A little?" Brian chuckled. "You cleared up *any* question in *anyone's* mind that they *may* have had, that you are *not* interested in Kyle or Shane...just Adam."

"I certainly hope so!" Stacey said, dropping her head onto her crossed arms on her desk. She felt a hand on her back, and jumped.

"Stace?" Shane said quietly.

Stacey groaned. "What now?"

"Duck Kyle," he whispered, and then left for his desk.

"Ooo!" Stacey clinched her fists, getting angry. "This is crazy!"

"What's crazy?" Mrs. McCoy asked, heading toward the front of the class.

Dropping her head back down on her arms, Stacey mumbled, "Nothing."

~

THE REST of the day went well for Stacey. During P.E., Kyle and Shane avoided her, and they did not run into that group at lunch either. They received some mean looks from that group though, which did not help her headache.

"Ready to start work tonight?" Adam asked. He and Stacey walked across the yard, holding hands as they headed toward their group at the tree.

"Think so. I need to stop off at home to get my uniform and some aspirin first."

"Not a problem."

"So?" Harmony smiled when they walked up to the group. "How are things?" She glanced down at their hands, then back up at the pair. She looked like she was about to burst.

"Good. You?" Adam smirked. He knew she wanted information, but he was being a brat about it. At lunch no one asked, and neither Stacey, nor Adam volunteered.

"Adam!" Marissa ran up to the group. Color drained from her face. "You can't...you guys..."

Brian chuckled. "Calm down and spit it out already."

"No." She had a hard time catching her breath from running. "Work tonight...not good!"

Adam furrowed his brow. "What?"

"Kyle...Shane...work. Not good."

"What's not good?" Adam asked.

"I heard..." She took a couple deeper breaths. "In class... Kyle's in my last class, and he...he said they were..." She shook her head. "You guys are in trouble."

"We'll be in a public place," Adam said.

"They don't care and you know it!"

"Wait. What?" Stacey asked. "Did Kyle threaten us?" When Marissa nodded, Stacey asked, "With bodily harm?" Marissa nodded again. "He won't do anything," Stacey said confidently. "There are too many witnesses. My dad will have that case blown sky-high, and he knows it. He said it to scare you."

"How can you…you don't know him!" She objected.

"No, but I *do* know he knows who my dad works for. He's playing a mind game," Stacey said. "I'm sure of it."

"Besides, the hostesses know better than to give me Kyle at one of my tables. There's no way we'll run into them," Adam added. "I'm training her. Who I have, she will have at her tables. We'll be fine."

"Boy, do I hope you're right!" Marissa said, still not convinced.

CHAPTER 6

"ONE WHO GAINS STRENGTH BY OVERCOMING OBSTACLES POSSESSES THE ONLY STRENGTH WHICH CAN OVERCOME ADVERSITY." ALBERT SCHWEITZER

On the way to Adam's, he and Stacey stopped off at Stacey's house so she could quickly change. Stacey also grabbed a couple aspirin while she was at it. Then they went over to Adam's so he could change.

"Since it's your first day, we'll go in a little early. You'll have a ton of paper work to fill out," Adam mentioned when they walked into his house.

"Sounds good," Stacey agreed.

"We can get a snack while we're waiting, and eat it in the break room," he said, heading back to his room to change. "I like their curly fries. They're the best in town."

"Good point," Stacey said.

While he was gone, Stacey studied the photos again. This time, she took a closer look to see if she could identify others in the pictures. One of them blew her mind. It looked to be a huge group photo of around thirty or so people. Kyle was on one end of the photo, with Adam on the other. She made a mental note to check with Adam about it later, before moving on to other photos.

"I'm ready," Adam said, coming down the hall. When he saw what she was doing, he asked with a smirk, "Studying me?"

"Just looking at the different faces of Adam," Stacey said. "There seems to be a picture of you at just about every age."

"Trust me, these have been filtered. There are a lot missing."

"Why?" Stacey asked.

"Long story. One that's for another day. C'mon, let's start your first day of work," he said, and they left.

ADAM AND STACEY were in the break room. As Stacey filled out her paperwork, she and Adam split an order of curly fries. Each one had a pop of their own.

Mikey walked into the break room. "Well, well, well, it seems that we meet again," Mikey said, as he half-bowed.

"Yes. We will be working together as well, my good man," Stacey said. "Whilst I do appreciate the bow, it is not necessary."

Adam shook his head, laughing.

"Sir Adam, why did you not share with me this fair maiden would be toiling beside us as we labored for our wages?" Mikey asked.

Adam struggled to keep a straight face. "I, um..." He bit his lip. "I was, um...saving it for a surprise."

"And a lovely one it is," he said. "Thank you for the kindness in supplying such a spectacular surprise! And welcome to the wonderful world of Slater's Diner, Lady Stacey. If I may be of any assistance, please do not hesitate to ask."

"Thank you, kind sir," Stacey said, and Mikey left to go clock in for the night.

As soon as he was out of earshot, Adam and Stacey burst out in laughter. "Oh-my-word! Is he for real?" Stacey asked.

"Unfortunately, yes," Adam said, chuckling. "He's one of the drama students at the School of the Arts down the road from Pine Crest."

"I didn't know there was one."

"Yep. Funny thing is you can tell what kind of play he's working on by his vocabulary. You should have heard it when he was doing one where he was a street thug." Adam smiled in remembrance. "That was hysterical! He was using words like 'dissing,' 'yo,' 'wack,' that sort of stuff. Right now, it's Shakespearian. He says he's a method actor, and needs to have a feel for how his character would act in the real world."

"I would have guessed it would have been somewhere in the Renaissance phase at the moment," Stacey said. "There, I'm done!" She finished her paperwork, and then grabbed for another curly fry. He grabbed at the same time, and they grabbed for the same one. "Oh, I'm…go ahead," Stacey offered.

"No, that's okay. I'll just take this one," he said. "Guess great minds think alike, huh?"

While Adam took the plate to the dish room, Stacey took the completed paperwork to Matt. Matt gave Stacey the quick run-down on how things worked. He jumbled her mind so much, she was sure it would take all night just to sort it out.

About an hour later, Stacey was given her first table with Adam. When Clarissa, the hostess for the night, pointed out the table, Stacey was flooded with relief to see it was her dad and Becky. "Thought we'd give you a break on the first one," Clarissa said.

"Thanks," Stacey said. Even though she was relieved it was her dad, she was also embarrassed. She felt like her dad was checking on her.

"Um, hi," Stacey said, walking up to the table with Adam beside her.

"Hey, Peanut. Thought you could use a friendly face on this side of things. You remember Becky?" Sam said, taking Becky's hand into his.

Stacey nodded in response as she stared at their hands. Taken aback, she was unsure what to say.

When Adam saw her struggling, he jumped in. "Would you folks care for anything to drink while you look at the menu?"

"Sure," Sam said, seemingly oblivious to Stacey's reaction. He ordered a couple of Cokes, so Adam and Stacey went to get them.

"Are you okay?" Adam asked, handing Stacey two glasses.

"I'm…I just…my mom just died in March. This is kind of…I don't know." Stacey shook her head. She glanced at her dad and Becky, and then back up at Adam. "I guess I expected a little more time. My mom's death is so fresh. I didn't think he would be dating so soon."

"There's not always a time table when it comes to love," Adam explained, resting his hand on her back. "You do, however, need to not let your feelings show on your face so much. That might affect the tip," he teased, trying to put her more at ease. When she did not smile, he leaned in closer to her, and said, "Stace, he's a grown man. He's going to find love."

"But my mom…" She looked toward the ceiling, forcing herself not to cry.

"I know. Just be supportive and happy for him," he said. "Sort out the feelings later."

Stacey nodded in response as she filled the glasses with ice and Coke. When they went back to the table, she said, "Here are your drinks. What can we get you this evening for dinner?"

"Are you okay?" her dad asked.

"Yes. I'm…yes. What can I get you for dinner?" Stacey asked again.

After they got her dad and Becky's order, she and Adam took it back to the kitchen where Marissa was working on the line. "Got an order for you." Stacey said, handing the slip to Marissa.

"Thanks," Marissa said flatly, snatching the slip from Stacey's hand.

"Riss, chill out!" Adam snapped. "We *do* need to work together."

"I just can't believe that you..." She shook her head. "Never mind."

"Marissa?" Matt asked, coming into the kitchen. "Is there a problem?"

"No sir," she said, and went to cooking the plates for Sam and Becky's meals.

"Good," Matt said. "Adam, you guys have another table."

"Thanks," Adam said, and they headed back out. "This one's all you." Adam nodded toward the table. "You got this. Just relax and smile."

"All right," she said, taking a deep breath. With that, they headed over to the table.

For the rest of the evening, Adam and Stacey alternated tables. Adam stood beside her all evening, encouraging her the entire time. Stacey was pleasantly surprised to find it fun to be a server. She knew this would not always be the case. Not surprising to her, Kyle and company did not come for dinner.

As they pulled up to Stacey's townhouse after work, Adam took her hand. "Tonight was fun," he said. "I'm glad you work there."

"Thanks. I liked it too," Stacey said, and then quickly added, "and the money's not bad either."

"Well, I think the twenty-dollar tip from your dad helped a lot. You should know that isn't normal."

"I know. But it *was* nice!"

"That it was! Glad we split the tips."

"So, school tomorrow? And skating on Saturday?"

"Yep," he agreed. Then a thought hit him. "Oh, wait!" He got out and ran around to her side of the vehicle, opening the door. "Let me walk you up?"

"Definitely," she said pleased, accepting the hand he put out to help her out of the car.

Together, they walked up to her townhouse front door. He then took her other hand into his and faced her. "I really like that you're here," he said.

"This place would be pretty close to perfect, if it wasn't for Kyle, his friends, and their families."

"Oh, he'll get over it," he said, looking down at her. "May I?"

Stacey nodded, so he hugged her tightly to him and kissed her head.

"Thank you," Stacey said, and then kissed his cheek.

Resting his hand on the side of her face, he looked into her eyes. After a few moments, he said, "For skating on Saturday?"

"Yes? What about it?"

"Would you consider that a date, and let me pay for you?" Adam asked.

"If you want to, I would like that," she agreed.

"May I pick you up?"

"I'm sure my dad would appreciate it. He was trying to figure out the scheduling for Saturday. He has a deposition to do on Saturday in Cleveland, and the time frames were going to run into each other."

"Well, since we both have to work on Saturday, I could pick you up for that if you want as well. That way he won't have to worry about that either."

"I think that's a great idea," Stacey said.

He looked into her eyes again. "I should..." He pointed over his shoulder toward the car. "My mom might be wondering where I am."

"Okay." Stacey fumbled around in her purse for her key. When she found it, she held it up. "Here it is."

"I'll see you in –"

"Do you...?" she started, but realized she cut him off.

"What?"

"Nothing, I didn't mean to...I'm sorry."

"No, what do you want to know?" Adam asked.

"Well," Stacey said, "if you *want* to, you could pick me up for school." She put her hand up. "That is, only if you want to."

A grin spread across his face. "I'd love to. Do I need to ask your dad?"

"No. I'll talk to him about it."

He continued to smile as he looked at Stacey for a couple moments, rubbing his thumb on her cheek. "I should..." He gave her a kiss on the cheek, and then left for the car before she could say anything else.

"Yeah," Stacey said on a sigh, watching him get in the car. He sat there until Stacey was in the house before he took off for home.

When she got inside, she talked to her dad about riding with Adam to school and about Adam driving on Saturday. He said it was fine, and to have fun, but be careful.

"So, you two are dating, huh?" Kyle asked Stacey, as she sat in her seat in math the next morning.

"Seriously? Are you still on this?" Stacey rolled her eyes. "I will never go out with you, so you can quit asking."

"I wouldn't be so sure about that," he said.

"What do you mean?"

"Well, I have two tickets here," he said, pulling them out of his math book. "I happen to know they're your favorite band."

Looking at the tickets, she narrowed her eyes as she asked, "How would you know what my favorite band is?"

"Social media is a wonderful thing," he hinted. "You can find friends of friends, as well as see posts from the past. Oh! And there's this cool thing called the *about* section that will tell you everything about the person."

"Mine is not set to public, and I *know* I never friended you," Stacey said.

"Well, your friend from Michigan did. Her name is Andi. When I told her I was one of your new classmates, she was all over talking to me via chat about you."

Stacey looked at him, stunned for a moment. She quickly pulled her phone out and looked Andi up. Sure enough, she was friends with Kyle. She texted Andi, explaining who Kyle was, so Andi blocked him. Unfortunately, the damage was already done. He already found out all he would need to know about Stacey from Andi. Afterward, Stacey texted all of her Michigan friends, telling them not to friend Kyle or his friends. As a matter of fact, she told them to ask her before they friended anyone from Ohio.

"Well," Kyle huffed. "You're quick on that phone. I'm already blocked by all your friends."

"They now know who you are," she said.

"Why are you so afraid of getting close to me?"

"I'm not afraid of you," Stacey said. "I don't like you. You keep trying to inch your way into my life. It's not cool at all."

"Why don't you like me?" Kyle asked.

Stacey raised an eyebrow. "Is that a trick question?"

"No. I really want to know. Even before you started dating Adam, you didn't like me. I want to know why?"

Thankfully, at that moment, Mr. Wexford got up to start class, so Stacey did not have to answer right then.

During swim class, Stacey partnered with a new girl, Shannon. Alex and Marissa partnered for class. Stacey was happy to see them finally getting along again. After class, Stacey headed out to the bus to wait to head back to the school. As she got on, Kyle was in the front seat. He snagged her backpack off her shoulder before she knew what happened.

"What are you doing? Give that back to me!" Stacey insisted.

Holding up the tickets, Kyle said, "Not until you agree to go to the concert with me."

"No. I'm dating Adam. I don't like you. Do you not understand that?" Stacey asked. "Now, give me my backpack!" She reached for it, but he slid out of the seat, and headed down the aisle, holding the bag behind his back.

"One date? One concert. That's all I want," Kyle pressed.

"No!"

Stopping, he got within a few inches of her face, and asked, "Do you not remember what happened last week? Do you not remember what I told you?"

"I will *not* go out with you!"

"You *will* or you and your friends may find themselves in more accidents," he said quietly. "You have until Monday to change your mind. The concert is next weekend," Kyle said, and then handed her back her backpack before heading toward the back of the bus to sit with Shane.

Stacey moved closer to the front of the bus to sit down. She was shaking. It was a mix between anxiety and anger. She was not sure which one was winning. Deciding that talking to Adam and her dad were the best option, she decided to talk to them tonight after work. Taking a couple more aspirin, she then just tucked herself into the corner of the seat with a book and her ear buds until they went back to school.

"Okay, *what* is going on?" Adam asked, as they got in the car after work.

"I need to talk to you and my dad," she said.

"Stace, you've been lost all day. It's like you've only been halfway there since lunch."

"I know. Just head home. Dad said he would wait up for us."

It was a quiet ride home. Stacey could feel the anxiety

coming from Adam. She hoped he did not think she was breaking up with him.

❧

"HEY, Stacey. What's on your mind?" Sam asked, as Stacey and Adam walked into the house.

Sitting on the couch together, Stacey took Adam's hand into hers, as she said, "I have a problem."

"What *kind* of problem?" Sam asked. "This looks big."

"Kyle's still demanding that I go out with him, or all of my friends and me will end up in more accidents. Dad, before you say anything, I know for a fact that he was not lying about hurting them."

"I don't understand," Adam said. "He knows we're dating. Why is he still pushing?"

"I don't know. He has concert tickets for next weekend, and is insisting I go out with him. What do I do?" Stacey asked.

Sam sat back in his chair, stroking his chin in thought. Adam sat in his spot, on edge, as he bounced his leg.

"Not helping," Stacey said after a few minutes of complete silence. "What do I do?"

"My first instinct is to tell him no," Adam said.

"I did. That's when he threatened all of you," she explained.

"With tomorrow being Saturday, you won't have school tomorrow. That will buy us a few days," Sam said. "Let me get with the old gang here in Pine Crest to see what they suggest."

"Sir, there's something you need to understand," Adam said. "This is something very few people actually know."

"What?" Sam asked.

"I used to have an older brother, Allen, who pushed too much as well. He had a healthy interest in Logan Mason's girlfriend, and she in Allen. Logan is Shane's brother. They killed Allen. I was at home with him. He had me hide in the cupboard in the kitchen, because he knew it was them. He knew what was going to happen."

"What?" Stacey and Sam asked, horrified.

Adam continued, "Afterward, they came in and cleaned it up. Then, they snuck his body out the back door, labeling him a runaway. My dad was furious and wanted to leave, but mom didn't. She's the sister to Kyle Chandler's mom."

"Wait...*what?*" Stacey's jaw dropped. "He's your *cousin?* Are you serious?"

"That's why the rivalry is so intense with us. Anyway, my mom didn't want to leave, but my dad did, so he left without her. He tried to fight for me, but the courts gave her full custody of me. Part of that was because Chandler's dad represented my mom, and the other part was because Mason's dad was the judge, who obviously ruled in her favor."

"But that's –"

"Trust me. I know," Adam said, cutting Sam off. "That's how it works around here. You had to have all of the facts before you make a decision on how to handle Kyle."

"I had no idea," Sam said, stunned. "This goes deeper than even I thought it did. Stacey, try to stay clear of him as best as possible. I'm calling Shawn," he said, and left the living room to make some calls.

"Who's Shawn?" Adam asked Stacey.

"Shawn's my Uncle on my dad's side. He works for the FBI in the Cleveland office. He'll know what to do. This is no longer a high school situation. What you told him made it bigger than that."

"No one else knows. Those I've told wouldn't listen. And when I tried to tell anyone else, that group threatened to make me a runaway next," Adam explained.

"I don't doubt it. Just give Dad some time," Stacey said. "He'll figure this out."

"All right. In the meantime, I need to get home. We have to

work tomorrow. Do you still want to go skating tomorrow night?"

"Definitely," Stacey said, as they both stood. Walking him to the door, Stacey said, "If there really is a God, please pray for all of us?"

"Daily," Adam said, and then kissed her cheek before he left.

Closing the door, Stacey looked toward the heavens, and whispered, "God, if you're there, we could really use some help down here."

CHAPTER 7

"WORRY DOES NOT EMPTY TOMORROW OF ITS SORROW; IT EMPTIES TODAY OF ITS STRENGTH." CORRIE TEN BOOM

fter work on Saturday, Adam dropped Stacey off at her house. He told her he would return in an hour to pick her up for skating that night.

When she went inside, her thoughts were filled with Adam. While Kyle was in the back of her mind, she refused to let him ruin their date that night. Daydreaming in the shower about Adam, she had to remind herself a couple times she was on a schedule.

When it came time to choose her outfit, she had even more difficulty. She wanted to look nice, but not *too* nice for roller skating. Nevertheless, it *was* considered a date, so she debated a lot on what to wear.

After trying on several outfits, since it was the beginning of October, she finally decided on a cream-colored sweater with a light blue turtleneck under it, and a pair of nice jeans. She also wore her hiking boots that were not really hiking boots. She could use them for hiking, but they were a little too nice for that. All put together, she looked country-casual.

True to his word, Adam rang the doorbell at five o'clock to pick her up. "Wow! That was a wonderful change...and in just an hour too!" He smiled as he stepped into the townhouse. He was wearing his high-tops, jeans, and an off-white sweater with a royal-blue T-shirt under it. Stacey found it amusing that their outfits matched without even trying.

"You look good too," she said. "And is that cologne you're wearing?"

"Yeah." He smiled as his cheeks flushed. "After working, I figured between the shower and cologne, that…well, yeah."

"I like it," Stacey said.

He grinned. "Do you mind if we pick up Alex and Marissa?"

"Is *she* going to mind?"

"No. They both called me separately to ask. She knows we're on a date, so there are no surprises."

"Good," Stacey said. "Then nope. I don't mind."

"We should go. They're waiting."

When they got to the car, Adam still had not taken his eyes off her.

"What?" she asked. "Do I look okay?"

"Yes. I just…" He leaned over and kissed her cheek. "You look *really* good," he said, and then started the car. "Oh! I figured we could share my Bible tonight…unless you want to use one of your own."

"No, that's okay. This is new to me, so you would have to look everything up twice. I don't know where anything is in the Bible."

"This is true."

They chatted for the remainder of the ride to Alex's house. When they pulled in, Stacey could not believe her eyes. The Crestwood home was massive. It was more of a mansion. There was even a gate where you had to call someone on an intercom to get through.

"You would *think* a Crestwood would have his own car," Adam commented, as Alex got into the car.

"We're working on that," Alex said, "but I'm being picky on which one to get."

"A license would be a good place to start," Adam teased.

Alex blushed. "Yeah, I don't want to take the driver's test in case I fail. I'm afraid if I do, my parents would *really* be disappointed in me."

"They're not disappointed in you."

"It's not that hard either," Stacey pointed out. "Take it in the car you learn in. Also, keep it a small car and you should have no problem. I have my license. My dad is leery on getting a car since my mom's accident."

"Understandable," Adam said.

"I'll be working on getting my license in the summer. Until then, I have to rely on the kindness of my friends," Alex said, as they headed toward Marissa's house.

When they arrived, Alex got out to get Marissa.

"Is this a date for them too?" Stacey asked Adam.

"No. Well, on his side there's always hope," Adam said. "Ya know, I just wish she'd open her eyes and see Alex standing there. He's a great guy, but she's not looking at him."

"No. She's looking at you."

"And I'm..." he kissed her cheek, "looking at you."

Just then, Marissa got in the car. "What the –?"

Adam sighed. "We're dating Riss. It's *going* to happen. Get over it."

After Alex got in, they went to church to meet up with the others. Marissa sat in the backseat with her arms crossed for the entire ride, not saying a word.

When they got to church, Stacey was pleasantly surprised to find that Marissa was right. She did know most of the youth. Randy and Harmony, and Brian and Melody were already there, along with about ten to fifteen other students she knew from school.

Shortly after they arrived, the group loaded up into the vans and cars, heading over to the skating rink. It seems the owner of the rink went to the church, and shut it down for the youth outing. There were two other church youth groups attending as well.

Skating was fun! Stacey enjoyed skating a few times growing up, so she did it pretty well. She and Adam were inseparable as they skated. The group had fun on the skating rink, playing around together.

"Now we're headed for our lady's choice," the announcer said, after they were there for about an hour. He dimmed the lights as he said, "So, if you are not in a couple, please exit the rink. Ladies, choose your partner."

Stacey and Adam looked at each other. Stacey smiled as she asked, "Adam, will you –?"

"Adam!" Marissa called, cutting Stacey off. She and Harmony skated toward the pair.

Adam shook his head with a groan. "Oh boy."

Stacey quickly looked up at him. As Marissa skated up to them, Stacey asked, "Please skate with me?"

Before he could open his mouth, Marissa asked, "Adam, will you skate with me? I need to talk to you."

"I can't," Adam said, still looking at Stacey. "Stacey already asked me, so I'm skating with her," he said as he took her hand into his.

"But I–I *really* need to talk to you," Marissa objected.

"Another time," Adam said, and the pair skated off.

Since Harmony already went to go find Randy, they left Marissa standing there by herself. Marissa huffed, crossing her arms.

"She's not going to be happy," Stacey said, glancing back at her.

"Don't worry about her." He shook his head. "Alex will ask her."

"Are you sure?"

He pulled her over to the side of the rink, and took both of her hands. "Stacey, she'll be fine. I'm happy and you're happy. Look at it this way," he said, thinking how to word it. "Are you upset about telling Kyle no?"

"No."

"I'm not either. It's the same thing."

"But –"

"*It's the same thing,*" he enunciated. "Kyle likes you, but you like me. It's the same as Marissa likes me, but I like you. Both think they can dictate who we date. However, neither should have that power. Make sense?"

She nodded. "In a way, it does."

"Good. Now, let's relax and enjoy our couple's skate," he said, "as a couple."

Stacey smiled and nodded, so they took off onto the rink. She had to admit, it was nice to relax and not have to look over her shoulder for Kyle. She was able to have fun and not be on guard.

About halfway through the night, Matt had the kids get some snacks if they wanted, and then sit down at the tables while he spoke. Stacey sat between Harmony and Adam, while Adam and Stacey shared curly fries. They each also had a piece of pizza of their own, along with a Coke.

Stacey was so engrossed in what Matt said, she was too distracted to eat. He spoke on mistakes people made in the Bible, and their reputations even after their mistakes. He spoke of the redemption The Lord granted them. He told the story of David, and even after the massive mistakes he made, how he still had the reputation of being a man after God's own heart. Then he told the story of Saul in the New Testament. It was regarding when Saul was converted, and his name was changed to Paul. He talked about how horrible Saul was before that point – how he used to kill Christians. Then Matt said, later Paul was used to be a miraculous man of God, and a spectacular witness for The Lord.

Stacey sat thinking about Kyle and Adam. Here were two guys who grew up in the same town, same school, and had a similar background. They were even cousins. However, because of this Jesus guy, they were two completely different guys.

After Matt talked some more, he prayed, and then sent them back out to skate.

"So, what do you think?" Adam asked, as people thinned out of the area.

Stacey picked up a curly fry. "I think this Jesus guy seems to be able to make a lot of difference in people's hearts and actions."

"What about you?"

"Well, since this is the first time I've ever heard –"

"Adam," Marissa came up to them, "I *really* need to talk to you."

"Marissa!" Adam shook his head. "Why are you being this way? We're dating. We're enjoying the evening together. Leave us alone," he said, his patience wearing thin.

"Just go," Stacey said. "If she needs to talk, then go and get it over with so we can be done. I'll just sit here and eat while I wait," she said, picking up another fry.

"Are you sure?" Adam asked, not wanting to lose the momentum of the conversation with Stacey regarding Matt's talk.

"Go ahead," Stacey said.

"I'll be right back. Don't go anywhere," Adam said, and then left with Marissa over to the side.

While Stacey sat, she snacked, watching all the different people around her. It was surprising how Jesus was able to touch each and every single person there.

"That's none of your business!" Adam snapped loudly, interrupting Stacey's thoughts.

Matt and Stacey both looked up at them, surprised. Matt was sitting a couple tables over from Stacey.

"You have no right to date her!" Marissa shouted. "She's not a Christian!"

"You have no right to tell me who I can date!" he shot back. "You are *not* in charge of me!"

"I'm-I'm concerned for you," she stammered.

"No, you're not." Adam narrowed his eyes at her. "You're trying to control me."

"No!" Marissa said, getting loud again. "We aren't supposed to date people who are not Christians. I mean, honestly! How can she sit there and listen to what Matt said, and *not* be a Christian? She's a cold-hearted –"

"Marissa!" Matt stood up from where he was sitting, stunned. He looked at her, then to Stacey, and then back to her again. He let out a slow breath of air, before he went over to where Adam and Marissa stood. Meanwhile, Stacey struggled to stop the tears that threatened to overflow.

Stacey set the curly fry she started to eat down on the plate, and took her skates off. Her stomach churned. Eating anything else was the last thing on her mind. At that point, it would be a matter of keeping down what she ate.

Stacey was too upset to continue the night. She wanted to go home. Marissa's statements and attitude lately dug deep. Stacey was almost to the point of not wanting to be around her or her attitude anymore.

Stacey turned her skates in, and got her boots back. Then she went outside by herself to think.

"Hey, you," Melody said, as she and Harmony came outside a few minutes later.

"What?" Stacey asked, wiping tears from her cheeks.

"What happened?" Harmony asked. "We were skating, and next thing we know we saw you turn your skates in. Did something happen between you and Adam?"

"Oh, didn't you hear? Marissa practically yelled to the entire skating rink that not only am I *not* a Christian, but I'm also a cold-hearted…well, at that point Matt cut Marissa off. I'm not quite sure *what* the rest of that was, nor do I *want* to," Stacey said. "Look, I'm not feeling well. You guys go finish skating. When Adam's done with Marissa and Matt, could you please send him out? I'd like him to take me home. I'm done for the night."

"Can I stay while Melody goes and gets Adam? I'm afraid if I see Riss right now, it's not going to turn out well," Harmony said, leaning against the wall next to Stacey. "I tend to get a little testy when people are mean to my friends."

"Isn't that the truth!" Melody rolled her eyes, and then went back inside.

"Listen," Harmony put her arm over Stacey's shoulder, "we don't think you're cold-hearted. We think you're searching. It takes time. Giving your life to Christ is a big decision. It's one I'll never regret, but a big one nonetheless."

"I'm sure," Stacey said, getting herself back under control.

They leaned on the wall in silence, watching the cars pass the skating rink. Finally, Adam and Matt came out with Melody.

"There you are." Adam took her hand. "I was getting nervous."

"Stacey, don't listen to Marissa. She's not thinking straight right now," Matt said, standing in front of her. "What she said was out of hurt and anger."

"She thinks just because I'm not a Christian, that I'm cold-hearted. She spoke to me like I was garbage the other day. Her attitude toward me for the last few weeks has been rude at best." Stacey sighed, looking toward the sky, fighting to stop from crying again. "Look, if this is what Christians think of those who are not Christians, I honestly don't know if I want to be one."

"It's not." Matt shook his head. "This environment is usually safe. I'm sorry for her actions. She *will* apologize to you, *and* have consequences for her behavior."

"I don't want her to apologize to me!" Stacey snapped. "I don't want her to talk to me at all! I thought you said that being a Christian was supposed to change people! If God changed David and Paul, then what? Did He give up now? If Marissa's changed, I'd hate to see what she was before!"

"She has a tender heart –"

"*Tender heart?*" Stacey yelled, cutting him off, feeling sick to her stomach. "If that's a tender heart, then –"

"Adam, go ahead and take her home," Matt said calmly, cutting Stacey off. "She's too hurt right now to listen." Turning to Stacey, he added, "Stacey, you are to be respected here. Under normal circumstances, this is a safe place to work through things. I'm sorry for what happened tonight. Will you give us another shot?"

Stacey only nodded in response, unable to look at anyone. She lost her temper. However, at that point, she was done with the evening.

"Okay," Matt turned back to Adam, "go turn your skates in and take her home."

"Thanks. I'll be right back," Adam said, running into the rink. He was back in a matter of minutes with his shoes changed and his Bible in hand.

"Why don't you make sure her dad is home before you drop her off? I don't think she should be alone right now," Matt said concerned. "I'll call Sam and tell him what happened."

"Thanks, Matt," Adam said, and they took off without another word.

FINALLY, after ten minutes of driving, Adam took Stacey's hand into his. "Stacey, I'm sorry for what happened. I'm sorry for being quiet. I'm not upset with you. I'm upset with her. She had no right to say what she did. That was wrong."

"I'm tired of hearing how hurt she is! I'm tired of hearing that what she's saying is out of hurt! I'm hurting too! What she's saying *hurts*!" Stacey said, crossing her arms.

"I know. I'm sorry. I'm not totally sure what's going through her head lately." He shook his head. "That's not normally her."

"I don't care," she said, staring out the window, resting her chin on her hand.

He just sighed. They drove for a little while longer, until he looked in his review mirror again for the third time in less than thirty seconds. "Hmm," he said, glancing in his mirror again, "it seems we have company."

Stacey turned to see a car behind them. "How long have they been there?"

"Since we left the skating rink. I've even made some turns that have taken us full circle. If they weren't specifically following us, they would have turned off somewhere by now."

"Matt said not to trust the police when we were at Slater's. We can't go home. Where do we go for help?" Stacey asked, heart racing.

"We'll go to Pastor John's house," he said decisively. He turned left, heading toward the house of his pastor. "He'll know what to do."

The car followed them all the way there. It pulled off to the side partway up the road from them. Its lights went off as Adam and Stacey got out of their car.

"Boy, do I pray they're home," Adam said, grabbing Stacey's hand as they jogged up to the front porch, continuously looking over his shoulder. He knocked on the door.

It did not take long for his pastor to answer. When Adam explained what was going on, Pastor had them come inside. After they went inside, Stacey called her dad. Then Adam called Matt and his mom to tell them where they were and why.

Stacey nervously sat at the table, picking at the dinner Mrs. Thompson got for them. Stacey was not hungry, but knew she needed to eat. She was more or less nibbling. The food she did eat was sitting on her stomach, threatening to come back up.

"So, you're Stacey," Pastor said, as he and his wife sat down at the table with Adam and Stacey. They were an older couple, probably in their sixties. They had friendly faces, and seemed to be at peace. Even with everything going on around them, they did not seem the least bit nervous.

"Is my reputation that bad already?" she asked.

"No." Pastor smiled, clasping his hands in front of him on the table. "We've just heard quite a bit about you."

"Marissa's their granddaughter," Adam explained.

"Oh, man!" Stacey put her head in her hands, shaking it. "Look, I swear it's not my fault."

"What isn't?" Pastor asked. "She just told us what's been going on."

"Riss got a little...well *a lot* upset tonight at the outing," Adam told them. "It was also a date of ours. She said some things that weren't very nice at all. They were actually rude."

Pastor raised an eyebrow. "What did she say?"

"She said Stacey wasn't a Christian, so I didn't have the right to be dating her. Then she went on to call her names, including cold-hearted," Adam said, still angry. "That was after she was also rude to her in Slater's the other day. Not even going to go into what she said there or what she's done at school."

"Well," Pastor cleared his throat, "looks like her temper and feelings are getting the best of her. So sorry to hear that."

"Look, Stacey's willing to look at Christianity with an open mind," Adam explained. "She's not shutting the door."

"To be honest, I've never really heard it before," Stacey said quietly. "This whole thing is new to me. The church thing, I mean."

"That's perfectly understandable," Mrs. Thompson said. "Give it a little time."

"What happens if I don't accept this Jesus guy?" Stacey asked, nervously. "Will I still be able to date Adam?"

"That's up to Adam. As far as the *not accepting this Jesus guy* thing goes?" Pastor Thompson chuckled. "Sorry, I have never quite heard it put that way before. Anyway, as far as that goes, the consequences will be a lot stiffer than having to break up with someone. In Romans 6:23, it says, '*For the wages of sin is death, but the gift of God is eternal life through Jesus Christ our Lord*'. You see, the consequences include a spiritual death as well. Jesus came to prevent that."

Stacey furrowed her brow. "I don't understand."

"Jesus came –" Pastor started, but was interrupted by a knock at the door. When everyone looked to him for instructions, Pastor said, "Sarah, take them into the bedroom and hide in the closet. Don't come out unless I call for you."

Mrs. Thompson did not say a word, she just headed toward the bedroom, with Adam and Stacey on her heels. "Be quiet," she said, as they tucked into the closet. She then reached down with her hand and closed the closet doors from the inside.

Hearts racing, they listened intently, trying to decipher what was going on in the living room. Stacey heard male voices, and thought she recognized them. She remained quiet, though.

After a moment, Pastor called for them, much to their relief. When they got to the living room, Stacey was relieved to find her dad and uncle standing there. She threw her arms around both of them. "I'm so glad it's you guys!"

"Happy to see you, too," Shawn said in a chuckle. "What's going on here?"

Adam opened the front door and looked down the street. The car was still sitting there. "See that car down there?" Adam asked Shawn.

"Yes."

"It followed us from the skating rink. I made enough turns that we went full circle to see if they were following me, and they did."

"I see," Shawn said. Then he turned to his partner, and said, "Pat, let's go have a friendly conversation with the people in that car."

After they left, The Thompson's, Sam, Stacey, and Adam sat back down at the table.

"Can we have a little time to continue our conversation before you leave?" Pastor asked. "I think it's important."

"I think that will be fine. Shawn and Pat are taking care of our visitors," Sam said. "We have a few minutes."

As they all sat down at the table, Pastor started, "Now, as I said before, as far as not accepting Jesus, the consequences will be a lot stiffer than having to break up with someone. If you recall, I shared with you Romans 6:23, which says, *'For the wages of sin is death, but the gift of God is eternal life through Jesus Christ our Lord'.* The consequences include a spiritual death."

"What do you mean by that?" Stacey asked.

"Can I try to explain it?" Adam asked.

"Certainly," Pastor said, pleased Adam stepped-up.

Shawn and Pat walked back into the house. "They took off before we could get to them," Shawn said. "Stacey, I'd like you to meet my partner, Special Agent Pat Holloway."

"Pleasure to meet you," Stacey said, shaking his hand.

"If you guys wouldn't mind waiting just a few, they were in the middle of a conversation," Sam said.

Shawn and Pat joined the others at the table. "No problem," Shawn said.

"Okay," Adam started. "Tonight, Matt explained how Jesus gave His life for you. In John 3:16, it says, *'For God so loved the world, that He gave His only begotten Son, that whosoever believes in Him should not perish but have everlasting life.'* Jesus came to give His life, so we can have eternal life with Him and God, The

Father. That's what Pastor meant by spiritual death. If you don't believe and accept Jesus as your Savior, you will experience an eternal death and separation from Him. Let's say tonight went bad. Let's say that car got us in an accident of some kind and we died. If so, you would not be in Heaven tonight."

"But you would?" Stacey asked.

"Yes. In that verse, it said all we have to do is believe in Him. We have to believe He's the one and only way to Heaven. We have to believe He actually came down from Heaven, *specifically* to save us from eternal death. He was perfect, so He was the only one who could do it."

"I still don't get it." Stacey shook her head. "I don't understand why He would die for us."

"Because He loves us. He loves *you*. If you were the only one He needed to die for to save, He still would have done it."

"He doesn't know me though. I have no idea who this guy was."

"You may not know Him yet, but He knows *you*," Adam said. "There's a verse in Jeremiah where it says He even knew you before you were in your mother's womb."

"That's Jeremiah 1:5," Pastor cut in. "It says, *'Before I formed you in the womb I knew you, before you were born I set you apart; I appointed you as a prophet to the nations.'* Now, while He was speaking of Jeremiah, the Lord knew all of us before He formed us in the womb. He has a plan for each of us...including you. He explained that in another verse in Jeremiah. It is Jeremiah 29:11, which says, *'For I know the plans I have for you," declares the LORD, "plans to prosper you and not to harm you, plans to give you hope and a future.'* Go ahead, Adam," he finished.

"Thank you," Adam said to Pastor. "I knew you would know exactly what verse I was talking about. Anyway," he turned back to Stacey, "Jesus loves you, Stacey. He wants you to have the confidence of knowing He'll be with you wherever you go. In Hebrews 4:16, it says, *'Let us therefore come boldly to the throne of grace, that we may obtain mercy and find grace and help in time of need.'* He's not going to turn His back on you when you need Him the most. He loves you and wants to take care of you."

"Then why did He put me in the middle of this mess? Why did He take my mom? Why –?"

"I don't have the answers to all your questions. What I *do* know, is Jesus said in John 15:13 that, *'Greater love has no one than this, than to lay down one's life for his friends.'* Jesus gave His life on the cross. He chose to put His life on the line for us. He also rose from the dead so we wouldn't have to endure Hell for all eternity. He didn't have to come down from Heaven in the first place, but He did. He did it because He loves us. He had, and *still* has the greatest love of all for us. He gave His life for us. In John 14:2-3, Jesus says, *'In my Father's house are many mansions: if it were not so, I would have told you. I go to prepare a place for you. And if I go and prepare a place for you, I will come again, and receive you unto myself; that where I am, there ye may be also.'* We only need to accept the gift of His sacrifice to get in to Heaven. He loves you, Stacey."

"But why? I don't understand the main question of *why*?"

"Because He loves us."

"If He loves us so much, then why did God even create Hell?"

"He wants us to *choose* to love and honor Him, so He gave us this thing called a free will. We have the free will to choose Him or not. However, that free will not only comes with the tough choices, but also the tough consequences if we make poor choices. A long time ago, an angel named Lucifer made a horrible one. He thought he was better than God Himself. The really bad part of that story? He convinced some other angels he was too, and tried to overthrow Heaven so *he* could reign instead. Well, of course, God would have none of that. He not only kicked him out, but also kicked out the angels who followed him as well."

"Kind of like how the government is stepping in to kick out the corrupt people of your town," Shawn said.

"Exactly!" Adam smiled. "Okay, imagine that Pine Crest is like Heaven."

"Have tell ya, that's *not* making me want to make the choice for Heaven," Stacey cautioned.

Adam chuckled before he continued, "It didn't used to be so bad. The taking over was subtle. Even now, unless you get in the middle of it, you really don't see it. What happened was, a long time ago Mr. Chandler moved into town – he can represent Satan for this example. Anyway, he came into town, and got together with the other leaders of the community. Slowly things began to shift, so *he* was the one in power and calling the shots, and not the government or their laws. We'll use the government as God for this."

Pat laughed. "Stretching it there too!"

Pastor had to laugh at that one as well.

"Bear with me here." Adam smiled. "*Anyway*, one day you and your dad came into town. You guys alerted the government to the situation, kind of like how God found out what Satan was doing. And just as God cleaned up Heaven, the government will clean up Pine Crest and the outer areas, leaving it free and clear of corruption. Now, a lot of people are going to get hurt in the process. The battle is going to get worse. But in the end, I have faith the government will win. I am going to trust that they'll prevail, just as God will win in the end too. And in the end of the Bible, God not only wins, but we also get to enjoy eternity with Him in Heaven. He is preparing a place for us, and is waiting to show it to us."

"Now," Pastor said, jumping back into the conversation, "you have a choice to make. You could choose Him, and enjoy eternity with love, acceptance, and peace, or you can continue to live by your instincts and what you know, leaving your eternity in the hands of Satan."

"Yikes!" Stacey's eyes widened. "That's quite a choice. How do I know I'm not already on Jesus's side? I've been good."

"Well, here's the thing," Adam said, "if you do not choose to accept Jesus's gift, you will not go to Heaven when you die. It doesn't matter how good of a person you are. When you're born, you're born into sin…Satan's side. You have to choose Jesus and God."

"How is *that* fair?" Stacey asked.

"Jesus has created an alternative option to Hell by dying on the cross. You see, because of Adam and Eve's sin, we were cut off from communication with God. We were destined to be separated from Him. The only way to atone for sin, was to sacrifice an animal. It had to be perfect, without spot or blemish. There had to be bloodshed."

"Okay, but –"

"Just a second," Adam cut Stacey off. She gestured for him to continue. "When Jesus came, He was perfect. He *was* the sacrifice. He shed His blood, therefore permanently fixing the communication with God and man. Now because of this, we now have an alternative to Hell. You see, Jesus didn't just die on the cross. He was also raised from the dead. When He did that, He created the alternative. He is now the go-between for God and man, allowing our prayers to reach the Lord without having to sacrifice an animal. Make sense?"

"Yes," Stacey said. "Actually, it does." She thought for a moment, before she asked, "If I choose Him, will He protect me?"

"My God is stronger than anything on this planet. If He's not through with me, I'm not going anywhere. There will be nothing in this world that can mess that up. God doesn't *do* surprises. Having said that, He may not protect your body, but He *will* protect your soul if you are one of His. It doesn't matter what goes on around you, Jesus will be with you if you are a child of The King. Jesus left us the Holy Spirit to guide and direct us. We are never alone if we are one of His."

"What would I have to do?" Stacey asked.

"Just pray and ask Him to forgive you for your sins. In Romans 10:9, it says, *'If you declare with your mouth, "Jesus is Lord," and believe in your heart that God raised Him from the dead, you will be saved.'* He's already paid the penalty for your sin and salvation. You only need to ask Him to let you into His Heaven, and allow Him control over your life. He has a plan for you. He'll lead you. He'll show you. All you have to do is believe. It's not a belief of the mind, but of the heart…your whole heart."

Stacey debated in her mind for several minutes. If she died, she knew as it stood, she would go to Hell. However, if she asked Jesus to help her, if she asked Him to forgive her of her sins and take over her life, she knew she would go to Heaven. There really was no other way to look at it.

The difference between Adam and Kyle was evident. The men Matt talked about in the Bible did bad things in their past. Even though they did those things, the Lord redeemed them. If the Lord could make that big of a difference in their lives, she was certain He would do the same for her.

"Okay," Stacey said. "I want to ask Jesus to forgive me of my sins, and take over my life."

"I don't want you to do it for me."

"I'm not. As much as I like you, I want the peace of not having to worry about being alone or protected. And from what you're telling me, the only way to get that is through Jesus."

"Yes."

"Then, I want to do it."

"Great!" He smiled, and then helped her pray right then and there to accept the gift Jesus was offering her.

After the prayer, Stacey, Adam, Shawn, and Pat said good-bye, and walked out of the house.

"Do you want to come to our house until your mom gets home?" Sam asked Adam.

"Probably wouldn't be a bad idea," Adam agreed. "I'll call her and let her know where I am."

"Why don't we all go together? That way if anyone gets followed, the others will know," Shawn suggested.

"Sounds good," Adam said. Then he asked Stacey, "Do you want to ride with me or your dad?"

"I'll ride with Adam if it's okay with you?" Stacey asked her dad. When he nodded, everyone dispersed into their vehicles to head over to Sam and Stacey's house.

CHAPTER 8

"We need to figure out what you're going to do on Monday," Sam said, as he, Stacey, Adam, Shawn, and Pat were sitting at the table in the townhouse. "The fact that they're following you, and have threatened you again doesn't make me comfortable."

"We could hide them?" Pat suggested. "From what I understand, we have some investigating to do around here. Can't imagine that will make them very happy."

"No. It won't," Adam said. "They're on edge as it is. When they figure out there are FBI agents around here, it'll be like you kicked a hornet's nest."

"We could take them to a Cleveland safehouse. Question is what your mom will say?" Shawn said to Adam.

"She probably won't care," Adam said in all seriousness. "She generally just likes to know where I am. We could call her?"

"Go ahead," Sam said. "If she's okay, we'll go ahead and send you two into protective custody."

"What about our other friends?" Stacey asked. "They'll all have targets on them. Kyle even said who he would use to do it."

"That's a good point," Sam said. "What if we figure out a safehouse here in town?"

"Does anyone have a house big enough for it?" Shawn asked.

"The Crestwood's do," Adam said. "Their house is huge!"

"Will they do it?" Sam asked.

"I don't know," Adam said. "Honestly, the only person's house I know for sure who would be willing to do anything about what's going on would be Matt and Tina. Their house is a decent size. We could camp out there until it's clear."

"Aren't they your neighbor?" Stacey asked Adam.

"Yes. Well, one of them anyway."

"I'll call him and see what he thinks," Sam said. He got up and left the room to call Matt.

"So, what you did at your Pastor's house," Shawn started.

"Yes?" Stacey asked.

"Well, we have this guy at work named Nick Locke," Shawn explained. "He has talked to me about Jesus. I've never heard how you explained it tonight, though," Shawn said to Adam.

"I just tried to make it clear through example," Adam said. "Do you have questions?"

"I do, but I think I'll talk to Nick about them. He's the one who has been talking to me about Jesus."

"Nick and Seth's team may get sent down here if things push forward," Pat said.

"That's true. He's a pretty cool guy. I would love for you guys to meet him," Shawn said.

Sam walked back into the kitchen. Setting his phone down on the table, he explained, "Talked to Matt. He said to take them over to his house. Matt will call your mom," he said to Adam.

"I don't know if it's wise for her to know where I am," Adam said. "It won't be much of a safehouse. She'll tell my aunt, who is Kyle's mom."

"Are you serious?" Pat asked. "Is everyone related in this town?"

"To an extent," Adam acknowledged. "There are several central families. These families have been here since the town was founded."

"So, basically you're telling us that this power has been going on –"

"Since the town was founded," Adam said, cutting Shawn off.

"I thought you said Kyle's dad came to town and got the group together," Stacey said, confused.

"I said Mr. Chandler. What I didn't say was *which* Mr. Chandler," Adam corrected. "This town was just forming when the Chandler's moved here. The Mason's, Strong's, Ross's, Foster's, Phillip's, Barnes's, and the James's were already here, along with several other families. Maxim Chandler organized it so the town was founded once he and his family moved here. It started off as favors owed. Soon it was a tight circle that no one could get into. After a few generations, the James's and Barnes's left the circle. They have been at odds with the other fraction ever since."

"Goodness!" Pat said, eyes wide. "So, basically each generation is teaching the next one how to hold onto power."

"Yes," Adam said. "And with each generation, the corruption gets worse. It's like this secret they think they have, only the entire town knows about it."

"Well, to answer your original concern," Sam started, "I never shared with your mom *where* the safehouse was they were taking you to. I only shared that they were taking the two of you to a safehouse."

"Good," Adam said.

"We'll just leave your car here," Shawn suggested. "If your car is parked in front of Matt's, or your house, it will be obvious where you are."

"True," Adam agreed. "Here are the keys," he said, passing them to Sam.

"Stacey, go pack a bag, and grab both of our sleeping bags,"

Sam instructed. "I'll go pack a bag for you to take for me. That way when I'm ready, I can just head over."

"Sounds good," she said, and ran upstairs while the others talked.

Once Stacey was packed, they headed out of the house. At first, they thought they were being followed, so Pat drove out of town to see if they would follow them. Shawn and Pat actually wanted them to follow, so they could talk to them.

However, as they left the town limits, the car tailing them turned off. Grateful, Pat and Shawn decided to head up to the Cleveland office in order to change vehicles to throw them off before returning to town.

THEY WERE IN BETWEEN TOWNS, when there were sudden flashes of light, along with loud bangs. Stacey knew instantly they were being fired upon. Both she and Adam ducked, as Stacey's window shattered by one of the bullets.

Pat swore, struggling to keep control of the car. The car spun, and then went over the side of the road, flipping a couple times. Glass flew. Yelling, screaming, and the smashing of metal created a deafening, ear shattering noise. Adam grabbed Stacey to keep her safe. It seemed like an eternity before everything finally stopped rolling.

"Stacey?" Adam asked, still holding her when the car landed.

She moaned. "I'm hurt."

"We need to get out of here," he said. Trying the door, it did not open. He kicked it until it gave-way. Afterward, he pulled Stacey out with him, and then dragged her off into the woods away from the wreckage.

"Uncle Shawn," Stacey asked. Her head felt like it hit a wall. She saw blood all over her hands and shirt from the cuts and scrapes.

"I'll get him in…uh-oh! Shh!" He covered Stacey's mouth, pulling her into some underbrush. Keeping an eye on the wreck, he whispered, "We have visitors."

Stacey saw four guys dressed in black with ski masks on. She gasped, as she watched them fire into the car at Pat and Shawn.

"Shh!" Adam hissed, close to her ear.

She nodded in response, while consciously trying to remind herself to breathe.

"We need to be quiet, or they'll find us," he whispered right near her ear.

Stacey nodded again.

The guys argued for a few moments as to whether or not this was the correct car before they left for their vehicle.

"Whew!" Adam said, relieved, when he saw them leave. "We need to see if Shawn and Pat survived."

Going over to the car, they kept an eye out in every direction. Adam pulled a cell phone from her uncle's pocket, along the map between the pair. Both Stacey and Adam's phones were cracked and unusable.

"They're unconscious," he explained to Stacey, as he handed her the phone.

Stacey looked at him, wide-eyed.

"They're alive for now," Adam assured her. "Let's see," he said, spreading the map open. "I think the last thing I remember passing was this mile marker. It looks like the next exit is only a couple hour's walk from here. When we get there, we'll find a diner of some kind and get help for them."

"Then we'd better start walking."

"First, let's clean up."

Adam cleaned Stacey's wounds with a water bottle he pulled from the car, along with one of Stacey's T-shirts. When he finished, she cleaned his wounds as well.

As they walked, Stacey called her dad's cell phone and explained what happened. Her dad said to keep him posted.

Since they were not exactly sure where they were, he said to let him know as soon as they knew their exact location. He also said he, Becky, Matt, and Matt's wife Tina were okay, and that he would be at Matt's when Adam and Stacey got back to town. He was not taking any more chances after they fired on a federal vehicle.

"I don't know how much more I have left in me," Stacey admitted after an hour of walking. "My head is throbbing and spinning. There are a lot of cuts and bruises all over me. I don't know where they all are. I just feel the blood."

"I got them all cleaned," he said confidently. Grabbing her hand, he said, "Come on, we need to keep moving. If we stay here not only will your uncle and his partner not get help, but those guys could also come back."

"Good point. Okay, just bear with me. I may need some breaks."

They talked while they walked, *and* walked, *and walked*, keeping an eye out for any vehicles. When they did see any, they hid in the underbrush until it was clear. Stacey had to stop multiple times to get a breather. Her head pulsated and pounded to the point that she was having difficulty focusing, but she pressed onward.

They were about ten minutes out from the exit, when Stacey's uncle's cell phone rang. Adam looked at Stacey. She shrugged, so he answered it in as deep a voice as he could get, "Spencer...uh-huh...actually, no," he said, in his regular voice. "This is Adam Barnes. I have Stacey with me. There was an accident...Yeah, they shot a tire out of the car...Well, we're almost to the next exit we told Sam about...You're there already? Good...She's not doing well. I hope we can make it. We'll see you in a few," he said, and hung up.

"We were so close. How much further do we need to go?" Stacey asked, her world spinning around her.

"I think it's this way," he said, and pulled Stacey with him.

"Please tell me we're going to Michigan?" Stacey said, dropping to the ground on her knees several minutes later. She grabbed her head in hopes of getting some kind of relief from the piercing pain.

"Stacey!" He crouched beside her, alarmed. He tried to help her off the ground. "I know you're tired, but we have to keep going. Come on."

"I'm sorry." Stacey slowly shook her head. "I can't."

He crouched beside her, keeping an eye out while she took a break. He was beside himself at the amount of blood on her. He did not want to alarm her, but she had blood streaking through her hair and soaked through her clothing. After a few minutes, they heard people calling for Stacey and Adam.

Hearing Sam's voice amongst those shouting, Adam yelled out, "Mr. Spencer! Over here! She needs help!"

Running toward the sound, Sam and the men with him finally found them. "Oh, Peanut!" Sam shook his head taking her into his arms. "That's it! You are going to keep going with these guys. You're getting out of this. I'm not even letting you stay at Matt's. I want you as far away from this as possible."

"Dad?" Stacey asked, squinting to see better. With difficulty focusing and her head spinning, she just closed her eyes. "It hurts. I need..." her voice faded. She did too, as her head dropped to the side.

"Stace?" her dad asked, when her head dropped to the side. "She's unconscious."

"She's beyond exhausted, and in a lot of pain," Adam explained. "We were all hurt from the accident. Did you guys find Shawn and Pat?"

"They're alive, but they're going to have a struggle. We found them about five miles back," he said, holding the unconscious Stacey close to him. The others moved around them, getting information from Adam. In the meantime, Stacey fell into a deep, painless sleep.

CHAPTER 9

"I LOVE THOSE WHO CAN SMILE IN TROUBLE, WHO CAN GATHER STRENGTH FROM DISTRESS, AND GROW BRAVE BY REFLECTION." LEONARDO DA VINCI

Stacey's eyes fluttered open. However, she was not where she expected. With the accident, she thought sure she would wake up in the hospital. However, there were regular navy-blue curtains on the window, as she lay in a queen-sized bed, with a navy-blue and white down comforter. There was a tall dresser made of walnut on one wall, with a long, shorter dresser matching the tall one on the other. On either side of the bed were walnut nightstands, with the same designs as the two dressers. She smelled what she thought was a turkey cooking. She looked up to see an IV in her arm, with a few different bags attached. No one was in the room at the time, so she called out, "Hello?"

"Hey, sweetheart," Sam said, coming in a few moments later. Adam, Becky, Matt, Tina, and another guy came in with him. The guy she did not know, went to the IV to check it before checking her blood pressure and pulse.

"What's going on?" Stacey asked.

"Well," Sam said, rubbing the back of his neck "we talked it over, and you're back in Pine Crest."

"Ugh!" She dropped her head onto the pillow. "I thought we were getting out of here."

"Well, the more I thought about it, the more I realized you were right in wanting to be with me. Stacey, this is Becky's brother, Scott. He's a paramedic. This is also Matt and Tina's house. We're using it as a headquarters. Downstairs in the basement are anywhere from fifteen to twenty FBI agents, about ten state police officers, and our little group – your friends included. By the way, don't worry about Marissa, she is very upset at what all has happened. She apologized up one side and down the other for what happened at skating the other day," he explained.

"Are all these people cleared?" Stacey asked.

"With help from Adam, Becky, Matt, and Tina, we've sorted through quite a bit. We're holding our own, and doing fairly well. They are a strong bunch, so we have armed guards around the house."

Stacey sighed. "Wow. That blew up fast."

"It did. Once the FBI rolled into town, things heated up," Sam explained. "The FBI are trying to handle it on their own. The governor doesn't want to have to call in the National Guard, but he said he will if this gets worse."

"Are you hungry?" Scott asked.

"Actually, yeah," Stacey said.

"Good," Scott said. "That's a good sign. Adam, want to go get her something to eat? We'll vacate, letting her move around on her own. Get up at your own pace," he said to Stacey. "Don't push it."

"All right," Stacey agreed.

With that, they all left except for her dad. He sat on the side of the bed, and took her hand into his. "Stacey, I know we're in for tough haul, but it will be worth it in the end. You get better, and you can do some footwork for us if you want?"

"I don't mind. What I don't understand, is how you grew up

in this town. Why didn't grandma and grandpa move? Why did they stay here with all of this mess?"

"We honestly had no idea this was going on," Sam said. "There were your standard bullies in school, but they didn't bother me or my friends. It's like Adam said earlier, unless you pushed it, you wouldn't notice what was going on. I also left after high school. Once I went away to college, I only returned for visits."

"I see. And now that you've seen it?" she asked.

"Once this is over, it should resemble the town I grew up in and loved to call my hometown."

"Okay. Are you sure we can't just move back to Michigan?"

"Would you really want to leave Adam?"

"No," she admitted.

"Do you really want to move back to Michigan, hearing the stories of your mom, and seeing her around every corner?"

"No."

"Okay. Then get some rest, and Adam will bring your breakfast shortly. We're having turkey, along with mashed potatoes and gravy, and green beans for dinner. Lunch will be sandwiches. You know," Sam said, in thought, "Adam's a good guy. He's a good choice."

"I'm not sure if dating right now is wise."

"Well, you don't have to go on dates to date. Just take it one step at a time. Under these circumstances, if anything good can come out of this, it'll be worth it."

"I agree," Adam said, standing in the doorway with a plate of scrambled eggs and a glass of orange juice. "It's not like we're heavily dating. We're just at the starting gates. We'll take it slow. I'm like that anyway."

"I'm going to...yeah," Sam said. He got up and left the room.

Stacey adjusted herself as she sat up on the bed, while Adam brought over her plate of food. "Here ya go," he said, sitting on the side of the bed.

"Thanks. So, what did I miss?"

"We've been at here for a few days. The good news is that we have a much stronger team than when we left. The town is beginning to divide, and those not on a side are more or less hiding or leaving. There's a battle growing, and it's not *going* to get uglier – it already is. Good thought in this? It can't get *too* much uglier before it gets better."

"That's true," Stacey said, eating her breakfast. "So, is Marissa really okay with this?"

He took her hand into his, as he calmly said, "I don't care if she's okay with *this* part of things. She doesn't have the right to tell me who I can and cannot date. She doesn't have the right to tell me who I can have as a friend or who I marry either. That's between the other person, me, and God."

Stacey nodded in understanding.

"Now, as the other person in this, would you like to continue this, or put it on hold for a bit until it's all done?"

"What do *you* think?"

"I asked *you* first," Adam said.

"Well, how about if we play it by ear? We can take it one step at a time."

"Okay, but how do we know what steps we can take?"

"Well, holding hands is a good one." Stacey smiled, as she squeezed his hand. "And I think I remember something about you saying you're a slow mover anyway."

"I did say that. And I am."

"Then I say to follow *your* lead. If the brakes need to be put on, we'll talk about them as they come."

"Sounds good," he agreed. "For the record? I'm really glad you're a Christian now."

"So am I. I'm still jumpy. However, I know if I die, I'm going to Heaven. I just wish I knew my dad had the same comfort."

"We'll work on him," he assured her. "But for now, since

you're done," he took her plate, "why don't you get some rest while we work on things downstairs?"

"That sounds like a good plan," she said, snuggling back under the covers.

He leaned down and kissed her cheek. Afterward, he left her to sleep, closing the door behind him.

Stacey was amazed at the good that still seemed to be prevailing, even though they were in the middle of all this mess. She shook her head thinking about it. Then she rolled over, falling back to sleep, dreaming about Adam.

STACEY WOKE up later to find Adam resting his head on the bed. He was holding one of her hands while napping in a chair.

"Adam?" Stacey asked.

"Hey. Are you hungry? There's some food for you on the nightstand."

"You keep feeding me like this," Stacey smiled and stretched, "and I'll get fat."

"Well, the alternative is just not a good one," he said, handing her a plate of food covered with saran wrap.

It contained a peanut butter and jelly sandwich, along with a small bag of chips. There was also an empty glass and a can of pop on the nightstand.

"So, how are you feeling?" he asked, pouring the pop into the glass for her.

"Think I might go ahead and venture out of bed today. Want to go get Scott to take this thing out of me?" she asked, holding up her arm with the IV.

"No problem," he said, and then went to get Scott while Stacey ate her food.

She was almost finished eating by the time Adam, Scott, and her dad came into the room.

Sam greeted her with a smile. "You're looking *a lot* better!"

"I feel better," she said. "I need to move around, though. I'm starting to wonder if this is what Rip Van Winkle felt like."

"Funny one, aren't ya?" Scott smirked, as he pulled the IV out, replacing it with a band-aid. "Look at that, she didn't even flinch," he said, impressed.

Scott looked to be about twenty-one or twenty-two. He had a decent build to him, blond hair, and baby blue eyes. When he smiled, it really lit up his face. From what Stacey saw of him up to that point, he was animated in his expressions as well.

"So," Stacey said to Scott as she rested her empty plate and glass on the nightstand, "am I free to go, Warden?"

He chuckled as he nodded. "As long as you stay close. If you don't feel right, come find me."

"Shower?"

"Most definitely," he said, wrapping the tubing. He put it, along with the bags, into the trashcan. "Finished," he said, and left the room.

"Do I have clean clothes somewhere?" Stacey asked her dad.

"Yes. There's your bag from where you packed it," he said, gesturing toward the bag on the dresser. "Have at it."

"Can I have a few minutes with Adam, please?" Stacey asked.

"No problem. See you downstairs," he said, and left, closing the door behind him.

"Okay, I have to ask. Why does he call you Peanut?" Adam asked, while sitting in the chair next to the bed. He propped his feet up on the side of the bed near to her, crossed at the ankles.

"Well, a couple reasons," Stacey said. "Number one, I was only six-and-a-half pounds when I was born."

"Wow! That's small."

"Yep. And number two is because I love to eat nuts – honey roasted peanuts being my favorite."

"Mine too."

"So, did you, or do you have a nickname from your parents?" she asked.

"Not really." He shrugged. "It must just be a girl thing,"

"So, you mentioned your brother before. What was he like?" Stacey asked.

"Allen was an athlete. He was strong physically, as well as strong-willed. He was dad's favorite. They always went to baseball games together up in Cleveland. He was popular and well-liked. He often butted heads with Logan Mason, Dylan Chandler, and their crew. He was a great brother. He always protected me…even until the end. He knew it was them at the door. He knew what was coming, but he didn't want them to get to me too, so he had me hide. I was eleven at the time. He was only seventeen." He looked up at her, tears brimming his eyes. "He was one of the good ones. He taught me how to skateboard. He didn't mind if I hung out with him, even though I was about six years younger than him. He had a great sense of humor. We laughed together a lot. Skateboarded together in the backyard and the skate park. He loved music and liked to draw. I still have the drawing he did of me in my Bible. It was of me jumping between ramps with my skateboard. It marks his favorite verse, Isaiah 40:31. Don't get me wrong. He had his faults too. He could be really stubborn. His attraction to Kara was prime example of that. She was attracted to Allen to, so they both decided to stand their ground when Logan tried to break them up. That's when their troubles started."

"I see," she said, as some pieces of the structure to the founding families fell into place.

"Yeah. When Logan found out Allen and Kara liked each other, he went through the roof! She was his girl. If he couldn't have her, no one could. She was there the night they killed Allen. They made her watch. Afterward, they told her if she ever chose to go with someone else, they would kill him too."

"That's horrible!"

"No kidding. But that's how they operate. They see something they want, and they lay claim to it. No one stops them... not even the people they're claiming."

"You mean like Kara?"

"Yes. You too. Kyle was interested in you from the start. That's the initial reason I stepped in. I didn't want you to be put into the same position as Kara." He glanced up at her as he admitted, "The other reason was because I like you...a lot."

She picked up his hand into hers, and said, "I like you, too."

After another minute, Adam asked, "Would be okay if I gave you a kiss?"

"You already have."

"No...well, if that's...don't worry about it," he said, flustered.

"Only when you're ready," she said, putting him at ease. "Until then, I need a shower."

"Sounds good," he said, and then got up to give her a kiss on the cheek.

She quickly turned at the last minute, and the kiss landed on her lips instead. He pulled back and looked at her in surprise.

"Did I –?"

"No. I did," Stacey admitted. "Just to let you know when you're ready, I am too."

He grinned, his cheeks still red. "I, um..." He pointed over his shoulder. "I'm going to go downstairs. Yeah. I need to go downstairs."

"Okay," Stacey said, as she smiled and waved.

When the door secured behind him, she gathered her stuff from her bag for a shower. It seemed like forever since she had one. According to her dad it was a little over three days since Saturday night skating.

Glancing in the mirror, she cringed. Dried blood was splattered throughout her hair. Her clothing was not much better. She had little cuts and scrapes all over her body from the accident. She shuddered as the memory of her car window getting shot out shoved its way into her mind. The glass from the window sprayed all over her and Adam. Her own screams echoed in her ears, as she remembered the feeling of weightlessness when the car flipped over the edge of the road twice before it landed, throwing her and Adam around the backseat like a ragdoll. Closing her eyes, she covered her ears, hoping to make it all go away. The smell of gunpowder instantly filled her senses from the exploding airbags. Seeing her Uncle Shawn and Pat getting shot again, the bright flash of the gun going off into the vehicle forced her to open her eyes. She sucked in a breath of air, bracing herself on the dresser. Looking in the mirror again, she gave herself a pep talk, "You're okay. You and Adam made it. Uncle Shawn and Pat are recovering in the hospital. It will be okay. God's got this."

Afterward, she took a few deep-cleansing breaths to clear her mind. Grabbing her stuff, she headed into the bathroom off the hallway.

Throughout her shower she chose to focus on Adam, pushing the memories from the accident to the back of her mind. Adam seemed to instinctively know what she needed to hear. He was protective, kind, caring, and a strong Christian. Her thoughts drifted to their many talks in the hospital. He discovered a lot about her during that time. She figured out a lot about Adam as well. Their bond grew stronger, the more they shared. Her thoughts continued as she got dressed, only half paying attention to what she was doing.

Adam usually had a smile on his face. She adored his smile. He was gentle, humble, meek, and fun-loving all wrapped into one. He protected her. He looked out for her. He had a tremendous heart, and a strength within she wished she had as well. Along with all of that, she was grateful he was a Christian. She did not know much about the Bible, but she knew if something were to happen to her in this mess, she would see him again in Heaven when it was their time.

As she tied her shoes, there was a knock on the door. "Come in!" she called out.

Much to her surprise, Scott was the one who walked in. "Hi. I was–Wow! You look different!" he said, pleasantly surprised. He left the door open as he came into the room. "I mean, you look *a lot* better. I-I mean…" He shook his head.

Stacey was tickled his reaction.

"I need your blood pressure and pulse," he explained. "You know, since you've been moving around a little bit more. You should probably eat some more too," he added, searching through his bag for his stethoscope, blood pressure cuff, and his pulse-oximeter.

She shrugged as she put her arm out for him. "Okay. Go for it."

He took her blood pressure, periodically glancing up at her as he took it.

"What's wrong?" she asked.

"What?"

"What's wrong? You have a different look on your face. I can't read what it means."

He shook his head. "Just my own thoughts."

"Oh," she said. When he finished taking her blood pressure, she mentioned, "My dad and your sister seem to be getting along really well."

"Yeah. Noticed that. It seems your family is full of personality *and* guts," he said, as he put his equipment back into his medical bag. Then, without looking at her, he added, "Looks too."

Stacey's eyes widened. Then, with a smile, she quickly asked, "You think my dad is cute?"

With all seriousness, he said, "No. His daughter is."

Taken aback, Stacey was not sure what to say. Much to her relief, Adam and her dad walked in at that moment.

"Well," Sam said with a smile, "you're looking much better!"

She grinned. "Thank you. A shower can make a huge difference."

"She'll probably need a little more to eat, but she'll be good to go shortly." Scott stood, resting his bag on his shoulder. "She's a tough little cookie." Turning back to Stacey, he said, "Please let me know if you have any dizziness, nausea, blurred vision, ringing in your ears, or confusion."

"Will do," she said, so he left.

Sam walked over and gave her a hug as she stood. "Can we please not do that again?" he asked.

"I'd like to not do that again either."

"Want to see the set-up?" Adam asked, excited. "It's pretty sweet!"

"Sure," she said, so Adam grabbed her hand and they headed downstairs.

Looking around the basement, she was in awe! Stacey was surprised they got everything in there, and just how elaborate the setup was within Matt and Tina's basement. There were tables with computers, telephones, cell phones, and walkie-talkies. There were bulletin boards with photos and maps of the two areas of town that were their primary focus. There were also a couple of dry erase boards to one side. One of the dry erase boards had a drawn-out map of the town. On the map were several houses and buildings they marked as places where they knew the other group operated. The other board contained photos and the names of everyone from the other group, along with their position within the city, and the hierarchy. She was not surprised to see Kyle's dad, Marcus Chandler, at the top of the adult version, and Kyle himself on top of the teen version.

As Sam and Adam showed her around, Sam introduced her to most of the people, giving her a brief description of their job. When he finished, they headed back upstairs for more food.

"So, good news is we're making progress," Sam mentioned.

He scrambled eggs in the kitchen, while she and Adam sat down at the table. "Bad news is they're getting meaner."

Stacey raised an eyebrow. "Meaner than they already were? Is that possible?"

"Yeah, the town's pretty much divided," Adam said. "We're making headway, but it's getting uglier. By the way, I haven't heard from my mom since the night of roller skating. The group downstairs has no clue what happened to her either. We don't know if they got to her, or if she got out."

"Would they hurt her?" Stacey asked. "I thought she was Chandler's mom's sister. Isn't that hurting one of their own?"

"They took out my brother. What would it matter if they took out another one of us?"

"They're not very nice around here, I'm afraid," Scott said, leaning on the doorway with his arms folded.

Becky slipped passed him, and went over to Sam, giving him a quick hug and a kiss on the lips. "Good afternoon," she said, smiling up at him.

"You, um, thanks," he said, glancing from the eggs, to her, and back to the eggs again, with a grin.

"We have a mission for you two. When you're done eating, go find Agent Nick Locke," she said to Adam and Stacey. "He'll fill you in."

"Sweet!" Adam smiled. "I've been feeling a bit confined."

"Am I ready for that yet?" Stacey asked.

"Yes. You are," Scott said confidently. "You bounced back pretty quick. You had a concussion from the accident. That's why you were so out of it."

"I see," Stacey said. "And now?"

"Where are you?" Scott asked.

"In Matt and Tina's house."

"What town is this?"

"Pine Crest."

"Count backward from fifty by threes."

"Okay. Fifty, forty-seven..." she said, and went all the way down to one.

"Yep. You're good," Scott said confidently.

"Okay," Stacey agreed, as her dad served all five of them scrambled eggs.

While she ate, Stacey studied Becky and her dad. They were already closer than she would like. However, as Adam said before, her dad was a big boy, able to make his own choices. When she brought up her concerns to her Uncle Shawn during the drive out of town, he said when most people lose their spouse, they get remarried within a year or after more than ten years...if at all. She did not want her dad to be lonely. She sorrowfully missed her mother, but seeing her dad and Becky, she could not deny how much they cared for each other.

STACEY GOT CHECKED out by Scott one more time when she finished eating. Afterward, Adam and Stacey went downstairs to get their instructions from Agent Locke for their first mission.

They left the house a couple hours after eating. Keeping to the unseen areas of town, they made their way to the school. Their job was to get into the school office and get files on Kyle and company. This was a test to see how they would do, and if they could get around town unseen by the other side. Stacey and Adam had the biggest target on them of the teens in the house, thanks to Kyle. With them being the highest risk, those from the command center in the basement wanted to see how much the other side was paying attention. There would be two agents shadowing them to make sure nothing happened to Adam and Stacey. They kept their distance, but stayed close enough to keep an eye on the pair in case of an emergency.

Becky gave the pair the alarm code for when they got into

the school. They used Becky's keys to get past the locks, and then entered the code. With everything open, they swiftly made their way to the office. Finding the files was easy. Their files were a bit thicker than they thought, so Stacey was grateful she thought to grab a backpack.

Once they secured the files, they grabbed theirs, as well as those from their group so the other side would not have the advantage of pulling theirs as well. Then they ducked back out of the school, locking it up as they left.

Again, keeping to the shadows, they made their way back to Matt and Tina's. Seeing those guarding the house, Adam let out a signal whistle. That way those guarding it knew it was someone from the house. Adam and Stacey knew they were being followed, but they never saw the agents, until they ducked into the house after them by a few minutes.

"Here you go," Adam said, taking the backpack off Stacey. He handed it to FBI Agent Nick Locke.

"Brilliant! Thanks, mate!" Nick said, flipping through the files. "How do you two feel?"

Nick fascinated Stacey. He had a thick Australian accent, and was built like a tank, but also had a light about him. There was something in his soul that shown bright. He also seemed to have a protective side for others, especially those in his team. While the teens were not his team, he was the one assigned to them. He went through several safety tips and tricks before even talking to them about missions. His entire team arrived the previous day, and took over until Shawn and Pat came back from the hospital.

"Fine," Adam said with a shrug. "I know this place like the back of my hand. If you want anything or need anything, any of the teens in this house can get it for you."

"And we can do it under there radar," Alex added, walking into the kitchen where the group was talking. "I also have a myriad of contacts throughout this town if there is information you need to acquire in a different manner. I will mention that a few are hackers if needed."

"Much appreciated," Seth Simmons, the Special Agent in charge for Nick's team, said. "We have our version of hackers, and we can do it legally. However, you guys know this town better than any of us. We'll set up a meeting with you all in a few hours, along with your parents, to discuss how we would like to utilize those connections and strengths you bring."

"I will alert the others," Alex said, and then left the kitchen.

"You will keep them safe?" Sam asked.

"That is not guaranteed. We will do our best to do what we need to do on our own," Seth explained. "Having said that, as they stated earlier, they know this place better than any of us. They may prove to be more useful to us than some of us doing what needs to be done."

"Dad, we stepped into an issue that has been effecting this town for generations," Stacey said. "They're not going to let go without a fight. Our best chance of success is for us teens to do what the agents cannot do as easily."

"This is true," Sam said. "I just don't want anything to happen to you."

"If you don't do anything, something is *guaranteed* to happen," Nick pointed out.

"It already has," Stacey said.

Looking at Sam, Nick asked, "Do you want your town and daughter safe?"

"Of course."

"Then be prepared for a fight."

OVER THE COURSE of the next couple weeks, Adam and Stacey paired for several missions to gather information or rescue people from their homes. Each time, they got away unharmed.

"So, where's your other half?" Scott asked Stacey, as she was reading a book on the back deck one afternoon.

"Not sure. I think he's with Alex and Brian somewhere."

"I thought you two were inseparable," he said, as he closed the sliding glass door behind him when he walked out onto the deck.

Closing the book, with her finger marking the page, she explained, "Not always. We're close, but we do give each other breathing space."

Smiling, he asked, "Is that possible in this house?"

"It is."

"Mind if I sit so we can visit?"

"Sure. What's on your mind?" she asked, gesturing toward one of the deck chairs.

Pulling the chair over, he said, "Well, my sister and your dad are getting close. I thought it would be a good idea to get to know each other since we may be family members soon."

Hugging the book to her chest, she sighed. "Yeah. I've seen that."

"Does that bother you?" he asked, crossing his arms.

"It does, but not in the way you think."

"Mind explaining that?"

"Well," she looked toward the sky, searching her mind for the right words, "it's like this: if something happened to Adam, I don't think I could fall in love with someone else so quickly. I can't figure out why Dad can fall for someone so fast, when he and my mom were married for over eighteen years. She died less than a year ago."

"I can see that as a concern. However, most people fall into one of two categories: they either fall for someone quickly; or they never fall in love again."

"Adam and my uncle said the same thing. I can't figure out why it has to be an all or nothing. Why can't he just give it time?"

"Why can't you just be happy he found love again? Not everyone finds love after losing the love of their life."

"I *am* happy for him. I also like Becky. I'm struggling with it being so close to my mother's death."

"Stacey, the heart wants what the heart wants," Scott said, leaning forward. "If this happened a year from now, would you be objecting?"

"No, but –"

"What's the difference?" he asked, cutting her off.

"Time."

"We all mourn differently. What works for one person may not work for another. Yes, it was quicker than you would have liked, but why not just be happy they found each other?"

"My mom."

"You're not dividing your loyalties here. Your mother is still your mother. No one can take her place in your heart. You can like Becky, without being disloyal to your mom."

"I don't feel like it."

"Why is it an all or nothing with you? Why can't you just love your mom for herself and everything she was to you, and also love Becky, and everything she can be for you?"

"I just miss her."

"I'm sure. Let me see if this will clear up my line of thinking," he said, rubbing his hands together. "When I was thirteen, my parents got a divorce. Becky and I lived with my mom, per the court order. My dad got us every other weekend. A few months after their divorce, my mom started dating again. Becky and I struggled. We watched my dad spiral after the divorce. He often said mom took everything away from him, and dove into the bottle. Of course, that made Becky and I not want to go on our weekend visits, which spiraled him deeper. During this time, mom and Noah, her now husband, got closer. I felt guilty for the longest time, because I actually like Noah. He's a good guy. He takes care of my mom, and loves me and Becky like his own.

My dad fought it for the longest time. He tried every trick in the book to make us not like Noah. When Mom and Noah got married, Dad got worse for a bit. When he realized Noah was not going anywhere, and he was about to lose Becky and I as well, he sobered up. He turned his life around. He started going to AA meetings. Now, it wasn't a complete one-eighty. He slipped here and there. He even went to rehab for a bit. He finally claimed victory over it about five years ago. Once he cleaned up his life, and got back on the right track, he found someone. Once he was healthy, only then could he be in a healthy relationship. Now here we are, many years down the road, an interesting family. Becky and I still switch-off holidays between Mom and Dad. We love both of our step-parents. We don't harbor any ill will toward either of them. They each have their good points, and their bad points."

"How did you get over the guilt of liking Noah when your dad was going through everything?"

"It was tough. I struggled. Dad and I were two peas in a pod. I was his little buddy growing up. When they divorced, and he was pretty much yanked from my life, I got angry. I didn't know what to do with the anger."

"How did you fix it?"

"I saw how Noah was with my mom. I saw that two people could be married, and not fight all the time. I saw how Noah spoiled my mom. I saw how much he loved her. Then, I watched my mom change. She went from a shell of a woman by the time of the divorce, to a woman who loved life. She had a smile on her face almost daily. He brought out the best in her. Now, I'm not saying your mom was bad for your dad. They may have been each other's soul mates. My point in this story is to say, take a look at how your dad is with Becky. Does she bring out the good in him?"

"She does," Stacey admitted.

"Watch them. See how they interact. See if she's good for

him. Take yourself out of the equation. Take your mom out of the equation. Look at your dad as a human being. Is he happy?"

Stacey mulled Scott's words over in her mind.

Scott patted Stacey's knee as he stood. "Just think about it."

"I will. Thank you," Stacey said. As Scott put his hand on the door to open it, she asked, "Will you stay and talk some more?"

A grin spread across his face. "You want me to stay?"

"Well, I think you're right. If they get closer than they already are, I think we need to get to know each other."

"Okay," he agreed.

As he headed over to the chair again, Stacey said, "So, tell me your favorite movie."

They talked and laughed together for over two hours that night. Stacey found herself enjoying Scott's company.

OVER THE NEXT FEW WEEKS, Scott and Stacey frequently talked about their lives, their likes, and their dislikes. It got to the point that Adam reached his patience point. "What's going on?" he demanded, as he pulled her out onto the back deck.

Stacey furrowed her brow. "With what?"

"More like with *who*," Adam corrected.

"I don't know what you mean," Stacey said, pulling her arm back from him. Crossing her arms, she asked, "What is wrong with you?"

Matching her stance, he said, "You and Scott are super close."

"So."

"I'm not comfortable with that."

"Adam, Scott is Becky's brother. My dad and Becky are dating. He may be family at some point."

"*May* be doesn't mean he *will* be."

"Adam," Stacey cocked her head to the side, "are you jealous?"

Adam looked away.

"Adam, honey, Scott and I have a lot in common, but *you* have my heart," she said, resting her hand on his arm. "I don't understand why you would think otherwise."

"I see the way you two look at each other."

"So, let me get this straight," Stacey said, crossing her arms again. "You're telling me that you can have friends who are girls, like the Kelley twins and Marissa, but I can't have friends who are guys, like Scott."

"You have Brian, Randy, and Alex as friends. You have friends who are guys."

"Friends who you approve of," Stacey pointed out. "They were your friends first."

"So."

"So, it's okay for me to have guy friends, as long as they are your friends first. Does that mean I can't have my own friends?"

"I don't...this isn't going the way I thought it would go," Adam admitted.

"Of course not. You thought I would bend to your demand of not being friends with Scott. Adam, this isn't you. You are not the jealous type."

"I am when I feel threatened," he admitted.

"Do you need a hug?" Stacey asked.

Adam shook his head, but she hugged him anyway. At first, he kept his arms crossed.

"Seriously?" Stacey said, taking a step back. "You are seriously upset about me being friends with Scott?"

"You are both so close."

"As are you and me!"

"You two are always talking and joking around."

"So."

"I just...I don't know what to do here. This is new territory for me," he admitted.

"Adam, my heart is yours. If you're jealous regarding Scott, quite honestly, it's not my problem. It's yours."

"Please don't say that."

"Why not? You're putting your feelings on me. Why do I have to stop being friends with someone just because you think something is there that isn't?"

"I don't-I don't know," he admitted.

"I already put the olive branch out. If you want to stop being so possessive, feel free to let me know if you want to keep going with us. I'm not going to stop being friends with him," she said, and went into the house, leaving him on the deck.

CHAPTER 10

"IF YOU CAN'T FLY THEN RUN, IF YOU
CAN'T RUN THEN WALK, IF YOU CAN'T
WALK THEN CRAWL, BUT WHATEVER YOU
DO YOU HAVE TO KEEP MOVING
FORWARD." MARTIN LUTHER KING JR

The next two days, Adam and Stacey's relationship seemed forced. Stacey was frustrated, but knew Adam would have to be the one to make the next move. If he wanted to continue their relationship, he would have to initiate their next conversation. For those two nights, Harmony slept beside her where Adam used to sleep, with her dad on her other side.

"Okay you two, time to go play superhero," Agent Nick Locke said to Adam and Stacey, as he walked up to them watching a movie in the afternoon.

"Who is it for?" Stacey asked, pausing the movie.

"Sherry Townsend. She called an' asked for help. We could send a team of ours, but I think you two would do a better job. You know this town inside and out," Nick explained. "You've done well so far."

"I know where she lives," Adam said. "We can get her out. She has woods behind her house, so we can duck in there."

"She said she would leave a basement window open in order for you two t' get into the house. She'll be waiting in the basement for you," Nick explained.

"Sounds good," Adam agreed.

"Are you sure you two can do this?" Nick asked, sitting on the coffee table across from them.

"What do you mean?" Stacey asked. "We've done a ton of these."

"You two are off lately. Can you still work as a cohesive unit together?"

"Of course," Stacey said, surprised by his question. "This isn't about us. It's about Mrs. Townsend."

"While I understand that, as partners in this, you have to be at your top in order to help her. Yes, this is about Mrs. Townsend," Nick said. "However, you have to be focused and working as one. I know Seth's weaknesses and strengths, and he knows mine. The other partners in our unit are much the same. When we go out, people can die. Because of that, if someone is off, we make them stay in the office if we go into the field. Otherwise it could cost them their life. You two are going out into the field. Do you feel strong and focused enough? This is not only your life on the line, but also Mrs. Townsend's."

"We can do it," Adam said confidently.

"Fair enough. Be safe," he said and left the pair on the couch.

Looking to Adam, she quietly asked, "*Are* we ready for this?"

"We'll be fine," Adam assured Stacey.

"Okay," she said, and turned back to the television, resuming the movie.

THAT NIGHT ADAM and Stacey took off from the house, making sure to stick to the shadows. They were in their usual all black outfits in order to blend into the darkness.

They slipped through the woods to an older woman's house, who called the Slater house for help. Mrs. Townsend knew what they were doing at the Slater's, so she called and asked for help to get her out of town safely.

Adam and Stacey did several of these before, for people who were going to try to stay in their houses and ride it out. They later called for help to get out, because they were either threatened or scared. Sometimes Adam and Stacey made it in time to help them. Sometimes they got there just as they were attacked. There were a few times where Adam and Stacey had no idea where the people were, and just prayed they got out on their own.

"There's the basement window," Adam whispered. Mrs. Townsend was to leave it open. That was how Adam and Stacey were to get in unnoticed by those possibly watching the house.

They ran over and slipped in through the window into the basement. The basement was dark...and full. Stacey tripped over a couple boxes, catching herself on another box. Adam stubbed his toe on a wood chest of some kind.

"Sherry?" Stacey whispered loudly, after about five minutes of looking around. "Sherry, it's Adam and Stacey."

"I'm here, but they were here earlier," she said, as she peeked out from a little storage room under her staircase. "We'd better hurry in case they come back."

"We're going to go right out your back door, directly into the woods," Adam explained. "Stay close, and move as fast as you can. Understand?"

Sherry nodded in response; terror written all over her body.

"Good. Let's go," Adam said. He took Sherry's wrist and went upstairs, with Stacey trailing behind them.

Once upstairs, they went through the living room. "May I?" Sherry asked, grabbing a photo of her and her departed husband at their fortieth anniversary party. He died five years after the photo was taken.

"Of course," Adam said. Stacey could hear the sorrow in his

voice. "He was a good man. Keep it close to you, and try not to drop it."

"I won't," she said, as she clutched the photo to her chest with one of her arms, while Adam still had her other hand. With that, they left.

While they crossed Sherry's backyard, the trio heard the cars pull up to the front of Sherry's house. People started yelling when someone caught sight of them ducking into the woods. The trio pushed harder. Stacey heard a couple bullets hit the trees around them while they ran. She was not sure they would make it all the way to the Slater's, but they did.

When they got near the house, the guards saw them and what was happening. They met Adam, Stacey, and Sherry with their guns ready. They fired-off a couple warning shots at those following them. Those chasing, turned and ran the other way. By the time the trio got into the house, they were exhausted.

"Okay, can we have a break for a bit?" Stacey asked, dropping onto the chair at the table. "I'm feeling worn out."

"I agree," Adam said, sitting beside her at the table. "I'm usually up for these, but they almost got us tonight. Can we have at least a couple days off?"

"Can you do one more tomorrow night, and then take the break?" Stacey's Uncle Shawn asked. He arrived from the hospital that afternoon, his left arm in a sling. His partner had a couple more days before he would be released. "There's some information Becky has in her desk that we need. She's been keeping track of various things, including names, dates, and even some accounts and cell phone numbers we can track. We *really* need this."

Stacey looked at Adam, who nodded. So, she looked back to her uncle and nodded.

"Excellent! I'll get all the information you'll need for tomorrow night. Just think, you get a break after that...for a couple days anyway," he said, and then left the kitchen.

"So, the dynamic duo strikes again," Brian said, smiling as he walked into the kitchen with Melody, Harmony, and Alex. "So, what grateful person did the wonder twins save tonight?"

"Sherry Townsend." Adam smirked at Brian's nicknames. "She was hiding in her basement. We almost didn't find her ourselves."

"But you did, and everyone's happy," Melody encouraged.

"Are you guys hungry?" Harmony asked. "We're going to be starting dinner here shortly. You can have a snack while you wait," she offered. "You just look like you need it."

"Here." Alex tossed them each a bottle of water, which they promptly sucked down. Then he got them each another one, while the ladies started dinner for the group.

∿

AFTER DINNER THAT NIGHT, Adam asked Stacey, "Can we go out onto the deck and talk?"

"Sure," Stacey said, so they got up from the table.

"So," Adam said, as they sat on the porch swing together, "I hope this doesn't last for too much longer."

"What? What's going on with the town or your distance from me?"

"Ouch!" Adam cringed. "I deserved that one."

"Well?"

"Both. Look, I'm sorry. I shouldn't be upset about your friendship with Scott. You two just seem to fit together."

"As friends, yes. You and I fit together in the heart," Stacey said.

"I agree."

"Then, what's your problem?"

"Jealousy is an ugly beast. It doesn't help that Marissa keeps pointing it out."

"Why are you still listening to her regarding our relationship?"

He sighed. "I don't know."

Hoping to change the subject before it blew up again, Stacey said, "Not that I'm not enjoying sleeping next to you at night, but this running for our lives *is* getting a little old."

"I agree. I'm sorry for not taking advantage of being able to hold you while we go to sleep the last few nights."

"No problem. Are you going to join me tonight?"

"Will you have me?"

"Of course," she said, giving Adam a hug. "All you had to do was ask."

He wrapped his arms around her as well. "I'm sorry for being mean. Please forgive me?"

"I forgive you. Just know that I will continue to be friends with him."

"I know," he said. He took her hand into his, and they walked over to the deck railing. "Man, I wish we could just take a walk in the park. We took what little freedom we had for granted, and now we don't even have that."

"While you had *some* freedom, imagine how free you'll *really* be when this is all done," she said, hopping onto the railing, facing him. "No more jumping when you see any of the Chandler's or their friends. No more running from the police or government officials."

"That *will* be a relief! I mean, not all of the police are corrupt. As a matter of fact, most are really good officers," Adam said. "The trick is figuring out which ones are in Chandler's pocket."

"I know Matt said not to trust them. I don't know if he knows which ones are safe either."

"I know there are some who are trying to protect us. I've seen it."

"A few bad apples ruin the bunch," Stacey said.

"More like a few bad apples ruin the reputation of the bunch."

"True," Stacey agreed.

Standing in front of her, he rested his hands on her waist. "Do you know what you mean to me?"

"I do. Do you know what you mean to me?" she asked.

"I do."

"Then you have to understand why I am upset you even remotely question my loyalty to you."

"I know. I'm sorry. I don't know why I thought you would do that to me."

"Marissa."

"I know. I'm sorry. She can be pretty convincing."

"Why are you listening to her regarding our relationship? She's been against us from the start."

"You're right. I'm sorry."

"While she has a good heart, maybe in regards to us, you should only listen to me and you?" Stacey suggested. "Let her alone with her relationship with Alex, while we take care of *our* relationship. Just like we don't butt into Harmony and Randy's relationship, no one should butt into ours."

"I agree."

Resting her hand on the side of his face, she said, "You have a trusting heart. That heart is what guides you. Your heart is what I fell in love with in the first place."

He sighed. "You're really beautiful, on the inside *and* out. You know that? You have a gorgeous and caring heart. There are days where I am amazed at what God has given me in you."

Stacey stared at him, her heart overflowing with love.

He hugged her. "Someday, I would love to be able to walk around with you, free from the stress of those around us."

"I know."

He rested his forehead on hers, with his hands on the sides of her face. "I have to tell you that…I love you."

"I –" Stacey abruptly pulled away. "What did you say?"

He smiled. "I said I love you."

"I love you too. I just…you've never kissed me more than a quick kiss."

"I don't have to passionately kiss you to know I'm in love with you," he said. "Kissing is just one of the many aspects of dating."

"I know, I just…" Stacey pulled him back to her, resting her forehead back on his, looking into his eyes.

"I'm really sorry for doubting you," he said.

"Thank you."

He brought his hands down, resting them on her waist. "One of these days, I might get up the courage to *really* kiss you," he said. "I just don't want to do that yet. I'm afraid I'll have a difficult time if I do."

Stacey furrowed her brow. "Why?"

He looked at her, with a different, more intense look in his eyes. "Because I know if I kiss you the way I want to, I won't want to stop."

Wide-eyed, Stacey had no words.

"You're so kind, so loving. You are stronger than you think. And the fact that you are in love with me, and put up with me, it just, well, let's just say it does something to me when I think about it," he explained, with a smile. "And if we start kissing, we could be in trouble."

"Oh, I think we'll be able to control it." She smiled. "After all, God won't like it if we do that before we're married."

"No." He shook his head. "He wouldn't."

"Hey, are you two coming back in anytime soon?" Sam poked his head out. "It's getting dark. We shouldn't be out, unless you guys want to do your mission now."

"No. We'll do it tomorrow night," Adam said, stepping back, turning toward Sam.

"We're going to be turning in soon," Sam hinted.

"We're coming," Stacey said with a smile, as she hopped off the railing. She and Adam followed him inside.

They relaxed as a group for a little bit, while some of the agents and officers worked downstairs in getting Mrs. Townsend out of town. Watching a couple movies before getting ready for bed was always a good way to relax.

Afterward, the girls changed in the rooms upstairs, while the guys went down to the basement to change. Any female officers or agents down there at the time, came upstairs for a few minutes while the guys changed.

When they finished, they grabbed their sleeping bags, and headed down to the living room. The group nicknamed their sleeping in the living room *the pack*. Most people slept in shorts or sweatpants, and a T-shirt. The guys were already there with their bags out by the time the girls got downstairs, so the girls picked their spots, and spread out their sleeping bags where there was room. Then they turned out the lights, and talked until people drifted off to sleep.

"Good night, Peanut," Sam said and kissed Stacey's head. Then he laid in his sleeping bag, cuddling with Becky who was on his other side.

"Good night, Dad," Stacey said, and turned to cuddle into Adam, who had already laid his arm out for her as he lay on her other side. When Stacey rested on Adam's chest, he wrapped his arm around her, and then kissed her head.

"I missed this," he whispered.

"Me too," Stacey whispered back, cuddling in closer.

"So, are you ready for tomorrow night?"

"Think so," she said. They whispered so they would not disturb anyone. "I'm a little nervous though. That's pretty close to one of their known houses."

"I was thinking the same thing. That's why I wanted a night of rest. That way we would be in better shape for it."

"Adam?" Stacey picked up her head, looking at him. She could see his face with help from the security lights outside.

"Yeah?"

"I know I have Christ in my heart, but is it okay to still be scared?"

"Stace, everyone gets scared. We're human. I have to tell you I was scared tonight too! I didn't think we were going to get away from them with Mrs. Townsend. She wasn't running fast enough, and that *did* scare me."

"I was scared too. And for the record, I love you too," she said, and quickly kissed his lips. She laid back down before he could say or do anything.

"I love you too," he said, and hugged her tightly.

He closed his eyes in prayer for the next day's events. By the time he finished, Stacey was sound asleep, so he kissed her head, and joined her as they went to sleep in each other's arms.

THE NEXT MORNING, and for most of the day, Adam and Stacey prepared themselves for the mission. The idea of being so close to one of their known houses concerned Stacey, but Sam and her Uncle Shawn continuously assured them it would be easy. They said Adam and Stacey ran these multiple times, and it would be no problem.

About an hour before they left, Becky gave them the setup of the school offices in detail, specifically her office. Becky hid an eight-by-ten manilla envelope in a drawer that had a false bottom. She explained exactly where it was and how to get it.

Before they left, Stacey gave her dad and Uncle Shawn a hug. Then Adam and Stacey prayed with those in their friend group before they left out the back door through the woods. They went at night, hoping not to get caught. Once again, they stayed in the shadows as much as possible.

When they got to the school, they climbed in a bottom floor window, and slowly, but silently, made their way upstairs to the offices. Stacey punched in the code to turn off the alarm system. Then Adam used the keys Becky gave him to get into the offices.

"Here it is," Adam said, pulling it out of Becky's desk drawer, smiling satisfactorily. Adam tucked it into the back of his pants, and covered it with his shirt.

"Great! Let's get out of here!" Stacey said, but he grabbed her arm, pulling her down with him. "What?"

"Um..." He looked at her, and in less than a split second, he kissed her.

It was not a quick one like normal. It was a long passionate kiss. It was a kiss Stacey felt through her entire body.

"Uh, I'm..." Stacey pulled away a little bit. She looked at him for a second, and then she kissed him back.

"I love you," he whispered a minute or so later.

"I love you too," she said, and kissed him even stronger.

"We, um, we should..."

"Yeah," Stacey said, and they kissed for a few more moments.

"Probably should go before we get caught," Adam finally said, and got off the floor. He reached down and helped Stacey up.

"Thank you," Stacey said, collecting her mind. "Whew! Now I know what you meant when you said you probably wouldn't want to stop once we kissed. That was...your lips are so soft," she said, face flushed as she touched her lips with her fingertips.

"Yours are as well. So is your skin," Adam said with a smile. Still holding her hand, Adam said, "Okay. Ready?"

"Yes."

"I need you clearheaded."

"Then you probably shouldn't have kissed me that way," Stacey teased.

"I couldn't wait any longer."

"I understand. Let's go," Stacey said, and they left the office.

Sneaking through the hallways, they kept close to the walls. Stacey had memories from her first few days of school go through her mind as they passed the award case.

Running across the lawn, they almost made it to the woods when they heard yelling, shouting, and gunfire coming in their direction. They ran faster.

Adam grabbed Stacey's wrist, pulling her with him. "Come on!" he yelled, as they ducked into the woods of the park across from the school.

While they ran, they heard those chasing them make it to the tree line. They spread out looking for them.

"Come out, come out wherever you are!" one of the guys chasing them taunted.

"Keep running!" Adam breathed out.

"I'm going as fast as I can," Stacey said.

"They're getting closer. We need to run faster!"

Stacey's heart raced. She could hear them getting closer. They only made it about another hundred yards when she felt the unmistakable searing heat of a bullet bite into her leg. She hit the ground, smacking her head on a rock. She barely got her eyes open in an attempt to find Adam. She saw him get shot twice, and then fall to the ground motionless.

Fighting consciousness as long as possible, she heard those chasing them run up to the pair. She passed out as they dragged them away.

STACEY OPENED HER EYES. She groaned. Once again, she was not where she hoped to be when she woke. She reached over and touched the dirt wall next to her to make sure it was real.

Barely able to see, due to it being dawn or dusk, she could scarcely make out the area around her. Above her was a cloudy sky, partially obscured by trees. The stench of death was unmistakable around her. Forcing the vomit to stay down, she covered her nose and mouth as she tried to get a better idea of where she landed.

Unsure of exactly where she was, she did see she was in a pit about six feet wide, and ten to twelve feet deep…and she was not alone. Sitting up on her elbows, she felt a sharp pain jet out from the back of her thigh, about mid-way up. She winced, grabbing it. "Ah-eee!" she growled through gritted teeth, grasping at her leg, breathing heavy.

Struggling, she finally got the pain to a tolerable level. Covering her mouth with her hand, she glanced around the area to ensure no one heard her initial noises. Once her eyes adjusted, she screamed and jumped back. There were dead bodies everywhere!

Looking down, she realized she was lying on dead bodies! When she reached down to brace herself, she touched an arm and a leg…and not from the same person. Grasping at the dirt wall to stand, she looked around in utter terror at all the carnage surrounding her. That's when a bloody set of hands moved around her. One covered her mouth, while the other wrapped around her body, holding her in place. Stacey momentarily lost it. She screamed bloody murder for several minutes, as she dropped to her knees. Everywhere she looked was carnage! And worse yet, she had no idea who was holding her there!

Finally, she calmed down enough to hear Adam's voice. He was talking to her the entire time, only she could not hear him over her screams.

Quoting Psalm 23 in its entirety, he then moved on to other verses, "*Surely goodness and mercy shall follow me all the days of my life, and I shall live in the house of The Lord forever,*" Adam said, rocking both of them. "Stacey, shh, peace *be still, and know that I am God.* He's here. Father, You have heard my voice, and You know my name. Please, Father. Shh, Stace, it's me. Shh. Calm down. Father, I pray You grant her calmness of spirit. Give her Your comfort to know it's me. Give us both Your strength, Father. Give us both Your peace that passes all understanding. We are acknowledging You. Father, please direct us! Please help us!" He said, and then started singing Amazing Grace.

Hearing him sing, the words penetrated the fear that encompassed her, wrapping her in a blanket of comfort.

"...*Than when we first begun.* Good job, Stacey," Adam encouraged, after he had sung all five verses of Amazing Grace. "It's me, Adam. Just remember, God'll never leave us, nor forsake us. He loves us. He'll take care of us. Just claim it! Even in the middle of this, claim His peace," he said, and kissed Stacey's head, still gently rocking. "Now, shh. It's okay. We're alive," he said, as he hugged her closer to him. "You know it's me, right Stacey?"

Stacey nodded, as her breathing finally started to slow down.

"Good. I'm going to take my hand off your mouth in a minute. You're not going to freak out again, are you?" he asked.

Stacey shook her head in response.

"Okay, then before I let you go, I need to tell you a couple things."

Stacey nodded for him to go on.

"Yes, these are dead bodies. You know that. Right?"

Stacey wildly looked around at the dead bodies.

"No. Calm down, Stacey," he said soothingly. "We're not dead. Just relax. We're *not* dead. It's okay. God's not done with us yet. Listen, you're going to have to help me," he said, as Stacey sat there close to hyperventilating. "Stacey, please calm down. Please calm your breathing," he coaxed for another few minutes. When she calmed, he explained, "Stace, I need you to get these bullets out of my leg and side. They'll get infected even worse than they already are, especially since this is *such* a sanitary place. Can you do that for me? Will you help me?"

Taking a few deep breaths, Stacey then nodded in response.

"Good. On the count of three I'm going to let go. Okay?" he asked.

She nodded again.

"Okay. One…two…three," he said, and let her go.

Stacey leaned forward with her hands out in front of her. She inhaled a deep breath of air. Turning toward him, she hugged him, bursting into tears.

"I know," he said, holding her. He kissed her head as he stroked her hair. "Shh, I know, but He's here. Believe it or not, the Lord is here with us. Remember you are never alone. He's here with us, Stace. Trust me." He kissed her head again. "Now, I really need you to calm down so you can get these out."

Stacey sat back, her hands resting on her knees. Taking a few moments to collect herself, she finally asked, "Okay. You want me to get the bullets out. Take them out with what?"

"I have a pocket knife."

"Are you-*are you kidding me?*"

"You're going to have to do it. I'm already starting to feel the effects of an infection. They have to come out. We also have to get out of here. You can't go too long without food."

"We won't have to worry about food if these gun shots kill us. Look at these people," Stacey said, gesturing toward the bodies all around them. "They don't intend for us to get out!"

That was when Stacey got a really good look at what was in the pit with them. Unable to control it anymore, she spun away from Adam, throwing up everything in her system.

There were not just a few dead bodies tossed here and there. It was a mass grave! These people were not neatly embalmed either. They were tossed in without another thought. They were tossed in just like Stacey and Adam. As far as that group was concerned, Adam and Stacey were dead.

The stench infiltrated every sense in her body. There was blood everywhere. The maggots and the flies feasted on every-thing in sight.

"Oh! I can't," Stacey said. She threw up and heaved for a few more minutes.

"I know. I did the same thing," Adam said, wrapping his arms around his legs. "I got my answer by the way."

"About?" Stacey asked, wiping the vomit off her mouth. Breathing heavily from heaving so much, she asked, "Answer for what?"

"My mom's over there." He nodded toward the other side of the pit where there were bodies piled. "I discovered her a little while ago as I was stacking them."

"As you were–you were *what?*"

"I was stacking them to get us closer to the top. That's what all the blood is on me. Most if it is not mine."

"Um…" Stacey said, and turned back toward the ground again, dry heaving. The thought that he was holding her with all those people's blood all over him was too much for her to handle. Thankfully, they were each wearing a black turtleneck shirt, black pants, and black boots, so she could not see the blood all over his clothing.

"Relax. Trust me, I know. I've done my share. Stacey, we have to get out of here."

"I'm…" She crawled on the ground to an area with no bodies. Feeling shaky from all the throwing up, along with the lack of food, she lay her head on her arms as she curled up on the ground.

"It's okay. Just rest," he said, kneeling beside her, rubbing her back. "Just rest, Stacey. We'll get through this."

She slid her head over to his lap, and fell asleep with him stroking her hair.

WHEN SHE WOKE AGAIN, there were several more bodies added to the stack, but he was asleep on the ground next to her. When she reached up and touched the side of his face, he woke with a start.

"Shh, it's just me," Stacey said.

"I'm…oh, wow. Sorry. You scared me."

Moving her hand to his forehead, she said, "You're hot."

"I know," he said, and then winced in pain, grabbing the back of his leg. "You really need to get these out of me. I started getting the chills along with this fever about a half hour ago."

"The sun is out. I should have enough light through the trees," she said, glancing up at the massive oaks and maples above. Then she looked back toward him, and asked, "Are you sure you want me to do this?"

"You have to. Infection has already set in."

"It's going to hurt. I don't know if I have it in me to hurt you like this."

"Stace," he groaned. "I *really* need you to do this. If you don't, then kill me and put me out of my misery now. You really don't have a choice here. If you don't get them out, the infection will kill me anyway.

Reluctantly, she agreed, "Okay. I'll do it."

He reached into his pocket and pulled out the knife. "Here," he said, handing it to her.

"So, how are we going to do this? One of them is in a precarious position."

"I know. Modesty is going to have to go out the window. Think you can handle seeing me in my underwear?" He chuckled again, and then winced and groaned. "Oh boy! Stacey, you have to do it now. They need to come out."

She gulped. "Okay. I–you have to take your pants down a little bit."

He unbuckled his pants, and pulled them partway down. Then he grabbed a stick from the ground near them and put it in his mouth. "Go ahead," he said. He bit down on the stick, while clenching his fists, bracing for the pain.

Studying the area around the wound, she did her best to decipher its exact location before she cut. "Shouldn't we sanitize this some way?" she asked.

"Just do it already!" Adam hissed through gritted teeth. "It hurts!"

"You asked for it," Stacey said, and then cut into his leg just below his underwear line.

He let out several howls, amidst his moans and groans of pain and agony. She was not sure how much more either one could take. Her stomach churned, flipped, and flopped, as she concentrated on the area, convincing herself not to vomit or pass out. She forced herself to focus to stop her hands from shaking as she breathed slowly. Sweat dripped from her forehead while she fished around the hole for the bullet with her finger.

"Please be done soon!" Adam groaned while Stacey continued to feel for the bullet.

"Got it," she said, finally pulling it out.

Adam dropped his head onto his arms, taking slow, deep breaths until the pain got to a tolerable level. In the meantime, Stacey tore off a sleeve from her shirt. She tied it around his leg where she originally cut to slow the bleeding.

Then she went up by his head, moving it onto her lap. He had tears of pain, along with more moans and groans. His body shook, while the sweat poured down his face.

She ran her fingers through fine, soft, light-brown hair. She really wanted to see his brilliant blue eyes, but she knew they would not be full of the love she was used to seeing in them. His eyes would be full of pain and agony. "Adam? Adam, honey?" Stacey leaned down. He looked up at her, breathing heavily. "Is it calming down yet?" she asked.

"No," he moaned.

"Not at all?"

"A little," he admitted. Then he winced and jumped again, groaning.

"Ready for the other one?"

"Not really."

"I have to get it out. You were right. The area I just cut into was infected."

"I know," he said, taking a deep breath. "Can you...five minutes?"

"Okay," Stacey agreed. She continued to stroke his hair until he was ready.

"Now," he said about ten minutes later. He reached down and pulled his pants up, and then took his shirt off. The bullet hit toward his waist on the lower right side, about two inches from his side.

He laid on his stomach on top of his shirt, with part of his shirt in his clutches. "Go ahead," he said, and then put the stick back in his mouth. He dropped his head onto the shirt, burying his face.

"Oh, Adam, I can't." Stacey shook her head, tears in her eyes as her heart broke. "I can't do it to you again."

"Yes, you can," he insisted. "You have to."

"I can't!"

"Yes! Do it!" he yelled, the stick still in his mouth.

"I..." Stacey took a deep breath, and then went in for it.

He immediately jumped. He broke the stick in his mouth from biting down so hard. Wide-eyed, he let out a yell, "Ahhhhh!"

"I'm sorry! I'm sorry!" Stacey panicked. "I'm so sorry!"

"Stace! Finish!" he shouted, and then buried his face back into the shirt. "Just do it already!"

Stacey took a deep breath, and then went back into the hole

with the knife to feel around for the bullet. When she hit metal, she pulled the knife out. "Almost done," she said, and then reached in with her fingers, finally pulling it out about two agonizing minutes after she started.

Once again, when she finished, she had him lay his head on her lap. She ran her fingers through his sweaty hair until he calmed down.

When he was calm enough, she had him lay his head back on his shirt. Taking a look at the seeping wound, she then tore the other shirtsleeve off her shirt. She tried to be gentle as she put a pressure on the wound with her sleeve. Leaving the sleeve on the wound, she had him lay his head back on her lap. She stroked his hair until he finally passed out.

Once he was asleep, Stacey lay back on the ground and closed her eyes. Resting her arm over her eyes to block the sunlight, she was finally able to drift off to sleep.

"STACE?" He said groggily, a couple hours later. "Stacey, wake up." He reached over and shook her. "Stace?"

"What? Huh?" She quickly sat up. Then she laid back down, closing her eyes, waiting for the rest of her body to catch up with her head. "What?"

"How are you feeling?"

"I need food, but I'm okay for now," she said, breathing slowly. As the dizziness subsided, she added, "I'm stable anyway."

"Were you shot?"

"Yes."

"We need to get that out."

"I know." Stacey sighed. "We should probably get it over with."

"*Where* are you shot?"

"In my thigh, just above my knee."

"You know we need to –"

"I know," she said, cutting him off. She reached down and unbuckled her pants before she pulled them down.

"You can lay down on this," he said, handing her his shirt. "By the way, you, um, yeah," he nodded in approval, "nice legs."

"Hey! I didn't make fun of your legs."

"I wasn't making fun. They *are* nice legs," he said. "Ready?"

Stacey buried her face into Adam's shirt, bracing for impact. She nodded for him to do it.

"One…two…three," he said, and then went to go dig it out.

"Ahh-eeeee!" She screamed and jumped. It hurt before, but when he went in with the knife, he might as well have gone in with a hot poker as far as she was concerned. He did not go in gently. Extremely severe did not cover the level of pain she experienced. Pounding the ground with her fists, she did not know what else to do with the intensity of the pain. "Hurry!" she growled.

"Shh! I'm sorry!" he apologized. Then he leaned down and kissed her cheek. "I'm really sorry, but we have to get this out. We also have to get us out of here…*preferably* before you crash on me. We've been in here for too long," he said, and went back to digging it out again.

The torturous agony went on for several more minutes before he finally stopped. When he took his shirt from her, she rested her head on her crossed arms. Tears poured down her cheeks, while sweat dripped from her face.

Adam tore the shirtsleeves off his shirt, and then put the rest of the shirt on. Afterward, he tied one of the sleeves around her leg to help the wound clot. The other one, he tied around his own waist to hold Stacey's balled up sleeve over the wound on his waist.

Stacey took several moments before she felt she could move. Then she pulled her pants up.

He wrapped his arms around her, holding her to his chest while she cried. "I know. Shh. I know. Just relax," he said. He rocked her in his arms until she calmed down enough to sleep.

WHEN SHE WOKE up once again, they were leaning against the side of the pit. She was still in Adam's arms. Seeing how red his cheeks were, she touched his face. "Adam?" she asked, concerned. "Adam?"

"I know. I'm…yeah," he said, breathing heavily, dropping his head back onto the wall behind him. "Hot."

"We need to get out of here."

"I haven't heard anyone else around us. If our screams didn't bring them running, then they're not around. I've stacked the bodies enough that –" He stopped and shifted to get into a better position. "If we're going to get out of here, we'll need to climb."

Stacey glanced at the pile he created. The heap had to have been at least seven feet high, still leaving about five feet where they would have to help each other climb out. They would have to work together to do it. One would not get out without the other one.

"Stacey?" he asked, after another minute.

She did not move any more than Adam did. She felt drained. "What?"

"Stace, I need to ask you something."

"What is it?"

"I know this probably isn't the best place, but I don't want to have any regrets. If I'm going to die, I need to ask –"

"You're not going to die. We're going to get out of here. You made sure of that by stacking the bodies to get us closer to the top."

"Please?"

Stacey gulped. "Anything."

"Would you-would you honor me by wearing this?" He asked, taking off his class ring. "Would you wear it for me?"

"Definitely," she said, accepting it. She placed it on her right-hand ring finger. She admired it for a few moments. The emerald stone signified his birthstone. The year of their graduation was on one side, with a skateboard on the other. "It's pretty. Thank you," she said, cuddling into him.

"I want you to keep it. If anything happens to me, I want you to have it," he said, tears brimming his eyes. "Please tell me you'll keep it?"

"Adam?" Stacey said, surprised by his statement. "Nothing is going to happen to you. We're going to get out of this."

"I'm really hot, Stace. I don't know if I'm even going to be able to get back to the safehouse. Here," he said, handing her the envelope from Becky's desk. "You need to get this back."

"No, I'm not leaving here without you."

"I know. I'm just saying –"

"Well *don't!*"

"Just letting you know, I love you very much," he said, resting his hand on the side of her face. His hand shook. His face bright red.

Tears came to her eyes, as she saw his weakness and frailness. Her heart broke for him.

"Shh, no." He shook his head. Rubbing the tears off her cheeks, he said, "Please, no crying." He gently kissed her head, which made her cry harder. "No. Please don't." He rested his forehead on hers. "Now, none of that, *Peanut.*" He smiled with a wink.

Even though she was scared, she had to smile at that one.

"That's better. Now, we need to get out of here. I'm not going to make it much longer."

"Me neither."

"They need that information."

"Adam?"

"Yes?"

"I need *you*."

He stared at her for a moment. Then he kissed her with the love he felt inside.

The kiss sent tingles through her body. It was stronger than the one he gave her in Becky's office. After a moment, she rested her hands on his cheeks and kissed him back to show him how much she loved him.

Before they knew it, several minutes passed. "We need to go," Adam finally said. "For both our sakes, we need to get back to the safehouse."

Climbing the bodies was one of the most traumatic things Stacey ever experienced. There were some people on the pile who Adam and Stacey did not get to on time. She finally had her answer on some of those missing. Knowing their fate not only made her sick to her stomach, but also heartbroken.

These people were people they knew. People they saw every day. There was the head librarian of the school library, a secretary at the courthouse, a grocery store clerk, a bank teller, even Adam's mom. There were others in the pile she did not know, but she still felt for them. Knowing these people were dead, and that the group killed them…it was a little more than Stacey could handle and process at that moment.

When they got to the top of the mound, he had Stacey go down on her hands and knees. She forced herself not to consider that she was on top of actual human bodies. When she got on her hands and knees, she saw some of the faces looking up at her, so she closed her eyes.

Adam climbed on top of her to go out of the hole first. He did not want her to go first in case there was someone waiting for them. He would also be able to pull her out. He did not think she had the strength to pull him out.

There was no one waiting, so Adam lay down on the ground,

bent in half at about his middle. He reached down, and said, "It's clear. Give me your hands."

Stacey's body trembled at the trauma surrounding her. She reached up, grasping his hands. Using her legs, she walked up the wall with her feet to get her closer to the top, until she could pull herself the rest of the way out with Adam's help.

"There," Adam said, out of breath when she finally climbed out, and was lying on the ground beside him.

"You can't rest," Stacey said. "We need to keep going."

"I know," he agreed. "They can come back any time."

"I'm hot too."

"I thought you were. Um, Stace?"

"Yeah?"

"I'm seeing things," Adam said. "I see shadows out of the corner of my eyes. I also see spots and sparkles. You're even wavering, when I know you're completely still. We need to go… like now."

"I know," Stacey agreed.

She slowly got up, and then helped him off the ground. Both of them had sore legs, but he was in worse shape than Stacey. Thankfully, there was at least one thing in their favor…it was nighttime.

Adam looked around a bit, before he pointed in a direction. "Go that way," he said. "I'm not completely sure where we are, but this looks somewhat familiar."

"I trust you. Please stay awake. I need you for direction."

"I'll do my best," he promised.

He put his arm around Stacey's shoulder, and leaned on her. She wrapped her arm around his waist, and held his other arm around her shoulder, partially carrying him as they left.

～

It took them a good half hour before Adam was sure where they were. Then it took them *another* half hour or so to get back to the safehouse.

They were about ten minutes from the safehouse when Adam collapsed. "I-I can't go anymore," he said as he shook his head.

Stacey knelt on the ground beside him, wrapping him in her arms. He was breathing heavily, and his fever was immensely high. "Adam," Stacey said, "You can't quit on me now. We're almost there."

"I can't go any further."

"Yes. You can. Lean on me. We're almost there. Please, Adam?" Stacey begged.

"That way...ten minutes. Just go down to Smithfield Road, and turn right. They'll be almost to the end of that road."

"You're coming with me."

"Just leave me," Adam said. "You can bring help back. You've already carried me for most of this with strength you didn't have."

"You said before that I can do all things through *Christ* who strengthens me," Stacey said. "I'm using His strength to get us both home."

"While I appreciate that, we have to be sensible."

"Adam, the trees and houses are moving. I am not sure I can find my way back to you in the shape I'm in. So, either you come with me, or we both die right here."

"Stacey, this is no time for arguing."

"I'm not arguing. I'm making a point. We get to the safe house together, or we both die together right here. Which one is it?"

"Stace, I can't."

"Yes," she said as she stood. She slipped her arms under his, and pulled, dragging him with her, praying the whole way for God's strength. "Lord, please help us. We are not going to make this without You. I know You got us this far. I know You will not leave us. Please give me strength to get us both back. Please keep Adam conscious until we get there. Please..." she continued to pray, as they turned down Smithfield Road.

When they got within visual range of the house, Stacey saw several guards running their way. Their guns aimed, the one in charge of safety, Luke, shouted at them, "Stop, or we'll shoot!"

"Help!" Stacey shouted, as she dropped to her knees.

"It's Adam and Stacey!" Luke yelled.

Stacey could not help it anymore. She closed her eyes and collapsed from exhaustion. Adam had been unconscious for a few minutes by that point. She barely heard the men run up to them. One of them picked Stacey up and threw her over his shoulder. Knowing she made it, and they were getting help, she rested in the blissful peace that surrounded her.

CHAPTER 11

"A HERO IS AN ORDINARY INDIVIDUAL
WHO FINDS THE STRENGTH TO PERSEVERE
AND ENDURE IN SPITE OF
OVERWHELMING OBSTACLES."
CHRISTOPHER REEVE

Stacey's fever continued to rise. She would go in and out of consciousness over the next few days.

"Stacey?" She heard, and looked up to see a man with a kind, gentle face.

Stacey stood. "Yes?"

She was not in the safe house. Mountains loomed in the distance, as she stood in the middle of a field of daisies. She looked down to see she was dressed in a flowing, flower-printed sundress, as a slight breeze went through her hair. "Who are you?" she asked.

He smiled. "A friend. Come, walk with me."

"I don't know you."

"Oh yes, you do." He took her hand, and they started walking. "Think deep and hard. You will find me within you."

"Are you –?" Stacey stepped back, staring at him wide-eyed. "You're not Who I think you are. Are you?"

"Yes." He chuckled. "I am."

"Wow! I..." She got down on her knees, covering her face as she lay prostrate.

"No, no, my child." He reached down and picked her up by

her hand. "I appreciate the respect, but you are one of Mine. I want to see your beautiful face."

"Am I supposed to look at you? I didn't think..." Her voice faded as she turned away.

He reached up and turned her chin back to Him. "I love you. I want to see the beauty of your soul. I want to see your face."

"Um, if I'm here, then..." She gulped. "Am I dead?"

"Do not be afraid. You need encouragement. You need to know you are not alone. You need to know you all are not fighting this battle by yourselves."

"What about...is Adam going to be okay?"

He nodded. "For now."

"He looked really bad."

"He will pull through for now. He is not done yet. He still has some work to do."

Stacey crossed her arms in thought. "The battle still going on down there?" she asked.

"Yes."

"I may be way off base, but is this more along the lines of good versus evil?"

"Ultimately, that is what they all boil down to," He said with a smile. His smile brought an instant peace.

"Um..." Stacey looked down, but once again He lifted her chin so she was looking at Him. "Is my dad going to be able... he's not a Christian."

"I know. Keep praying for him. Let *Me* work on his heart. The choice is his. Having said that, I would like them *all* to come home."

Stacey nodded.

"You need to go now," He said after another minute.

"Can I come back?"

"Anytime." He smiled and hugged her. "But for now, there are some people who would love to see you open your beautiful eyes."

"Thank you," Stacey said, hugging him back.

"You are most welcome," He said, and kissed her cheek. "Make wise choices and be strong. You are a daughter of The Most High."

She grinned. "Thank you."

"Go. The Spirit is with you."

She took a few steps forward. When she turned to look at Him again, she only saw a curtain of white. When she turned back to the direction she was walking, everything swirled together within the white curtain. Stacey's head spun, so she closed her eyes and took a deep breath.

When she opened her eyes, she was in a bed in the Slater house. Only this time, Adam was beside her in the bed. He was still unconscious. Sam, Becky, and Scott were asleep on various chairs throughout the room.

Taking a few moments to collect her thoughts, she finally squeaked out, "Dad?"

As soon as she did, Scott jumped up. "Stacey?" He went over to her side of the bed and knelt down. "You in there?" he asked, brushing her hair out of her face.

Stacey nodded.

"Good." He leaned over and jostled Sam and Becky. "She's awake," he explained when they both sat up startled.

"Adam?" Stacey asked, turning her head toward him. She reached over and grabbed his hand.

"I'm afraid he's not awake yet," Scott explained. "We're glad at least one of you woke up."

"Why isn't he awake yet?" Stacey asked, heartbroken.

"Oh, Peanut. He'll be okay. Just give him time," Sam said, running his fingers through her hair. He sighed, as he sat on the side of the bed. "Been a long time this time. What happened to you two?"

"The group," she said. "They caught us as we were running from the school." She groaned, closing her eyes. There was a lot of pain jetting from her leg. "They, um, they caught us in the woods, and then dragged us, throwing us into a mass grave."

Becky gasped, looking from Adam to Stacey. "Are you serious?"

"His mom was in there," Stacey said, turning toward Adam. "He stacked the bodies so we could climb out."

"That was good thinking," Sam said.

"He'll be okay, right?" Stacey asked.

"We don't know yet. His fever is still pretty high," Sam said. As tears rolled down her cheeks, Sam said, "No. Don't cry, sweetheart. You need to just relax and eat something."

Stacey rolled onto her side, facing Adam. She reached up, running her fingers through his still soaking wet hair. "Please wake up. Adam?"

"Stacey, honey, he might be a while longer. You guys were really sick. You were both unconscious by the time they got to you," Sam said.

"Adam, please wake up?" she pleaded.

"Just rest, Stace. Why don't you get a little more sleep for now?" Sam coaxed.

"Okay," she whispered. Looking at Adam, she slowly drifted off to sleep.

"Let's leave them for a bit," Sam said. "Hopefully, they will get some good rest."

"Good idea," Becky said. "Plus, we need to eat."

With that, they left, closing the door behind them.

Stacey woke to a dark room. As she lay there, she remembered everything that happened since they broke into the school. She sighed as she closed her eyes. It all seemed like a horrific nightmare. She remembered getting shot. She remembered pulling the bullets out of Adam, and when he pulled the bullet out of her leg. She remembered climbing the body mound, sometimes slipping and having to reclimb in spots, as the faces of those passed stared at her, haunting her nightmares. She remembered half-dragging Adam to the safehouse. Then she remembered the peace she felt when she saw the face of Jesus, so she stayed there, resting in that peace.

Adam moaned, as he woke up several hours later.

"Adam?" Stacey asked.

"Was that him?" Scott asked, jumping up from his chair.

"Think so. Adam?" Stacey asked.

"I'm here," Adam said weakly.

Scott went over to Adam's side of the bed. "Here, tuck this under your tongue," he said, slipping the thermometer into Adam's mouth. "Very good," he said after a minute. "How are you feeling?"

"Better," Adam said. "Do I still have a temperature?"

"Just a low-grade. Believe it or not, Stacey's is actually higher right now," he pointed out. "How do you feel? Any dizziness? I know you were up earlier, but your temperature was still high."

"I really could use some food," Adam said.

"I can get it after I check out Stacey."

"That's okay," Adam said, getting off the bed. "I'll get hers and mine."

"You shouldn't jump out of bed just yet," Scott said.

"I'll be back in a few," Adam said, ignoring Scott's directions.

Scott sighed, shaking his head. "He's stubborn."

"Yes. He is," Stacey agreed. "But that's how he is."

"Your turn," Scott said, as he went to Stacey's side of the bed. He slid a new cover onto the thermometer and stuck it in her mouth. While the thermometer took her temperature, he took her blood pressure. When he finished her blood pressure, he asked, "So, after this mess is over, what's next on your agenda? Being a superhero in a different city? You know, there's good versus evil everywhere."

Stacey reached up and took the thermometer out of her mouth. "Not really *everywhere*."

"What do you mean? And before you answer that, I need your temp so leave that in," he said, putting the thermometer back in her mouth.

After a minute, he took it back out, and Stacey simply said, "Good and evil cannot co-exist."

"Well that was profound."

"But it's true. Where God reigns, evil cannot exist. In Heaven, there is no evil."

"So, knowing that you're a Christian, is it good to have you and your boyfriend in the same bed?" Scott asked, changing the subject.

"Considering that neither of us have been conscious enough for anything to happen, I think it was okay. However, I am going to ask for a new room, or roommate, now that we're both more coherent."

"Afraid you're going to get denied. If you weren't in here, you'd land back in the pack," he said. "You know only those in need of medical attention, along with Matt and his wife, have the bedrooms."

"That's true. So, how far off are we from being done with this mess?" Stacey asked.

"Not sure. I heard a couple agents say they're pretty close. I can't imagine it'll be too much longer. The town's kind of being held hostage in this. If it goes on too much longer, they'll have to call in the National Guard. I *do* know they want to make sure they have all the evidence they need to convict. Speaking of which, think you can remember where that mass grave is?"

"Not sure." She shook her head. "My fever was pretty high, and I don't know my way around here enough. I honestly don't ever want to see that place again!" She shuddered.

"Aww, my image of you is shattered," he said with a smile. "Here, I thought you were one of those tough girls."

"I threw-up for like ten minutes straight...and totally freaked out when I realized what was around me!" She shook her head. "It was terrifying! Sorry. Tough girl, I'm not."

"I think you're tougher than you give yourself credit for."

Just then Adam walked in. "Hey guys! Here ya go, Stace," he said, bringing her a plate of food.

"Thank you," Stacey said, appreciatively.

"When you two are done, Adam, you're going back to the pack. Stacey, I'd like you to stay up here for tonight. I'm keeping close tabs on your fever. It's still a little higher than I would like," Scott said.

"It probably didn't help that her bullet was taken out after mine," Adam said. "We should have pulled yours out first."

"If we did, you may not have made it," Scott said. "You were touch and go for a bit...both of you were. I can't image it was all that sanitary."

"It was sketchy at best," Adam agreed.

"Okay then," Scott stood. He handed Stacey two aspirin, as he said, "Take these when you're done eating, and get some more rest."

Stacey jokingly saluted him before he left. "Yes, sir."

Adam and Stacey ate dinner before Stacey took her medicine and went to sleep. Adam closed the door as he left the room. He did not want to leave her up there, but he knew he had to follow the instructions given. Scott had full authority when it came to medical and everyone had to follow.

LATER THAT NIGHT, Stacey heard someone in the room. She went to turn on the light, but stopped mid-reach when she heard a male voice say, "Don't move."

Heart racing, she gulped.

Scott opened the door as he lightly knocked on it. "Stacey," he whispered, "I need to check your temperature."

"Scott, are we the only ones in here?" she asked, hoping with every bone in her body they were.

As soon as he flipped the light on, Brad and Shane jumped on Scott, while Kyle lunged for Stacey. She could not believe her eyes, when she saw Marissa just standing in the corner with her arms crossed, glaring at Stacey.

"Please let this be a nightmare?" Stacey asked.

"Nope. This is justice," Marissa said, as Kyle placed a cloth over Stacey's mouth.

As she was going unconscious, she saw Scott knock Brad out. Just as he did, Shane immediately took Scott out, and they both lay on the floor unconscious.

SHANE AND KYLE CARRIED STACEY, with her going in and out of consciousness. It took them over forty-five minutes to make their way through the backwoods to the other side of town. They took her to one of the warehouse buildings, which the Slater house group already targeted as one of their hideouts.

"Tie her up," Kyle said, nonchalantly, as he dropped Stacey's feet. "I'll be over there in a minute," he said. Then Kyle went over to talk to his dad.

When he dropped Stacey's feet, Shane grabbed under her shoulders to stop her from dropping to the ground. Stacey groaned, but he continued to drag her across the warehouse to the other side, where there was a chair and a mattress.

"Come on! Work with me here, Stacey!" Shane snapped, dropping her onto a chair. Then he swore when she fell forward a bit. "Trying to tie you when you're like a ragdoll isn't easy."

"Sorry...maybe I'll...go easier on you next time. I..." Stacey said, and then felt her head drop as she closed her eyes.

"Hey, Chandler? Can't we tie her to a bed?" Shane yelled across the room to him. "She's passing out on me."

"No. Leave her there."

"Fine," Shane said on a sigh. Then he swore under his breath again before he said, "Sure, he gets to sit back and relax while I have to tie you up." He shook his head, as he wrapped her arms behind her, securing her hands with zip ties. Then he tied Stacey's ankles to the chair with zip ties, before he got up and went over to the others.

Her head swimming, Stacey periodically opened and closed her eyes, trying to look around. Shaking and dizzy at the same time, she finally raised her head, and asked, "Um...Kyle?"

"She speaks!" Kyle smiled as he walked over to her. "Shane must have forgotten the tape."

"Kyle, I need food."

"Not until you talk to me."

"I'm hypoglycemic. If you don't give me food, I'll die...and you won't get the answers you want," she said, and then dropped her head. "I need food."

He walked over and crouched in front of her. "Well, this is an interesting situation," he said as he reached up with his hand and moved her hair out of her face. "Want to talk to me first?"

"Food."

"Talk."

Stacey sighed as she rolled her eyes. "What do you want? I don't have time for games."

"You're pretty demanding considering the position you're in."

"Kyle," Stacey said, and then felt her head spin even worse. She moaned. "I need to lay down."

"Nope. Just relax. *If* I get the urge, I *might* feed you something."

"I can only go so long, and then it won't matter," Stacey said. Then she looked up, trying to refocus. "Please?"

"You're begging me? Oooo! I like that!" He grinned. "But you see, now that we've lost, not only one of our inside people, but also Brad...well, we need to know what you guys know. Not that Marissa wasn't just chockfull of information, mind you, but her main concern was with you and Adam. And golly gee, since he's not here..." his voice faded.

"Adam's your cousin."

"What?" he said, his hand near his ear as if he could not hear her. "You need to speak up."

"He's your cousin," Stacey said. "You shouldn't hate him this much."

"Oh, it's not him. It's what he stands for."

"God?"

"Yep. It's kind of like this, we're on opposite sides in that particular war. He's all nicey-nice, and I'm more on the...hmmm, how can I word it? Well," he said, resting his elbow on his knee, "I'm on the side that enjoys our power." Then he got louder, and more in Stacey's face with each syllable, as he said, *"and-don't-like-it-when-people-take-it-away!"*

"Kyle...food," Stacey begged.

"I'll tell ya what," he said, still within an inch of her face.

Stacey barely got her eyes open to look at him.

"You deny your God, and I'll give you all the food you want. We can talk information later."

Stacey shook her head, confused. *"What?"*

"You don't really believe that a God who loves you would put you through this, do you? Would He let what all has taken place happen to you if He loved you? Would He *really* take your mom away from you, only to have you end up *here* of all places? That's not including everything that happened to you that has since you moved here? Come on! If someone *really* loved you, would they *really* do that to you?"

"I..." Stacey shook her head, trying to think. Between whatever he knocked her out with, along with the lack of food, her head spun out of control. It was difficult for her to focus on anything.

"You're on the wrong side, Stacey. You need to be on *this* side of things. This is the side that gets what we want. I'm talking the best of everything. On *this* side, people do what you tell them to do. People listen to you. Have you ever felt that people weren't listening you?"

"Yes," Stacey admitted.

"Have you ever wanted something so bad, that to not have it actually hurt?"

Stacey thought about Adam, and longed to be with him so she nodded.

"Have you ever wanted to be with someone, and they choose to be with someone else?" He asked.

"Yes," she admitted.

She felt his breath on her face as he talked to her in a low voice. His eyes drilling deep into her very soul. "Well, on *this* side, *that* doesn't happen. On *this* side, you get *what* you want *when* you want it. Would you like that?"

Stacey squinted to see better. Everything around her swirled, blurring together.

"Stacey, all you have to do is say that God doesn't really exist. All you have to say is you don't believe in Him. Just admit that you don't believe in Jesus."

"That's...a lie," Stacey said.

Her eyes got huge as he stood up and pulled back his arm. She braced for impact as he slammed his fist forward, punching her square in the jaw. It felt like he hit her with a bat.

As her face pulsated in pain from where his punch landed, she felt the warmth of the blood fill her mouth. She spit a mouthful onto the ground beside her.

"He *doesn't* exist!" Kyle shouted, getting back in her face. "If He did, then He would free you from this!"

"Yes. He *does* exist," Stacey said defiantly.

She shut her eyes and braced for what she knew was coming. Kyle punched her in the jaw again, this time on the opposite side. Then he punched her stomach. She gasped for air, hoping to get the precious air into her lungs. Then he went to punch her on the jaw again, but missed, hitting the side of her head. Stacey moaned and groaned, with not enough air in her system to yell as loud as she wanted. It came out more as a squeak, while she continued to gasp for air.

Down near her face, Kyle growled, "*Obviously*, I need to make my point more forcefully!"

"No." Stacey shook her head. Blood dripped from her mouth, landing on her clothes. Every part of her body throbbed in pain. "They…exist," she said, barely a whisper. Then she looked up at him. A blood-soaked smile appeared on her face as she added a little louder, "and…in the end…we win."

Seeing him stand up, she braced for what she knew was coming again. He picked up his foot, and then kicked her front left side, mid-section. Stacey groaned in agony, praying the precious air she needed would fill her burning lungs quickly. Feeling at least a couple ribs crack under the pressure, the pain and agony was unbearable. The chair actually went back onto the ground, hitting Stacey's head on the concrete under her.

Kyle set her back up. His strength was astounding. "They don't win!" he said, picking up the back of her chair, and then slammed it down. *WE DO!*" He roared, from behind her. Then, moving back around to the front, he continued, "And *this* battle? You *will* lose!" he said, and then squeezed her collar bone until he heard it snap.

"Ahhh-eeee!" Stacey screamed in excruciating pain. The tears streamed down her face, as she did her best just to get air.

"Ooooo! That worked!" Kyle smiled. "I'll bet that will get you to say *whatever* I want!" He tightened his grip.

Stacey felt the bones move, scraping each other. She

screamed at the top of her lungs. This was a new level of pain for her – a level she never experienced in her entire life!

"Is the Slater house the only house they are in?" Kyle demanded.

"I'm not..." Stacey shook her head. Before she could say anything else, he squeezed her collar bone again. "Ahhhh-eeeeee!" she screamed in horrific pain through gritted teeth.

"Answer the question! Is it the only house?"

Stacey did not say anything, so he pulled back on her hair. Less than an inch away from her face, he asked, "Would a God of love *really* do this to one of His? Deny Him and I'll set you free."

"Never," Stacey said, and spit blood out of her mouth. The blood splattered all over Kyle's face and shirt.

He stepped back. And then he did a round-about kick, his boot landing on the side of her head, knocking her over. When she was on the ground, he kicked her in the stomach a couple times.

"Hey! Take it easy, Chandler! If you kill her, we *definitely* won't get any information," Shane's dad snapped.

"She's finished...for a while anyway," he said, disgusted, and kicked her one more time. "Just for good measure," he said with a shrug when Shane's dad narrowed his eyes at Kyle.

Stacey lay on the ground, still tied to the chair, ready to pass out. She fought through the pain and agony as she listened to them talking.

"You should feed her if she's hypoglycemic," Marcus Chandler said, thinking. "If she dies, she won't be worth anything."

"Fine!" Kyle said in a huff.

"I'll do it," Shane said, getting up from the table where he, Amber, Erin, and C.J. were playing cards.

"Is this like feeding the dog?" Erin asked in a chuckle.

"Erin, knock it off!" Shane snapped, as he went over to the kitchen. He grabbed a candy bar, as well as a sandwich and a water bottle. He set them on the ground next to Stacey's chair. Then he set her back up, chair and all. Once she was upright, he knelt in front of her and quietly said, "All right, can you eat this for me?"

"I...no...pain," Stacey moaned.

"You have to. You're going to crash. And unlike the rest of those cretins, I actually care what happens to you," he said in a whisper so only she could hear him.

She looked at him with only one of her eyes partially opened – the other was already swollen shut. "What?" she asked, dumbfounded by his change of attitude.

"You didn't see what happened after we knocked you out at the Slater's. Kyle made us leave Brad since he was unconscious. We needed to carry you. I don't like that he made us leave Brad behind. You *never* leave a man behind. I don't like any of this either. I hate that they killed Allen. I hate that they killed the other people from town. The only reason they killed them was because they had the guts to go against them. I hate that they get to pick and choose who dies and who lives. I hate that I have to put up with Erin too." He rolled his eyes. "She's as evil as the rest of them, but I *have* to." He shook his head. "I was born into it," he explained, while feeding her a bite of the candy bar. "I didn't have a choice. Good job, Stacey. Keep eating. Just know I'll make sure you get food."

Stacey raised an eyebrow.

Shane chuckled. "Your face gives you away every time. Look, I'm not like them, I have a heart," he said, giving her another bite, still talking quietly so only Stacey could hear him.

"Then...why?" Stacey asked. She slowly chewed, and then swallowed the bite.

"Because they'll kill anyone who opposes them. Adam's brother and mom are perfect examples," he said as he fed her the rest of the candy bar. Then he moved onto the sandwich and the water. When she finished, he said, "There, that should help shortly."

"Pain," Stacey moaned.

"I know. Just relax. Get some rest, okay?" He said, patting her knee.

"Shane!" Erin snapped. "It's taking you long enough. Come on already. She's just a dog," she said. She got up and walked over to Stacey and Shane. Standing beside Stacey, Erin smacked the top of her head, as if to pat it really hard, making Stacey dizzy. "Did you eat your food? Good doggy," she said, and then laughed. She tapped Stacey's cheek, and then she walked off.

Shane watched her leave. He rolled his eyes and shook his head, disgusted. "*She* needs a leash!" he said under his breath.

"Tired...pain..." Stacey said, her head dropping.

"Do you need more sugar?" he asked, concerned.

Stacey nodded, so he got up and got her a small bag Peanut M&M's. "Here ya go," he said feeding them to her.

"Shane, leave her alone already." His mom shook her head. "She's just another pathetic –"

"Mom!" Shane snapped.

"Shane Michael!" His mom looked at him, appalled. "What is wrong with you?"

"Shane," his dad warned.

"I'm fine. Just give me a minute," he said, shaking his head. Kneeling in front of Stacey, he said, "See? They gang up on me all the time. If I don't listen, they get mean. Have you heard about my brother?"

Stacey nodded.

"My parents are worse, and they double-team me."

Stacey nodded in understanding. He fed her the rest of the M&M's before he got up, leaving her sitting there by herself to drift off to sleep. Between the pain and her sugar levels bouncing all over the place, she was so far beyond exhausted that she literally could not see straight. She finally fell asleep still attached to the chair.

∾

PARTWAY THROUGH THE NIGHT, Stacey felt someone jostle her. Her entire body hurt. She was sore, yet stiff and in pain everywhere.

"Stacey?" Shane whispered. "Stacey, wake up."

"Shane?"

"Shh!" He hushed her. "Here, I got this for you," he said, and then fed her a bag of M&M's, another sandwich, and a bottle of water.

"Um..." she said, finishing her food.

"What?" he asked.

"I have to go to the bathroom. I drank too much water."

"I don't know if I can –"

"Please?"

"Promise not to pull anything on me?"

"I won't. I just need to go to the bathroom," she said, her bladder feeling as if it would explode.

He cut the zip ties on her wrists and ankles, and then helped her to the bathroom. She was too weak to do anything else. When they returned, she let him secure a new set of zip ties.

"Good," he said, kneeling in front of her.

"Good...what?"

"I feel we can trust each other. I also think if we're going to get out of here alive, we will *need* to trust each other."

"Will you go let Adam and my dad know where I am?"

"I'm afraid I can't do that."

"If you tell them where I am, then you can get out of here. You'll also be able to make a deal for your information. And if you get me out of here, I can testify for you."

"Stacey," he narrowed his eyes, "what's in it for you?"

"I get out of here."

"Stace, I…" He shook his head. "I'm sorry. I can't do it."

"Shane, do you or don't you want out?"

"I do, but –"

"Then go tell them where I am. Tell them everything you know. If they raid these places simultaneously, they'll get everyone at once."

He smiled. "You're starting to wake up, aren't you?"

"Please?"

"All right," he finally agreed. "Just do what you can to stay alive until they can get back here. Okay?"

Stacey nodded, and then closed her eyes. Exhaustion and pain were taking over once again.

"Just stay alive," he said, and then he quietly left through one of the side doors.

With her eyes closed, she said a long prayer for Shane's safety, bravery, and courage to do what he needed to do. Then, she went to sleep.

CHAPTER 12

"I SURVIVED BECAUSE THE FIRE INSIDE
ME BURNED BRIGHTER THAN THE FIRE
AROUND ME." JOSHUA GRAHAM

"Hey! Wake up!" Kyle said, slapping Stacey across the face. "We need to talk!"

Stacey shook her head.

He got in Stacey's face. "Yes."

"Um, Kyle?" Amber said, her voice on edge. "Why do you have to get so close to her?"

"Shut up!" He snapped, looking over his shoulder at her. "*You* can be dealt with later."

"Sorry," she said, looking down, fiddling with a piece of paper on the table.

"Now," he said, looking back to Stacey. He was within three inches of her face. Bent in half, with his hands on his knees so he was at eye level with her, he said, "It *seems* that we're missing someone. You wouldn't *happen* to know where he went, do you?"

"Who?" Stacey asked.

"Shane! That's who! You were talking to him last night when he gave you dinner. What did you say to him? Hmm?"

"Nothing." Stacey shook her head. "He just fed me."

"Liar!" He said, and slapped her across the face. "Tell me where he went!"

"How am I supposed to know?"

"Tell me!"

"I don't –"

"Liar!" He shouted, and squeezed her right collar bone tightly.

"Ahhheeee!" she screeched. "That...Kyle! Please stop!" she begged.

"Then tell me what I want to know!" he shouted, not loosening his grip on the collar bone he broke. "I want to know the location of the other safehouses. I also want to know where Shane went."

"I don't–ahhhhh!" she screamed again.

His hand was like a vice. "TELL ME!" he roared.

Stacey could not speak due to the immeasurable pain she was experiencing.

"Tell me!" he demanded. "Where is he?" When she did not answer, he stood and rubbed his chin in thought. "Say, just how hungry are you?"

"I'm not!" She glared at him, breathing through the pain. The sweat mixed with the blood from where he slapped her as it dripped off her face onto her T-shirt and jeans.

He crossed his arms. "You were hungry last night."

"I'm not now," she said through gritted teeth.

"Oh, I think you look thirsty. Don't you guys?" he asked over his shoulder.

A couple rather large, burly guys got up from the table. One of them grabbed a few bottles of water, and then they walked over. Kyle grabbed Stacey's hair and pulled back. He then pressed down on her left shoulder so she could not move. Then, while one of the guys held her mouth open, the other one poured the bottle of water into it.

Stacey could not breathe. When she tried to get air, the

water went down the wrong pipe, and she started to choke. She felt like she was drowning sitting in the chair.

Ease up a sec, guys," Kyle said, covering her mouth while he plugged her nose. "Suck it down, babe!" he said. "Then we'll give you some more."

Unable to breathe, she tried to swallow the water to get it out of her mouth. She saw sparkles everywhere, but tried to fight her way out. Kyle held on tighter to her hair and mouth until she passed out.

STACEY WOKE up coughing several minutes later. When she gasped for air, her eyes widened. That's when she saw movement near the ceiling of the warehouse. Squinting to see better, she would swear Scott and Adam were up in the rafters of the warehouse. They were in the shadows wearing all black clothing. Even their faces were painted black. The only reason she saw them, was because of Scott's blond hair. Unsure if she was dreaming or not, she shook her head to clear it. Then she took another look toward where she saw them. Scott put his finger in front of his mouth for her to be quiet. She nodded in response as she coughed up more water.

"Oh good! She's awake for more." Kyle got up from the table. "Come on guys!" He went over to Stacey and yanked her head back by her hair. "Thirsty?"

"No!" she shouted, trembling in fear. If they did it too much, she knew they could kill her.

"Then tell me where Shane went!" Kyle demanded.

"I don't–ahhhh!" She screamed when one of the other guys grabbed her right collar bone.

"All she does is whine." Kyle shook his head. "Let's shut her up again," he said with an evil grin.

The guy tightened his grip on Stacey's broken collar bone.

When she screamed, one of the other guys poured the water in, and then Kyle covered her mouth and plugged her nose.

She felt like she was in a horrible nightmare! She struggled to get air, but every time she did, she ended up sucking down more water.

Just when she thought she would pass out again, she heard a loud commotion. It was followed by agents and police officers with guns running in to the warehouse. They fired their guns into the air before shouting for everyone to freeze or get down.

When the gunfire slowed down, one of the agents aimed his gun at Kyle, and shouted, "Let her go!"

Kyle let go of Stacey, and put his hands in the air. Stacey gasped for air. Instead of getting air, she sucked in a lot of the water still in her mouth. She started choking again.

Adam and Scott were on their way down as soon as the agents burst through the door. As Adam and Scott hit the ground, gunfire came flying in from behind the agents, and a gun battle ensued.

Scott ran up behind Stacey, with Adam at a close second. Adam cut the ties, while Scott tried to help Stacey get air. He tilted her head forward. "Cough it out, Stace!" He yelled, patting her back.

"She's free!" Adam shouted after he released her hands and ankles.

Together, they pulled Stacey over to the side, ducking the gunfire swirling around them.

"Breathe!" Scott said, as they huddled in the corner. "Come on, Stacey, breathe!"

No matter how hard she tried, she could not get air. The black cloud threatened to overtake her once again.

"Oh, I don't think so!" Scott said, and laid her flat. He did two breaths of air, a couple chest compressions, and rolled her to the side. He repeated this until Stacey coughed up water. Scott turned Stacey's head to the side until the water drained, and she finally got a huge gulp of air. "Good job!" Scott encouraged.

Adam picked Stacey up, holding her to his chest. "I'm sorry we didn't get here sooner," he said, holding her tightly to his body.

"It's..." She shook her head and closed her eyes.

"Stace?" Scott slid in front of Stacey, blocking them from the view of anyone watching. "Stacey?" He asked, tapping her face.

"Pain...hurt...tired," she moaned, breathing heavily. "He broke my collar bone and a few ribs."

"I know. We saw a little bit of it. I'm sorry," Adam said, heartbroken. Then he said to Scott, "We really need to get her to the hospital."

"I know. Once this mess clears," Scott explained, as there was still yelling and fighting going on around them. "There is too much commotion right now."

"Stacey, can you hold on for me?" Adam reached up, putting his hand on the side of her face. Stacey nodded in response. "Good, because I would have a hard time living life without you now that I've had you in it." Looking to Scott for help, Adam said, "She doesn't look good."

The gunfire slowed. There was still a lot of yelling while the agents tried to get things under control.

"No, she doesn't. I'm going to call for life flight to come and get her and take her to Cleveland." Scott walked over to where it was a little quieter so he could hear on his cell phone.

"Stacey," Adam said, looking back down. He laid her down on his lap. Running his fingers through her hair, he said, "I'm so sorry. I wish we could have been here sooner."

"I'm fine," Stacey said between coughs. Then she reached up and touched his face. "Your eyes are such a pretty blue."

"Thanks." He smiled, a few tears escaping onto his cheek. "Your eyes are very pretty too. I didn't think I was going to see them again by what Shane told us."

"Is he okay?"

"He will be. He gave us a ton of information, and is willing to testify as well. Since he came voluntarily, they're considering him a federal witness, and will be granted immunity for testifying. They're also going to place him in the witness protection program afterward." He smiled as he looked down at her. "He said you were the reason he did it."

"I asked him to," Stacey explained.

"How are you feeling now? Your coughing has slowed."

"I'm –"

"Adam! Look out!" Scott shouted, cutting Stacey off as he ran toward them.

Several men looked up, trying to get their guns up in time to shoot Kyle, who had had a gun in his hand aimed directly at Adam and Stacey. Kyle got off one shot before they killed him where he stood. It all happened in what seemed like slow motion, but it was done in a split second. Adam and Stacey did not have any time to react.

"Adam!" Stacey stared at Adam horrified

Adam looked down. Kyle shot him, grazing his neck, severing the carotid artery. Adam's eyes wondered back to Kyle in time to see Kyle drop to the ground dead.

"Adam! God, please help him!" Stacey shouted, as she went hysterical. Her adrenaline kicked into high gear, as panic took over. "Adam!"

Scott dropped to his knees in front of them. "Stacey, are you okay?" he asked her.

"It's not me! It's Adam! Help him!" She sobbed. Reaching up, she touched his face as he put his head back on the wall. "Oh God! No!" Stacey screamed. "*Please no! Save him! Adam!* Scott, help him!"

"Adam, buddy," Scott said, struggling to concentrate through Stacey's hysterics without losing it himself. He pressed his hand onto Adam's neck in an effort to slow the bleeding. Meanwhile, he kept track of Adam's weakening pulse, feeling it through the wound. "You can't do this, Adam! It's over! You made it! It's done!" he said. The tears crawled down his cheeks as he struggled to keep himself composed. "Come on, man! She needs you! Adam, stay with me. We've been through too much for you to go now. Come on!"

Stacey continued to cry and scream for Adam over and over again, unable to move off his lap.

When Adam looked down at her, Stacey put both hands on his cheeks. "You're-you're still here," she said, tears streaming down her cheeks.

Hearing the chopper landing down the road at the airport, Adam gulped. He had a look of peace and serenity in his eyes. "I love you," he said, rubbing his thumb on her cheek. "Always remember how much I truly love you," he said. Then he took his last breath of air, dropped his head back to the wall, and closed his eyes.

Stacey gasped. "Adam? Adam! Adam! No-no-no-no-no! Please, no!" she screamed, sobbing uncontrollably. "Adam! No! Please! Please come back!"

Scott slid Stacey off Adam's lap and held her as they both cried. "I couldn't do anything. I'm so sorry, Stacey," Scott whispered, as he rocked her back and forth amongst her sobs.

One of the other agents came over and checked for a pulse. He just shook his head. Standing, he placed his jacket over Adam. "You should get her away from here," the agent said to Scott. "They need to get to him, and she's a mess."

The life flight paramedics ran in and looked around. "Oh wow!" one of them said, looking at the carnage. "We need more than a chopper and an ambulance. This is a war zone!"

"It's for this one," Scott called out from where he was holding Stacey. "The others are probably dead."

"What happened here?" one of them asked as he knelt next

to Scott and Stacey, while his partner went to see if anyone else was alive.

"A raid gone bad," Scott said, holding Stacey. Her sobbing downgraded down to a steady stream by that point. "Incredibly bad," Scott said as he shook his head.

CHAPTER 13

Stacey woke up off and on over the course of the next several days. Every time she woke, she remembered what happened in the warehouse, and cried herself back to sleep without a word.

"Stacey?" Scott asked, about three days after the raid. "Stacey, can you please wake up?"

Stacey opened her eyes and looked at him, immediately bursting into tears. She had the figure-eight splint on her right arm, securing it to her body with a sling. This made her movement limited until her collar bone healed.

"Okay, you need to calm that down. I know you miss him, but you know where he is."

"You're not a Christian. You don't believe in God. You said it yourself."

"I do now. Adam and I did a lot of talking the night they took you."

"How can you –?" She shook her head, tears pouring down her cheeks.

"Please stop," Scott said. "You're scaring everyone. They're worried about you."

"Why would a God of love do this to me?" Stacey demanded. "Maybe He's not real after all."

"I need Matt!" Scott shook his head, not sure what else to do. He quietly got up and left to find Matt, while Stacey cried herself back to sleep.

~

STACEY WOKE the next day to hear Matt quoting Psalm 23, much the same as Adam did when they were in the pit. She cried as memories from the pit flooded her mind. When he finished with the Psalm, he went on to the next verse Adam also quoted, *"Be still! And know that I am God."*

Stacey turned and glared at Matt. "God? If He were *really* God, then why did He let all this happen?" she shouted through her tears. "How can I have peace, when it seems that anyone I get close to dies? Peace? Ha! That's a crock!"

"That's a lie planted in your head by Satan himself," Matt said, and then bowed his head silently in prayer.

"You can quit that." Stacey rolled her eyes. "If God was *really* a God of love, He wouldn't have let things get so bad. He would have stopped this." Stacey pushed herself up in the bed with her left hand, getting angrier by the second. "Why would He take away my mom? My *mother*! And why would He take Adam? Adam had the most tender soul of anyone..." Angry tears streamed down her cheeks. "Of anyone I have ever known! *Why?*" she demanded. "*Why would He do this*? If He were real, why didn't He put a stop to all of this? Why would He let this stuff happen to His children if He were real?"

Matt hung his head and sighed. "That's the question we've all been struggling with lately. It hit you harder because of Adam."

"I'll bet Marissa's pretty happy now. Adam's not in my life anymore. He's not in *anyone's* life anymore. Because of she self-ishness, she turned me in to them. Did you know that? *She led them into my room so they could kidnap me.* Do you understand what happened? The end result of her actions was that Adam was killed. They almost killed me too. I hope she's satisfied," Stacey shouted, her body trembling.

"Please, don't be bitter," Matt said calmly.

"Bitter? Bitter! You want bitter? I'll give you bitter!" Stacey swung her legs over the bed as she gingerly pushed up with her left hand due to her ribs. Grabbing the IV pole, she pulled herself up.

Matt jumped to block her. "Where do you think you're going? There is no way you are leaving here. Look at yourself."

Scott, Sam, Becky, Harmony, Melody, Brian, Alex, Randy, and Marissa walked into the room. Zoning in on Marissa, Stacey narrowed her eyes at her.

"What's going on?" Scott asked. "Why are you out of bed?"

"You want bitter, Matt?" Stacey said, glaring at Matt, ignoring Scott. "*I'll* show you bitter!" she shouted, and went to jump at Marissa. Scott and Sam jumped to stop Stacey, as Marissa backed against the wall, petrified. "*That* girl is the reason Adam is dead!" she shouted, as Scott and Sam held her back, doing their best not to injure her even worse. Struggling in their arms, Stacey's face was red with anger. Running completely on adrenaline, she shouted, "It's *your* fault! *You* were the one who let them into the house! *You* were working with Kyle the entire time!" Then Stacey looked at the others, "How *dare* you bring this...this wretched, vile piece of venom into my room! Get her out of here! I don't *ever* want to see her again!"

Melody grabbed Marissa by the arm. She and Brian left with Marissa out of the room. Marissa was in tears.

"You need to calm down!" Sam said sternly.

"No! I need to let her know what it feels like to get the life beaten out of her!"

Scott and Sam slammed Stacey against the wall to try to get her under control. She groaned in pain before she remembered seeing Marissa, and then she struggled to get free again. "Where'd she go?" Stacey demanded. She was livid. The anger consumed her to the point that she could not feel the pain anymore. "Let me go!" she shouted, struggling. "Let me go!"

"Someone go get the nurse!" Matt yelled over her shouting, as he also had a hand on her midsection to keep her against the wall.

"We'll go," Randy said, as he and Harmony left the room.

"Let me go! Let me go! She killed Adam! She's responsible for killing him! It's all her fault! Let me go!" Stacey shouted while struggling to get free.

Randy and Harmony were back in a matter of seconds with the nurse. "I'm sorry, I was on my way in," the nurse said with a syringe in her hand. "I heard her."

"Don't you dare!" Stacey stopped struggling as she narrowed her eyes at the nurse. "That girl betrayed us all, and you're going to just knock me out? I'll wake up again. And when I do, I will get my hands on her and –"

"You'll *what?*" Alex got in her face. Matt put a hand on Alex to keep him separated from Stacey. "*What* are *you* going to do?" Alex demanded.

"I'll let her know what it feels like to have her heart ripped out! I'll let her know what it feels like to see the one you love literally die in front of your very eyes! He had his hand on my face. He told me he loved me as his life drained out of him," she said, feeling a warmth circulate through her body. While Stacey was yelling, unbeknownst to her the nurse put the medicine into her IV. "I'll let her know what..." Stacey shook her head, starting to melt. Things blurred together and swirled in the room around her. "I'll let her know what it feels like to...to feel death so close...so-so many times in a matter of days...to...whoa," she said, her legs buckling.

"Time for bed, Stace," Sam said, while he and Scott dragged Stacey back to bed.

"She has no idea!" Stacey said, tears still pouring down her cheeks in a steady stream. "None of you have any clue what it's like," she said, as Sam covered her up. Stacey's breath shuddered, and then her head fell to the side. The medicine took over as she went unconscious.

"I gave her a little more than I probably should have," the nurse confessed. "As riled up as she was, I didn't think the normal amount would take. I'll let the doctor know what happened."

"Thank you," Sam said appreciatively.

Harmony shuddered. "That was...wow!"

"*That* is a hurting woman," Matt said. "The hold that's on her right now is strong. We need to pray, and we need to pray hard. There's a struggle going on inside her that's shredding her from the inside." He shook his head. "I don't know what they did to her while they had her, but..." his voice trailed as he crossed his arms.

"It was scary," Scott said. "At least what we saw was. They were trying to drown her with a bottle of water. They would pour it in, and then cover her mouth and plug her nose. When she didn't open her mouth, Kyle grabbed her collar bone. We didn't know he broke it earlier until she told me on the way to the hospital. He would grab it, so she would open her mouth screaming in pain. Then they would force the water down her throat. Afterward, Kyle would plug her nose and mouth until she went unconscious. He would literally drown her in the chair. If Shane didn't come and tell us where she was, she could have died by Kyle's hands. Pretty sure that was his intention."

"Kyle kicked and hit her in the head and stomach, cracking a few ribs. He also tried to starve her on top of it," Shane said, as he walked in with two agents on either side of him. "I'm going to go soon. I just wanted to see if she was all right."

"She's not. Thanks to you, she will be with time," Sam said, shaking his hand. "Thank you."

"It was her idea. Tell her I said thank you," he said, and then turned to leave. He stopped and turned back around at the door. "I'm really sorry, guys. I know you won't believe me when I tell you I was just as much a prisoner as you were, but it's true," he said, and left.

"Dad?" Stacey moaned.

"Hey, Peanut, can you open your eyes?" Sam asked, tucking a portion of her hair behind her ear.

"Adam?"

"I'm sorry, honey. He didn't make it."

As soon as he said sorry, tears fell down her cheeks.

"I'm sorry, but I can't stay," Harmony said, wiping her eyes from crying.

"I'll go with you. This is heartbreaking," Randy said.

Together, they left holding hands.

"Can we join hands and pray for her?" Matt asked those who were left.

Stacey fell asleep to the sounds of their prayers to God on her behalf.

"STACEY?" she heard, and then looked up from the field of wild flowers where she sat, to see Jesus again. The feeling of hate and anger welled-up inside her, while her bottom lip trembled.

"What is wrong?" He asked, crouching in front of her.

"*You* let this happen!" she shouted, tears crawling down her cheeks as her body shook. "You let *all* this happen! Every last little bit of it! How could you do this to me?" she asked, looking up at Him. "How? Why?"

"Yours is not to question, my child. Yours is to trust Me."

"Trust You? *Trust You!*" Stacey stood. She clenched her fists around the bundles of wild flowers she had in her hands. "How am I supposed to trust You, when You took away everything I've ever cared for? You took my mother! You took away Adam! He was on *Your* side! How could You do that?"

"Have you ever read about my servant Job?"

"I don't *care* about your servant Job! I *cared* about your servant Adam! I *cared* about people like…like the ones who were at the bottom of that pit we were thrown into," she said, and hung her head. "Those people loved You."

"You have to give all that you are, for all that I am. That is trust. '*Greater love hath no man than this, that a man lay down his life for his friends.*' I did that. You need to be willing to do that."

"I am!" Stacey shouted, exasperated. He calmly stood there, not moving. "Adam did just that! We were *done,* though! Why did you let Kyle shoot him when it was finished?"

"Trust Me."

"I don't trust *anyone* right now."

"You need to trust Me. I am not going to leave you. I have a plan for your life. You only have to trust Me."

Stacey turned away. "I-I can't."

"Stacey?"

Stacey heard Adam's voice, and gasped. She released the flowers, and they slowly fell to the ground at her feet.

"Stacey," Adam said, "you need to trust Him."

She turned and saw his beautiful blue eyes looking right at her. As soon as he touched her shoulder, she dropped to her knees. Tears streamed down her face, as she covered her face with her hands.

"Stacey, there is a struggle within you." Jesus knelt beside her, resting his hand on her back. Lowering her hands from covering her face, He explained, "The struggle is whether or not to believe the words Kyle planted into your head, and ultimately in your heart. The Father did not put those words in your heart. They were sown there by Satan himself."

Stacey looked from Jesus to Adam, her mind a jumbled mess.

"Come. Take a walk with us," Jesus encouraged.

When Stacey stood, He and Adam each took a hand, and they walked for hours.

"See that?" Jesus asked, after about three or four hours of walking and talking.

Stacey saw the most stunning city she ever laid eyes on! There were gold and jewels everywhere. There was even a lake, clear as crystal, along with gates made of pearl.

"Oh my!" Stacey said, awestruck.

Jesus tugged on her hand. "Come."

"To where?"

"This is the Father's house. He wants to see you."

"No...I..." Stacey pulled back, but they held on. "No." Stacey shook her head. "I-I can't."

"You need to see Him," Adam encouraged.

"It's the medicine! I'm either going crazy, or it's the medicine!" Stacey said, her eyes shut tight with her feet planted.

"No. There's a struggle deep within you. It'll all become clear once you go see Him," Adam said, as he gently tugged on Stacey's hand again. "Come with us."

Stacey relented, and let them pull her into a luxurious castle. There were amazing works of art throughout the castle. The walls were lined with gold. The scent of frankincense filled her lungs. Music and song filled the halls.

They walked through the castle where Jesus and Adam seemed to know everyone they walked past. As they walked, Jesus showed her all the various rooms and told of their function...until they stopped in the middle of a hallway. When Stacey looked to see where Jesus gestured, she was met by two very heavy doors made of solid gold with sparkling jewel insets. The elegant and beautiful doors left her in awe. "Is this...?" her voice trailed off.

"Yes. It is the Throne Room. Come," Jesus said, and gently pushed on the doors. They opened without resistance.

They took a couple steps in, and Stacey instantly dropped to the ground, prostrate. Jesus and Adam knelt down on one knee on either side of Stacey with their heads bowed.

"Come closer, my child," The Lord God Almighty said.

She shook her head, unable to make eye contact. She said The Lord was not real. However, there He was, right in front of her. The light was so intensely bright, she almost forgot anyone else was in there with her. The warmth of the light encompassed her completely.

Adam and Jesus remained where they knelt, as the Father reached down and took Stacey's hands into His, pulling her toward the throne.

Stacey shook her head. "This must be a dream."

After He took his seat on the throne, He had Stacey climb onto His lap. When she settled, He wrapped His loving arms around her, holding her close to Himself. "Does this feel like a dream?" He asked.

Stacey shook her head, and then laid it on His chest. A feeling of peace washed over her. She struggled to remember the last time she ever felt that tranquil and relaxed. "They said You weren't real," Stacey said. "They said You didn't care."

"I am...and I do."

"Then why?" she asked, and then immediately regretted asking the question. "I'm–I'm sorry. Please don't be mad at me. I didn't mean to –"

"I know what you meant. I know what is in your heart. You *did* mean to ask the question. That has been your continuous question. However, yours is not to know. Yours is to trust Me, and let Me direct your paths. I will take care of you. And when it is your time, you can come back. It was Adam's time. His journey was complete. The reason he made it out of the pit was to plant the seeds in your father and Scott, and to harvest those seeds within Scott. He did that. He was able to see a lot of harvest in his young life. He fulfilled his purpose. He finished his race. You are not done. There is much you have not seen or done. I have big plans for you that have yet to be fulfilled. Yours is to trust Me, and let Me guide you."

Stacey nodded in response.

"Yours is to *also* go after the one who has wondered," He said. "She needs you, as much as you need her."

"Marissa?" Stacey asked, knowingly. When He nodded, Stacey said, "But she –"

"Is one of Mine," He cut her off. "You two are sisters in the same family. My family. You need to forgive one another, and let Me judge the heart. Trust Me when I say she has been reaping what she has sown. She feels much the same as Judas. Can you be as loving and gracious as I have created you to be, and forgive her? Your sins are no less than hers. Hers may have bigger consequences, but they are the same in My book. And for the record, *Mine* is the one that counts. You not forgiving her, is as much a sin as her betraying you and Adam, and ultimately Adam losing his life. This is a stiff penalty she now has to live with every day of her life."

Stacey mulled His words in her mind. Then, looking up at His kind and loving face, she asked, "You'll take care of me?"

"Always."

Stacey glanced at her hands for a moment, debating in her head. Tears welled-up in her eyes as she forced herself to ask the next question. "You'll-you'll take care of Adam?" she asked, bottom lip trembling.

"Yes. Do not cry for him. He is well taken care of and happy. He is very excited to show you around when it is your time to return home. This you have seen for yourself."

Stacey weighed His words. After a few more moments, she knew what she had to do. "I'm sorry," she said. "Do you forgive me?"

"Of course, My child. All you need to do is ask. All you need to do is speak, and I am listening. I love to hear from each of my children. Now, the answer may not always be yes. It may be no, or even wait, so you have to listen closely. However, never doubt that I *am* listening, and I *am* looking out for you. I know what is best for you." He smiled. "I am here. I love you, my child. I have a great plan for you, you only need to trust Me."

"I trust You and believe in You. Thank You for Your patience and understanding."

"You were misguided. You were deceived. I needed you to understand and clear your heart and mind. It is now time for you to go. You need return and guide the lost sheep back to the fold."

"I'm ashamed of the way I acted toward Marissa."

"You acted out of anger. You were confused, and now you have been enlightened. Go and do what you now know is right," He said, and then set her down.

Adam and Jesus both looked up. As they stood, each took one of Stacey's hands, and together the three left the Throne Room.

"He said I had to go," Stacey finally said, once they returned to the field. She let the Father's words marinate in her mind so she could process during the walk.

Jesus nodded. "Yes. You do."

"I don't want to."

"I know. You will return when it is your time. In the meantime, stay focused on the path in front of you. Keep listening for Our voice to guide you. The Spirit will help you know which direction to take."

"Thank you," Stacey said, and then looked down, thinking.

"Stacey?" Adam asked. "Are you okay?"

"I don't want to leave you."

"You know why I'm here now. I will be fine. There are people willing to look out for you. You may even find love again."

"Adam! No!" she said, hurt.

"Stacey?" He turned her toward him. Resting his hand on the

side of her face, he said, "I love you. You know that. You also know you have your whole life in front of you. If the good Lord chooses to give you another partner to do life with, please don't reject His gift."

"But –"

"I love you. I know you love me. Don't worry about that. We will always be each other's first love," he said, and kissed her cheek. "But there may be another. If you have the gift of finding it twice in one lifetime, take it, receive it. Just know that I love you and always will," he said, and lightly kissed her lips as she closed her eyes.

When she reopened her eyes, she was in the hospital room. Scott was asleep with his head on the bed. "Scott?" Stacey asked, touching his arm with her left hand, her right arm still in the sling.

"Hey you!" He looked up, smiling. "I'm afraid you've had a rough couple of days, but you're looking much better now. You don't look like you're so full of anger anymore."

"How long have I been asleep?"

"It's been about three days since we knocked you out. You had us all scared."

"I'm sorry. Would you please get me something to eat? I'm hungry."

"I really don't want to leave you alone. I haven't left yet, and don't want to start now. Can you wait a little while? Becky and your dad will be coming in soon."

"You haven't left?"

"Not since we flew you in. Well, except to change, go to the bathroom, and take a shower. I do all that in the bathroom off this room, so no, not really."

"You *never* left?"

"No. You were never alone. After everything that happened to you, I didn't have the heart to leave you alone. I didn't want you to wake up in an empty room."

"Thank you."

"Your friends feel really bad for you," he said, uneasy, "but they're also nervous about coming back in after what happened last time."

"I have to apologize to them," Stacey said, toying with her blanket. "I didn't mean to –"

"They know," Scott assured her. "They just don't want to trigger you again."

"I shouldn't have done that."

"It's understandable. After everything you've gone through over the last two months, it's not something uncommon. The fact that you haven't lost it before now is amazing."

"Will you call Marissa? See if she'll come see me?"

"You want...*who*?" he asked, taken aback.

"I need to talk to Marissa."

He shook his head. "Oh, I don't know about that one."

"Please?"

"If you...okay," he relented. "If that's who you want."

"I want you to stay. I want Dad here, too."

"You really..." A grin spread across his face. "You want me to stay? Really?"

"If you want to, I–I would like it if you would. I would enjoy the company. I really could use a good friend right now."

"Sure!" he said happily. "So, you want me to call your dad and your friends then?"

"Specifically, Marissa."

"All right," he said as he got up.

Stacey struggled to sit up and get comfortable while Scott called her dad. He was talking to him for a few minutes, when the nurse came in with some pain medicine.

"Thank you," Stacey said after she took it.

"Since it's been a few days, the medicine is a lower dose," the nurse explained. "How do you feel otherwise?"

"I'm okay," she said with a shrug.

"Okay. I'll call your doctor and get you some food."

"That would be nice. Thank you," Stacey said, and the nurse left.

"So, you're looking a lot better," Scott remarked, tucking his phone into his back pocket. "I'm amazed at the difference a three-day nap gave you."

"Thanks. Did you get a hold of everyone?"

"I talked to your dad, Marissa, and Randy. They'll catch everyone else up. They said to expect the group here in a couple hours."

"Thanks."

"It's kind of boring in here," he said, sitting in the chair next to the bed. "I feel really bad for you. They'll probably keep you here for quite a while."

"Like for how long?"

"You flipped-out. Not that there wasn't a good reason mind you, but still." He shook his head. "What you've gone through has been horrific."

Stacey nodded. "I know."

"But you survived it. You lived to talk about it."

"Adam didn't," Stacey said. She picked up his class ring from the table next to the bed, turning it in her fingers.

Scott reached over and slid Adam's ring onto her right ring finger. Due to its size, it wasn't secure, so he moved it to a bigger finger before taking her hand into his. "Stacey, he loved you with all his heart. You also know you *will* see him again."

"Would you think I was crazy if I told you I had a dream about him...in Heaven."

"No–I...no." He shook his head. "That's understandable."

"It was real. I felt everything. I *know* I went up there. I *know* I was there. I sat on God's lap. God hugged me. I *know* I held Adam's hand. I felt him kiss my lips and my cheek. I *know* it was real."

"I believe you. I had a dream, too," he admitted. "I dreamt I went to Hell, though."

"But I thought –"

"It was when I was on the floor the night they took you. When I woke up, I told Adam about it. He and I talked long into the next morning. It was so real." He shook his head. Then he shuddered. "It was *too* real."

"What about now?"

"I'm just saying I understand. I've never been so scared in my life! I thought you people were crazy until I had that dream. There was like a lake of fire...and the smells...the screams..." He shuddered again. "Then, when Adam told me about Heaven and Hell, and he actually read to me from the Bible about what Hell was really like, I almost had a heart attack right there! I've never even picked up a Bible, much less *read* one. However, what he read to me was *exactly* what I saw. It was as if he was in the dream with me. It was scary!"

"I haven't read a huge amount myself. I'm kind of curious to know if there is anything about what Heaven looks like."

"There is. Here." He pulled a Bible from the nightstand drawer. "It says..." He read all 27 verses from Revelation 21 about the New Jerusalem.

While he read, Stacey closed her eyes, remembering what the castle and surrounding area looked like in her dream. It was almost a perfect match. "I was there!" she said when he finished. "It *was* real!"

He smiled. "Cool." Closing the Bible, he looked at her.

"What?" she asked after a minute.

"Nothing. I'm just glad to see you're back. You were totally not yourself the other day. It was terrifying just how scary you looked. It was like you were possessed or something."

"I *was* possessed with anger and hate," she admitted. "That's why I need to talk to Marissa. That wasn't me, and she needs to know that."

"I'm sure she does."

"Even if she does, I really *do* need to apologize."

"Okay." He shrugged. "So, did you –"

"Hi," the nurse said, coming in with a wheelchair.

"What's that for?" Stacey asked.

"With your flying leap, Dr. McMillan wants a new set of x-rays, so he can see if you did more damage."

"Oh. Okay," Stacey agreed.

The nurse got Stacey into the wheelchair, and wheeled her down to x-ray. It took several minutes to get all the x-rays of her clavicle and ribs.

By the time they returned, Sam and Becky were in the room talking with Scott. Scott helped the nurse get Stacey back into bed before the nurse left.

"You're looking *much* better today," her dad said, pleased.

"I feel better," Stacey said, "but I really want to get out of here."

"That will be up to the doc –"

Dr McMillan walked into the room, cutting Sam off. "Howdy, folks!"

"Great timing," Sam said.

Dr. McMillan pulled a chair next to the bed and opened Stacey's file. Spreading it out onto the bed, he said, "I have to tell you that I'm impressed."

"About?" Stacey asked.

"Well, after your excitement the other day, I was seriously concerned you may have done more damage."

"And?" Stacey asked.

"Nope. None. Your bones are healing extremely well." He got up, placing the x-rays on the lightboard for Sam and Scott to see. As the three stood there studying the x-rays, the doctor continued, "The breaks are here, here, here, and there. They were hairline fractures of the ribs. The clavicle is the worst of the breaks, but even that's still in place." Then he turned to

Stacey and Becky, and said, "The nurse said your disposition has vastly improved as well. I'm considering sending you home."

Becky smiled. "Sweet!"

As soon as she said it, Stacey's head spun toward her, bottom lip trembling.

"What's wrong?" Scott asked.

"Adam said that all the time. I-I can't," Stacey said, shaking her head as a few tears escaped. "In here, I don't have to see places where we've been. In here, I don't have to remember he's gone. That's why we moved from Michigan. The memories of Mom were too much."

"We cannot keep moving because it's too hard," Sam said. He understood her pain, but this was a different circumstance. "There are some things you can't run from."

"Was he buried yet?"

"Yes," Sam admitted, sitting on the side of her bed. "His dad buried him a few days ago. We were trying to wait for you. It became apparent you wouldn't be out anytime soon when you went lost it the other day. Ben decided to go forward with his funeral. We can have our own memorial service once you're out of here."

As soon as he said *memorial service*, Stacey burst into tears. She lay down, rolling over onto her side. She stared at Adam's ring, lost in thoughts of Adam.

Harmony, Randy, and Marissa walked into the room.

When no one said anything, Marissa said, "Stacey, you have every right to say what you said to me the other day. I'm really sorry."

Stacey knew she needed to say something. At that time, she could not form a single thought, except to see Adam's face in her mind smiling and laughing.

"Can you forgive me?" Marissa asked.

Stacey nodded in response, not taking her eyes off Adam's ring.

"I don't know why we're here. I need to go. I can't take this," Marissa said and turned to go, but Scott stopped her.

"She specifically wanted you here...not to torture you either. She wanted to apologize to you. You have to understand the emotional roller coaster she's on." Scott turned Marissa toward Stacey. "If something happened to Alex, would that not be you? What if you and Alex had been going out for a while and were as close as they were. If the two of you went through what they went through together, would you not be where she's at right now?" Scott asked. "I can guarantee the thoughts going through her head are only of Adam. Look at her eyes. She's not there."

"No, she's not." Marissa shook her head. "I'm sorry. I need to go. Can I come back later?"

"That is probably a good idea," Scott agreed.

"We'll...um..." Randy pointed toward Marissa. "Yeah, we'll be back later too."

"Sounds good," Sam said, and the three of them left. After the door closed behind them, he sat on the side of her bed. Resting his hand on the side of her face, he said, "Stacey, honey?"

Stacey sniffed, staring at Adam's ring. "I miss him, Dad."

"I know."

"He was a good guy."

"He was."

"I loved him, Dad."

"I know. He loved you too," he said, and then kissed her head.

"I want him back," Stacey said, and then started crying again.

"I know. I do too."

"I second that one," Scott said. "He ended up being a good friend."

"One of the better students in the school," Becky added. "He was a strong leader as well."

"I know he's in good hands," Stacey said, "but I..." her voice faded as she shook her head.

"I know, honey. I know." Sam lifted her to a seated position. Then he sat on the side of the bed and held her while she cried for over an hour.

"Want me to go get the nurse?" Scott finally asked. "I think she might need a sedative."

"No. She's almost asleep," Sam said, running his fingers through Stacey's hair as she drifted the rest of the way out.

CHAPTER 14

"TEARS SHED FOR SELF ARE TEARS OF
WEAKNESS, BUT TEARS SHED FOR OTHERS
ARE A SIGN OF STRENGTH." BILLY GRAHAM

When Stacey woke the next morning, she was *really* hungry. "Food," she said, and then opened her eyes to see her dad, Becky, and Scott still there. "Dad?"

"Hi, Peanut. You need something to eat?" he asked.

Stacey nodded, so he left to get the nurse.

"How are you feeling this morning?" Becky asked, sitting on the side of the bed.

"Shaky, tired, but okay. I'm going to have rough spots, but..." She looked back down at his ring on her hand. "I do know he's good where he is, and God is taking good care of him."

"You know, I have the perfect necklace for that. That is, if you want to wear it around your neck," Becky suggested, gesturing toward Adam's ring.

Stacey nodded. "Thank you."

"Well, well, well, Sleeping Beauty awakes, eh?" the nurse said with a smile as she walked into the room with Sam.

"Yeah. Sorry," Stacey apologized.

"No problem. You made my night pretty easy for this room," she said with a smile. When she finished taking Stacey's blood pressure, pulse, and temperature, she asked, "So, your Dad says you're hungry?"

Stacey nodded. "That would be...yeah."

"How bad?"

"Really bad."

"Can you hold up your hand for me?" the nurse asked, concerned.

Stacey held her hand up. It was shaking.

"Yeah, okay," the nurse said. "I'll get you a quick fix, and then order you a tray for when you're done."

"Actually, can you get her the quick fix, and I'll run down to the cafeteria and get her some *real* food?" Scott asked.

"A person who understands hospital food," the nurse said with a chuckle. "Go ahead," she said, as she left the room.

"So," Scott came over to the bed, "what are you in the mood for?"

"Whatever. Surprise me."

"Well, are you a pizza, slash junk-food junky type person, a salad and soup type person, or a meat and potato person?" Scott asked.

"That's quite a lot of different type people," Stacey pointed out. "I'm a little of each, but I think my stomach might only be able to handle the soup and salad right now, with a small bag of potato chips on the side?"

"Sounds like a plan." Scott half-bowed. "Your wish is my command." He looked up and smiled as he waggled his eyebrows.

Becky, Stacey, and Sam laughed at him.

Sam stood. "I'll go with you. Becky, are you hungry?"

"Yes, please?"

"What do *you* desire? Your wish is *my* command." He half-bowed, and winked at Scott, who laughed.

"Same. Thank you, kind sir." Becky nodded in appreciation.

With that, they left. "Well, you've made quite an impression on my little brother," Becky said when the door closed.

"He's a nice guy," Stacey said. "A good friend, too."

"Who is doing a great job of holding back."

"What?"

"He likes you. You know that, right?"

"Becky, I'm..." Stacey shook her head, looking down at Adam's ring.

"I know. I'm just saying he's not normally as coy as he seems to be right now. He's usually pretty cocky and arrogant when it comes to women. Now, your dad on the other hand..." she said, and Stacey glanced up at her. "He's quite the suave and debonair guy. He's kind, sweet, and very much a gentleman."

"He would appreciate you saying that."

"I'm going to be transparent with you, because your father and I are getting close."

"Uh-oh, this doesn't sound good."

"No. It's good. See, I like you, and I like your dad. You two are very close. I admire that."

"Sounds good so far. It also sounds like there is a *but* in there?"

"Nope." She shook her head. "I've seen a lot of family relationships in my line of work, and you guys are solid. I admire that. I think it's healthy and a good thing. You *should* be an important part of his life."

"What about you?"

"I've just walked into the picture. I don't have the right or privilege to be the least bit demanding. Now, when it comes to Scott, I just ask that you try not to hurt him. He may seem tough, but he does have a heart."

"I know. I like him as a friend. With Adam's death so fresh, I don't even want to look at anyone else right now. I have a lot to work through. My mind is a bit clouded right now."

"I know he'll respect that."

"Thanks for being honest."

"Stacey, you *have* been through a lot with Kyle and the rest of that group. You've seen and been through more than any person should *ever* have to go through."

"It hasn't been very nice," she admitted.

"Want to talk about it?" Becky asked. "We obviously have time."

"It was scary."

"I can't imagine."

Stacey sat back and told her everything that happened to her over the last several months. About halfway through, Scott and her dad returned with the food. As they ate, Stacey finished the rest of the story. "After he said *I love you* again, he was gone," she said, tears rolling down her cheeks. Feeling like a bowling ball was sitting on her stomach, she set her fork next to her plate. "He told me to remember that. I always will. It just–it hurts."

"I know. I'm sorry," Sam said, giving her a hug. "You've gone through a lot, but know your God is with you and him. He told me about this God of yours."

"He's real, Dad! He really is!"

"I don't doubt that. I'm having a hard time seeing where He was in all of this, though."

"Well," Stacey said, thinking about it, struggling to keep control over her emotions, "He gave Adam a clear head through it all, especially when I was in the middle of losing it. He kept me alive when I was in the hands of Kyle. He also let Adam live long enough for him to talk to you guys, and for Scott to meet Jesus and accept His gift for him."

"You're a Christian?" Sam asked Scott.

"A new one, but yes," Scott said. "This stuff is really new to me, so I'm wading through it. Matt's helping a lot."

"Yeah, he's a pretty smart guy," Sam said, returning to his chair.

"Good morning, campers," Dr. McMillan said, walking into

the room. "I hear you guys got brunch for four this morning from our wonderful cafeteria?"

"Yep. It was good, too," Becky said.

"Good!" The doctor smiled. "So, how was your night?" he asked Stacey

"I don't remember it," she admitted.

"She slept it off," Scott explained, setting the tray on the counter. "She cried for a good couple of hours, until she cried herself to sleep."

"Well, at least you slept. That's a good thing," Dr. McMillan said. "So, how are you this morning?"

"Okay." She shrugged. "I *would* like to get out of here. Being in here gives one *way* too much time to think. I also need to get out and move around before I get fat," Stacey joked.

"Oh," he chuckled. "I don't think that would be something you'll have to worry about any time soon. As far as going home," he turned to Sam, "as long as you keep a close eye on her for any signs of depression, I don't have a problem sending her home with you today."

"I can do that," Sam agreed.

"Good. It's settled then." Dr McMillan pulled out her IV, replacing it with gauze and medical tape. "You're ready to go home. I'll get the paperwork ready for you to sign," he said, and left the room.

"So, looks like you're free," her dad said, pleased.

"Then I'll get changed and we can go ho–" Stacey looked up at him and asked, "do we still *have* a home?"

"Actually, yes we do," he said. "We had to spend the last few weeks cleaning up what they ransacked, but it's there. It's even in good working order now too."

"What about school?" Stacey asked.

"It starts in several weeks," Becky explained. "The town is still trying to put things back together while the investigators are cleaning up."

"All right. Well, I'll go change." She got up and grabbed her bag. She then headed into the bathroom. While she was changing clothes, she could hear them talking, despite them trying to keep their voices down.

"She's going to be okay, right?" Scott asked.

"She's a tough little cookie. She'll be fine. Give her a few months," Sam said confidently.

Scott crossed his arms as he raised an eyebrow. "Months?"

"They loved each other. Any fool could see that. Her losing Adam hit her hard. And to have it happen right in front of her? That's going to deeply scar her."

"A lot of what she told me is going to scar her," Becky added. "You guys only heard part of it. It sounded like a horror movie she lived for real."

"Maybe I should schedule her with a counselor?" Sam debated. "After losing her mom and her boyfriend both within a year, that cannot be something easy to work through and process by herself. I was going to find her a new counselor here from the loss of her mom, but there wasn't time before things hit the fan."

"Matt's a youth worker *and* a Christian," Scott suggested. "He should be able to help her put things into perspective. He also knew Adam for years. He'd be a great one for her to talk to."

"That's true. I'll talk to him in the morning."

"I'm ready," Stacey said, coming out of the bathroom. "And no, I don't want to talk to anyone. I'm fine. I'll be fine. I'll hit low points, but I'll be fine in the long run."

"But –"

"Dad, if I need to talk to someone, *I'll* ask them. Please don't do this to me. I'm not a little kid. I'm seventeen years old."

"I know, but you've had so much loss. You've had so much done to you at such a young age. I don't want –"

"Please?"

"Are you sure?"

"Yes," Stacey said, relieved he wasn't going to push.

"All right then," he agreed.

"Looks like I'm right on time," the nurse said, walking into the room with the release papers and a wheelchair. "Just sign on the dotted lines, and she's all yours," the nurse said to Sam. When he finished signing, she added, "Here are the going home instructions. Since she doesn't seem to have any serious injuries and her bones are healing, just take it easy and continue to take your pain medicine. Also, keep an eye on her emotional status. Dr. McMillan prescribed anti-depressants until you can get an appointment with one of the counselors suggested in the paperwork."

"Will do," he agreed.

"Call Dr. McMillan's office for a follow-up sometime next week. You're good to go," the nurse said. "Do you need help into the chair?"

Stacey waved her off. "I don't need a chair."

"Sorry. Hospital rules," the nurse explained.

Stacey reluctantly got into the wheelchair. As Becky and Scott gathered Stacey's belongings, Sam left to get the Cherokee.

"Well, are you guys ready?" the nurse asked.

"Yes, ma'am," Stacey said, and they headed downstairs.

When everyone was in the Cherokee, and they pulled out of the parking lot, Sam asked, "How about going to the house for a bit? We will figure out from there what to do. I think it'll be good for Stacey to see the townhouse. Then later we can go play pool in the clubhouse."

"Dad, I..." Stacey shook her head. "I have no problem going to the townhouse, but I don't want to go to the clubhouse."

"That's fine. Can I ask why not the clubhouse?" he asked.

"Because when Adam and I first got together on our first date, we were there."

"Okay." He shrugged. "So, no clubhouse."

"Thanks," she said, relieved.

On the way home, Becky, Sam, and Scott filled Stacey in on what the final outcome was on the raids. Most of Chandler's group was killed, including Kyle. Those in the group who were seriously injured, were still recovering in the hospital.

Shane was going to testify in all cases against everyone in that group still alive, in exchange for immunity and the witness protection program. Since Shane was eighteen, he could go alone. He chose to let no one in his family go with him.

Erin, CJ, and Amber were arrested at the warehouse. They were discovered hiding in a closet in one of the upstairs offices.

As far as Brad, he was caught on the day they kidnapped Stacey. He was arrested, and also offered a deal in exchange for information.

Marissa was granted immunity, also in exchange for the information she was going to provide. She chose to remain in Pine Crest afterward.

Stacey was certain they would all be called in at some point to testify. She knew she would be able to handle it though, after all she had God on her side. And according to Matt and Adam, that included His peace.

CHAPTER 15

"YOU HAVE POWER OVER YOUR MIND – NOT OUTSIDE EVENTS. REALIZE THIS, AND YOU WILL FIND STRENGTH." MARCUS AURELIUS

The next several weeks were extremely rough. Everywhere Stacey looked, she saw Adam. After going through this not that long ago with her mother, it tore her apart to now be going through it regarding Adam.

As she went through town, she saw places where they attempted to rescue people, as well as some places where they acquired information. The places where they went to together as a couple were the most difficult. Places like Slater's, the skating rink, Trina's, and the clubhouse.

Adam's dad, Ben, came up a couple days after Adam's death to get Adam and his mom's belongings and estate in order, and setup a memorial service for Adam. He let his ex-wife's family handle her funeral. Stacey was in the hospital at the time of Adam's funeral, so she could not attend. Instead, she went to his gravesite for her own memorial service once she was released. She would also go at least once a day after that, even if it was just for a few minutes. When she was there, she would have conversations with Adam and God.

"Hey you," Stacey said, sitting next to where he was buried. She rested a rose on his grave. "I'm back."

"Somehow I knew I'd find you here."

She jumped. Then she looked up to see Scott walking up to her with a white rose of his own to put on Adam's grave.

"You've been pretty predictable lately," Scott said when she made a quizzical face.

She sighed. "I know. I can't help it."

"Well," he set the white rose next to her red one, "at least he's a good listener."

"That's sort of not funny."

"Hey, he was." Scott shrugged. "And he still is."

"True."

"So," he crouched next to her, "mind if I join you?"

"Go ahead."

He sat beside her, taking her hand into his.

"Scott, I..." Stacey's voice faded as she shook her head.

"I know. This is a support thing," he explained. "You know my feelings, but I also know you have a lot you have to work through."

"Thanks." She knew Adam's body may have been under the freshly laid sod, but his soul was not there. His soul was free, enjoying Heaven. "Adam's dad called last night," she said, absentmindedly running her fingers over the grass.

"Oh yeah?"

"Yeah. He said talking to me helps him. He also said he ordered the gravestone."

"Did he say what it would look like?"

"Yeah. It's a black, grey, and white marble. It's going to say, *Adam David Barnes*, along with his birth date and passing date. He also said it would say, *'Dear friend, and great soldier. A good and faithful servant in the Lord's Army. We look forward to seeing him again in Heaven. Psalms 23'.*"

"Wow!" Scott said. "I would love to have that on mine. What an honor!"

"He *was* a good and faithful servant."

"He still is," Scott added.

Tears brimmed Stacey's eyes. She cried so much lately. She did not want to cry anymore.

"You can't tell me he's not still looking out for us up there. He's scoping the place out, so he can show us around when we get there."

Stacey nodded, wiping the few tears that escaped off her face.

"Stacey, he loved you. He still does. You can't tell me he doesn't love you, because I won't believe it. It took all I had to hold him back when we had to wait for the others and watch what Kyle was doing to you." He shook his head. "Frankly, I wanted a crack at Kyle too. We knew the others were coming. We understood if we waited, fewer people would get hurt. I'm sorry we couldn't do anything sooner."

"They had guns."

"I know. And we didn't. Those few months were the worse I have ever seen in my life. I wasn't even with you guys directly. You guys saw more than I did. I just saw the aftermath."

Stacey nodded, lost in her own thoughts of the events.

"Stacey, you guys were brave. You guys gave for this town, and should be honored for it."

"No. I just want to forget it."

"It's part of you though."

"A part I want to forget."

"Don't forget Adam. Learn from him. In the middle of everything going on, he was still telling others about Jesus."

"I know," she said. "I'm trying to sort things out, but I'm having a hard time."

"You have to start school tomorrow? Right?"

"Yeah. I'm *really* not looking forward to that."

"I'll tell you what, what if I take you out to dinner at Trina's afterward, as friends of course?"

Her bottom lip trembled. "I don't know if I can handle

tomorrow. Every time I think about it, I feel like I'm going to throw up."

"I know it's going to be rough. I'm hoping dinner will give you something to look forward to."

She reached over and touched the white and red roses.

"He was a good friend," Scott continued. "The things he taught us for the short time we knew him will be extremely valuable to us for the rest of our lives together. And no, that wasn't a hint. I think my sister and your dad are going to be getting married here soon, so we'll be seeing a lot of each other. Besides, I consider you a very good friend."

"I consider you one, too." She sniffed, wiping her tears. "I don't know how I'll be able to face everything and everyone tomorrow."

"Why don't I pick you up from school, and we'll see what you're up for." He shrugged. "If it's just a walk or a really good cry, then so be it. I don't think you should be alone tomorrow after school."

"Thank you. I would appreciate that."

"I'm glad you got that brace off yesterday so you can start school without it."

"Yeah. Being right-handed, I was trying to figure out how to write with my left hand. Dr. McMillan had compassion on me and took it off yesterday. He was satisfied with the healing of my collar bone and ribs. He said to take it easy for a few more weeks. He was also impressed by my mental state."

"Not to offend you, but you still concern me in that department."

"I have my days," she admitted.

"They're getting further apart, but I still see the flashbacks in your eyes."

"I'm doing my best."

"You do what you need to do."

"Thank you."

They talked for another hour, before deciding to go to Stacey's house. They decided to cook dinner for Becky and Sam.

"So, what are we going to make for the wonderful couple?" Scott asked, putting her dad's apron on.

Stacey sat on the stool at the breakfast bar, her chin resting on her hand. "I don't care," she said on a sigh.

He put his chin on both of his hands in front of her face. "Stacey?"

"What?"

"You *really* need to get out of this slump. I know it's justified, *but* Adam wouldn't want you living like this."

"Like what?"

"Like this. There *is* life after Adam. He wouldn't want you to be like this. I happen to know he loved your smile. Whenever we talked about you, that was one of the things he brought up the most."

"I know. He told me."

"Is there anything I can do to cheer you up?"

"Not really. I'm just going to have to work my way through it."

"Stace, we will never truly be able to work through losing him...losing anyone for that matter. We just learn to live with the hole in our hearts the loss created."

"How did you get so smart?"

"Years of practice." He smiled. "Now, can you set aside your thoughts for a few moments, and help me with dinner for when the dynamic duo comes home?"

She slowly got up. "Yeah, I guess."

"Okay, could you set it a little *further* aside?"

She noticed he had adorable dimples when he smiled, but even those were not working for her tonight. "I'm trying, it's just..." her voice faded. She went to the living room, curling up on the couch.

"Hey, the kitchen is this way," Scott said, leaning on the doorway with his arms crossed.

"I know."

"The longer we wait, the longer *they're* going to have to wait. Come on, work with me here."

She sighed as she got up and returned to the kitchen. "Fine."

"That's better. So, what do we want to make?"

"I'm not hungry."

"Yes. You are. Okay, that's enough of this. Let's go get take-out," he said, taking off the apron, replacing it on the hook in the kitchen. "This isn't working."

"No. We should save our money. What do you want to eat?"

"What about, say…oh! I got it! I'll fry some chicken breasts in a pan, and we'll smother them with swiss cheese, sautéed onions, and mushrooms. Sound good?"

"Actually, that does," Stacey agreed, thinking about what to have with it. "How about some green beans and rice to go with it? Of course, we'll have a salad as well."

"Of course." He nodded. They always had salad with dinner. "And that's more like it. I knew you were in there."

"It'll take a while, but I'll snap out of it," she said, pulling a can of green beans from the cupboard. "I just need some time." Emptying the can into a pan of the stovetop, she started those cooking while he worked on cutting the fat from the chicken breasts.

"So, are your friends excited for school tomorrow?" he asked.

"Some are…some aren't. The first few weeks are going to be really tough. We're missing about two thirds of the student population, including the entire popular circle. Many moved away, but some were killed or arrested. Losing the most popular kids in school will make it that much more difficult."

"I don't know about that. Becky said your group was more

popular then Kyle's crew. This could be a good thing. I know you won't have Adam, but the rest of your group is still intact."

"True. It still won't be the same. I had Kyle and Shane in front of me for first-period, and Adam in the next row over. Then I had Adam in front of me for second-period. This is going to..." She shook her head. Tears brimmed her eyes as she imagined what the next day would hold.

"Come here," he said. When she walked over to him, he held her. "It's going to be okay. Give it time," he said after a few moments.

"Thanks." She sniffed. "I know."

He let her go. "Are you okay?"

"Think so."

"Okay, let's get dinner going again."

"Yeah," she agreed. She worked on the rice while the green beans cooked. When she got that going, she worked on the rest of the salad, while he sautéed the onions and mushrooms for the chicken. He was also frying the chicken while those sautéed.

"Wow!" Stacey's dad said with a smile, when he and Becky arrived about twenty minutes later. "Smells delicious!"

"I'll say! You two should be assigned to cook more often if this is what we get!" Becky grinned.

"Well, I can't do it *every* day. I still have to work, you know," Scott pointed out.

"Sure, if you call it that. I think working an average of ten days a month is hardly working," Sam countered.

"But they're twenty-four to forty-eight-hour shifts. Sometimes those shifts get ugly!" Scott shook his head. "There are times we have multiple calls, one right after the other. Those are the days I count down the hours until I'm off."

"Wimp!" Becky smirked. She went over to Stacey, resting her hands on Stacey's shoulders from behind. "So, how are *you* doing today?"

"Depends on when you ask," Stacey admitted. "I'm not looking forward to tomorrow, if that's what you're asking."

"I'm not either. Just make sure to take plenty of tissues. I'm going to be having a moment of silence for each student and faculty member lost as I read the names. I'm not sure if *I'm* going to make it through." She sighed. "I was looking at the list today. It's a long list."

Stacey crossed her arms, hugging herself. "I can't go tomorrow."

"You have to, hon," Sam said, giving her a hug. "You need to go. The rest of the group will be looking for you."

"I know, but..." Stacey shuddered. "I-I just can't!" She shook loose of her dad, and ran to her bedroom in tears. She shut her door in hopes they would leave her alone. They left her alone for the rest of the night. She cried herself to sleep, dreading the next morning.

"STACEY?" Sam gently shook her. "Come on, Peanut. You have to get ready for school."

"I-I'm...hungry," she mumbled.

"I figured. Come on," he said, helping her out to the living room. "Scott said to tell you he'd pick you up after school today. Is that a date?"

"No. It's just a friend thing. He said he knew I would need company."

"Good idea. He's a good guy, Stace."

"I know. I'm not ready for anything right now. It's only been a few months."

"He won't wait forever."

"Then he'll date someone else. I'm not ready. If he can't handle that, then I'm sorry," Stacey snapped. "I will not be pushed until *I* am ready."

Sam put his hands up in surrender as he walked into the kitchen. "Okay, okay, just making a point." He returned from the kitchen a moment later with a plate of food and a glass of orange juice. "Here's your breakfast. Eat up, and then go get a shower. We leave in about an hour."

"Thanks, Dad," she said. As she ate, she looked around the room, lost in her thoughts. "I'm sorry I snapped," she said a few minutes later.

He looked up from his iPad where he was reading the morning news. "It's okay. You've got a lot on your mind. And the idea of school starting back up with this still fresh is going to be difficult for everyone."

"I know. Thank you for breakfast," she said, cleaning her plate. She then downed the remaining orange juice. Afterward, she took a quick shower, and then got dressed just in time to leave.

"Try to keep your chin up today. Okay?" Sam said when they pulled up to the school. "Today will be the worst. Each day will get better. I promise. Time will heal your heart."

"I know. Thanks, Dad. I love you."

"I love you, too," he said, as Stacey got out of the Cherokee after they hugged each other.

"Stacey!" Marissa called. She and Alex jogged across the front lawn. When she caught up to her, Marissa gave Stacey a hug. "People are saying Miss Schmidt is going to read everyone's name who died. Is that true?"

"Yes," Stacey said. "She told me last night."

"She can't! This is going to be awful."

"It's out of respect. I have to go to class," she said, and went to leave.

"Stacey?" Alex grabbed her arm. "Are you going to be okay?"

"No. Just let me go. I need to be by myself today."

"You really shouldn't be by yourself," Alex said. "We should go through this together."

"Just...please? This is going to be hard enough." Stacey pulled away from him, and headed into the school. Several people tried to talk to her, but she would quickly excuse herself. Finally, when she got to class, she put her head down on her desk praying for people to leave her alone.

"Ms. Spencer?" Mr. Wexford looked up from his desk. "I'm surprised you're here today."

"I have to be," she said. "I wasn't given a choice."

"I want you to know that you have my sympathy regarding Mr. Barnes."

"Thanks," she said. Everywhere she looked, she saw Adam. *Today was going be heart wrenching.*

After several more minutes, the rest of the kids slowly drifted into class. The class had a quarter of the students normally in attendance.

A couple minutes after the first-period bell rang, Becky's voice crackled over the loud speaker. "Good morning, students and teachers. Under normal circumstances, I would be welcoming you back, but in the wake of what transpired over the course of the last several months, I'll just say I'm glad to see each and every single one of you. To start, we will have a moment of silence for each of those dear ones that we have lost. Please say a prayer for each as I read their names..." She said, and read the names. She paused with each one. By the time she got to Adam, Stacey thought she would vomit. Forcing herself to focus on something else, she pulled a book out of her backpack.

It took over fifteen minutes for Becky to read the entire list. Afterward, she said, "For some of us, those lost were our best friends. There are some we hardly knew. However, we are small enough that we all knew each's name and face. There will be a memorial placed in the garden outside the front doors within the month. It will include a plaque with each name read today, that will allow us to always remember those we loved and lost. Please keep those families touched by this in your hearts and prayers. Listen and reflect while I play the Star-Spangled Banner for those brave soldiers of our town who fought to bring peace. There will also be counselors in the auditorium all week for those who need to talk to someone. Thank you," she said, and played the anthem.

There was not a dry eye anywhere by the time it finished. As a matter of fact, over half the class that *was* there, ended up going to the auditorium after or during the anthem.

They did not do any math in class. Mr. Wexford allowed them to have an open discussion and quietly talk amongst themselves. About halfway through class, Mr. Wexford sat in Kyle's seat in front of Stacey. He faced her, as he quietly said, "Ms. Spencer, I know you've been through a lot. Do you want to go talk to someone?"

"Nope," she said, reading the book from her backpack.

"Look, I know you not only went through some pretty violent things, but you also lost Adam."

"Mr. Wexford," she looked up at him a little irritated, "if I wanted to go down, I would have asked. I don't want to, though. I'm working through things just fine, thank you," she said, and returned to her book. He remained in his seat. She sighed, frustrated and annoyed. "*What?*"

"Well, I saw you crying earlier. However, as soon as Adam's name was read, you stopped. It was like you shut down when you heard his name."

Stacey was angry by that point, so unfortunately her tone was stern and short as she said, "*Mr. Wexford*, I've been at his grave site every day since I've been out of the hospital. I've ran my fingers through the grass he's buried under." People were beginning to stare, but she did not care. She was not going to do this all day. "I wear his ring around my neck. I have his picture next to my bed, so I see it *every* morning and *every* night. There are not too many moments that go by where I *don't* think of him. Trust me when I say I have mourned. Right now, I'm just trying to not completely lose it in front of everyone," she said. She grabbed her books and backpack, leaving the classroom. Not sure where she was headed, she just walked. She needed to go somewhere. She needed to be anywhere but there.

She must have made her point, because Mr. Wexford did not send anyone after her. As a matter of fact, any teachers who did see her let her keep walking. She walked out the doors without anyone stopping her…that is, until Becky ran up to her outside the school.

"Stacey!" Becky called. Stacey headed toward the track, figuring that would be a safe place to blow-off steam. "Stacey! Wait up!" Becky said, finally catching up to her.

"*What?*" Stacey snapped.

"Mr. Wexford told me what happened in math. He was worried about you. He said you were like a loose cannon about to explode."

"That's probably because he wouldn't leave me alone," Stacey said, clutching her books to her chest, while her backpack hung on her shoulder. "He kept pushing, even after I told him I was fine."

"*Are* you fine?"

"In time I will be, but not right now. Having said that, I don't want to talk to some brainiac psychiatrist wannabe who thinks *they know how I feel!*" she said, tears brimming her eyes once again. "*No one* knows how I feel! There is *no way* in this world *anyone* could have *any* idea what I've been through!"

"No one does. However, Matt is down in the auditorium. Maybe you could talk to him," she suggested.

"I'm sure he has his hands full."

"Actually, he's been waiting for you. As soon as Mr. Wexford called me, I called down there. Matt's been looking for you. We thought that was where you were headed."

"Well, I'm not."

"Stacey, we love you, but there's so much going on in there. You need to talk to someone and get it out."

"I *have* been," she said. Looking up at the sky, she silently prayed for some type of intervention.

"To whom?"

"Adam and God."

"Well," she considered Stacey's words. "Those *are* good people to talk to, but how about someone who can hold you while you let things out and cry for hours?"

"Scott does that. He usually ends up down at Adam's grave with me at least once every few days."

"Honey, listen," she rested her hands on Stacey's shoulders, facing Stacey toward her, "this morning wasn't to throw you into a tailspin. It was to honor those lives lost."

"I know."

"You are a strong young lady, who has been through a lot. These kids need you. They need your strength and leadership."

"I'm fine."

"I know you will be, but you're going to have to put up with some nosey people for a while. They're not doing it to be rude or obnoxious. They're doing it out of concern."

"They're smothering me!"

"I know. Just do me a favor and smile and nod, and then talk to your dad, Scott, or me about it later. Okay?"

Stacey nodded in response.

Becky hugged her. "We love you. You know that, right?"

Stacey nodded again.

"Good," Becky said, and then kissed Stacey's head. "How about talking to Matt now?" she asked. Becky looped her arm around Stacey's as she directed her back toward school. "Matt wants you to have something of Adam's that he's been waiting to give to you."

"You're just trying to trick me into going to the auditorium."

"Well, that too," Becky admitted. "So, how about it?"

"Fine." Stacey sighed. "I'll do it if it'll get people off my back."

"You can stay there for as long as you want. That should keep you off people's radar."

"That's okay. I'll just get what Matt has and leave."

"Fair enough," she agreed. "You know where to find me when you want to go home, right?"

"What do you mean?"

"Your dad said if you wanted to go home early today, to have me call Scott and he could come get you. He didn't tell you?"

"Well, I kind of snapped at him this morning," Stacey admitted. "I wasn't in the best of moods."

"Yeah, let's get you to the auditorium," she said, and walked Stacey the rest of the way.

"Hey, Stace," Matt said. "I was wondering where you were."

Stacey shrugged. "I've been around."

"Well, on that note, I'll leave you two," Becky said. She gave Stacey a hug before she left.

The auditorium was full of groups of two scattered throughout. It looked like most of those who *were* in school that day, were in the auditorium.

"Why don't you come on over here with me?" Matt asked.

When she nodded, they went over to an area where there were not a lot of other people and sat down.

"I've had a lot of concerned individuals come up to me over the last few weeks about you," Matt started.

She nervously played with the piece of paper marking her spot in her book. "I'll bet."

He moved to a seat in front of her and turned to face her. Stacey glanced up at him. "They're doing it out of concern," he said. "They're worried about you."

"I'm dealing with it."

"How well?"

"Well enough. Look," Stacey said, looking him square in the eyes, "I've had a lot go on in my life over the last year. The last thing I want to hear is someone telling me, *Oh, I know how you feel*," she said dramatically. "Or, *You'll get through it.* Or my personal favorite, *God took him for a reason.* You know what? I don't *care* what the reason is! There was a kind, gentle, humble, fun-loving guy in my life, who loved me unconditionally, *and* who protected me to the point of him giving his life. *That's* the point!" She crossed her arms, looking away.

"Stacey, we *do* care. We know exactly what Adam was like. Good grief, Tina and I even babysat him when he was still in diapers. I had the privilege of leading him to the Lord and baptizing him. I watched him struggle through the same thing you are when they killed his brother right in front of him. He saw it. He saw what they were doing, and was helpless to stop it. Allen knew what they were going to do, so he hid Adam. Allen told him not to move. Adam went through the same thing you are going through right now. You don't think we didn't have some massive conversations then?"

Stacey did not respond.

"Let's talk this out," Matt coaxed.

"I've talked it out with Adam and God...*a lot.*"

"I'm sure, but how about talking to someone who can hold your hand while you talk? If not me, then let me call Scott. You trust him, right?"

"I do, but he's got a life. He doesn't need to hold my hand through all of this. We created this mess, not him."

"What do you mean *you created this mess*?"

"My dad and I were the ones who came here and rattled

their cages. We were the ones who stirred this up, and got the government involved. We're the reason it blew up into this," she said, gesturing to the others in the auditorium. "These people lost friends and family because of me."

"These people lost friends and family *before* you! Those people were holding the town hostage, and you guys set these people free," Matt said, exasperated. "They don't hate you, they're *grateful* to you!"

"Oh sure, grateful they no longer have Kyle, Shane, Adam, or any of those who were lost? How can someone be grateful to someone who had someone close to them killed?"

Matt narrowed his eyes, as he said, "How *dare* you say that! You have *no idea* what it's been like living here! We've looked over our shoulders for years, making sure not to offend the wrong person. You guys were a God-send. You were a blessing. The ones who died in that pit? They knew it was coming. Many were surprised it didn't happen sooner. As far as Adam's mom? She was living on borrowed time. As far as Adam? He was an innocent, but God used his short life to impact many. Look, this is what I wanted to show you." He handed Stacey a piece of paper. "Several months back, I did a lesson on perspectives. I wanted everyone to write down how they wanted the world to remember them after they died. They were to write what they wanted their tombstones to say. After they finished, I had them write what they wanted God to say to them. You know what he put for God's?"

"What?" she asked, holding the paper still folded in half. She did not want to open it and see his writing.

"He wanted God to say, *Well done thy good and faithful servant.* You know what he wanted the worldly one to say?"

"What?"

"He wanted it to say he was *a faithful servant of God's.* Adam *was* a faithful servant for God to the very end. God was there through all of it. The Lord saw it *all*. *Nothing* is a surprise or coincidence to Him…*nothing*. To God, there are no surprises."

"I know," she said, looking down at the piece of paper.

"Stacey, Adam's job here was done. His life was spared many times just to make sure he would have the opportunity to do what God had planned for him. Adam did it, too. He did his job to the best of his ability, and then God took him home."

"Yeah, see, *that's* the part I'm having trouble with," Stacey said. "Why would He wait until this was all finished, and *then* take him home? Why didn't he give him some time to enjoy it first?"

"Because he's enjoying something *way* better right now. And he can't wait to be the one to show it to you."

"I need…" Stacey turned and walked out, tears streaming down her face once again. She could not handle it anymore. With Adam's paper in hand, she left and walked home…by herself.

CHAPTER 16

"THE MORE YOU CARE, THE STRONGER YOU CAN BE." JIM ROHN

The phone rang several times that afternoon, but Stacey ignored it. Instead, she stared at the paper containing Adam's handwriting. After a few hours, she had the courage to finally open it. It said exactly what Matt said it did, but to see it in Adam's handwriting stung.

Around three o'clock, Becky stopped by to check on Stacey. She brought Scott with her.

"Hi," Stacey said, unenthusiastically, as she opened the door. Then she went back to the couch and laid back down.

"You had us worried," Becky said. "We were looking all over for you. We tried calling, but you didn't answer."

"I just wanted to be left alone."

"Well, see, *that's* going to be a problem," Scott said, crouching next to the couch, up by her head. "You see, in the state you're in, that could be a very bad thing."

"I need to think," she said.

"No. You need to work through things, and not marinate in those feelings. You do need to face what you're going through right now, but not alone," he said. "That could be dangerous."

"I have an idea I want you to think about," Becky said, as she sat down on the coffee table slightly behind Scott. "There's going to be a dedication to the students and faculty lost through this in a few weeks when we place the memorial in the garden. When we do, each person is going to have something personally said about him or her. I've talked to Adam's dad, and he agreed. We want you to do Adam's."

Stacey shook her head, looking down at the paper. "I–I can't."

"I think it'll be good for you. You weren't able to go to his memorial service. I think you need to do this. I also think people need to hear what you have to say. Adam was a strong leader. He might not have had the muscle behind him Kyle did, but he didn't need it. Kyle was a dictator. Adam was a leader. There *is* a difference. The school has lost one of its key leaders, and you need to pick that up for him and help guide them through this. You've given up a lot for this town, and they know it. You've also *done* a lot for this town, and they know that too. They need to know you're still behind them. They also need to know how to live without the corruption they've been used to for so long. The school *and* the town need you, Stace."

"Fine. I'll do it. Will you leave me alone now?"

"Nope." Scott shook his head. "She may, but you're stuck with me."

"Scott, I don't want to lead you on. I *do* like you, *a lot*. It may even be borderline love. However, I'm not ready for a relationship yet. I'm going to need a lot of time and space. If it's too much to ask, I'll understand if you date someone else. I'm also only seventeen, you're what...twenty-one, twenty-two?"

"Twenty. And that's only three years," he said. "But that's not the point. The point is I'll wait."

"I'm not asking you to."

"I understand that. But right now, dating is the furthest thing from my mind. Helping out a very close and dear friend through the loss of the one she loved is my priority."

Stacey took a staggered breath.

"Stacey, you need someone right now…not as a lover, but as a friend. I want to be that for you. If something comes of it later, that's fine, but that's not my motive. I want you to understand that. Adam meant a lot to me, too. I wouldn't be a Christian if it wasn't for him. I would have no idea who Jesus is, let alone know and believe He died specifically for me. Adam ran his race. He ran it with patience, perseverance, and strength. And when he wasn't strong enough, he leaned on God to finish it."

"I know."

"You know that here," he pointed to Stacey's head, "but do you know that here?" he asked, pointing to her heart. "Adam loves you, but God loves you more."

"I know."

"He's not just a peace giver, He's a life giver. Let Him give you life right now. Let Him show you *your* purpose. Let *Him* give you strength. You gave this town a reason to fight. You showed them a strength inside them they didn't even know they had. Why don't you give them another purpose? Give them another victory to fight for. Use Adam's life to show them the way."

Stacey sat there with the paper in her hand. After few moments, she finally said, "I'll do it."

"Good." He smiled. "Now, how about some dinner?"

Stacey shook her head. "No."

"Why not?"

"Because I have to get started."

"Okay, you go get started while Becky and I work on dinner. Deal?"

"Deal," she said as she stood. He gave her a hug before she left for her bedroom.

She worked on what she would say for days. She even went out and talked to people who knew Adam, and heard their stories about him. She wanted this to be special. She wanted this to make an impact. None of it was for her. It was all for Adam and God.

~

THE DAY FINALLY ARRIVED. Stacey was a nervous wreck! By the time she got to the school with her dad, there were people and news cameras everywhere. They were not going to play the entire service on the news, just segments. The news crews were also planning on interviewing people afterward for the news segment.

Stacey sat in her chair with her paper in hand the entire time. She would not let anyone see it.

"Are you ready?" Scott whispered, as he sat on one side of her, holding her hand through the service to that point.

Becky told Stacey she would be last. Becky said she knew what Stacey was going to say was going to have to be the closer.

"Yeah," Stacey said.

"You'll do great, Peanut," Sam said quietly, as he kissed her head. He was sitting on the other side of Stacey, with Adam's dad Ben, on his other side.

"All this morning, we have paid tribute to those lost who were dear and near to us," Becky said from the stage. "This final one I saved for last on purpose. Adam Barnes was not only a dear friend, but also a leader in the community, in his church, and in this school. He did not need the popularity status, nor did he desire it. He did not need people to answer to his beck and call. He was a servant to all, and a faithful one," she said and paused, looking around at those in attendance. "Leadership is a position that is *given* by those who choose to follow you...not by those *forced* to follow. Adam was a prime example of this type of leadership. Please allow Stacey Spencer, Adam's girlfriend, a few more minutes of your time. She is the person who knew his heart best. Allow her to show us a bit of who he was," she said, and stepped away from the microphone.

As Stacey made her way to the stage, she felt awkward. With all eyes on her, she prayed for strength to be able to read what was on the paper. She prayed through her speech as she wrote it over the past few days, so she knew words given were from The Lord. She understood what needed to be said. She knew it would be big in the hearts of those who heard the words. However, she was not confident she would make it through without crying.

Stepping up to the microphone, she cleared her throat. Taking a deep, cleansing breath, she started, "When I was asked to do this, I wasn't sure what I was going to say. That is, until a dear friend told me to use this opportunity to show the world who Adam was at his core. Use it to show you Adam's purpose for being here. Adam wasn't here for Adam. He was here for God. He lived his life that way too. He lived it for others, and that showed in the many people I spoke to regarding Adam.

"Now, I'm not a writer by any means, but this is the only thing I could come up with to best show you Adam. This may sound strange, but I wrote it from what I believe would be God's perspective of Adam's life. It's called, *I Was There*," she said.

Nervously clearing her throat, she then dove into the poem. "I was there before you were born. I gave you your heart of humbleness. I gave you your strength to be bold when you needed to, and your sense of discernment as to when to back off," Stacey read. "I gave you your heart of compassion for others. I gave you your sense of justice and stubbornness to stand and fight for things when you felt it wasn't right. I gave you the strength from within to make it through each day with bravery and courage. I was there the day you were born into your family. I picked them for you. I picked your father for his wisdom and discernment. I picked your mother for her tenderness and tenacity. I picked your brother for his protection and strength. I gave them to you not by accident, but for a purpose. They each needed to teach you these values. I was there for you for your entire life. I was there when you took your first step. I was there when you got your first tooth, and made your first friend. I was there when you were five, and you helped Marissa home because she skinned her knee riding her bike. I was there when you were six, and started your first day of school with excitement and anticipation. I was there when you gave Joel your lunch money to eat, because some kids took his lunch money from him. I was there for all your scraped knees and elbows when you learned to skateboard. I was there when Matt led you to Me at age eight, and were baptized at ten. I was there when you said hello to the new students to help make them feel welcome and comfortable. I was there when you had to watch as they murdered your seventeen-year-old brother for his love when you were eleven. I was there when you struggled with how to trust anyone after that again...including Me. I was there when you found the resolve to show others that it's not okay to be controlled. I was there when you stood up to the others for a friend. I was there when you comforted people in tough situations. I was also there with you in the cupboard, while you hid for your life. I was in the pit when you were stacking the bodies, trying to get out. I was there when you had to sit helpless in watching the abuse taking place around you. And I was there to hold your hand on the day they took your life. I was there. I saw it all. I will never leave you nor forsake you. I *was* there. I *will* be there. I was there on the day I brought My good and faithful servant home, so he could enjoy peace after all the fighting. And I'll be there for you too, if you'll let Me."

Then she looked up at the audience, and continued, "God *was* there. I don't know how many times He saved my life personally, just so Adam could share the gift of Jesus with me. Adam didn't shy away from sharing either. Even in the middle of the chaos around us, he still paused to tell me about Jesus. Even when I was being held prisoner, and he was scared for me, he took the time to share Jesus's gift with Scott. Adam's mission wasn't to protect this town. That was his privilege. His mission, and even greater privilege for him, was to share the story of The One who was with him from the beginning, was with him until the end, and is now with him forever. Jesus will take care of Adam by letting him rest in The Lord's peace. Adam loved the people of this town, but he loved Jesus and God more."

Stacey glanced back down at her notes for a moment, before she looked up and continued, "In John 15:13, it says, '*Greater love hath no man than this, that a man lay down his life for his friends.*' Adam did that for his friends. However, Jesus did that not only for His friends, but also for His enemies. Jesus doesn't want *anyone* to live in fear. He wants everyone to live in peace. Jesus wants us to tell others about His love and sacrifice, so they don't have to live in eternal fear. Now, I'm not here to preach at you. I'm here to tell you about my closest and dearest friend on this planet, Adam Barnes, and what was closest to *his* heart," she said, tears welling in her eyes. "*People* were. Marissa James, Harmony and Melody Kelley, Brian Dalton, Randy Taylor, Alex Crestwood, Sam Spencer, Scott and Becky Schmidt, Matt and Tina Slater, even Kyle Chandler was close to his heart. As much as Kyle hated him, Adam loved him. Not because he was his cousin, there was animosity on both sides, but he wanted to show Kyle Jesus's love. He wanted to protect others, so they would be able to have the time to stop running long enough to hear about Jesus."

Stacey looked at each of the faces in the audience, as she said, "Now Adam wasn't a saint, but he did love God. Adam wasn't perfect, but he knew his purpose. Do you know your purpose? Do you know your life goals? Matt Slater gave me this paper a few weeks ago." She held it up. "Several months back, he asked his youth group to write down two separate entries. He did it so they would gain perspective on their life. The first was to write down what they wanted the world to say about them when they died. What they thought the world's perspective would be on their life? What made them successful? Adam wrote down, *'To be known as a faithful servant of God's'*. Do you know what's actually written on his tombstone?" She looked at Ben, as she explained, "It says, *'Dear friend, and great soldier. A good and faithful servant in the Lord's Army. We look forward to seeing him again in Heaven. Psalms 23.'* He got his dream. He wanted the world to remember him as a faithful servant of God's, and he got that." She paused before she continued, "The second half of the assignment was to write down what they wanted God to say about their life. Adam wrote, *'To hear God say, well done, thy good and faithful servant.'* His goals were clear. He wanted to do what *God* wanted him to do. And I believe, with all my heart, that when Adam got to Heaven, God looked down at him with love, and said, *'Well done, thy good and faithful servant',*" she said, and left the stage with the sound of applause ringing in her ears. She did not go back to her seat. Instead, she went straight to the car to wait for her dad.

Scott came shortly after she got to their car, and got in. Without a word, he simply reached over and wrapped his arms around her while she cried for hours. They ignored anyone who came to the car to talk, while they cried together. People left, but they remained.

FINALLY, three hours after it was over, and people cleared-out, Sam, Becky, and Ben (Adam's dad), walked to the car. Scott and

Stacey got out and leaned against the car, with Scott holding her hand for moral support.

Ben was the first to speak. "Thank you for what you said. I know that was tough for you. You did a beautiful job. Adam would have been the first one up on his feet after your speech."

"Adam loved you," Stacey said to him. "He only wanted to spend time with you."

"I know," he admitted. "I had no idea what to do. I didn't want to do anything that was going to get him into trouble, or worse yet killed when he got back. I wanted him out, but there wasn't anything I could do about it. Even from South Carolina my life was being threatened."

Stunned, their jaws dropped.

"I couldn't get away from them no matter what I did," Ben continued. "What you and your father, and those behind you guys did, was nothing short of a miracle. I thank you from the bottom of my heart for what you did for this town and these people. It was a bit of a bloody mess, but to be honest it would have been worse had it gone on without being stopped. This town owes you a lot, whether they know it or not."

"They do," Becky said.

"Thanks," Stacey acknowledged. "I tried to honor his memory. I tried to get his purpose across to others, in hopes that they would pick up the baton and carry it for him."

"They did. Matt was pretty busy after you left, along with a lot of others from the church," Sam said, and then added, "He was busy with me too."

A grin spread across Stacey's face. "You?"

He nodded in response.

"That's great!" She threw her arms around him, excited. "I'm so happy for you."

"After what you said, and after what he told me, I couldn't *not* do it," Sam said.

"Sam! That's awesome!" Scott hugged him as well.

"For the record?" Ben said, "I already was one, but if you're passing them out, I'll take a couple of those hugs," he said. Stacey gave him a hug as well.

Afterward, they talked in the parking lot for a bit until they went back to the townhouse.

CHAPTER 17

"THE MORE YOU CARE, THE STRONGER YOU CAN BE." HERMANN HESSE

Over the course of the next year, the town was able to get a healthy restructure on all levels. They saw new people come into the town, settle, *and* feel safe and happy. After a couple of months, people even felt secure to disagree with someone without fear of retaliation. They were also able to work on rebuilding the school and government, along with their systems.

During that time, the churches and their people were extremely busy. The town leaned on them quite a bit through the restructuring. The reasoning stemmed from the news crews in attendance on the day of the memorial service. They played Stacey speech in its entirety with a couple interviews from people afterward for the segment. This made Stacey feel good for a couple reasons. First that the gospel got out, and many lives were changed. Some seeds were also planted that God could use later. Another reason she was because she knew Adam would be honored to know his life changed many hearts for Christ.

As they went into the next school year, Stacey stepped back

and let others lead. She felt she did enough leading over the last year, and wanted others to step up.

Marissa and Alex both worked on a school paper. They got it published and working on its own, so when they graduated at the end of the year it would run smoothly.

Melody and Brian hooked up a while ago, and made a formidable team in their own right. They worked with the student government in setting school guidelines. They also created a new set of rules for the students and faculty to work and live by while in the school. As president and vice president of the student body, they had a lot of say in the rules and regulations. They were fair in making decisions for future students.

Even though Harmony and Randy were active in school sports, they decided to go a different route in influence, becoming more active in youth group. The work they did helped the community with organizing different projects. Those included: cleaning up the city parks; helping rebuild the homes destroyed; or even cleaning some of the houses ransacked.

Everyone in the group changed over the last year, and became bolder in their stance in life and for Christ. Also, for the first several months, Stacey was active in getting people headed in the directions needed to make effective positive changes. After that she needed a rest. She continued to work at Slater's as a server, which opened three months after the raid. While she did not have Adam as a trainer, Brian was a good second.

After her junior year, Stacey knew her senior year would be a big one in life choices. She knew the decisions she made from that point would directly affect her future, and she wanted to focus. There were a few constants around who helped her work through those choices. One was her dad. Sam asked Becky to marry him a few months into Stacey's senior year, and of course she said *yes*. They would marry a month after Stacey's graduation. Becky felt it was important that Stacey had her dad's full attention for the last year she would be in high school.

One of Stacey's other constants was Scott. While he had a few dates here and there with other girls that friends of his set him up with, something always seemed to get in the way. There would only be one, maybe two dates before he stopped seeing them. Even though he went out with other girls, he was always there for Stacey. She did her best not to take advantage of him. She always remembered to respect his space

Stacey did not want to date anyone throughout that time. She was asked, but always said no. Even when prom came around during her junior year, and homecoming during her senior year, she chose not to go. Her dad vocalized his concern, but she needed the time. She needed to take those nights that should have been with Adam, and spent them with him in a different way. She went to his grave on those nights. She needed to do it for herself.

"STACEY, CAN I TALK TO YOU?" Scott asked one night after dinner. Becky came over for dinner every night. Scott came over as well, except for the nights he had to work or his occasional dates.

"What's up?" Stacey asked. They were sitting on the back deck of the house her dad bought about a month ago. Becky, her dad, and Stacey finally decided on one. It took a while to find one they all liked.

"Well, with your dad and Becky cleaning up dinner, I figured this would be as good a time as any," he said, nervously fidgeting with his hands.

"For what?"

"Well, I know you don't want to go, but your prom is in a week."

"I'm not going," Stacey said, looking down at Adam's ring still around her neck on the necklace Becky gave her.

"Would you go if I escorted you?" He asked.

Stacey's jaw dropped.

"It can only be as friends if you want. I just think you should go. I would be honored if you would allow me to take you."

Stacey stared at him, wide-eyed.

"I've already asked your dad's permission, in case you were wondering."

"I don't know. I mean, I don't have time to get anything."

"Would you at least think about it? I'm sure Becky would help you find a dress. You also have some very creative friends who I *know* have been wanting you to go."

"Harmony, Melody, and Marissa?"

"Yep," he said, and then took her hand. "Look, I know you hate it when people tell you what to do, so I'm not going to tell you what to do. I'm *asking* you to allow me the honor of escorting you. You know I'm safe. You know I won't try anything. You know I respect you. And you *also* know I get along with your friends."

"If I do, it's as friends. Right?"

"Right. If that's what you want."

"What do *you* want?" she asked.

"You *know* what I want. But right now, what *you* want is what counts."

"All right," she agreed after another minute of debating in her head. "I'll do it. I mean, I accept. I mean...oooooo!" Stacey growled. "I can't even accept a date right!"

"I get it. And if you need it to be as friends, that's fine."

"Thanks," Stacey said, relieved. "I want you to know I really do appreciate you taking time to consider my feelings in all of this. That speaks a lot to me."

"So, do I get a few brownie points for that?" he asked, hopeful. "At least that'll get me in the right direction, right? Maybe a real date down the road when you're ready."

"But not for prom."

"But not for prom," he agreed. "I'm just happy to be the one who gets to take you."

"Thanks," she said, and gave him a quick kiss on the cheek. "You're a true friend, my best friend actually. Thank you."

He looked at her, not saying a word.

"I need..." She stood, and pointed over her shoulder toward the house. "Um, I should call the girls and see...shopping...that sort of stuff."

"Stacey." He jumped up, catching her by her arm. When she turned toward him, and he took her hands into his. "You know I love you. You also know I respect your space. I don't want to overstep. You have made it clear you're not ready. I know that. But may I have a hug?"

She nodded and gave him a hug.

"You are a brave and strong young lady," he said, and then kissed her head. "I admire you. And if I have to do that as a friend for the rest of our lives, it's fine with me. I understand. It'll kill me, but I'll understand. Your heart was Adam's. He was a lucky man."

"Scott, I..." She took a moment, and then hugged him tighter.

"No pressure. You know how I feel. I just wanted you to know the next step in this is yours," he said. "Until then, know I will always be here."

"Thank you," she said, relief washing over her. *She liked Scott, but wanted to remain loyal to Adam. After all, Scott was the one Adam accused her of having an affair with during the siege. While Adam said in the dream if she could find love again to take it, would he still approve if he knew it was Scott?*

"Uh, Stace? I need to, um..." Scott stepped back, his face flushed. "Do you want to take a walk?"

"Sure," she said, and grabbed his hand.

They told Sam and Becky they were taking a walk before they headed down to the park to walk around.

"I remember this place," Stacey said in a whisper when they neared the area Adam and Stacey were taken on the day they got beat-up. It was also near where they got shot the night the other side threw them into the pit.

"Stacey, you need to come out of the past," Scott said. "Adam is gone."

"I know he's gone, but I'm left here picking up the pieces."

"You've made leaders out of followers. You made people, who didn't think they had it within them, become influential in the community. They are making decisions which will impact this place way into the future. Stace, you believed in them."

"Adam believed in them."

"He did, but you helped them see their way through this, so they were able to come through it stronger than ever," Scott said. When she did not respond, he got a good look at her face. "What's wrong?"

"Adam...Kyle...the day they beat us up on my second day of sc-school," she stammered. She shook her head. When that did not clear her mind, she closed her eyes, forcing the pictures out of her head. "It was here. The other side also shot us over there before they threw us into the pit." She shuddered. "I-I can't be here. I'm trying, but I can't do it!" she said, with a pained expression. "I need to get out of this town! The memories are beginning to swallow me whole!"

"Stacey!" he said, getting in her face. "You need to focus!"

"I need Adam!" Tears brimmed her eyes, as her body trembled. "I need him to come back."

"He's not coming back! No matter what you do. No matter what you say. No matter where you go. You will always see things that will remind you of him." He let a slow breath of air out. Then he looked back up at Stacey and calmly explained, "You have to understand he's not here. He's with God in

Heaven. You helped others move in the right direction, but you're still losing yourself. You are a strong person, but I am continuously seeing you shrinking away day after day. Let us believe in you the same way you believed in us. Lean on *us* until you can stand on your own again. Let God show you what His plan is for *you*. It wasn't just that wonderful speech you did. It wasn't just helping those of this town to find their way through this either. God has something bigger for you. I'm *sure* of it! As sure as I'm standing here, I know God has something bigger for you or *you* wouldn't still be standing here."

Stacey stood there, tears mixing with the rain that started during Scott's speech. She could feel the warmth of her tears as they slowly trickled down her cheeks.

"Stacey, I love you. I know you love me. It's okay to love someone else. I'm sure Adam would approve if he knew it was me. He knew how I felt about you. He also knew I respected him too much to do anything about it." Scott thought for a moment. Then he asked, "Do you really think Adam wants you to be alone for the rest of your life?"

Stacey thought about the dream she had in the hospital, and shook her head.

"Would he want you to be stuck in the past with him so much, that you couldn't see your own future?"

Stacey shook her head again.

"Once again, I'm not going to pressure you, but I *am not* going to let you throw your life away either!" he said, the rain coming down harder, soaking their clothes through to the skin. "You have become one of my best friends over the last few years. You are stronger than you think. You haven't seen what I have," he said calmer, not taking his eyes off hers. "I have seen you go through being beat-up; attacked multiple times; kidnapped and tortured; and even saw your love die right in front of you. You went through that, but you had the heart and strength to turn around and help this town to find not only

God, but also a strength that was always inside them to move on. You have shown those who didn't know Jesus, who Jesus is and the love He has for them. You have shown those who thought they were just followers, and thought they would always be just that, how to be influential leaders, and teach others to be as well. You are as powerful, as you are passionate. And you made one heck of a formidable opponent to the ones who held this town captive. You showed that group they weren't the ones in charge, but that the people of this town were in charge. You wouldn't take their crap, and you didn't feel anyone else should either. They felt threatened, and rightly so. You had a huge hand in taking them down. Don't think for a second they didn't know who was behind the mutiny against their generations of power. They knew who to blame. You and your father were on the top of that list. There is a strength within you that you are trying to hide." He looked down and sighed as he thought for a moment. Then he looked back up at her and said, "I guess what I'm trying to say is –"

"I know what you're trying to say," Stacey said, wiping her face. "And I got it. I'm just having a hard time with it."

"Then go talk to someone about it," he said, relieved to finally be getting through to her. "Let someone else carry the load for a while."

"That would be nice. I just don't know if I can."

"You can! All you have to do is let others carry you for a bit while you heal on the inside. Come on, let us help you," he encouraged, and he hugged her. "We love you too."

"Thanks," she said, wrapping her arms around him. He went to let go, but she hugged him tighter.

"Stace, I..." his voice faded.

"No," she shook her head. "Shh."

"Okay," he said, and held her in the pouring rain for about twenty minutes, until she finally let him go. "Are you okay?"

Scott asked, tucking a portion of her sopping wet hair behind her ear while he looked into her eyes.

"Yes. Thanks."

"Well, let's head home. They might be starting to worry about us. Besides, you need to get dry before you catch a cold."

Stacey nodded, so they headed home. When they got there, they sat down with Sam and Becky. Wrapped in blankets on the couch, they shared what all they talked about. Becky said she would set up an appointment with a counselor for Stacey for the next day. They were also excited Stacey was going to the prom, and were relieved Scott was the one taking her.

Before she went to bed that night, Stacey called Melody, Harmony, and Marissa. They decided to go shopping for a dress for Stacey the next day after school. They, of course, already had theirs. They were thrilled Stacey was going to the prom, and could not wait to talk about it at school the next day.

THE WEEK FLEW BY, while Stacey scrambled to get ready for the prom. The girls found a dress for Stacey after a couple nights of searching. It was a floor-length dress made of pure satin. It was fitted at the top, and flowed to the ground with a slim-lined, straight skirt. The dress itself was a bluish-gray color. She was able to find a gold choker necklace to go with it, and a purse to match the dress as well. There was a shawl that came with the dress made of the same material. That was nice, because the dress itself had spaghetti straps, and it still chilly in May.

The day of the prom, Stacey picked up his boutonniere from the florist. It had white roses with light blue, white, and gold ribbon.

After she picked up the boutonniere from the florist, she met Melody, Marissa, and Harmony, at a friend of Marissa's family's salon. They all had appointments to get their hair and nails done.

"Oh! You ladies look absolutely gorgeous!" the salon owner gushed when they finished.

Marissa grinned. "Thanks! And thank you for squeezing us in."

"Not a problem, honey. Happy to do it."

The group of girls had a permanent grin on their faces as they paid, and then left for their homes to get ready.

Harmony and Melody may look identical, but the way their hair was done, it made them look like two completely different girls. Melody's hair was done in soft curls that surrounded her face. She also had a small part of the sides loosely pulled back with combs and baby's breath. Meanwhile, Harmony had hers pulled back in a twist, with the part at the top of the twist where the hair ended, curled. There was also a little of bit hair on the sides pulled down, just enough to make a curl or two.

Marissa had her hair down and styled very nicely. Hers was shorter than the other girl's hair. Since it was so short, there was not much she could do with it. Her stylist was able to dress it up with some curls here and there.

"Stacey, you look great!" Becky said, as she helped Stacey get ready. "Scott's not going to believe his eyes!"

"Thank you." Stacey smiled, looking in the mirror one last time. Her hair was straight, but curled toward her face in layers. She liked her hair down better, so that's how she did it.

After she got her dress on, she fluffed her hair a bit to give it a little more body. It made it look fuller. She did her own make-up, but tried to keep it on the lighter side since that was how she normally wore it. She wanted to stay as close to being her true self as she could.

"Stacey?" her dad knocked on the door. "Scott's waiting for you downstairs."

"You ready?" Becky asked.

"Yeah," Stacey said.

"Good. Here's his boutonniere." Becky handed it to her, and then kissed her cheek. "Have fun, hon."

Stacey gave Becky a hug. "Thank you."

"Try to keep my little brother out of trouble, huh?"

"I don't think that'll be a problem. He's usually pretty good at keeping *me* out of trouble," Stacey countered.

Sam knocked again. "Stacey?"

"Coming!" Stacey called. Then she turned back to Becky, and said, "I guess it's time to go."

"You'll have a great time!" she said, and hugged her again. "Now, let me go down first, so I can get the camera ready. Count to twenty, and then you come down. Okay?"

"Okay," Stacey agreed.

"Great!" she said as she smiled and left.

Stacey counted as she did one last check before heading down the stairs.

"Oh my!" Scott's eyes widened when he saw Stacey on the stairs. "I–wow!"

"Is that good or bad?" Stacey asked at the bottom of the staircase.

"I–wow!" he repeated, with a look of shock on his face.

"Take that as good," Sam said in a chuckle. "You look spectacular, honey!" he said, giving her a kiss on the cheek. "Your mother would be proud of you. You know that, right?"

Stacey blushed. "Thank you," she said, pinning the boutonniere on Scott's jacket.

Scott stared at her the entire time, not saying a word.

"Okay," Stacey said after she got it pinned on his jacket, "you're starting to give me a complex. Can you say anything?"

"I..." He shook his head to clear it, before he turned and picked up her wrist corsage from the foyer table. He looked at Stacey for a moment, and then slid the corsage onto her wrist. The corsage matched Scott's boutonniere, but was bigger. "I–

I'm just...I'm going to have a really hard time *not* wanting to kiss you. That's just a warning," he quickly explained, realizing what he said. "It wasn't meant to scare you or anything. You just look...yeah," he said, flustered.

"My brother tongue-tied?" Becky laughed. "I have *never* seen *that* one!"

He looked up at Becky and smiled, his dimples in full view and his cheeks bright red. Gesturing toward Stacey, he said, "She just looks –"

"I know," Becky agreed. "It's just funny!"

"And I'm sure at your wedding here in a month, you'll be equally as tongue-tied when you see my dad in a tux," Stacey pointed out.

"Oh, I'm sure." Becky looped her arm through Sam's. She nudged him as she said, "He's handsome anyway. In a tux, well, I'm sure that gorgeous isn't going to cover it."

"You look stunning tonight," Sam said with a smile. "I'm sure stunning won't cover it for the wedding."

They were dressed to go as chaperones for the prom. They were supposed to be at the gym thirty minutes ago, but they wanted to wait until Stacey was picked up.

"Nothing personal, but I'd like to...can we go?" Scott asked Sam. "I want to take this young lady to the dance floor, and dance with her all night long," he said. His baby blue eyes were twinkling with joy as he grinned, looking down at her.

"Yeah, just have her back by one," Sam said. "Or at least a phone call if you have a change of plans. If you need to adjust it, we'll talk then. Deal?"

"Deal!" Stacey grinned, excited. Her dad letting her have some free reign like that was rare.

"Wait! Pictures!" Becky said, and took a few photos of the pair.

"Thank you," Scott said after she finished, and they left.

When they went outside, he grabbed Stacey's hand. "You look amazing."

"I think you said something along those lines."

"May I at least kiss your cheek?"

"Sure," she agreed, as they stood by his truck.

Scott opened the passenger's side door, and then stood in front of Stacey. "You are an amazing young lady. One, that I am honored to be with…even if it's just as a friend," he said, putting his hands on the sides of her face. Then he leaned forward and gently kissed her cheek. "Thank you for coming with me."

Stacey could not form words at that moment. Her heart raced. She looked into his eyes. They were so tender as they searched her eyes for some sort of idea as to what was going through her mind.

"Want to go?" he asked.

"Not really."

He furrowed his brow. "Change your mind?"

"No. I just–" Before she changed her mind, she kissed him on the lips.

He was taken aback for a second, before he joined her in the kiss. They stood there for several minutes lost in each other, before Stacey moved back a little bit.

She took a moment, and then confidently said, "*Now* we can go."

"Does this mean what I think it means?"

"That depends on what you think it means," she said, getting into the truck.

It was a Ford F-150, in two-tone hunter green and silver. The interior was gray as well, with gray leather seats.

Scott closed the door and shook his head. He grinned from ear to ear while he went around to his side and got into the truck.

"So?" Stacey asked, while he put his seatbelt on.

"So what?" he asked, still smiling.

"What do you think it means?"

He started the truck, and they took off. "Well," he said, "I'm afraid to answer, and be way off base. So, why don't you just tell me?"

Stacey said, "I love you."

"That's an already previously established fact. Can you clear up as to what *kind* of love?"

"Well," she said, a thousand thoughts flying through her mind. She looked over at his hands, and took one of them into hers, as she said, "If you'll have me, I'd like to try this in a different phase then we've been in?"

He was quiet the rest of the way to the school. When they arrived, he parked the truck. Then he got out and went around to Stacey's side. When he opened her door, he put his hand out for her to help her down. When she was out, he then took her other hand into his so she faced him, and said, "Am I making an accurate assessment in my thinking, or am I overstepping when I ask you to finish off this night as a *real* date, and not a *friend* date?"

Stacey did not want to mess this up. She carefully considered her words, as she said, "It would by *my* honor if you would allow *me* the privilege of being escorted by you to my prom as my boyfriend." When his eyes got huge, she quickly backed away a step, and asked, "Is that overstepping? I'm sorry."

"No! I –" He shook his head. "Would you really be my girlfriend? I know it's a trivial title that people use, but..." his voice faded.

Shaking her hand free, she put it on the side of his face. Moving closer toward him, she explained, "I put Adam's ring into the box on my dresser earlier today. There'll always be a place in my heart for him. The ring will always be in that box. You're right, though. I need to move forward. So, yes, if you so desire, I would be honored to be your girlfriend if you'll have me."

He shook his head in amazement. "You have no idea how long I've waited for you to say those words to me. You have no idea of how much I've wanted you to look at me the way you're looking at me right now." He leaned forward and kissed Stacey, wrapping his arm around her waist.

She melted in his arms and in his kiss. It was so loving and tender.

"Thank you for waiting," Stacey whispered, a few minutes later, their faces inches away.

"Thank you for –" He kissed her again.

After a few more minutes, Stacey said, "We should, um, the prom?"

"Yeah." He nodded. "Let's go." He locked the truck, and then they headed into the gymnasium.

Everyone from their group was already there. "Stacey!" Brian called when he saw them. "Over here!"

When they got to the table, Melody looked at Stacey suspiciously. "You guys look...um, Stacey, let's go to the bathroom. I need to go, and I want the company."

"We just got here," Stacey objected.

"Now!" Harmony said, realizing what Melody was honing in on. She got up and grabbed Stacey's wrist, pulling her from the table. Melody and Marissa followed them out to the hallway. "Spill it, Spencer!" Harmony said, smiling ear to ear.

"Spill what?" Stacey asked.

"There's something different. Your face is almost...I don't know. What's going on?" Harmony asked.

"Yeah, I haven't seen you look this happy in a long time," Melody said. "You're glowing. Did something happen?"

"Where's Adam's ring?" Marissa asked.

"It's in my box on my dresser," Stacey said.

"Oh, so it's just off for tonight?" Marissa pressed.

"No. I'm going to go ahead and keep it there for safekeeping," Stacey said.

"You...*what?*" Marissa's jaw dropped. "Why would you do that?"

"Riss, back off!" Harmony said. "You tried to rule Adam's life when he was here. Give them peace and let them move on."

"I can't believe –" Marissa shook her head, crossing her arms. "He loved you!"

Stacey stood there, jaw-dropped.

"Marissa!" Melody snapped. For Melody to snap, it stunned everyone around them. "Back off! Just let her be happy!"

"I–I'm sorry!" Stacey shook her head, holding herself. "I-I wanted to honor him."

"You have!" Melody said. She glared at Marissa, as she loudly said, "But her life doesn't have to end with Adam! She can be happy with Scott too!" She was almost at a yelling stage. For Melody to yell was *extremely* rare.

"Mel?" Brian poked his head out the door. "What's–oh, this isn't good," he said. He waved for the other guys to come out with him.

"What happened?" Scott asked, when the guys walked into the hallway. "She left happy."

"Big mouth over there thinks she can control how people should act and feel!" Harmony said, crossing her arms. "She's giving Stacey a hard time, because she took Adam's ring off, and is dating you now."

"Really?" Randy said, patting Scott on the back. "Dude! That's great!"

"Well, it seems everyone thinks it's great except the high and mighty princess!" Melody gestured toward Marissa.

Alex looked at Stacey, and then at Marissa. "Riss?" he asked. "What's going on? Why are you so mad at her for taking off Adam's ring?"

"Because she..." Marissa and Stacey both had tears in their eyes by that point, but both were too mad to cry. "She *had* a great guy!" Marissa tried to defend her actions. "Adam was the best! And now she's throwing that away for *him*!"

"Stop it!" Stacey shouted. "I took the time to work through his death," she said sternly. "I took the time to make sure I wasn't going to the first guy who came my way. I *do* love Adam, but he's gone. He's not coming back. I love Scott too. He has been a pillar for me over the last year and a half! While I was trying to help others pick up the pieces, he stood beside me holding *me* up!"

"Yep!" Marissa put her hands on her hips. "He was just waiting for his shot!"

"*Marissa!*" Scott's jaw dropped. Clenching his fists, he said, "If you were a guy, I would punch you!"

"I'm trying to figure out what to do myself!" Alex looked at her, stunned by her actions. Marissa stood there shocked, as Alex said, "You didn't want me. You've always wanted Adam. You wanted him so much, that you've been pining away after him since his death. What? Have you been living vicariously through Stacey all this time? Is that why you chose to stay here? Did you stay just to keep an eye on her?"

"Come on, Stace." Scott grabbed her wrist, and they left out the front door.

"Where are we going?" Stacey asked.

"I don't know, but we can't stay here." He was livid. "At least not right now."

"Scott." Stacey pulled back and he stopped. When he turned toward her, she said, "She's hurting."

"She's obsessed!"

Glancing at the school, and then back to Scott, Stacey said, "Scott, she's still lost."

"She's trying to live her life through you. She's trying to make you feel bad for moving on with your life."

"I know I made the right choice. I don't regret anything I've done. I do love Adam, and I always will. I love you too. While I love both of you, *you* are the one who is here. You know that though, and told me you would respect that."

"I do, and I will."

"Then," Stacey said, getting her emotions under control, "then we're fine. I'm not going to let her rule my life. If she wants to ruin hers, that's for her to decide. But I'm not going to let her run my life, and you shouldn't either."

He stood there looking at her for a few moments before he said anything. It was almost too long for Stacey's comfort. Wrapping both of his arms around her waist, he said, "Stacey, I *do* love you. I also respect Adam's memory. If you want to, we can go back inside. I will do my best to protect you from her, but only if you want me to."

"I want you to do what you feel you should. I'm not going to stop you. Just think about any future repercussions she's going to have to face. She's probably in the process of losing Alex right now. I feel bad for him, but there's nothing I can do about that."

"No. There isn't."

"What if we just go and enjoy ourselves?" She asked. "If we need to avoid her, we can. This is my prom. This only happens once in my life. I am not going to let her ruin it for me."

"Sounds like a plan to me. You're probably going to want to stop off at the bathroom first," he suggested.

"Why?"

"Your make-up is a mess. You're still beautiful. I'll gladly take you just the way you are, but I know you won't like the prom pictures if this is what they look like." Then he gave her the most wonderful, sensual kiss she ever experienced. It was as if he was set free from having to hold back for so long. She joined him in the kiss for a few minutes...that is, until Marissa came storming out of the school.

"I...*why you*..." Marissa narrowed her eyes at Stacey with her fists clenched to her sides. "How *dare* you!"

"What is wrong with you?" Stacey asked.

"Adam loved you! You show him disrespect by dating *him*," she said, disgusted. "He's the one Adam broke up with you for being in love with in the first place! That's just a slap in the face to him! I'll bet you he's rolling over in his grave right now!"

"*Marissa!*" Stacey said, wide-eyed.

"Lost or not, that's unacceptable!" Scott shouted. "You have exactly thirty seconds to leave us alone!"

Marissa crossed her arms. "Or you'll do *what?*"

"Or I'll call the police for you harassing her! We left, so you'd leave us alone. And now you're coming back at us once again. This time your words are even more malicious than the original ones! You *will* leave her alone, or I *will* file harassment charges against you!"

"You wouldn't!"

"I would!" He glared at her. "You see, in the real world, there are legal ways of dealing with people. A restraining order might be necessary if you continue, but I have a feeling one visit by a police officer to your home might just make my point clear."

Her eyes widened.

"I don't throw things around lightly. If pushed far enough, I *will* use what I have to protect the ones I love." When Marissa started to cry, Scott put his hands on his hips, and more calmly continued, "Marissa, this girl has been through hell and back over the last couple years. You have no clue what she's been through. And for you to have the nerve to accuse her of what you did tonight was not only offensive, but also inappropriate and reprehensible. You didn't take her feelings into consideration. You, for some reason, thought you had the power to control who Adam dated in the first place. And since it wasn't you, you thought you should be able to control Stacey when Adam died. Adam didn't let you control him any more than Stacey's going to let you control her. She's a grown woman. She's perfectly capable of making her own choices. She *has* mourned for Adam. She *does* still love him, but she's choosing to let go and move forward. God has a plan for her, just as He has a plan for you."

Marissa wiped her eyes.

"Riss, people love you, but don't want to be controlled by you," he continued. "God has a plan for them, just as He has a plan for you. I promise you that neither plan includes you being in charge. Look, you had a great guy in there. I'm not sure if he's still there for you or not, but he was a really good guy! Instead of focusing on your own relationship, you chose to continue to try to control Adam and Stacey's...and he's not even here." He walked over to her, leaving Stacey for a moment. He rested his hands on Marissa's arms, as he said, "Adam wasn't here for you. He was for Stacey. Now that he's gone, I'm the one who gets the honor to continue the journey with her. God had a plan for Adam. Adam fulfilled it. God has a plan for Stacey, and for you. They are not the same plan. You two are *not* the same person. God loves you for you. He has a plan specifically designed for you, if you'll let Him show it to you. Riss, we love you. You know that, right?"

Marissa broke at her core. The tears streamed down her face as she nodded.

"Adam, Alex, Randy," he said, "Harmony, Brian, Melody, and Stacey, and even me – we all love you. *You* have to love the person who God created in *you*, before you can do anything else. You have to accept the person God made Marissa James to be. You have to love the person He created you to become. He gave you special gifts and talents He hasn't given anyone else. That's how He does things. You should know that by just looking at the Kelley twins. Harmony and Melody may look alike, but they are in no way, shape, or form identical in person-ality *or* character traits."

"No, they're not," she said, processing his words.

"Adam and Alex aren't identical either. Marissa, *Alex is a good guy*. You can't compare anyone to Adam though. You have Adam on such a high pedestal, there's no way any other man will ever compare. You're setting every other guy who likes you up for failure. Adam had his faults. He wasn't perfect."

"I know."

"He loved Stacey."

"I know that too."

"Then know Stacey and I are now together. Know Adam is enjoying his time with Jesus, up in Heaven just waiting for us."

"Riss," Stacey said, as she stepped closer, "I had a dream while I was in the hospital. I went up to Heaven and saw Jesus, God, and Adam. I know it sounds crazy, but bear with me here," she said, as Scott stepped aside to let Stacey finish. "In one of our conversations, Adam and Jesus were concerned. Their concern was for you. God called you lost. He wants you back. He specifically asked me to help you come back. Now, I can only do so much to help you, but you have to work at it too. I like being your friend, but I won't be your puppet or dartboard."

She shook her head. "I would never do that to you."

"Yes. You have. You placed me in both. That isn't right. You tried to use Adam as a puppet and dart board, too."

"I would never!"

"Then why did you tell him you saw Scott and I kissing when we didn't? Adam told me you told him that during one of our arguments about me and Scott. You knew Adam would be hurt. You used his heart as a dartboard. You lied to him to make him do what you wanted him to do. Then, when we didn't do what you wanted, you *really* took matters into your own hands. You gave me to Kyle *knowing* what he was going to do to me. I saw you in the room that night. I *know* you were the one who let them in."

Marissa shook her head. "Stacey, I'm so sorry!"

"I'm not trying to open old wounds here. I'm trying to make a point. It seems if you don't get your own way, you take matters into your own hands to shape it the way you want it to be. You had to learn the hard way that you're not the one in control. Adam and I both paid dearly for that lesson. If it worked, then it was worth it. You are not in control, Riss. God is. This world is a chaotically jumbled mess, that I for one, am more than happy to handoff to God. I wouldn't *want* to be in control *or* responsible for this," she said, gesturing around her. Stacey took Marissa's hands into her hands. At first, Marissa tried to pull away, but Stacey held firm until Marissa gave up. "Marissa, I forgive you for all you have done, or had a hand in, in the past. You have to let me live my life, though. It's taken me a year-and-a-half to work through Adam's death to even *consider* another man. Scott is an admirable gentleman. He was patient with the process, and has never pushed me into anything. I have come up with the decisions I've made between me, Adam, and God."

Marissa did not move.

"I still have conversations with Adam at his grave. Granted, they're not as often as they were, and chances are they'll even get further between them as time goes on, but there will always be a place in my heart for him. Scott not only honors that, but also respects it. I will always keep Adam's ring in my jewelry box, but there needs to be room in my life to love again. And just like I'm moving on, you need to move on as well. You should start with a conversation with a man that, as of a half hour ago, was totally enamored with you. Alex is a really great guy, Riss! Don't waste that! Let him show you how nice love can be when it's freely given and freely received. See Alex for who he is. He's seen the good in you. You two are a formidable team together. Let God work through the both of you."

"You two are too," she mumbled through her tears.

"Thanks," Scott said, coming behind Stacey, resting his hands on her waist.

"I'm sorry," Marissa said. "I've really messed everything up now."

"No. It's not too late," Stacey said. "Go talk to Alex. I have to go to the bathroom and fix my make-up before we go back into the gym. We'll be in shortly."

Marissa hugged Stacey. "Thanks, Stace," she said, and then she went back into the school.

"Bathroom?" Scott put his arm out. Stacey nodded as she looped her arm through his and they headed inside.

AFTER A LONG TALK AS A GROUP, they talked things out between themselves. Then, while everyone else had a blast, Alex and Marissa had a talk by themselves for a few hours. They finally decided to try it again. Marissa then went around, and individually apologized to the others in the group again.

While everyone had fun on the dance floor, at about eleven o'clock Becky got up to make an announcement. "It is my great honor to announce the King and Queen of this year's prom. Now, some of you are aware that they are not on the court," Becky explained.

Some exclamations of shock were heard around the room.

"This year we're doing something a bit different," Becky continued after it calmed. "After everything we've gone through as a town, it was voted by an overwhelming majority as to who was to be our King and Queen for this year's Senior Class."

They waited in anticipation as she opened the envelope. "As unusual as it sounds, our King this year was an outstanding student and leader, and will always be remembered as such. It will be remembered that this year, the position of Prom King will be dedicated to Adam Barnes," she said, among the shouts, whistles, and cheers from around the room.

Stacey stood there with tears in her eyes. Scott held her up by her waist.

After Becky quieted everyone down, she continued, "And *his*

Queen was none other than Stacey Spencer, who is *our* Queen this year as well."

Stacey covered her mouth in shock as the spot light was suddenly on her.

"Stacey, you've led us through, and showed us how to live life again," Becky explained. "You've given us a freedom we never thought possible. This year's dance is dedicated to our King and Queen, you and Adam. Since Adam cannot obviously be here, would you choose the suitor you would like to share this next dance with?"

Stacey nodded as she grabbed Scott's arm around her waist. "Please?" Stacey asked Scott.

"Of course," Scott agreed.

Becky came off the stage, and crowned Stacey in the middle of the dance floor. She then placed Adam's crown in the honorary seat beside his picture in the chair as the music began.

"Stacey, I love you," Scott said, as they danced. "You make an excellent choice for Queen."

"Thanks, but I'm..." She looked around the gym. "I'm having a really hard time with this," she admitted. Things were spinning around her, and her anxiety amped. She was having trouble breathing.

"I'm sure," he said. "Please slow down your breathing. They're honoring both of you. You know that, right?"

"I do, but..." She looked around at the other couples dancing, and shook her head as the tears slowly crawled down her cheeks.

"Just breathe, and focus on me," Scott coaxed.

"My...anxiety," she said, still breathing heavy.

"Stacey, tell me five things you see around you," Scott said calmly.

"What? Why?"

"Just do it. Focus on finding five things you see."

"Um, there's a crystal ball in the center of the room."

"Good. Four more," he said.

"There's my dad and Becky off to the side."

"Good. Three more."

"There is a center piece of flowers and candles. There is also a table with pop. And then, there is you standing in front of me."

"Good. Now, touch four things around you."

"Why?"

"Just do it," he said.

Taking slower breaths, she reached down and touched her corsage. "My corsage is one. Your face is another," she said resting her hand on the side of his face. Running her fingers through his hair, she continued, "Your hair is three. And your boutonniere is four," she said touching it.

"Great job. Now, tell me three things you hear?"

"Okay," Stacey said, closing her eyes. "I hear the music playing. I hear kids laughing and talking. I hear your steady breathing."

"You're doing really good. Now, keep your eyes closed, and tell me two things you smell?"

"I smell your cologne," she said. "I also smell the bubbles in the bubble machine."

"Well done. Now, tell me one thing you can taste."

She opened her eyes, and glanced at his lips. Leaning forward, she gently kissed his lips. Afterward, she smiled as she said, "I can taste your Chapstick."

"Great job. How are you feeling now?"

"Much better. How did you do that?"

"You did it. I just guided you through."

"I have had high anxiety since my mom passed," she admitted.

"I can only imagine. Listen, you're going to have those moments. Just remember the five senses. You don't have to remember the exact sense with the number. As long as you do all five, it will center you."

"Thank you," she said, resting her head on his shoulder.

They danced for the rest of the night, never leaving each other's side.

After the prom, instead of going to a after-prom party, the group split-up. Scott already knew where he and Stacey were going, but would not tell her.

"Why won't you tell me where we're going?" she asked.

"Because I have a special spot I want to share with you," he explained. They drove for about thirty minutes, before he pulled into a park.

"Is this even open?" she asked.

"Nope. Just trust me," he said, turning off the truck. He handed her a pair of her tennis shoes. "I got them from your dad. Trust me. He knows where we are," Scot explained when she raised an eyebrow.

After they both changed their shoes, they headed down a trail. While they walked, they talked about the prom. Finally, twenty minutes later, they walked into an open area in the canopy of trees to a waterfall dropping into a small pool of water. With the bright full moon, the moonlight gave everything a unique tint.

"Oh, Scott! This is stunning!" Stacey said in awe.

"I know. Here. We'll sit over here," he said, taking her over to a rock. "Thank you for trusting me."

"Of course," she said, sitting down.

"Tonight, at the prom?" he started, as he sat beside her.

"Yeah?"

"I'm sorry for the bad that happened. I saw your face. I wish I could carry that hurt for you."

"What doesn't kill us, makes us stronger," she said on a sigh.

"I want you to have only the best, no second rate. I want to be able to give you everything you've always dreamed of. I want –"

"You have to know you can't do that," Stacey cut him off. He had a look of sorrow in his eyes, so she clarified, "You can only give me what God has intended me to have – nothing more, nothing less. If you try to go against that, we will not be blessed."

"Okay, how did someone so young become so wise?" he asked with a smirk.

"Well, youth has its privileges, but also its consequences. When things happen to you at such a young age, it tends to make you grow up faster."

"True," he agreed. "So, any other wise counsel?"

"Just love me with all your heart, and it will be more than enough for me."

"That was...I'm not sure how to respond to that," Scott admitted.

"I haven't said anything you haven't already said to me at one point or another over the last year or so," she explained. "You have loved me, even through my mess of emotions. You stood there waiting for me. Thank you for your patience. Thank you for loving me with an unconditional love. All I ask is that you keep that unconditional love for me and I'll be a happy woman. Even if we end up in the poor house, I'll be happy as long as you love me."

"For real?" he asked, stunned. "You don't have any dreams?"

"Scott, growing up, every girl has their dreams. For the most part, it's to find their knight in shining armor, and live happily ever after. Mine wasn't any different. But when my mom died, my perspective on life changed. And when we moved here, things started to happen. Life was no longer a fairy tale, it was survival. I was just trying to fight my way through things. Then when Kyle was –" she stopped. "Then with Adam..." She shook her head. "With everything that has happened in my life, my perspective on life will never be the same. I'm not looking for the top of the line car, the best house, or the perfect job. I'm looking for a Godly man who will love me, and protect me and any future children God may give us, with everything he has. I am looking for someone who is not going to elevate his own agenda, but simply honor God's perspective on life. To me, *that* is being successful."

"I'm impressed," Scott admitted.

"We're not guaranteed a certain amount of time here on earth," she continued. "Something may happen to me one day. I may be in an accident like my mom, and not come home. I have to agree with Adam's parting thoughts in that matter. To hear God say, *'well done thy good and faithful servant'* would be the best thing ever. Having said that, I want the world to remember me much the same. If that means God blesses me with a wonderful man in my life while I'm here, that's great. If that means God blesses me with children, even better. If that means we have some money, time, or talents we can offer along the way that will reap some more lives for Him, that's excellent!" She paused before she finished, "But all I ask of God is to love me. All I ask of the man He has granted me time with is the same."

"Stacey, I..." He shook his head. "I would love to be that man, if that's the position God would grant me. I will be not only the most excited man on this planet, but also the most content. I know we only started dating tonight, but you've known how I've felt for a year and a half. Someday, I may ask you for your hand in marriage. But right now, I am more than content to just be your love." When she looked at him in surprise, he explained, "You are very mature for your age. You were before this whole thing started, but even more so now. I want to be with you every waking minute of the day. I want to see you smile. I want to know you'll look at me the way you are right now...forever."

Stacey pulled him toward her, kissing him with the love she felt. He immediately responded with the same. Afterward, they sat and talked until it was time for her to go home.

CHAPTER 18

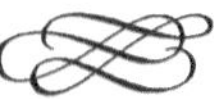

"BUT THOSE WHO HOPE IN THE LORD WILL
RENEW THEIR STRENGTH. THEY WILL
SOAR ON WINGS LIKE EAGLES; THEY WILL
RUN AND NOT GROW WEARY, THEY WILL
WALK AND NOT BE FAINT." ISAIAH 40:31

The next month was a busy one. Stacey had a graduation ceremony, along with a graduation party. This was interspersed with the last-minute preparations for her dad and Becky's wedding. Stacey was Becky's maid of honor, so she had quite a bit to do for the wedding.

Graduation day was amazing. After graduation, the group, along with Scott, went out to the park Scott and Stacey went to on prom night. They enjoyed a picnic and hiking. Later that night, they met back at Stacey's house for a bonfire and night of talking.

"You know, Stacey, we all know where everyone is going to college, except you," Brian pointed out. "Whenever we ask you, you say you haven't decided. You're cutting it awful close."

"I'm going to college." Stacey waved him off. "Don't stress."

"Where?" Scott asked. "Did you finally decide? I know you had a stack of thick envelopes from colleges on the counter for months."

"I'm going to stay local," Stacey said. "I'm going to Cleveland State University."

"Really?" Scott asked, with a grin. "You're going to stay around here?"

"Yes. I am going to stay in the dorms the first year, just to get the experience. I'll commute afterward. I'm going to major in Psychology."

"So, none of us are going to the same school?" Marissa asked, upset.

"That's not necessarily true," Harmony said, holding up her left hand.

The girls squealed in excitement at the diamond ring on her ring finger. While the girls talked, gushing over Harmony's engagement ring, Scott asked, "When did that happen?"

"Last night," Randy said. "I asked her dad the night of prom. He said it was okay as long as we didn't get married until after we both graduated college. We're going to Ohio State University together."

"That's awesome!" Scott said, giving him a high-five.

"What happened?" Marissa asked Harmony. "How did he ask you?"

"Well," Harmony said, with a dreamy look on her face, "he conned Melody into taking me shopping last night to get me out of the house."

"Of course, I already knew what was going on," Melody confessed. "He asked me to get her out of the house. I told her I needed a dress for graduation."

"Sneaky little bugger!" Harmony jokingly narrowed her eyes at Melody. "*Anyway,* when I got home, I was greeted by a path of rose buds at the door, leading to the back of the house. Mel refused to go with me to investigate. My parents, were in the kitchen, and told me to keep going."

"They helped set it up?" Marissa asked.

"Yep!" Harmony grinned. "So, I went out to the back deck. From the deck, to a table on top of a sheet on the grass, there was a pathway of candles in votive glasses. On the table were two candles, along with a formal table setting. There were two salads. Melody waited on us for a three-course meal that *he'd* made. Afterward, she flipped on the stereo, and went inside, closing the blinds."

"Oooo! What happened next?" Marissa asked.

"Well, he got down on one knee, and asked me to marry him!"

"That's so sweet!" Stacey said with a grin. "I'm so happy for you!"

"Thank you! Of course, we're not getting married until after we graduate college, but I promise you it won't be long after graduation."

"Speaking of marriage," Melody said, "Your dad and Miss Schmidt are getting married next week. How are you about that?"

"Honestly? I'm okay," Stacey said. "She didn't have to wait until I graduated. She didn't even have to ask me to be the maid of honor. I'm excited to have her as a second mom. Dad's happy. She's happy. I'm even happy."

"Glad to hear that," Scott said, coming up behind her. He kissed her cheek, before he sat down, wrapping his arms around her from behind as he rested his chin on her shoulder.

"I think all this great news deserves a toast!" Alex said. Everyone raised their cans of pop, as he said, "I am thankful for friends who have become family. I'm thankful for the all of the ugliness because it made us into who we are today. I am thankful for Jesus, our Lord and Savior, for bonding us all together, and for carrying us when we did not think we could walk again. I am thankful for Adam and his leadership. I am thankful for the future God has in store for us, whatever it may be."

~

Finally, the big day came for Sam and Becky's wedding. It was a chaotic morning, as they rushed around getting finishing touches done before the wedding.

"How's my tie?" Sam asked, coming into the room while Stacey was fixing her hair.

"Not too bad...here," she said, and adjusted his tie.

"I'm nervous."

"Really? I never would have guessed," she teased. "In all seriousness, you'll do just fine. She's a good lady."

"I wanted to talk to you about that. I've been wondering for a while now how you felt about Becky."

"Dad, as long as you're happy –"

"Stace, I've seen your face while you watch us."

Stacey sat down on her chair. He knelt in front of her, as she tried to explain, "I just –"

"You know how I feel," he said. When Stacey furrowed her brow, he clarified, "Having lost Adam, you know what it's like to lose the one you love. You also know what it means to find love again. I've seen you and Scott. You're getting close fast. Not that it's a problem, mind you. After all, you two got together on a different level than most people. You guys had the foundation of a terrific respect and friendship before you added the physical aspect to it. What I'm saying is, if you stay with him, I approve. I just want the same respect from you regarding Becky."

Her eyebrows arched in surprise.

"You wear your emotions on your face." He chuckled. "Let me see if I can clarify this. I loved your mom. Lauren was my first true love. Once we came together, we were inseparable. We were married for eighteen years. She gave me you. Moving forward was not something I took lightly. When she died, a lot of things died inside me. Becky revived those feelings. She makes me happy, Stace."

"I know. I've seen it," Stacey admitted. "I get it. I *do* know. That's why I haven't given you a hard time. Yeah, at first it was hard for me to see you with someone so fast after mom. But the more I saw you together, and talked to her, the more I saw why. She's a great lady. You would be stupid to turn your back on that. She respects you, and our relationship. How many women do you know would put off a marriage, just so their soon-to-be husband can make sure to give his daughter his undivided attention during graduation?"

"Not many."

"See? She's great, Dad. I approve."

"Thanks!" he said. "Would you do me the honor of a dance tonight? I know Scott's going to want you for most of it, but I just want one."

"Dad, you can have as many as you want. Becky might have a different theory, though," Stacey teased. "With the way you look, she might not want you to dance with anyone else."

"Thanks," he said, and they both stood. He gave her a hug. "I'm pretty sure she'll let me have at least one dance with my little Peanut."

"Okay, we need to finish getting ready so we can get to the church," Stacey said, and then turned, grabbing her make-up and hair utensils.

"Thanks, Stace," he said. Then, he headed out of the room to finish any last-minute preparations before they left for the church.

WHEN STACEY and her dad arrived at the church, the other bridesmaids were already there. They were in the middle of finishing their hair and make-up. The bridesmaids were friends of Becky's, leaving Stacey as the youngest in the bridal party. There was no flower girl or ring bearer, since neither Scott nor Becky had any kids. They were the only siblings in their family.

"Becky, you look amazing!" Stacey said when Becky walked in, ready to go. "Stunning!"

"Thank you. You look beautiful too. Scott's not going to believe his eyes," she said. "He thought you looked good on prom night." She shook her head. "You look ten times better today."

"Becky," Stacey said, taking Becky's hands into hers, "Dad and I had a talk this morning."

"Uh-oh." She smiled. "Am I in trouble?"

"No. I told him I had a really hard time when you two first started dating. But after a while, I saw how happy you make him. So, if my dad is happy, I'm happy. Now, if you hurt him..." Stacey said with a smile.

"I'm pretty sure we have that covered on both sides," she agreed. "Regarding Scott too? He really loves you."

"I know. I love him too," she said, and gave Becky a hug. "I love *you* too. You'll be a great second mom."

"Thank you!" she said, grateful.

"If you were looking for it, you have my blessing."

Becky hugged Stacey again. "Thank you so much."

"Ladies?" Stacey's Uncle Shawn knocked on the door. He was the best man. "It's time."

"Coming!" Becky called out, and then they all left for the doors of the sanctuary.

The ladies heard quiet whistles from their counterparts as they came down the stairs.

"Okay, the only reason I'm fine with you walking her down, is that you're her uncle," Scott said to Stacey's Uncle Shawn, as he stood in front of them. "Otherwise, I would be *majorly* objecting! You look great!"

"Thanks." Stacey blushed. "You look great as well."

Scott smiled. His partner yanked on his arm, as it was time for them to go down the aisle. Shawn and Stacey were last, before Becky and her dad. Sam was up front the entire time.

The wedding could not have gone any better. Everything went according to plan. The songs were the right length. There were enough bird seed packets made for everyone. There were enough wedding favors made. They had enough cake and food. And the best part? Becky and Sam had an absolute blast all day! She could not have asked for a better day for the two of them.

SAYING good-bye to her dad and Becky as they left for their honeymoon was tougher than Stacey anticipated. They would be gone for two weeks to Aruba. That was the longest she and her dad had ever been separated.

"So," Scott said, as they sat in his car in front of her house after the reception, "you really want to go in there?"

She looked at the dark house, the pit in her stomach growing by the minute. "Not really."

"How about a walk?"

"That sounds good," she said, relieved. "I plan on avoiding the empty house for as long as possible."

As they walked toward the park hand-in-hand, Scott said, "You *really* look beautiful today."

"Thanks. You look handsome yourself."

"I don't think it was fair for you to look prettier than the bride."

"Scott, she is your sister."

"And *you* are my girlfriend," he said. "I'm allowed to be biased."

They walked and talked for over an hour, until they landed back in front of Stacey's house again.

Stacey groaned. "Oh, I don't want to go in there."

"Why not?"

"It's too dark. I'll be lonely. I'm not used to being alone."

"So, you plan on going to college. What are you going to do afterward?"

"I'll marry some rich guy," she joked.

"Lofty goals," he said in a snicker. "However, what are you *really* going to do?"

"Go to Disneyland?"

"Stace?" he said, impatience evident in his tone.

Wanting to put the conversation off for a bit, she pulled her key out of her purse and unlocked the door. Scott followed her in, so she got them both something to drink.

"Okay, you've stalled long enough," Scott said, as they sat on the couch. "What are you planning to do?"

"I really don't know." She shook her head. Taking a sip of her pop, she said, "I've prayed about it, and I really don't see myself going anywhere."

"What do you mean?"

"I don't see myself going to Cleveland except for college," she said. "I know I'll have to go for my Master's Degree in order for my degree in psychology to be of any use. I'm just not sure where I'll go for that, or what I'll do with it. I thought about the FBI."

"The FBI?"

"Yes. I talked to Nick Locke about it a lot. He said I could be a profiler."

"That's unique."

"I thought so, too," she said, her mind drifting to her future.

They both sat for a few moments, lost in their own thoughts.

"Okay, this is *so* not helping the lonely thing," Stacey said. "It would help to actually *talk* with the person who's here."

"I just..." his voice faded.

Seeing him struggle, she asked, "What is it?"

"Your dad and I have talked about you."

"Oh really? I can imagine how *that* conversation went."

"You'd be surprised."

"Really?"

"Yeah," he said with a serious tone. "He wants what you want. He doesn't care what you do, as long as you're happy."

"Really? My dad always said he wanted me to be successful and go to college."

"I want the same thing your dad wants for you," he said. "I want you to be happy."

"I have to tell you that I *am* surprised," she admitted. "My dad always talked about success. He said we needed to always work hard, fast, friendly, and furious to be successful."

"What did you tell me was *your* definition of success?"

"To have a husband who would always love, honor, and respect me and our children. Most importantly, I wanted him to love, honor, and respect God, and the plan God has for us."

"Do you think I would do that for you?"

"Of course!"

He nodded, deep in thought. "Do you-do you think I'm successful?"

"Definitely! I don't know too many men, except for the ones you've introduced me to from the fire and police station, who would give their lives, time, and effort for someone they don't even know. To me, that's admirable."

"Would you –?" He turned and faced her. Taking her hands into his, he said, "Maybe not any time in the immediate future, but that's up to you."

She shook her head, confused. "What?"

"Would–I've already talked to your dad, and he said it was fine with him, but it is up to you."

"What are you talking about?"

He slid off the couch onto his knee, still holding her hands. "Would you marry me?"

Her jaw dropped, as her eyes widened in shock.

"Like I said, maybe not in the immediate future, but..." His hands shook as he pulled a ring out of his pocket. "Would you be my wife on the date of your choice? I would be a happy man just knowing someday down the line you would be my wife."

Stacey glanced from him, to the ring, and back again, still in shock.

"I know we've just recently started officially dating, but I also know we've loved each other long before that. Like I said, I don't care if it's one year, two years, three years, or six years down the road. I would be ecstatic to know you would marry me some day in the future. So, Stacey Marie Spencer, would you do me the honor of being my future wife?"

"I..." She had a trillion thoughts fly through her head at once. She tried to control them, with not a lot of success. "Yes," she finally said.

He grinned. "Really?"

"Yes."

"For real?"

Stacey laughed. "I said yes!"

He pulled the ring out of the box and put it on her ring finger. His hands trembled with excitement. Once the ring was in place, he leaned forward and kissed her with so much love, it sent her thoughts flying a trillion other different directions.

It was at that moment, she knew God *had* provided another love for her. She knew she would not only be okay, but she would also spend the rest of her life with a man who loved, respected, and honored not only her, but also God as well. She was excited to see what God had in store for her, and the future husband she would have in Scott.

GOD *IS* A GOD OF LOVE. God *is* a God of comfort and understands us. After all, He created us. God does not do surprises. Nothing throws Him.

God is also a God of peace and justice. Of that, you can be

sure! He equipped you with the tools you need to pass whatever test is placed before you, as long as you lean on Him for *His* strength, and His Words of encouragement found in the Bible. He sent Jesus to die for you. Jesus was resurrected, so you can have the faith and understanding of knowing you can be with Him after you die. All you need to do it trust in Him. He also provided you the Holy Spirit for courage and guidance. All you have to do is search deep within yourself, and you will see that God is a God of strength, honor, trustworthiness, and loyalty. All you have to do is trust in Him, and have faith that He has a plan for you. There *is* a strength within you that can be found in Him.

MATTHEW 17:20 – He replied, "…if you have faith as small as a mustard seed, you can say to this mountain, 'Move from here to there' and it will move. Nothing will be impossible for you."

Exodus 15:2 – The LORD is my strength and my song, and he has become my salvation; this is my God, and I will praise him, my father's God, and I will exalt him.

Philippians 4:13 – I can do all things through him who strengthens me.

Psalm 46:10a – Be still, and know that I am God.

Isaiah 40:31 – But those who hope in the LORD will renew their strength. They will soar on wings like eagles; they will run and not grow weary, they will walk and not be faint.

RONALD REAGAN: "If we ever forget that we are 'One Nation Under God', then we will be a nation gone under."

BOOKS BY C.J. PETERSON

GRACE RESTORED SERIES

BOOK FIVE
SPRING
SHADOWS
BOOK THREE
GRACE RESTORED SERIES
C.J. Peterson

SUMMER
SECRETS
BOOK FOUR
GRACE RESTORED SERIES
C.J. Peterson

FOREVER
FALL
BOOK FIVE
GRACE RESTORED SERIES
C.J. Peterson

Katie MacKenna experienced one storm after another in her life. When Leukemia stole her mother from her and her father, Katie was only seven-years-old, and her father didn't know how to cope after such a catastrophic loss. His response was to shut down and become abusive. The overwhelming devastation which surrounded Katie throughout her journey in life forced her to shut down just to survive as well.

Trust is a difficult thing for many people, but for Katie it's virtually impossible. Every life has Seasons of Change. Will those seasons open Katie to new opportunities or will they forever isolate her in survival mode? Will she be able to overcome the storms that have surrounded her to answer a call for help?

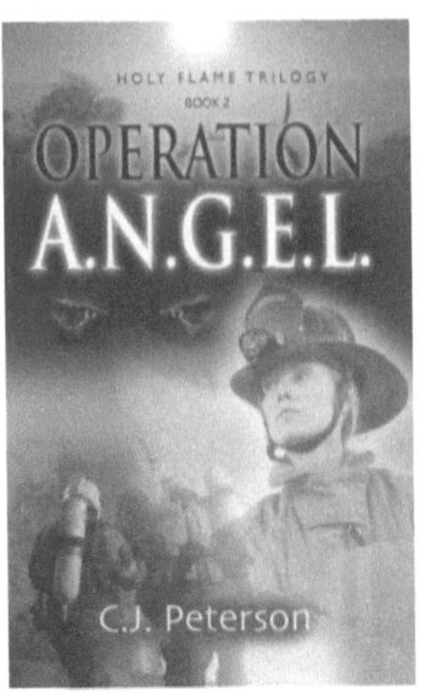

Courageous. Brave. Fearless. Valiant. These synonyms are often used to describe firefighters/paramedics, police officers, and military personnel. They face danger and lay their lives on the line when they leave for work. What are their struggles? Could that hinder their job proficiency? Who is taking care of those who are taking care of the citizens of this country?

Casey Carter is a 'newbie' to the firefighting family of Engine Company 15. Not only does she have to prove herself as a probationary firefighter, but she also has to battle misconceptions of females within her newly chosen profession. As situations begin to arise, can she count on the firefighter brotherhood to have her back? Will she be able to pass the tests placed before her, or are there aspects that she was not even aware existed?

Often in life there are two realms in play. There is the physical realm - what is right before you; the other is the spiritual realm - what is unseen. Each can directly affect you, whether you believe they exist or not. Can Casey keep them in balance when she is not exactly sure what she is fighting? Can a group of men help her see what cannot be readily seen, hear what cannot be readily heard, and be able to overcome what she never knew existed? Will they be able to show Casey her true Call To Duty?

THE NEXT GENERATION
IS TAKING OVER
DIVINE
LEGACY
2019
First Place
Texas Authors
Christian
Fiction
Series
BOOK ONE
DIVINE LEGACY SERIES
C.J. Peterson

As two of the children of Nico and Kit Sullivan, along with Mark and Casey English's, make up the new members of the A.N.G.E.L.s, their job is to gather their remaining teammates. In the process of acquiring the two members listed in the United States, they run across a situation that isn't on their agenda. Amber Jones was in need of miraculous intervention, and God answered her call with the next generation of A.N.G.E.L.s. The A.N.G.E.L.s find some unique help along the way, and learn valuable lessons that will change how they function and see the world from that point forward. Read along as the next generation picks up the torch, claiming their Divine Legacy.

Joel 1:3

Tell it to your children, and let your children tell it to their children, and their children to the next generation.

Hebrews 13:2

Do not forget to show hospitality to strangers, for some who have done this have entertained angels without realizing it!

Connect with CJ – CJPetersonWrites.com